BLOOD & MAGIC ETERNAL

JESSACA WILLIS

BLOOD & MAGIC ETERNAL

JESSACA WILLIS

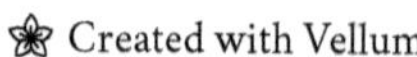 Created with Vellum

BOOKS IN SERIES

PRIMORDIALS OF SHADOWTHORN

Shadow Crusade, Book 1

Blighted Heart, Book 2

Immortal Return, Book 3

BLOOD & MAGIC ETERNAL

Hunger & Cursed Shadows, Book 0

Blood & Magic Eternal, Book 1

Death & Wicked Monsters, Book 2

N
NW
NE
W
E
SW
SE
S
The Capital
Unresting Mountains
Neveridge Castle
NEVERIDGE
Va
THE UNITED REALMS

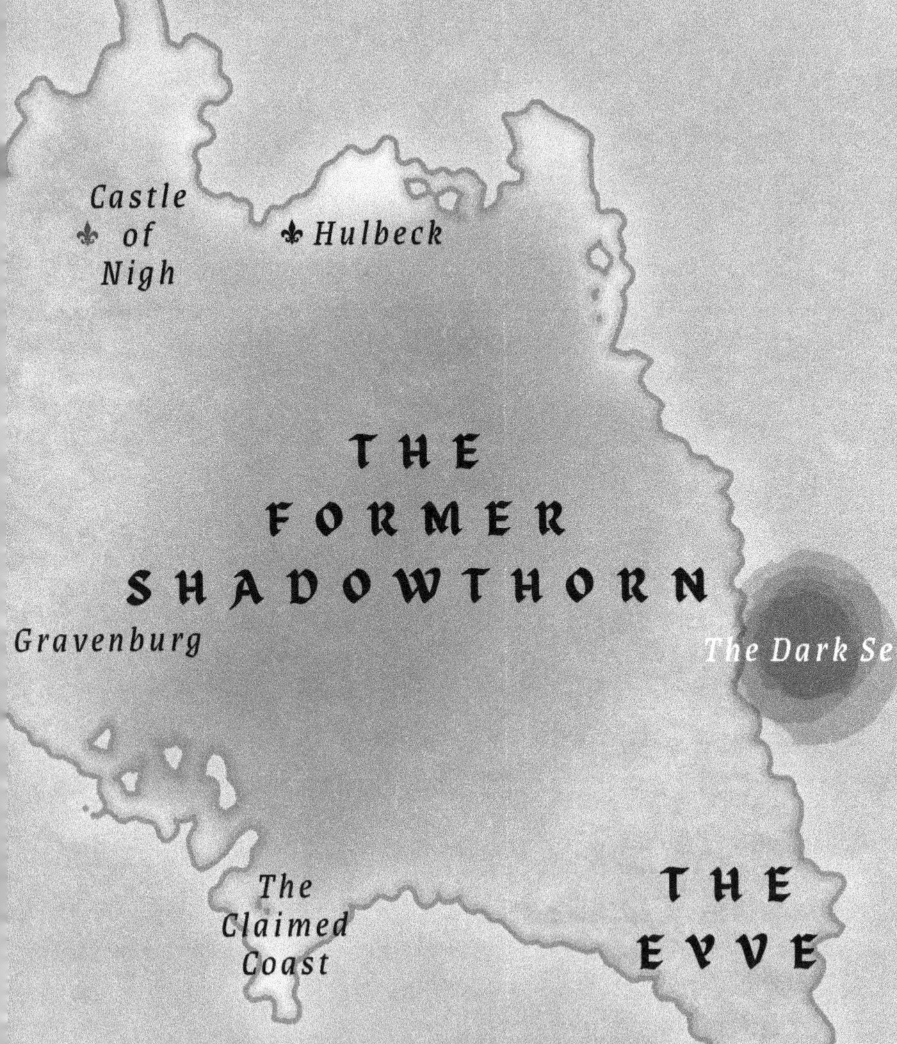

Castle of Nigh
Hulbeck
THE FORMER SHADOWTHORN
Gravenburg
The Dark Sea
The Claimed Coast
THE EVVE
nholm Ocean

For my readers,

Who love the dark shit as much as I do.

CONTENTS

THE SCARS OF YOUTH

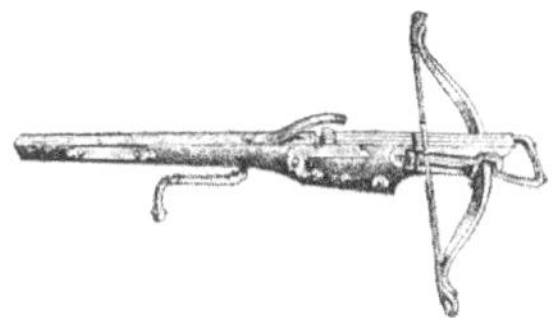

"The sewers?" My mother's head jerks up from where she's just finished planting the last of the radish bulbs. She wipes at the dark wisps of hair pressed against her forehead, smearing dirt into her freckled complexion. "What in the realm makes you two want to play out there?"

Abashed, I lower my gaze. I've lied to my mother every day for fifty-two days now. What's one more going to hurt?

"I wouldn't call it *playing*. It's more like…a scavenger hunt for things that people threw away that we could still use."

"We already have everything we need." The summer sun beams down on us both, making her hairline prick with sweat as she grumbles in distaste. "I don't want you wandering off out there, Charlotte. It's not safe. And Rowland Barret should know better."

He does. I'm not sure there's a single person in Hulbeck who doesn't know better than to find themselves alone on the outskirts of our protected sanctuary. It's out there where the monsters roam, where they await any opportunity to feast.

Truth be told, I don't like the idea any more than my mother, and I begged for an alternative option. The problem is, the reason the monsters like it is the same reason it's good for our purposes: no one will see us out there. No one will know what we're up to.

Rowland says the best way to conceal a lie is to hide it in the truth.

"I promise we won't be long, Mother. Besides, you know I can't stand the stench. It's horrible! Smells like fish that's been left in the sun for years."

She chuckles, but the usual joy that accompanies her smile doesn't quite erase the worry from her tired eyes. I'm told that when she was younger, she'd had eyes as vibrantly ambered as mine, like beads of honey shimmering in the warm, summer sun. Now they're as dull as the dirt drying beneath her fingernails.

After a long, scrutinizing moment, she sighs. "Stay within earshot of the sea," she warns. "And if you hear anything—"

"We'll return, right away." I nod vigorously, desperate to leave before she can change her mind or before the nausea climbing up my throat can spill forth. "I promise."

One of her slender brows arches at me, and for a moment I fear I've given something away. Thankfully, the moment passes.

"Well, alright. Give Rowland my regards," my mother says, squatting back down to resume her work. She starts humming a familiar and soothing tune, one I've often heard her singing when she's planting a new crop, but she stops as soon as she's started. "And if you see his mother, tell her to swing by. Gregory will be working the salt mines all day and I'd love the company. Tell her I have a fresh pot of that lavender tea she loves so much, just waiting for her."

"Okay. Will do."

With my heart in my throat, I wave goodbye, completely unaware that it'll be the last time I ever see my mother alive.

I scurry through the streets, sure that each person I pass

somehow knows what we're up to and are seconds away from dragging me back to my mother to confess. If Rowland were with me, he'd tell me I was just being paranoid, and he'd probably be right. He often is about these sorts of things. It's one of his many talents, knowing how to get away with small lies, and knowing when the small lies will blow up in our faces.

For courage, I pretend he's racing alongside me until I finally find him, sitting on a busted cart, looking so bored that he'd rather die.

"What took you so long?"

When he sees me, Rowland jumps to his feet on the uncoordinated limbs of a young boy who is only just starting to become a young man. An injury to his knee makes him wince on impact, even though it's been more than a year since he fell from that rooftop. That, with his recent growth spurt, makes him even wobblier than usual on the landing.

"It was my mother," I whine while he regains his balance. "She started asking me questions about where we were going and what we'd be doing. I had to lie to her. *Again.*"

"It's not lying if—"

"*If it's the truth,*" I finish for him, fingers nervously twining around themselves. "I know, I know. But she made me promise...and...and that was *not* the truth."

His eyes roll back. "It's not a crime to lie, you know? And, if it was, it's not like it'd be a bad one. They wouldn't feed you to the sirens."

My jaw drops wide. "They're not...they don't do that... Do they? I thought that was just a legend."

His shoulders bob, but I never get my answer because Rowland becomes distracted by his itching scalp. "I hate these things," he grumbles, scratching at the tightly bound locks.

This happens every time his mom re-braids his hair. She worked on them almost all day yesterday, and it's why we had to postpone our gathering until today.

"I kind of like them." My cheeks warm when his brown eyes shoot up at me and self-consciously I begin rubbing my arms. "My mother stopped doing my hair a long time ago."

Deeming it an acceptable response, he gives his head another vicious scratch that looks like it could break the skin, let alone tear out his hair, before he allows his attention to scan our dingy surroundings.

Abruptly, Rowland tears away from the wall and begins to pace, a growl lying in wait somewhere low in his lungs. "Where is she?"

It's only then that I realize who he's talking about and notice that we're missing someone from our party.

"Where's Agnes?" I ask him, a bit needlessly.

He throws his arms in the air, a look of contempt about him when he spins around.

"She's late," I say slowly, and rub the hair standing up on my arms. "But…she's never late."

Agnes was a warrior. For a decade or more, she served on the Shadow Crusade, a feat that almost none of the other Crusaders ever accomplished. She was there all the way up until the final battle when the mages were defeated and demonkind was destroyed for good.

Or at least, demonkind as we knew it.

It's why Rowland asked her to train us. She's encountered more monsters, survived more battles, and held the title of warrior longer than anyone else in Hulbeck. Perhaps in all the realm at this point.

"She's probably just…she must've lost track of time?"

It's the best I can do, but even I know that her losing track of time is about as unlikely as a Crusader surviving a decade of service. The values of loyalty, duty, and diligence practically flowed in her veins. It would be against her nature to lose track of her commitments. Especially to us.

We don't have to wonder for long though. Because it's not

long after we notice her absence that the screams begin. Screams like hissing tea kettles and distraught animals. Screams that make my skin prick and clench my heart in an iron-cold fist. Dozens of shrieks tear through the air, perhaps hundreds, surrounding us like the sea barricades the shore.

My eyes lock with Rowland's, his pupils as wide as walnuts.

"What's happening?" I begin to say.

But before I can finish listing all the questions buzzing in my mind, his lips move, forming a single word. "Mother."

His feet slide out from under him and he's running, bolting headfirst into the storm of terror before I can even make sense that he's moving. Wide-eyed and lip quivering, I can only watch him as he disappears. I'm only eight. Whatever horrors we thought we were training to face, I never actually imagined facing them. It was a pastime born of boredom, never a necessity. Hulbeck has stood here for years. Undisturbed. Safe.

Never had I dreamed that one day we might actually need to use the skills Agnes was training us with.

And never before have I felt more helpless, more childlike.

All the times I argued that I was mature, or insisted that I could handle something as well as any adult, I know now that was a lie. I am petrified. And I am defenseless.

Something solid and warm wraps around my arm and tugs me into the shadows.

"Let me go!" I writhe, tears stinging my eyes at the thought of one of the monsters grabbing me. Feasting on my blood. Killing me. "Let me go!"

A hand clamps around my mouth. Agnes' wrinkled face leans into view. "Hush now, or they'll hear us."

Trembling in her grasp, I nod, but I wonder how anyone could hear anything over the horrific wails filling the town. I watch her with wide eyes, waiting for her to tell me what to do, like she's done in every one of our lessons. Instead, she's quiet, and I find myself staring at a diagonal spray of blood that covers her cheek and eye.

"We have to go," she murmurs, but then another thought occurs to her. "Rowland?"

"H-he went home. I think to find his mother."

Solemn, Agnes shakes her head, limp, grey curls swaying around her face. "He's gone then. We have to head inland."

She tugs on my arm to lead me away.

"G-gone?" I yank myself out of her grasp. "What do you mean *gone*?"

In that moment, the warrior flashes before me, the one who's seen more pain and suffering than I can even fathom. Her eyes shine like steel, cold and sharp. There's a forced sort of tenderness in her hands when she takes mine into hers, almost as if she doesn't feel fear or sadness or worry for Rowland at all.

"There is nothing back there for you, I promise," she says. "If the two of us are to survive this, we have to go. Now. The noctis haven't made it this far into the village yet. We can still—"

"The noctis?"

Hot and throbbing, my heart lurches into my throat. Every story I have ever heard of the bloodsucking demons that we call the noctis attacks my fragile mind, sending me into a frenzy of worry. I've heard tales of them devouring entire towns, leaving nothing left but skin and bone. There are other legends that say they don't even leave that much, that the bones they tear from their victims are fashioned into spears or worn as necklaces and earrings to lavish events at the king's castle in Neveridge. Tales of noctis engorging themselves on human blood until their bellies burst.

"The noctis? Here?" My eyes spill with tears. "My mother—"

"Your mother is gone, child. There will be time for mourning her later. But right now, we—"

When I make the turn and run, it's not a conscious choice. One second, I'm clutching onto Agnes as if my life depends on it, the next my feet are thump-thump-thumping down the street. It's the only thing I feel, my feet moving and my heart setting the pace. The rest of my body is just…gone. I hardly see the wooden huts or their thatched roofs that blur by, my mind entirely engulfed repeating thoughts:

Find Mother.

It's not too late.

Find Mother.

It can't be too late—

But of course, it is.

By the time I make it back to our neighborhood, the seafoam on the coastline is tinted pink, the sand stained an unnatural shade of red that glistens in the sunlight. It's not until the road beneath my feet becomes slick, red splashing up my calves, the same color sprayed on every door, every cart, and every barrel, that I realize with sinking dread the reason.

"Mother!"

The word tears from my lips like a colony of bats fleeing a cave at dusk and I burst through our unhinged door.

But then I stop.

Everything is wrong. Chairs thrown across the room. The loom laying on its side. My mother's basket tossed on the ground and vegetables scattered all over the floor like a game of jacks.

Most upsetting of all is the blood. It covers every inch of our home so thoroughly that it's even dripping from the ceiling.

"Mother?" My voice warbles, drowning behind a wave of grief that has yet to swell and crash, just waiting for the final proof that my world has unraveled, and I am alone.

It's not my mother's relived voice that answers, or even her faint whimpering, or any sign of her at all.

But the monster inside hears me. His neck snaps around, hungry eyes pinning me in place. Red dribbles from his mouth, and it's then that I finally find her. It's then that I finally break. A woman with long hair as black as mine. But her skin has gone too pale. The eyes that had been a duller shade of mine just earlier, are almost a void of color now.

My knees give out. I crumple to the floor and land in a pool of blood, blood that I don't want to think about who it belongs to.

Something thuds on the floor. I can only barely make out my mother's body where she's been dropped, hair splayed over her neck but doing nothing to hide the ghastly, gaping bite mark beneath it. Footsteps hammer against the wooden planks until a shadow looms over me, a blanket of darkness that I know I should run from, but almost feel myself leaning into its embrace. I know it's him. I know it's the noctis and he's come to feast upon my blood, but I can't move. I can't stop him.

All of the training, however limited it had been, is gone from my mind because I can't even fathom a life without my mother. She cared for me. She loved me. She kept me safe and shielded me from this…this nightmare of an existence that we live in.

Instead of running, instead of fighting, I lean forward and sob into my hands.

The noctis stands over me, his shadow cold against my back.

I reach for my mother's hand. I just want to feel her one last time. I want to hold her and have her hold me in return as the life is drained from my small body. But she's too far out of reach, and before I can even attempt to crawl closer, I'm hoisted off the ground by the back of my neck.

Some primal instinct kicks in, and I thrash in the noctis' grip.

"Let me go!"

Blood-soaked fangs peek out from his menacing smirk. "Go ahead and squirm. I like knowing you humans fear me."

Without another moment's notice, his jaw widens. He leans over me, fangs bared, tongue salivating, and I brace myself for whatever painful death my dear mother just endured. Perhaps it's best this way. I froze when Rowland ran, after all. I froze when I entered my home. Since the screams began, I've been useless. Defenseless. Without my mother or Rowland or Agnes to tell me what to do, I am nothing.

My eyes squeeze tight, and I await the puncture of death.

But it doesn't come.

My eyes snap open when his fingers loosen, and I watch blood gurgle from his mouth as I fall to the ground. The noctis before me paws at his chest, a sharp, wooden stake jutting from the place where his heart should be.

The woman behind him jerks on the weapon, drawing him nearer as she says into his ear, "Go ahead and squirm. I like knowing the monsters fear me."

Agnes withdraws the stake with a sickening squelch and the noctis falls.

She keeps a wary eye on him as she steps over his limp, bloody body, and crouches down beside me. "Are you all right?" When I don't reply, she looks up, spies my mother a short distance away, and sighs. "I tried warning you, child. There is nothing left for you here. Hulbeck has fallen. We can't stay—"

Hooves thunder through the streets.

As fluid and swift as a coursing river, Agnes wraps her arm around my torso and hoists me onto her hip. "Where is it? Where did she tell you to hide if the noctis ever came?"

My finger lifts without my doing. To the naked eye, there's nothing where I'm pointing, just my mother's loom and a few dozen spools of thread that she'd been spinning. But Agnes knows better. Hulbeck was the town she'd called home before the Shadowthorn overrun it, and when the darkness was finally cleansed from it, the people rebuilt every home inside this village with a safe haven in mind, just in case evil ever returned. They were right.

Agnes leaps across the room and sets me on the ground. As she shoves the loom away, clearing the floor, I make the mistake of peering out the window and I see him for the first time. A noctis male with hair as silken as spiderwebs and just as pale as the dead that litter the ground around him.

The king of the noctis.

The king of devastation.

King Tor Devonshire.

"Did you find him?" the king asks the rugged man on the horse behind him.

The other noctis shakes his bearded head. "No, sir. No sign of him yet. But we'll find him."

Agnes glances over her shoulder out the window every few seconds as she taps on the wooden planks, searching for the hollow beneath the floor. When her knuckles finally strike it, it only takes her a few seconds before she has the floor opened wide, revealing the hiding hole beneath the house that I never thought I'd have to use, no matter how many times my mother reminded me of it.

Agnes ushers me inside.

It's not until the door closes that I realize she's left me alone.

It's not until I hear weapons slicing through air and flesh that I realize she's fighting the noctis because she has no choice. Because I've given her no choice. Because she told me to flee with her and instead...I brought her back here.

Her guttural cry as she meets her end buries me where I lay, this hole feeling a lot like a tomb I will never climb out of.

For days I remain there, petrified and lost. The noctis enter my home and finish off what they began, draining the rest of my mother dry and lapping up the spill on the floor. They even bring in other humans to feast upon, and for hours I listen to their screams, wondering why I can't go up there and fight, why I'm so useless that I'm just stuck down here, waiting out a death that everyone else has already met.

I'm not sure how long I stay. Day gives way to night, and night to day. It's only once I'm sure the noctis have left Hulbeck, only once the town has been silent for days and all those who had been left near death and in agony have at long last perished that I muster the courage to crack open the floorboards and escape. When I finally crawl out of from the hole beneath my home, I force myself to look at every dead body I pass, to gaze upon all those who were too weak to survive so that I will always remember what the noctis are capable of.

Laying my eyes on the carnage, I finally understand why Rowland wanted us to train. Why Agnes agreed to it.

Hulbeck had become weak.

The people here stopped worrying about the noctis because they believed we were safe by the sea. They believed that because our village was so large and populated, that the noctis wouldn't dare fight us. But they were wrong. That's exactly why they came. We painted a target on our backs. A thriving community of fresh blood just waiting for a bloodthirsty army to come and drink their fill.

We weren't safer behind these walls, allied together. It drew the noctis to us like moths drawn to flame.

I grab the crossbow and quiver that hangs beside our front door, and as I race down the streets of Hulbeck, headed for the shoreline that my mother always instructed me to follow in case of an emergency, not once do I look back at the town or the life I'm leaving behind.

2

TEN YEARS LATER

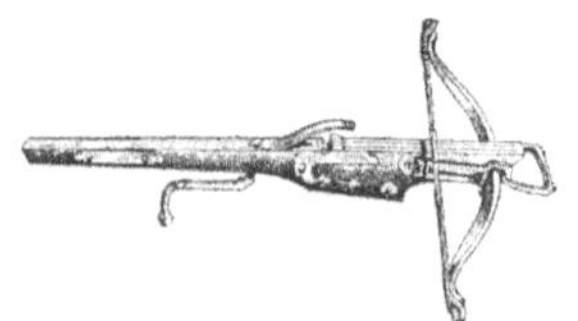

Every now and again, I catch myself staring into the blackened shadowood of my mother's crossbow, mesmerized by the lethal beauty hiding beneath its iridescent shine. Sable, I've come to call her, courtesy of her dark and captivating allure. There's always been something eerily magical about her, but today I feel it more profoundly than usual.

Unease skitters down my spine and I force myself to look away from her before I can fall too far into her black void. It's just superstition, I remind myself. Just the paranoid ramblings of commonfolk to distrust weapons made from shadowood. Nearly two decades ago, when the Shadowthorn fell, it wasn't uncommon for blacksmiths to forge weapons from the dead wood that had grown inside the cursed forest. It was believed that perhaps the trees of the Shadowthorn had protective properties that could fend off against the evils of the new era, just as the shadowsteel weapons had been designed to protect them from the demons they eventually eradicated.

Of course, they soon discovered that shadowood was no more effective against the monsters of our time as any other weapons were. No magical qualities. No noctis-killing power. Our predecessors were fortunate in that regard. They had an advantage that we do not.

A weapon is a weapon.

Which means I could opt for another, since Sable's shadowood has no special effects against the noctis. But I wouldn't. I tell myself it has nothing to do with her having once belonged to my mother and therefore being some kind of symbolic source of comfort, and instead assure myself it's simply because I know where my strengths lay. I'm no good with short-ranged weapons. Knives and swords are awkward in my grasp, and my fists never pack as big of a punch as I mean for them to. But put me on a rooftop with a crossbow in my hands? I'll be damned if I don't hit every target I take aim at.

With Sable securely in my grasp, I go about gathering the rest of the supplies I'll need for my run today. I fasten a leather belt around my waist and pluck one of the small vials it carries free from its chamber. I hold the glass up to my line of sight. Empty. I examine the others one by one, giving each vial a shake just to be sure none of the contents that should be there are hiding, but it's to no avail.

"Fuck," I mutter and glance to Sable where I have her wedged in the crook of my free arm. "How did we let this happen?"

Almost obligingly, the previous day plays out in my mind. How I'd used the last of my blood supply to bait a ghoul away from the brook on the outskirts of town long enough so I could finish washing my latest catch of fish. The plan had been to check my various traps and snares around town afterward, and therefore replenish my blood supply, but nightfall came faster than I'd anticipated, and Sable and I had to hurry back to our hovel before it became too dangerous out and about. For whatever reason, the ghouls are most active at night.

I cram the empty vial back into its slot.

"We need to check those traps today." I try taking a deep breath to calm myself, but it doesn't help. "Fuck! I was really hoping to focus on one of those jobs today."

There's a job board at *Fort Barret* with postings from the civilians who dwell there of special requests. Some of them you'd have to have a death wish to attempt, like breaking into a noctis stronghold to search for and free someone's loved one whom they haven't seen in months. I don't bother with requests like those. They're just a waste of everyone's time, and needlessly put my life on the line on a fool's errand. But there are others, people in need of a bushel of arrowroot, protection for newcomers traveling into town, or finding lost family heirlooms that have just been sitting in dust-covered houses in neighboring villages. It's one of the ways I trade for goods, plus it helps the long, quiet days go by.

Closing my eyes, I massage the sharp twinge pinching between my eyebrows. "Blood first. Everything else can wait."

Or more importantly, every*one* else. Soon the people will turn to other mercenaries to finish their jobs for them, and I'll have to find someone else to barter with. These raggedy boots aren't going to re-sole themselves…

It's a tough decision, one that could cost me, but it's the only option I have. Wandering around the streets of Gravenburg without any vials of blood falls smack dab into the category of rookie mistakes that I no longer permit myself to make. In my years of survival, I've learned a few hard lessons. I've lost track of the number of ghouls I've slain with this crossbow, but I distinctly remember each and every one of the noctis, for every time I've faced one of them it could've been avoided.

Six. In a whole decade, I've had to kill six noctis because I was careless.

They don't make it easy. So rarely do they travel alone anymore that it's usually safer just to hide when I see any. Even when I do find the odd noctis on a solo hunt, I can never be certain there isn't another nearby, somewhere just out of view, waiting for someone like me to make the wrong choice and reveal myself. It's usually not worth the risk to shoot one unless my life depends on it. And, as a general rule, I don't like getting myself into those kinds of situations.

It has happened, though. Six times, to be exact.

Once when I forgot to walk quietly on a road in shambles with far too much gravel and debris to be wandering about. Another time when I was careless in my assessment of my surroundings and hadn't seen the bloodred eyes blinking from the shadows. Then there was the evening I stayed out later than I should've, and the time I became too bold and greedy on a supply run. Once when I ran when I should've remained hidden.

And, then of course, the day I stopped caring whether I lived or died. We all have one of those days. A story about our darkest moment and how we overcame it. It's not a day I care to remember often, but it is one that taught me the most. The noctis who came and was more than willing to finish the job made me realize that I was done being a victim who could be robbed of my life at any given moment. It taught me that I was done making avoidable mistakes. No more lapses in judgment. That was the promise I made myself. This life? It might not be much of an existence, but it's still better than not having one at all.

That's what I keep telling myself anyway. Things *have* to change. Some day. Someone will eventually find a cure or an immunity, or maybe we'll get lucky and someone will find a way to obliterate every single monster.

Whoever it is to make the discovery, I want to be around when it happens. I want to be alive long enough to see what Arcathain had been like in its glory before it became the lie of the *United* Realm. Before the noctis. Before the demons.

I want to know what this world was like before it was cast in the shadows of monsters.

And so, I shove all thoughts from my mind and focus on the present. On the near-silent thud of my door closing behind me as I exit the false safety of my hovel. On the narrow, grey corridors I slink through, looking for any signs of life—or lack thereof. On the dank stench in the air, and the pockets that reek of gore, decaying skin, and rot.

I move through the streets of Gravenburg like a cat prowls through the night. I know the safest paths, the spots that require precise footing, and the best places to hide in case a predator comes lurking. And I leave all thoughts of job boards, my dead mother, and the notion of a cure back in my hovel.

No distractions. Not while I'm outside.

There are jobs to complete. Traps to check. Food to find. Ghouls to slaughter. And hopefully, if I play my cards right, I'll make it back home without spotting a single noctis.

I'm already deep into the city when something as cold as a dead man's finger taps my nose. The wet pitter-patter of rain plays a macabre melody that draws me to a complete stop.

"You've got to be fucking kidding me." My glare falls from the grey clouds clogging the sky down to the menacing, almost taunting, gleam of Sable's shadowood. "You couldn't have warned me?"

Sable knows better than anyone just how much I loathe the rain, even if she is just a crossbow. But only she was there the day I hid beneath the floorboards of my home as Hulbeck fell. Only she witnessed the showers of blood that splattered everything in a grotesque hue of red. Only she saw me days later when I dragged myself out from underneath the floor, my hair and face crusted with the blood of a dozen pour souls.

I don't just merely hate the rain. It makes me want to dive into the nearest lake and scrub my skin raw until I can no longer feel their blood.

It takes me less time than the last rainfall to gather myself, to remember that I'm standing in the middle of a Gravenburg street and recall the work I have left to do.

"Stupid!"

I curse myself, ducking into a small cave of rubble nearby. I should've noticed the signs, should've paid closer attention to the darkening clouds when I left. Not only does the rain repulse me, but it's not exactly a friend to stealth either. It dulls my ability to hear. Rain leaves puddles that, in turn, create tracks that the noctis—and maybe even the ghouls—are capable of following.

The alcove carved into the felled balcony is barely large enough for me to fit inside, and so my forehead and nose still stick out like lightning rods for the incurring downpour.

As much as I'd love to wait it out and avoid being pelted by raindrops and traumatic memories alike, there's no telling how long it will last.

I have to keep moving.

I have to check my traps before I can head back to my hovel.

For good measure, one more "fuck" slips from my lips and I emerge back onto the street.

I do what I can to avoid the already-forming puddles, but on roads made of stones, there are ample places for water to collect. And collect it does. Pretty soon, my squelching boots are all that I can hear as I sneak through the narrow streets, my fingers icy where they clutch Sable to my chest, my mind a monsoon of blood and screams and terror.

Not without having to stop a half dozen times to desperately try to wipe my face clean, finally, I make it to the first trap.

A pigeon is tangled in my snare, its head hanging limply against its grey breast, wings cocked at awkward angles from its thrashing. It wasn't a swift death; of that I am sorry. This trap wasn't meant for birds, and as such, it wasn't meant to hold a creature that would try to fly away and inadvertently knot itself up until it started suffocating.

My eyes burn, tears threatening to pool, but I bite the feeling down.

Setting Sable down at my ankles, I begin unknotting the bird. It never does get easier taking their cold bodies in my hand and unwinding the rough ropes from around their broken limbs and necks. It also doesn't get easier to ignore the gentle, somber melody that always drifts into my thoughts when I'm doing it.

When I was younger, my mother set traps in the garden to keep rabbits, mice, and other small critters out who might've otherwise been interested in snagging a free bite at the expense of her hard labor. She'd taught me how to tie snares such as this one. Despite the traps being necessary for our family to have the food we needed to eat and trade with, she was always upset whenever she'd find a dead animal caught within one, but I only ever knew because of the songs she'd sing as she'd twist the poor things free from the ropes and wires.

There was one song in particular that she favored in these moments, a tune soft and low that made me think of the journey we'd all take to our eternal slumber one day, the song like a guide or a doorway to glimpse what that might feel like.

It felt cold. Empty. And I always shuddered whenever she sang it.

Now, I have to clamp down on my tongue so that same melody doesn't find its way out of my mouth. Not while I'm out and vulnerable to any ghouls or noctis who might be around.

Once I've freed the dead bird from the snare, I grab my knife and an empty vial from my belt. I cradle the pigeon's breast in my hand, pinching the head to prop it up and make space for the vial beneath. Then, I slide the knife against the bird's throat, careful not to nick my own fingers and I collect the blood that is willing to spill.

But I'm a fool because I forgot about the rain.

I don't know if the ghouls can tell the difference between watered-down blood and the untainted kind, but I'd rather not risk finding out.

With the bird and the vial tucked beneath my breast, I retrieve Sable from the ground, angle my body over my work to try to prevent as much water from mixing with the blood as possible and race to the nearest awning. I look about as awkward and uncoordinated as I feel, I'm sure. And of course, as I run, I can't really see what's happening. I have no idea how much blood is falling into the vial and how much is splashing onto the ground until I stop to check it.

When I'm finally free from the downpour, I dare hold the pigeon and vial out to check my handiwork.

My stomach sinks. Not even a full vial's worth of blood— the amount I can usually get from a bird of this size—sloshes around when I give the container a shake. Judging from the thick consistency, that's either because the bird has sat too long and the blood has already coagulated, or because I wasted half of the bird's blood as I clambered over here.

Blood is blood though, I guess. I'll take what I can get.

Growling through my irritation, I cram the cork into the top of the vial and place the half-full container back on my belt. For a moment, I consider leaving the pigeon here. If the blood is this thick already, there's a chance the meat has also spoiled. But I can always make that choice later once I'm out of the rain and can better gauge the state of the creature, maybe even get a second opinion.

I tie the pigeon's legs together with some twine and secure it to the back of my belt.

One trap down, just a few more to go.

But with the rain, I'm not sure I can make it to them all. Not without losing my shit in the process.

One of them is fairly close though. Just a few blocks away, outside the old sewage system, so it might be more likely to have snagged a large rat, or perhaps even a fat racoon, and I can't afford to let a kill like that spoil just because I couldn't tough it out and shrug off a little rain.

There and back. I can afford that much.

Securing my knife back into its sheath at my hip, I begin my trot to the next trap.

I make my way toward the old marketplace in the center of town. Because of the ghouls who frequent here, it's one of the more dangerous neighborhoods in Gravenburg to travel.

That is, unless you know the safe way.

I turn down an alleyway, my feet nearly sliding out from under me on the wet stones, but I grip the ladder rung just in time. The metal bars are as slick as melting ice, making the contraption almost too slippery to climb. But it's only a story up, and I've fallen from greater heights before, so I propel myself up the rusted scaffolding anyway.

I keep low once I'm on the roof, blinking away the rain that pelts me in the eyes so that I might scan the other buildings for signs of danger. The ghouls rarely make their way up here. They're fueled by hunger alone, and they lost most of their basic functions during the final days of their human lives. But the noctis, however, *can* climb. And more importantly, so can humans. The kind of humans who prefer an aerial view so that they can ambush other fellow survivors. The kind who are desperate for meat, no matter what kind of creature it comes from. The kind who have all but lost their humanity.

One sweep of the surrounding rooftops is reassurance enough that I'm alone. On a dreary day like this one, I'm not surprised. Nonetheless, I swing Sable over my shoulder, ready in case I need her—one can never be too safe—and continue my trek.

From here, the path to the other trap is a lot more direct. Some of the buildings have connecting terraces, while others I've fashioned with makeshift bridges of fallen beams and boards, allowing me to cross the many corridors that I otherwise would have to weave in and out of.

It takes barely more than a hop, skip, and a jump to make my way to the building I'm searching for, the one that overlooks the hub of what had once been a bustling market. From my vantage point, I crouch even lower and fall silent.

Thankfully, the torrential downpour has slowed to a drizzle. My clothes might be soaked through, my fingers sodden to the bone where they rest on Sable's trigger, but at least the familiar sounds of Gravenburg are becoming more discernable.

And what I find makes my skin pinprick.

The truth is the city is never in absolute silence, not even after it's complete demise. It's as if the screams of the fallen have imbued the cobblestone streets, and they chase after you wherever you go, pleading for mercy, begging for justice. The dead don't sleep peacefully here, not in a place that has seen more death than a crypt. The ghouls are always hunting here. Always scavenging. Always making a ruckus. The noctis, too, don't care about being stealthy once they find something to devour.

Each monster moves about the city with their distinct noises. And today, I can tell it's not the noctis who are on the streets below me.

Slowly, I raise Sable's aim over the ledge and quietly pull myself up to peek over. Not all the way. Not so far that I could be spotted, but enough that just my eyesight can skim over the edge of the roof I'm leaning over.

At the base of one of the many heaping piles of refuse and

debris, stands a grey, emaciated creature. Its spine is so sharp, it looks like it might puncture through the thing's hunched back, its skin so thin and so pale that it's nearly translucent where it's stretched over its naked body. The ghoul looks more like a sickly birch tree in winter than the former husk of a human, all spindly branches rattling in the wind and ready to snap.

The sounds coming from it fuel my nightmares. Sounds that remind me of Hulbeck, of the worst day of my life. It's never one cohesive memory that pulses through me. Just flashes of images. Bursts of sound. None of it is ever in the right order—not that I can even remember what order that is anymore. Was I already beneath the floorboards when the noctis tore through our home? Were my hands already covered in my mother's blood by the time I found Agnes' lifeless corpse where she took her final stand outside my home? Sometimes when I recall running through the carnage days later with my eyes shut, I can hear the agonizing screams of my murdered neighbors, and other times only the silence of death. Sometimes it's my father's head among those stabbed on pikes along the beach, while other times I see none.

The one thing I know for certain is that all of them are dead now. Every single person who lived in Hulbeck with me.

Well, everyone except me and one other.

In memory of my family, my friends, and my neighbors alike, my finger twitches on Sable's trigger.

The ghoul before me could be one of them. We're a bit far south of Hulbeck, but if anyone had been left alive to turn, they could've made it to Gravenburg in the decade that's passed. Or perhaps the ghoul below me was one who swept through the town in the following days, and among the sloshing contents of its belly might've once been Agnes' face, my mother's intestines.

Making matters worse, the damned thing is eating my catch.

I steady my breath and take aim. All it will take is the slightest tap of pressure and my bolt will fly. From this distance, the ghoul's rotten brain has a very high chance of exploding out the back of its skull, not a mess that I'm going to be particularly thrilled about cleaning off my trap later but considering this foul creature has probably already tainted the meat of whatever vermin was caught down there anyway, I have nothing to lose. This way I get the satisfaction of reaping sweet revenge, I help rid the realm of one more monster, and I get to use the ghoul's corpse as a bartering chip when I head to the compound later.

It's a win-win-win situation, as far as I can tell.

My finger flexes against the curve of metal. The bowstring tenses where it's pulled taut, a loaded bolt just waiting to be launched.

But just as I'm about to make the kill, something hulking blocks my sights.

I peer around Sable to find a man, as tall as a carriage, standing behind the clueless ghoul. His broad shoulders block my shot, and I might be inclined to thank him for saving me one of my limited supplies of bolts if his proximity hadn't gone so alarmingly unnoticed.

No mere man could sneak up on a ghoul like that, completely undetected.

Which leads me to the only conclusion I can make: he is no mere man.

He is one of the deadly noctis. And I am in grave danger.

3

DON'T MAKE A SOUND

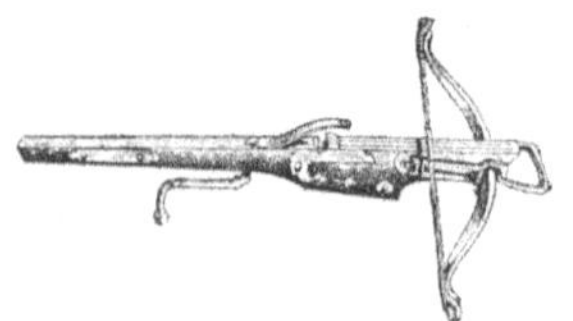

The noctis throws his head back, casting his long, greasy blond hair out of his face as he snatches the ghoul from behind. He sinks his fangs into the creature's throat before it's even had time to register what's going on and shriek out in protest.

Part of me wants to celebrate. Another ghoul taken off the streets and making this realm safer for humans again.

But part of me knows that ghoul's blood only serves to make this noctis more powerful, and for every ghoul he puts out of its misery, how many humans does he kill to satiate his appetite? How many more ghouls does he create whenever he inadvertently forgets to drain a body of its life completely?

In no time at all, the ghoul's translucent skin turns even more ashen. The lively limbs of the creature that had started to claw at the noctis, fall limp at its sides. Not a single drop of blood falls from the ghoul's neck, every ounce of it lapped up by the other monster gnawing on its neck.

If the ghoul is dead—or close enough to it—I might be able to finish the noctis. After all, my sights have already been set. My shot aimed and ready. I could kill the noctis with a single bolt to the skull just as he's finishing his meal and walk away victorious with new notches on my belt to boast whenever I make it back to town.

Once again, my shot is thwarted, and not a moment too late.

Another noctis steps out from the shadows from an alleyway below. He approaches the first noctis greedily, eyes hazed over with hunger. For a moment, I'm not sure if I'm about to witness the two predators fight to the death for their perceived entitlement on the kill, which would be foolish of the second considering he's about half of the other's stature. My wishful thinking is proven wrong when the first noctis tosses the half-drained ghoul to his friend, who wastes no time slurping up his sloppy seconds.

Sable and I are a prolific team, but we can only fire one bolt at a time. If I pull the trigger now, only one noctis would go down, and the other would disappear into the shadows before I could get another shot off. I'd blow my cover. I'd risk my life for no reason.

Killing them isn't an option. Either I can remain hidden and hope that they leave as soon as they're done sharing their meal, or I can run now, get a head start, and hope that by the time they notice my scent or tracks, I'm already long gone.

The larger noctis wipes the leftover blood dribbling down his chin. Licking his fingers, he grimaces and glares at the ghoul. "Fucking filth."

The second noctis finishes his grotesquely wet slurping and tosses the dead creature aside with a pucker of his own. "You could say that again. But hey, food is food."

"They're pests," the first noctis snarls.

Nervous laughter jostles the scrawny one's shoulders. "Yeah, well, the way I see it, it's like nature's looking out for us. This guy fed one of us when he was still human and was left alive to turn so that now he gets to feed one of us again—or in his case, two. He's a three-for-one." There's something about his voice that makes my skin crawl, and I'm grateful when he pauses, turning thoughtful. A shy hint of pride glints behind his wide, murderous pupils. "Come to think of it, that might not be such a bad way of doing things."

The other noctis sounds unconvinced. "They're the reason there aren't enough humans anymore. You can't honestly think that—"

He stops short, something catching his interest at his feet.

With swelling dread, I realize what it is.

My trap.

The large noctis assesses the compound, and I slide silently down to pin myself against the small wall of the rooftop's ledge, my neck torqued at an awkward angle.

"What's caught your eye, Gregor?" The scrawny one's voice is distinct in its nasally tone.

The other noctis responds with a grizzled grunt. "Look." He doesn't elaborate, but I know he's toeing my trap. "No signs of rust on the metal."

"Well, I'll be blighted. Would you look at that? There's a gift for us too." There's a brief pause, and it's not until I hear the metal chain of my trap clanking that I realize he's knelt beside it for a better look. "This rat looks like it's still fresh."

No one should ever sound so jubilant to utter such a sentence. And though I can't see him, the way I'm imagining the both of them licking their lips and salivating over the rat's corpse ties my stomach in knots.

There's a commotion below, more chains rattling.

"Fuck the rat," Gregor says, voice as harsh as a storm. He sniffs and my chest tightens. "You smell that? Fresh blood."

Fuck.

If I stay here, they'll find me. I know they will. Now that they've caught the scent of blood in the air, and they've found a trap—one clearly set by human hands—they'll stop at nothing to find whoever's responsible for its handiwork.

"You think someone set this recently?"

"Mmm," Gregor grunts. "Might even live near here."

I need a plan, and fast. One that doesn't involve me being seen. But that seems impossible until they leave the marketplace.

There's another hint of pride in the scrawny one's voice as the two of them start skulking around the compound. "Who knew someone could live in this disgusting dung heap, eh?" When Gregor doesn't respond, there's a thudding sound. "Me. I thought it. Looks like I was right to suggest we come this far. The others—"

"Boris, that's enough. We should alert the others."

Others? How many more could there be?

"Aye-aye, captain"—I hear the ruffling of clothes and assume he's lifting his arm in salute, but I don't understand the disappointment that follows— "Well ain't that just the piss-end of a horse."

Gregor grunts. "What?"

"The blood oath. Looks like the rain got to it."

The blood...what?

Clothes shuffle again.

"Fuck," Gregor says, and the two of them fall silent for a moment. Whatever the blood oath was, it sounds like something they wanted to hold onto, and therefore despite having no clue what it is, I'm grateful it's no longer in their possession. I listen to Gregor's thunderous pacing. "We search the area on our own then. See if we can find anything."

There's a long stretch of silence, punctured only by their subtle movements as they explore the marketplace ruins. My heart bangs against my insides, rattling my ribcage and telling every inch of my body to run far, far away. But maybe I'm thinking about this all wrong. They have no reason to believe I'm on this rooftop. They didn't see me up here. And the blood Gregor scented could easily be shirked off as belonging to the ghoul or the rat once they stop presuming a human is nearby. They will, however, see me if I move. They'll know I'm here if I so much as swallow too loudly.

I've made the mistake before of running when I should've stayed hidden. I've let my nerves convince me I'm in danger when logic could've assured me otherwise. Hiding is how I survived Hulbeck and it's how I've survived most of my days since.

"How long you think?" the one called Boris asks. "How long before they're back?"

"Meat spoils fast. A trap like this would need to be checked often. Every day maybe. Whoever set it, they'll be back. Soon."

There's a short pause, long enough that I start to fear that one of them might've heard my heart pounding and rattling Sable where she's clutched against me. I squeeze her tighter. I need a plan, one that won't draw their attention up here.

That's going to be nearly impossible given our proximity and the way these old, dilapidated buildings like to creak.

"Or maybe this guy, here—" To enunciate his meaning, Boris thumps something. The ghoul maybe? "—ate whoever it was. He's plump enough. Could've had a meal recently."

Gregor makes a frustrated sound. "True or not, we're here for one reason: to find the king some fodder for his fucking Hunt."

The king? As in, King Tor Devonshire? Fuck, of course he means *that* king; there are no others. Which means he's talking about the same king who strode into Hulbeck on horseback and commanded his noctis to go home-to-home searching for *him*—whoever *him* was.

At the mere thought of his name, my heartbeat triples its pace. I'm back beneath those floorboards again, those horse hooves galloping overhead, the noctis pillaging my home while I lay curled in a ball in a hole.

I'm so busy trying to catch my breath and convince myself that I'm not that frightened, helpless little girl anymore, that the second part of that sentence goes unnoticed.

"It doesn't matter what's in this ghoul's belly as long as we don't return empty-handed!"

"I know, I know," Boris groans. "You don't gotta remind me what's at stake here."

"Apparently, I fucking do," Gregor bellows, the sound exploding throughout the courtyard. "What did the prince say before we left?" He hardly gives Boris a chance to respond. "What did he say?"

Reluctantly, the other noctis does as he's beckoned. "That it's our hides if we don't bring back some live ones. Fresh blood pumping through their veins, or nothing."

"Mmm. So, you're not a complete idiot?"

"Only half," Boris says with an almost boy-like chuckle. "So, what do we do? Where do we start? Oh man, can you imagine the look on Malachi's face if we actually find a human? Do you think he'll give us a taste?"

"Doubtful."

A sorrowful moan whines from the scrawny noctis. "What I wouldn't give to drink some real blood—not that ghoul sludge-shit."

"Mhmm," Gregor mumbles his agreement, but even though I can't see him, I can sense his attention isn't on the ghoul, but on every alleyway, shadow, and even the rooftops.

I don't know what to do. They don't seem to be moving on. And if they need to return with a human and the only lead they've found is my trap, then what reason would they have to go before turning every inch of this place over?

"We start here," Gregor says, returning to Boris' original line of panicked questioning. "The ghoul was chomping on rat guts, for fuck's sake. I doubt he ate a human recently. I think the man who set this trap is still out there—"

Man?

Whatever. He can presume whatever he wants to presume. His underestimation of me can be forged into a weapon, one I intend to use if I get the chance.

"Even if he is long gone, it's the best chance we have in this ghost town."

"So, then…" Boris begins, skeptically. "We keep searching?"

"Mhmm. If we can get on the rooftops, we'll have a better view."

The air suddenly feels like acid in my lungs.

Shit. Shit. Shit.

Time is running out, and so are my options.

Whether out of desperation or instinct, my hands find their way to my belt and rummage over its contents. A knife could prove useful in close combat, but I've never been very good with one other than to clean game. The twine beside it that I use for tying snares? Even less effectual.

Next to it, my fingers glide over the soft feathers of the dead, bloodless pigeon. It wouldn't be a good enough distraction for a ghoul, let alone the two hungry noctis below. But the blood in my vial…

The blood might be enough.

Hastily, I tear the only vial from my belt with anything inside it and pour the contents over my fingers. With the tips stained a horrendous shade of crimson, I drag them down my chin.

My attention flits back below, to the plotting noctis, and the words that leave Gregor's mouth next fill my chest like cement.

"I go high. You go low."

Of course it would be the big one.

My hands are shaking. I try cramming the vial back into the belt, but my fingers and the leather won't cooperate. The notches feel like they've shrunk to the size of toothpicks, the jar suddenly too big to fit. And my blood pumps furiously through my veins, giving me far more strength than I need for the task, and thus, I make my seventh mistake.

My thumb slips from where it's gripping the vial, and the container springs out of my grasp.

I watch it fall in slow motion. It shatters with a crystalline chime that rings in my ears with deafening harshness.

The noctis fall silent.

They know I'm here.

The way I calculate it, I have three seconds until they're upon me.

Being silent is no longer useful, so instead I fling myself forward onto all fours, not bothering to hide the top of my head from their eyesight.

Two seconds.

I rip the dead pigeon from my belt.

One second.

And I sink my teeth into the raw breast and savagely tear at the meat.

I've seen the way monsters eat. The way they tear at flesh like they're pirates savagely digging for gold. They don't care about the mess they create, or how much destruction they cause. They only care about their rubies, about letting the blood flow into their mouth, no matter how many feathers they swallow in the process.

And so, I pretend I'm the same. I forget about the necessity of being quiet and instead take on a new survival characteristic, one that makes me as loud and insatiable as I've seen them become. I hunch over the pathetic meal as if it's a decadent feast and I bite and chew and swallow every piece of cold, plumy flesh I can muster. A flash of a memory tries to infiltrate my resolve, one of me trapped beneath floorboards while a torrential downpour of blood showers me, but I shove the unwanted thing aside. I'm not under those floorboards now. It's not the blood of my family and neighbors oozing down my throat, and that is the only reason I can keep chewing. I can keep swallowing, as long as I'm able if it means survival. Until—

Feet land forcefully somewhere beside me, behind me, as if they've just jumped all the way up the side of the building. Despite every instinct in my body telling me to look or flinch or run, I stay where I am. I keep eating the bird and tell myself that the churning in my stomach is just part of the fear. The adrenaline of being so close to monsters.

It's not until one of their feet steps into view where I'm knelt that I finally acknowledge them.

Dark hair frames my face in velvety curtains as I peer up, hunger alit in my deadly eyes.

Gregor's robust frame casts me in shadow. For a noctis, someone who is seemingly hunting for scraps for a king who can no longer promise them nightly feasts, he sure doesn't look as if he's starving. Maybe there are enough ghouls to keep them fed. For now.

After the briefest assessment, I growl, clutching my pigeon closer. "Oh. What a pity. You're no human, are you?"

Gregor watches me for a moment, his mind working somewhere inside that hard skull. Finally, he settles back onto his heels, unfolding his arms. "No."

"Figures," I say, something like relief washing over me that he isn't already biting into me. I'll take the small win. "It would be nice to dine on a human heartbeat again someday."

Though my stomach twists and turns, my heart begins to settle. The hardest part of this rouse was always the beginning. The noctis are smarter than ghouls, but still in many ways as dumb as humans can be. All it ever takes is a little blood, and maybe a fresh corpse for added effect, and they're almost eager to believe I'm one of them. After all, what human would ever dare face them instead of run?

Boris inches forward then. "It's a pity, isn't it? Eating scraps like a bunch of dogs."

"Worse than dogs," I say, and this appears to appeal to him, as if we're now bonded over our hardships. He has no idea what hardship truly is. He thinks that being forced to eat animals instead of killing humans is such a plight? The only reason there are so few humans for noctis like him to eat is because they've already feasted their way through the country. The ones they left for dead but didn't quite finish the job turned into ghouls that ravaged the remaining cities and cut mankind off at the knees.

My knife calls to me, the metal blade practically a siren serenading me to make the kill. But I remain strong. I can survive this, if only I keep myself in check.

"So, uh," Boris says, pulling me back into the conversation. "You haven't seen any live ones around these parts, have you?"

"None," I reply, maybe too quickly judging by the glance exchanged by the both of them. "I'm just passing through, really. What about you? You must track them down pretty easily between the two of you?"

"If only." Boris laughs. "It seems Gravenburg is just as dead as Neveridge, and every sad city between."

"Is that where you came from? Neveridge?" I'm mostly just trying to be casual, but I had already guessed that's where they were from since they are working directly for the king.

"Yep," he says proudly. "Home sweet home."

Under the guise of interest, I try milking him for information. "You traveled all this way? Just for food? Are we really so fucked?"

Why has the king lead them here is what I really want to ask them. Why are they so far away from the noctis castle?

Humor lights him up. "Oh, no. Not exactly. We're with the

Prince's envoy. Scouting ahead to collect donations for the Hunt."

My heart skitters to a halt. The words *the Hunt* are almost too foreign for my mind to comprehend. I remember hearing tales of it when I was a child. But as I grew older, I just assumed the Hunt was a legend spread around towns to scare children into obeying their curfews and the rules about staying within the compound walls, safely tucked away from the noctis who might snatch them out of the shadows.

The Hunt, as I recall, was said to be an annual game of barbaric delight. In the months leading up to it, humans were captured, imprisoned, and then released. But not back to the safety of their homes. No, they were released into a field of death, one where noctis from every corner of the realm were said to indulge their most primal and carnal desires in a race to kill as many humans as they could.

When I was a little girl, the idea of the Hunt had filled me with such soul-quenching dread that the night Rowland told me about it, I refused to sleep anywhere but in my mother's arms.

Hearing Boris mention it now makes me feel much the same.

Of all the ways to die in this world, being hunted for sport as a source of entertainment for the very monsters who have already made our lives miserable, ranks up there for the worst possible way to die.

I shouldn't be surprised it's real. Many legends are born from fact.

Besides, the job board has been more cluttered than usual lately with missing persons reports. All this time, I just presumed them dead. Or worse, that they'd been turned into ghouls by the hundreds still scattered about Gravenburg. Little did I know that perhaps some of them—if not most—were being rounded up by King Tor's Crimson Guard to be stored for the Hunt.

It's possible I never knew the truth because they've never had to come this far for recruitment before. The human population dwindles more each year, especially with the ghouls' numbers rising.

"Oh well." Boris shrugs. "We won't be in this graveyard for long. We'll be heading north to Nigh by week's end." Noticing my lingering confusion, he adds, "That's where the Hunt'll be this year. Taking us back to our roots into the Shadowthorn."

He's right to assume my ignorance. Practically everything he's shared with me has been a new piece of the puzzle that I didn't have until today. And valuable information at that. To think of what kind of price it would fetch back at the compound sends a trill of excitement fluttering into my stomach. If I mistakenly believed the Hunt was just a fairytale, it's likely I'm not the only one. More than that, the knowledge that this year's Hunt will practically be held in our backyard will be invaluable to every human nearby, especially the compound leaders.

I need to make it out of this alive and pay them a visit. If not for my sake, then for the boneheaded leader of *Barretsville*—or whatever they're calling it—whom I call friend.

And maybe that visit needs to come sooner rather than later. After all, now that I'm close-ranged, I can't take on two noctis. I'm not even sure I could handle one. Especially not when one is the size of an ox, and the other is slimy enough that I imagine he'd slip out of my grasp the moment I tried anything funny.

There are sentries outside of the secret town though. Sharpshooters with aims almost as true as mine. Almost.

If I could get Gregor and Boris to the outskirts of the commune, they wouldn't be a threat to anyone anymore. And they certainly wouldn't have any more opportunity of snatching away some of the locals.

"It's morbid if you ask me," Gregor says abruptly, upper lip peeled back and accentuating his bloodstained teeth. "Five years I spent trapped there. No need to go back."

It takes me a moment to realize what he's saying, but eventually the history of demonkind that had been taught ad nauseum finally catches up to me. The demons who lived in the Shadowthorn were venomous. One bite would kill a human. But for the druids, the bite was merely the start of a transformation.

Many of them lived among the demons for years, some for decades. But when balance was restored to the ancient Primordial, the blighted druids were cured. For a time. They at least return to their human form, but the bloodlust remained.

Thus, the noctis were born.

Boris merely shrugs at him. "Some like the thrill of it. Being back in those dark woods. Makes them feel strong again."

"Strong," he sneers. "A caged animal is no threat. We are stronger now than we ever were there."

The irony of what he's saying doesn't evade me. For someone who clearly has a disdain of being caged, he certainly seems to have no qualms doing the same thing to the humans he's procuring for his precious king.

Boris looks as if he's heard all this before and is quite exhausted by the repetitive conversation. "Sure, but at least caged animals aren't starved animals. They're fed daily, their strength kept intact. Look at her, for fuck's sake. Picking her teeth with pigeon bones. The ghouls have all but devoured the country."

"Not the whole country," Gregor says, and as he does, he strides to the edge of the building and looks down. "Someone's here. Laying traps."

The groan that escapes Boris is exaggerated and long. "One

sorry sack of life is hardly enough to sustain the entire noctis population." He meanders over to his friend, feet dragging the whole way.

Finally, I see my opportunity.

"You know," I begin, shoving myself off the ground and resisting the urge to wipe the blood from my chin. "There might be more than one sorry sack of life around these parts."

I pique their interests, Boris looking positively savage with glee, while Gregor is clearly still deciding whether I can be trusted. But at least he's curious.

"And what makes you say that?" Gregor asks.

I form a lie, and I do so quick. "Last night there was a massacre—actually, just a few blocks from here. Five or six ghouls slaughtered and left in a bloody mess. I doubt they killed themselves."

The crook of one of Boris' bushy brows hikes up. "They still had their blood in them?"

"Mhmm. Well, not *in* them. But definitely *around* them."

I let them draw their own conclusions. It makes them feel like they arrived at the information on their own, and everyone knows they can trust themselves more than they can trust a stranger.

Boris aims to give Gregor a triumphant pat to the chest, their problems all but solved, but the man is so tall that he barely grazes the bottom of his ribs. It doesn't deter Boris' excitement though. I'm not sure anything could at this point.

"Killed by humans then. Gregor, this is great!"

Not a reason I ever thought I'd hear a noctis celebrating...

"Mmm." Gregor sneers. "Almost too good to be true."

I give a careless flick of my hand and turn away. "Don't believe me if you'd like. It's of no consequence to me."

Gregor's glare burns into the back of my skull. Behind me, I hear them whispering, Boris begging the man to loosen up and trying to appeal to his senses. They need to find bodies. I'm the best lead they've got.

"We could run it by Malachi if you'd like?" I hear Boris shrug. "Send him word through the blood oath—"

It's the second time that name has been mentioned. It sounds familiar, but before I can place it, Gregor erupts in a fit of frustration.

"The blood oaths are gone, remember?" He thrusts one burly arm into the air, brandishing a wrist that's tinged burgundy.

Could that be...blood? And was it actually painted on his skin in some elaborate design? Judging from the crusted lines and shapes remaining, I shudder to think it is. But who's blood was it? And how would they possibly use it to communicate to the others?

"Why tell us?"

There's something sinister in his tone, something that suggests if I answer wrong, it'll be the death of me.

I make sure to answer right.

"I assume you've been traveling with others for a while, yes? Maybe you've forgotten what it's like to be on your own. It's not too different from what you've described, Boris. I'm eating scraps. I'm not as strong as I should be, and I'm only one"—the word *human* nearly slips from my lips, but somehow, I manage to catch it at the back of my teeth before I can blow my cover—"I'm only one. And to come across humans who could take down a half dozen crazed ghouls—with none of their own dead and left behind, I might add—needless to say, it wasn't anything I planned on sticking my nose in. I hid for the night and decided to leave town this morning.

"But between the three of us," I continue, turning back around and facing them with renewed hope—albeit faked. "With tall, thick, and grisly over here, and with the two of us, we might be able to feast like we once had. Like during the glory days."

Gleeful delight flashes behind Boris' dark eyes, and he claps his hands together like a small child witnessing whatever it is that children have to be excited about anymore.

"Feasting like kings, we'd be. Now, doesn't that sound like something we'd want to do, Gregor?"

The burly noctis doesn't blink, his noxious eyes never once relieving me from their sharp hold. I'm just about to give up, to excuse myself and hope that they'll let me leave in one piece, when he finally says, "You remember where you found them?"

"I do," I say, anticipation a flutter in my belly. My plan might actually be working.

"And you believe they have reason to return."

My shoulders bob. "I think they're local to the area. Whether they'd return to that spot, I don't know. But we could scope it out, see if they left any indication of where they might've gone, or where they'll go next."

Gregor thinks for a moment. "Fine. But we don't feast. We need the humans for the Hunt."

The words *fair enough* almost pass from my lips until I realize how foolish that would make me sound. I'm playing the part of a starving noctis who was just caught tearing into a pigeon. Being told I'm not allowed to eat should ruffle my feathers, at a bare minimum if I want to keep up the ruse.

Fortunately, Boris takes the lead on that.

"What? Are you out of your bloody mind? We've been at it for days. We need to eat!"

"And we will." Gregor's teeth grind together as he narrows his eyes at his partner. "When we return to Nigh."

"And what about me?" I push, hoping to sound convincing. "What's in it for me? I have no plans of going to Nigh with you."

The corner of Gregor's lip ticks up.

"Just one?" Boris begs. "The king would understand"—thinking better of it, he corrects himself— "The king doesn't have to know that we fed on one human if we return with three? Five? Ten?"

Gregor casts a glare his way. "Facing ten would be too risky."

"True enough. But if it's a small party, we could take them. One a piece at least."

"I could take two," I chime in and hope the bullshit I'm speaking doesn't reek.

Gregor considers the options a moment longer. He glances over his shoulder back down to where my trap and the dead ghoul still lays.

"Fine. If we find humans and there are more than six, we do nothing."

A toothy grin splits Boris' face, an orangish hue staining his teeth. "And we can eat one of them? Shared between the three of us?"

"Fine," Gregor grumbles.

"Great," I say, a wicked grin emerging that they mistakenly assume has to do with the prospect of drinking human blood. But I'm just excited that my plan is working. "Follow me then."

These noctis should know as well as anyone that there are rules to follow in this world, and they've just broken the most sacred. Whether it be human or monster, trust no one.

4

VALOR

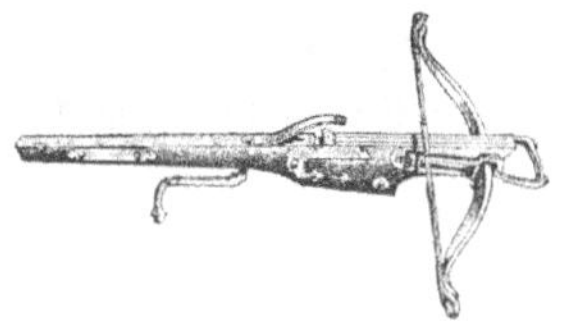

"We've gone more than *a few* blocks."

Ahead of me, Gregor marches with the intensity of a bull that's just been castrated, all seething discomfort and grudging trust. He doesn't want to keep moving. Part of him knows it'll be the death of him. But without proof, and with the promise of greener pastures on the other side, he has no choice.

He hasn't looked back at me once, not the way most distrusting people would. Then again, he's not a person. He's an apex predator. I am no threat to him. Even if I really was a noctis like he believes, his arms are triple mine in size. If I was leading him into an ambush—which I am, of course, and which he might be starting to suspect me of doing—it wouldn't take much pressure for him to lock my neck into the crook of his arm and pop my head off my shoulders.

It's a fate I'm not eager to accept, so I muster the charm I'm sometimes forced to use when bartering at the market.

"Sorry, that's my fault," I mutter, the illustration of coy innocence. "I was distracted by Boris' stories of dining from goblets in the castle. I think we might've missed a turn or two."

When Gregor aims his hateful glare over his shoulder it strikes the babbling idiot beside me, but the effect is all but void.

Boris waves, fending himself from the anger that might otherwise snuff his good mood. "Ah, give us a break. Will you? We've been at it for weeks. What's a quick detour, especially when we're enjoying such lovely company?" The way he turns to look at me, heavy-lidded and eyes aglow, makes the pigeon blood in my stomach curdle. "I never did catch your name, by the way, dove?"

Gregor rolls his eyes and I panic, spluttering the first name that comes to mind.

"Agnes. I'm called Agnes." When my rushed response seems to cause him some distrust, I add hastily, "I can't remember the last time I gave someone my name. Like I said, I usually travel alone. It's been a long time since I've actually...spoken to anyone." The lies become easier the more I suffuse them with the truth. Just as my dear friend Rowland taught me, all those years ago. "Let alone, heard lavish stories about how the other half lives. I guess it pays to know the king."

If you're into being associated with bloodthirsty monsters who singlehandedly killed mankind and set about a new era of terror.

"No apologies necessary, Agnes," Boris chirps, the crags of his face lighting up in a horrific way. "We'll keep you company as long as you'd like."

I'm thankful when Gregor jerks around, snuffing out the light and casting Boris back into gloomy shadow. The noctis don't deserve to feel things like excitement and elation. Anger, disappointment, and hunger are all his expression should ever know.

"Perhaps it's time you shut up and let the woman think," the large noctis roars. "I don't want to spend half the day walking in circles, listening to you two prattle on, just so you can get your cock wet by evening."

We both stiffen, but I'm sure it's for different reasons.

The chastisement has the desired effect though. Boris, with his hands crammed into his pockets, doesn't utter another word, or crack another smile for the remainder of our walk through the city. It's a good thing too because my mind needs a break. My stamina for social interactions is almost nonexistent, let alone ones that involve pretending to cozy-up next to the monsters I despise. Every word I've uttered, every smile or laugh I've feigned, has tasted like a betrayal. Every time I've had to pretend that I was interested in another one of Boris' kill stories, a pool of poison has sunk into my belly until my well became nothing but lies and death.

I shudder to think what would happen if someone from the commune saw me walking around with not one, but two noctis. What they'd think. What they'd do.

"How much farther?" Gregor asks, pulling me back to the present, back to the dismal streets that feel far more welcoming than the place I'd been in my head.

Shaking the useless worries out of my mind, I point ahead. "Just around the corner. Take a left here."

He takes the turn, his disgruntled nature softening at the prospect of our arrival.

When he sees the compound, he stops mid-stride.

It's not that it's so obvious to the naked eye. There aren't any signs reading *Fresh Meat! Come Eat Your Humans Here!* or pikes displaying the rotten heads of noctis and ghouls alike. At first glance, it's hardly discernable from any other street in Gravenburg. Some buildings are seemingly unscathed by the horrors that laid roots in this city, their shutters intact, and not a single weed breaking through the foundation. Then there are others that are in complete disarray. Eschewed doors hanging off their hinges. The collapsed buildings, the rubble, the dust.

But the one quality that the rubble possesses on this street that most others lack is tidiness.

The stones that crumbled from the walls when the demons plowed through the town have been stacked to one side of the road. The carts of discarded goods that didn't even have value in the aftermath like handcrafted jewelry, corsets, and pipes, have all been swept into a pile. If either of the noctis with me were to peer into the windows on this block, they'd find that the buildings are almost entirely free of dust and cobwebs. That's because they're put to use, on occasion, when the town runs out of room beyond the wall. The homes and shops out here have become temporary storing units, or prison cells for noctis and ghouls they've kept alive long enough to torture for information, or for science.

Having anticipated Gregor's keen eye to cause him to stop abruptly, I'm not the one to run straight into him.

"I don't get it," Boris says once he's had a chance to stagger back into place beside his partner. "What do you see? What are we looking at here?"

Gregor takes it in for a moment longer, a deep breath the only thing to puncture the silence as we anticipate his answer. "It's...clean."

Boris scratches the thin, wiry hair atop his head. "Well, I'll be damned. Not pristine by any standards, but it is clean, isn't it?" He leans forward, addressing me on the other side. "This is where you found them? Where they killed those ghouls?"

Fortunately, our ruse is over. Now that they're both in the line of sight, I don't have to put up with this game any longer. And when the corners of my lips twitch, I don't stop them from curving into the vile, satisfied smile I've been looking forward to since we left the rooftop.

"No. No ghouls died here," I say, voice laced with deadly intent. "But this is where *you* die."

Before his expression can even wilt with realization, an iron bolt—no doubt fletched by Elison Wade, the best fletcher around and the only one that I'll ever do business with—

pierces Boris right through the eye socket. His undamaged eye blinks in time with his sputtering lips, but it's only a matter of seconds before he collapses, utterly boneless.

Another shot fires, but it's slower than the first. Perhaps a grave mistake on their end. Or on mine.

The first bolt acts as a warning bell, giving Gregor just enough of a heads-up that when the second quarrel comes flying a split second later, he's already spun out of its trajectory. The noctis is smarter than he looks, and it's my fault for not giving him credit for that sooner.

He dodges the deadly blow and charges toward me.

"Fuck me—" The words I mutter are ripped from my lungs in a whoosh of air as the mountain of a man slams into me. My head cracks against the brick wall, a burst of white blinding my eyes.

"I knew you couldn't be fucking trusted."

"Apparently not," I say groggily. "Since you followed me anyway." I'm not sure what possesses me to provoke him. Adrenaline, I guess. But the foolhardy, taunting words will surely only be the start.

Pinning me in place, he grinds his forearm against the ball of my throat. "Oh, I knew you were up to something. You either set the trap, or you were gonna lead us to who did."

All things considered, I'm feeling pretty smug for a human girl who's cornered and struggling to breathe. Or at least, I am until he smiles.

"Never thought you'd lead us straight to the whole nest."

My eyes widen at the realization, a wriggling worm of dread sinking deep into my gut. All this time I thought I was the one with a leg up. I thought I was in control. But he was just using me. And like a naïve little girl who thinks herself smarter than anyone else, I fell for it.

I led him here. To a community no different than Hulbeck. And now that he knows where they are, if he escapes, he'll run back to his king and tell them where they can find a nice big catch for their Hunt.

An arrow whirs overhead, drawing the attention of both of our gazes. Thanks to a large stack of rocks beside us, the sentries can't get a good aim.

That just means I need to make it easier for them.

With as much force as I can muster, I cram my knee into his groin. Gregor staggers back, but the moment he exposes himself, instead of fighting me or waiting around for another archer to take aim, he hobbles away, dodging behind every source of cover he can find—upturned carts, beams, doorways.

I can't let him go.

My first instinct is to take aim myself, but Gregor would already be around the corner by the time I loaded Sable. And by the time I'd chase after him, he'd be around the next. And then the next. He's lumbering enough though that I might be able to catch him in a run. But then what? I can't take him hand-to-hand. And I don't even know how far away his gang is. What if they're close? If I chase after him, how long before I raced headfirst, neck exposed, into a den of fangs with appetites?

I'll just have to catch him before then, and hope that my knife and my bullheaded determination to survive will give me the edge I need.

Realizing with a heavy heart that I'll be faster without her and therefore less likely to find myself in a noctis den, I cast Sable aside and run after the big guy.

By the time I round the corner, feet slipping and sliding on the freshly damp cobblestones, making them even deadlier than usual, Gregor is already at the end of the street. Once again, I've underestimated him. I should've known his bulk is more athletic than sluggish, especially since I saw him make use of his impressive speed earlier when he suddenly appeared on the rooftop beside me.

I forgot how fast the noctis can be. It's usually limited, and once they use their preternatural burst of haste, they resume a more human speed. But even as brief as it is, that burst was enough to give Gregor a major advantage over me.

I'm in the very predicament I feared. It'll take me blocks to catch up to him at this rate, and by then, who knows how far away from the community I'll be, how far away from Sable, and how nestled into noctis territory I will have cozied.

Legs thrashing at full-speed ahead, Gregor glances over his broad shoulder. Something like glee flashes behind his dark gaze, like he thinks he can actually win this. Like he thinks a human girl couldn't possibly catch up to him.

But he's wrong.

I may be small, and I might not be as strong as someone of his stature, but I've been running my whole life. It's what I do.

Never underestimate someone who's greatest asset is the ability to survive.

He takes the next turn wide, his body too top-heavy for the tight corner-hugging that I'm able to do. It doesn't cost him much, but it's enough. Each corner we fly around, each pile of rubble we clear, I gain that much more on him, until eventually he's not even halfway down the road from me.

I'm so close to the racing noctis that the puddles he tromps through splash onto my pants as I race right behind him. I'm tempted to grab my knife now. Without Sable smacking my back, it would be a comfort to have at least some weapon at my immediate disposal for when I catch him.

But suddenly Gregor takes a hard right. He disappears into a near-black alleyway, and I follow after him, hell-bent on ending this chase and the terror he's likely inflicted upon hundreds of innocents once and for all.

It's not until I'm shrouded in the cool darkness that I realize that something is terribly wrong.

The glee I glimpsed in his expression earlier flashes before my eyes again. It was more than mere ego or arrogance that had him smiling. It was a primal sort of relishing. The sort of dark triumph reflected in a hawk's amber eyes the moment they lock onto their prey. The hawk knows the field mouse stands no chance against it, and watching it race for its futile life only makes the predator all the more excited for the kill.

And it means Gregor has fooled me again.

He stops at the end of the road. I don't have to look around to realize that I am completely, and utterly alone, and I made myself this way. We are so far from the sentries that not even Sable and I could make that shot were our positions swapped. As nice as it would be to rely on the aid of others, a lifetime of experience has also taught me that reliance on anyone but myself only breeds false hope. Those same sentries are the ones who didn't time their shots correctly and missed the one clean shot at Gregor they had. They're likely still standing in their towers wondering what the hell just happened and why I was with the noctis. If we were still within shot, they might've even shot me next, unsure if I'd have turned into one of the creatures myself—it's rare as fuck, but it does occasionally happen, if someone with druid blood is bitten.

Better to have no one around to further botch things up for me than to have clueless, frightened strangers holding my life in their hands.

I wish I had Sable though. With Gregor holding still now instead of dashing around every corner, my aim would be true. With his haste gone, I might've even had enough time to load her up and fire.

But none of that matters now.

All I have is my knife, my slippery and evasive size, and my will to survive.

And all three will be used to my advantage.

He exposes his left wrist and I catch another glimpse of the dark stain upon his flesh. It's too fast for me to get much of a look, other than to notice that the marking appears more faded now.

Whatever the design means, the sight of it makes him curse, and he shoves the sleeve down again.

"Dead end," Gregor growls, the words made of crushed stones.

I can't tell if the wrist thing is supposed to be a distraction, but I'm done underestimating him. I'm done letting this vile creature puppeteer the game of *who will win: me or the monsters* that I was thrust into the day I was born. I've been outrunning noctis and cheating death longer than he has. I've had practice with surviving the monsters because I know that my life could be forfeit any second of any day.

He, on the other hand, believes himself impervious. With any luck, it's that ego that'll get him killed.

"Cute," I say, leaning onto one hip and cocking my head at him. "But last I checked *you* were the one running like a scared little boy. What's the matter? Afraid to lose a fight against a mortal girl?"

The only warning I get that he's about to lunge is the slightest flash of his bared teeth before his feet are tearing back down the alleyway toward me. Arms outstretched, I'd expect to find claws at the end of his sausage fingers, instead of the gnawed down, bloodstained fingertips.

But his hands aren't the weapons I need to keep my eyes on.

Sharp fangs poke down from his upper jaw on a mighty roar that shakes my heart.

I grab my knife and raise it, blade shaking as panic climbs up my spine. I feel fucking ridiculous. It's been…I can't even remember the last time I used this knife on anything other than skinning the poor critters that wander into my traps. And something tells me that he's not just going to sit here and let me flay him.

One of Gregor's arms hitches back, a mighty blow prepping

to launch into my face once he's close enough. And in a few more strides, he will be.

I move my aim, positioning my knife at the large man's cocked fist—as if that's going to deter him in any way, shape, or form. As if seeing my tiny ass blade is going to make him stop dead in his tracks, and be like, *Oh shit. You have a knife? My mistake. I will be on my way then and let you resume your scouting.*

What the fuck was I thinking?

Never—*ever*—fight a noctis. Not in hand-to-hand combat. And certainly not when there was a choice to just let him *run*.

Instead, I foolishly thought of the town. Of the people I lost in Hulbeck. And I'd let my fragile, human heart feel sorry for them. Feel guilty for bringing about their demise. When in reality they chose to live with a target on their backs! Not me!

I should've let Gregor run, warned them about the information he had about their location, and then left the fucking city.

I guess it's too late now.

Frightened, and backed into a dark corner, I can't help but feel like the small child I'd been the day Hulbeck was destroyed. I'm not sure I'll ever outgrow her. Truthfully, the noctis will always terrify me. They will always be stronger, faster, deadlier. No matter how long I survive, or how many I fight.

I am just human. A nobody. A nothing.

With his arm still locked in position, Gregor grabs my wrist with his other hand and twists my knife down. The angle my arm snaps into sends an excruciating jolt of pain into my elbow, but not as excruciating as when his fist collides with my face. My jaw burns, a white-hot light illuminating my vision and engulfing my face.

My body wants to fly backward, across the alleyway and maybe even slam into one of the walls still standing nearby, but his hold won't allow it. When I bow backward, Gregor yanks me forward. My chest presses against his rotund belly, my cheek slamming up against a dried-up stream of blood that must've stained his shirt the last time he fed.

My thoughts are hazy clouds that have forgotten which way to drift. They slide upward and downward, back and forth, each one colliding into the next without rhyme or reason. The panic is there, but it's drowning at the bottom, unable to latch onto any of the half-formed ideas that keep slipping by it.

He's about to...

I should...

What will happen when...

Can I reach my...

I'm barely aware of my body or his. I feel the pressure of something wrap around my back and hold me in place. My head is yanked back by a fistful of hair, but I'm too dazed and too weak to fight for a more comfortable position.

Heat and steam fold over my exposed throat.

Suddenly, the cloud of disoriented thoughts is a gushing river that all points to the same conclusion: find the will to fight now or die.

My eyes pop wide. I can just barely see the top of his head as he's dipped down over me. His fangs skirt along my neck, the steam of his breath dampening my skin. He leaves a trail from the base of my throat all the way up to my ear.

I refuse to whimper, to give him that satisfaction.

"And here I thought you might be a challenge," he breathes into my ear. "It never is though. You're all the same. Pathetic. Useless. Frightened."

He's not wrong. And maybe that's why I hate them the most. Because we will never compare and it's not fair. We didn't choose to be helpless and defenseless. We didn't choose to be their food. We didn't choose to live in a world with monsters.

Pools collect in my eyes, but I refuse to let them fall.

"Sorry to disappoint." My clenched jaw throbs but focusing

on the pain might the only thing keeping my voice from cracking.

I struggle against his hold, if only to test what I already know: there is no breaking free. My arms are pinned between our bodies and my knife isn't even in my grasp anymore—I guess I must've dropped it the moment his fist tried inverting my face.

"Just fucking do it already," I tell him. "If I'm so pathetic and useless, do it."

He snarls, a sound that I can't decide is one of hunger, disapproval, both, or something else entirely.

He lowers his mouth to my neck, fangs mere inches from my skin.

Regret pierces me before he does, a twinge in my chest that bleeds into the rest of my aching body. I'll die here if I'm lucky enough not to be left to turn into a ghoul, and if or when anyone finds me, they'll leave my body for the animals they hunt because respect for my body, my passing won't matter as much as their need for another meal. I will fade in time just like every human who died before me. And I only have myself to blame for foolishly believing I could handle this noctis on the ground, in close range.

I'll be damned if the last thing I see is Gregor's smooshed face, so for one final time, I look up into the sky and relish what little of the violet sunset I can see.

At least it's not red.

My eyes shut, bracing myself for the worst.

But a new, guttural sound gurgles from Gregor's lips.

Something wet splashes against my neck as he gasps and splutters. I open my eyes as his grip on me loosens, the large man staggering backward and clutching his chest. There's a wound there, cavernous and ghastly. Blood seeps between his fingers like a flower blooming darker than night.

Gregor coughs one final time, red glistening on his lips and teeth. Then he crumples, revealing a silhouetted man standing behind him.

The man steps closer, skin so dark he nearly blends in with the shadows cast down by the tall buildings.

I'd recognize those short ropes of hair anywhere; I'd know his spiced cake scent.

Standing over Gregor's body, Rowland yanks a spear from his back, and brings the blood-dripping tip of the blade to the decorative but tattered red fabric at his hip.

"What were you doing out here?" he bites out, and every word possesses the powerful roar of an ocean. He marches closer. "My sentries spotted you with two noctis. They said it looked like you lead them straight to Valor's Rest. Straight to *my* front doors. To *my* people. And then you just ran off with a noctis that, from the looks of it, could've eaten five of you and still wanted more. Have you lost your mind?"

An eon stretches before I'm able to wrap my head around the fact that I've just managed to evade death once more, and with the help of Rowland Barret, nonetheless.

He's never going to let me live this one down.

Second only to my crossbow, Rowland is the closest thing to a friend I've ever had, or likely ever will. For years, I presumed him dead, lost somewhere in the mass grave that became of Hulbeck. But to my surprise, and perhaps some relief, our paths crossed again one summer a few years back when he was moving his people to Gravenburg, and I just happened to be traveling through.

Or at least, that had been the plan. He hasn't let me disappear again since. In fact, on more than one occasion, he's tried convincing me to move into *Valor's Rest*, but I've denied every request. He knows why. Yet, the poor man keeps trying. I imagine the thought of me being out here all alone terrifies him as much as the thought of belonging to a community of people just to watch them die terrifies me.

Knees still trembling, I think about thanking him for saving my pitiful life. But I can't bring myself to do it.

I muster a wry smile and shove everything else behind it.

"Valor's Rest? That's what you settled on? What was wrong with any of the names I suggested. I quite liked *Barret Town*. Or there's always the age-old classic *Rowlandia*."

"Are you serious right now?" The veins in his throat bulge, his nostrils flaring the same way they did when we were children and I'd beat him at a game of skip rocks. "What could you have possibly been thinking coming out here on your own?"

"I'm always on my own! Today was nothing different."

A humorless laugh cuts from his mouth. "Great. That's just great. Just a normal day in Gravenburg for you, narrowly escaping your own demise."

My jaw clamps shut. Not because I want to protect his fragile ego from my lashing tongue, but because he enrages me beyond my ability to form rational sentences—as he so often does.

I just want to scream at him sometimes. But I want to hug him too. It's never anything but complicated when he's around.

Dragging a hand through the braids that he still wears, the ones he used to hate, he looks me over again. His eyes linger on my quivering hands, on the ragged rise and fall of my chest that I can't seem to soothe no matter how much I'm trying to appear unscathed.

He sighs, the anger that had carved dark grooves out of his forehead softening. "Char, are you—"

"I'm fine," I say swiftly, but the edge in my tone is gone, replaced by the other emotions catching up with me.

If he hadn't come, I'd be dead. I should be dead, by all rights. I just spent the last couple hours wandering aimlessly in a ghoul-ridden town alongside two noctis, one of whom suspected I was a fraud from the beginning. No one survives this long by making reckless choices like that.

My head shakes in small, rapid movements, and I utter the very thing I would've rather not said. "I would've died if you hadn't found me…"

The statement is too true. Too vulnerable. Too intimate.

His hand finds mine in an instant, like he's been waiting for that confession all our lives. Perhaps because he has. It's not just a confession of the truth. There's so much more behind those words. I've just admitted to weakness, to needing him more than I've ever led on to believe.

Under normal circumstances, such a notion would've never left my lips, no matter how much it was true. But perhaps because I'm still too shellshocked to move, much less think, I don't flinch away from his warmth. He wraps me up in his embrace and I lean into the gentle, almost timid caress of his stroking fingers along my spine. Today has left me raw and shattered, and all I want is for him to hold me together before the pieces burst apart.

"Come here," he says into my ear. "Of course, I came for you, you fool. I'll always come for you."

I laugh. Something I hadn't expected to be able to do just yet. And in so doing, my frayed pieces begin smoothing back together.

At least for a fleeting moment.

A memory of the last time he held me like this awakens in my mind. It was only a few short days ago as we laid in my bed, arms and legs entwined and he counted the freckles along the curve of my hip. He declared the constellation there as the most beautiful among all the stars, which was saying a lot for someone who used to watch them every night when he was a boy.

But the comfort and affection he'd hoped to give me that night had the opposite effect. It had reminded me of how foolish we were being. How reckless with our own hearts.

In this world, there's no room for love. Only death.

Spice cake has no business in this shithole of a town. Neither does anything as intimate as him caressing my back. He is a distraction, and a damned fine one at that. But I think I've had enough distractions for the day.

"You're alright. You're safe now," he says, making the same mistake they all do.

Safety is a lie. One that I've never been able to believe. Not since I was a little girl. Not since Hulbeck. What I learned that day is that for as long as there are noctis, no human will ever be safe.

It's then that I finally step out of his embrace. I do so slowly though, perhaps because he just saved my life and I don't want to stir up any more emotions today for either of us.

"Thanks for coming," I say with a faint smile, avoiding eye contact. "Sorry that I had to lead two hungry noctis to your front gates. I had good reasons."

He answers with a snort. "That's what I told the sentries, and believe me, I can't wait to hear them." Tapping the blunt end of his spear on the ground, his gaze drifts down to the dead noctis at our feet. "You know, for someone who still can't fight without a crossbow, you'd think you would've picked a fight with someone you'd be better-matched against."

"And you'd think for someone who just scored himself two fresh noctis corpses, you'd be a little more grateful."

His expression turns dubious. "You didn't bring them all this way just for my research. So spit it out. Why are you here? Why did you bring them to me?"

Night approaches. Soon these streets will be black, and our human eyes won't be able to discern a single thing. It's too much to say out here in the open.

"Don't just make a girl stand out in the cold rain," I whine, my shivering limbs making it difficult to sound anything but pathetic. "Let's head back and I'll tell you everything these guys let slip about the next Hunt."

5

THE CRIMSON GUARD

"What an effulgent city."

Sarcasm is more Caz's thing, but after what feels like hours of ambling through this bloodless wasteland that our history books call Gravenburg, I almost can't help myself.

Before we left Neveridge, I'd heard the rumors of the deterioration of the realm, of course. That the human population was dwindling at alarming rates, thanks to the overpopulation of ghouls, and that if something wasn't done soon to replenish them—humans, not ghouls—the noctis race would follow suit. It was a difficult concept to believe for someone who's spent most of the last decade chugging blood by the goblet-full. Part of me merely assumed those rumors had been started by the humans themselves, meant to scare us into thinking that we should back off and find a new source of food.

I'd neither blame nor disagree with them.

But seeing as I've rarely ventured outside Neveridge these past few years, I hadn't quite fully understood the dire circumstances my people discussed in the banquet halls of the castle. After all, we keep blood on tap where I come from. The most decadent wines, as well. Every hallway of the castle is decorated with humans in chains so that our esteemed guests can snack as they please.

Their dying screams claw at the walls of my mind in every waking moment, as well as the dreaming ones. The wastefulness of killing them just because we can, instead of preserving their life, our source of nourishment, grinds against every nerve in my being.

When I'm king, it's one of the many changes I'll enact.

If I'm ever allowed to ascend.

My tongue pricks at the thought of tasting human blood—anything red and fluid, really. I'm not accustomed to skipping meals for so long, so my restraint is like the last cord holding onto a frayed rope.

Beside me, Caz throws his head back laughing. "You poor, overprivileged bastard. Prince Malachi, having to leave the comforts of his plush, goose feather bed to be here with us today, witnessing Gravenburg and all her *effulgence*. What a crime against humanity, but perhaps mostly against your fragile ego."

"Careful, careful." I flash him a crooked smile. "You mention my fragile ego again and you might do irreparable damage."

"Oh, we wouldn't want that. Now, would we?"

If he were anyone else, this would be the end of our playful bantering. He would smile and we'd continue our search through the quiet town, our conversation shifting to that of politics and courts.

Caz, however, has never allowed my royal standing to stand in between him and a good time.

Like a lion cub preparing to pounce, Caz crouches low. Something primal awakens within me, and I find myself mimicking his stance, my best pair of leather boots sliding in mud to lower my center of gravity as I contemplate exactly how I'll incapacitate him.

Two sharp fangs poke through his smile. "Who knew a prince could be so delicate? No wonder the king is disappointed with you so often."

Anyone else would lose their head for making such a remark, especially on a topic so personal, so tender.

But this isn't personal. This is just Caz goading me.

I should ignore the bait.

But where's the fun in that?

"You son of a—"

I lunge, but before I reach him, Caz is thrown across the alleyway by a blurred curtain of red. His back slams against the bricks, knocking a few of them loose. The woman standing before him, clutching his throat between long nails like fangs, kicks the debris aside with her crimson, satin heel.

"Honestly, you two. Do you ever think about anything other than messing around?"

Renee Vanderbilt, Caz's older sister, tosses waves of hair as thick and silken as orange marmalade over her shoulder and scowls at me. But even in her most infuriated states, hardly a wrinkle ever presses into her flawless, near-immortal flesh.

"I'd expect better from you, my prince."

Caz wriggles out of her grasp, brandishing a boyish grin as he reties the dark hair at the nape of his neck. "Yeah, *my prince*."

"Oh, shut up." Renee's fist cracks his shoulder.

He hunches over, cradling the poor thing, though I suspect it's all an act.

When Renee returns her expectant gaze on me, I bow as deep as I can. The garnet amulet around my neck dangles past my cheeks, and I wonder which one is a brighter hue of red right now. Chastisement, no matter how warranted or not, always has this effect on me. It must be the way I was raised.

"Happy to oblige," I tell her, straightening as I remember my place. "Wouldn't want my reputation of *disappointing* everyone to be sullied."

Caz chuckles, but Renee wasn't here for his earlier remarks and so she doesn't realize I'm joking. Her icy demeanor melts, allowing a flicker of her beauty to shine through. If only she would let those walls down more often, if only she would allow herself to enjoy the life we have rather than walking around with a stick shoved up her ass, she might actually find that she is capable of enjoying herself.

Caz waves her off.

"Ignore her"—he throws an arm over my shoulder, but it lands atop the sharp, rigged points of the cape I just had fitted for our journey— "Ow! What the hell did they make that out of? Sword tips?"

My grin is proud as I twirl so they can get a better look at my newest accessory.

"Watch it!" Caz yips, dodging the material as it livens.

Velvet and satin make up the large drapes that hang down my back when the cape is stagnant. But when I spread my arms, it becomes a living thing. The heavy fabric snaps open like a dark sail catching wind across an ocean at midnight. The way the seamstress sewed boning along the edges and to connect the various triangular patterns, makes it look as if I have two large bat wings stretched behind me.

"Not sword tips," I reply. "It's impressive though. Isn't it?"

As I finish peacocking my wardrobe, Caz groans. "Oh, for the love of—Now look what you've done. You've made her blush, you sexy fool."

He's not wrong. My gaze flits to Renee to find that not only have her cheeks flushed the color of freshly bloomed poppies in spring, but even her emerald eyes seem to hold a molten hue. She's cornered me in one too many rooms with that look in her eyes, the kind of look that says she would have me right here, right now, if I allowed it.

"Shut your fucking mouth, Cazimir," she snarls at her

brother. "Or the next time I pin you to the wall with my hands around your throat, I'll rip the fucking thing out."

"Relax," I say, trying to diffuse the situation. "It's alright. Caz just doesn't know good fashion like we do."

The crimson tingeing her cheeks threatens to brighten, but by sheer force of will alone, she clamps it down. With a whip of her long, scarlet evening gown—a garment that is certainly not suitable for travel, but one of the many delicate and provocative dresses she insisted on packing because, and I quote, *"I won't be caught dead in my Crimson Guard rags at the event of the season,"*—Renee pivots, headed back down the road.

"Now, if you two can take yourselves seriously for one second of your pathetic lives, I suggest we continue."

As we follow, Caz leans over me. "Always so bossy."

Renee spins around. "I wouldn't need to be bossy if you just did your job! Or do I need to remind you what will happen if we don't deliver? Hmm? Have you both conveniently forgotten what the king said—"

"That's enough."

It's not often I use my regal tone when I'm among friends, but that's precisely why when I do, they both know I mean business.

The casual Caz disappears behind the soldier of Cazimir, born and raised under noctis regime as a warrior to defend the crown. He is dutiful. Protective. Bound by honor—and our kinship, whether or not that be by choice rather than blood—to obey.

As a lady of the court, Renee's taught not to be a soldier and to stand tall, but to cower in the presence of power. Where her brother has been trained to meet the eyes of every adversary he faces in a show of respect, Renee has been trained to avert her gaze to show her obedience.

Some things can't be trained, however.

Renee has the spirit of wildfire caught on the wind. So,

although her head dips, her emerald eyes are stubborn. It's in her nature to challenge my command. Which is perfectly fine by me. I don't need her to bow, or act like a proper lady of the court. Unlike my father, I have no desire to rule under an iron thumb. True loyalty and friendship are far more valuable to me than obedience and fear.

As long as no one mentions *the great King Tor* for the rest of our journey.

Easing away the tension that always creeps in when I use my royal tone, I roll my shoulders.

"I know what we've been charged with, Renee. Why else would I have deployed my most fearsome team?"

My words are meant to lighten the mood. But Renee only sees them as more childish games. She always does. It's one of the many things she and my father have in common, always assuming I'm not taking things seriously enough.

"Fearsome?" She laughs. "Look at us. We've been traveling for days and only Ursulette has captured anyone."

"Exactly," Caz says, chest broadening. "That's because our mere presence terrifies them into hiding."

Renee looks ready to punch him again.

"We'll find more," I interject, stepping between them. "They've been in hiding for years. And the ones who aren't smart enough to hide find themselves a new member of the ghoul population."

I pause, the three of us wincing as we try not to think about the vile way ghoul blood tastes. Growing up, before I was a member of the royal family, ghoul blood was one of my main sources of nourishment—if you can call it that. It was like drinking mud, but worse. Ghoul veins seem to be filled with the same grainy sludge that sits in the bottom of ponds.

Having to stomach that repulsive flavor is one of the few things about my pre-prince life that I don't miss.

Swallowing the nauseating memory, I continue. "We knew

this wouldn't be easy. It's why my father dispatched most of the Crimson Guard. The humans are hiding somewhere. We just have to find them."

A hunger takes hold of Renee, one that has her sliding a slender finger down the crevice exposed by her deep V-line dress.

Frowning, I avert my attention elsewhere, to the damp, twisting street ahead, to the endless grey stone buildings, to whatever lies ahead. We can't give up though. Or at least, if we do, we might as well never return to Neveridge. If we don't procure enough donations for the Hunt—or rather, if my father can't force the noctis under his employ to secure enough humans in time for the annual festivity—the participating noctis will revolt. Then there wouldn't be a castle to return to anyway.

Planting my knuckles on my hips, I reassess our situation. "Maybe we need to cover more ground. If we each went a different way—"

Renee makes a disgusted sound. "Go different ways? Don't even joke. You know we're safer together. That's why you sent everyone off in pairs to begin with."

The notion doesn't seem to sit well with Caz, either, but as usual, he masks his concern behind humor. "Don't tell me you're sick of us already?"

"Not in the slightest," I say. "But Renee is right. We need a victory. And how long will we be on this wild goose chase? For all we know, everyone in Gravenburg is dead. It'll take us three times as long to search this neighborhood if we stick together."

"I'm not going out there on my own!" Renee shrieks. "You've seen what they do to us!"

"You forget," Caz says. "He hasn't."

That truth stings a little. It hasn't entirely been my choice to remain closed off from the realm. Or has it? I suppose my father wouldn't mind if I went out more, but what reason do I have to go? To see the devastation? I've witnessed enough of it for my short lifetime, thank you. To indulge in the carnage? The others enjoy the thrill of a good hunt, but me? I'm afraid I see no point in it.

Renee rolls her eyes. "Fine, but he's definitely heard about it. The noctis bodies they've been finding all over the United Realm?"

Oh, I've heard about the bodies alright.

Even during what limited time I spend in my father's court, I've overheard dozens of stories brought to him by distraught barons and advisors, all describing similar accounts of noctis who have been alleviated of their hearts, their brains, some even without flesh.

Someone is experimenting on us.

The reports are so vastly spread though that my father is unsure who's responsible, let alone where they're residing. It's one of the many reasons that he moved the location of the Hunt this year to the dreary Shadowthorn; most of the discarded bodies they've discovered have been from this region.

"Of course, I know about the bodies."

Frowning, I drag my fingers over my head and through the long, white hair I've been forced to grow out, cursing every tangle I snag on. When I was younger, I was foolish enough to think that when I finally became an adult, I'd be able to do what I wanted with my own hair. How wrong I'd been. Even at eighteen, my father still won't allow any of our hairdressers to cut off any of the length beyond an annual trim. It's a family trait, our white hair, and one that should be worn proudly for how iconic it's made us, according to him.

One of these days I'll finally lose my patience and hack it all off, toss the tail at my father's feet, and tell him I'm done being a Devonshire.

Soon. Once we reach Nigh, the time will come all too soon enough.

"What if we regroup with the others instead?" Caz offers, pulling me out of my head. "For all we know, they might've had better luck with all of this."

Renee's laugh is haughty, her slender nose pinched. "Right, because I'm sure Ursulette and Rhain aren't off somewhere fucking; Harland and Davorin aren't feasting upon whatever pathetic souls they happened upon; and Gregor and Boris didn't botch whatever scouting attempts they've been trying to make."

The accuracy with which she depicts our laughable situation is painful. While the two of them continue arguing, I massage my temples, wondering why my father even let me leave with these fools. Each and every one of them is a formidable opponent and a skilled killer. But as far as being the best for a search and capture mission? We might've had better luck bringing along rabid ghouls.

Unless, of course, he expected me to fail.

With dawning irritation, I realize he must've. Why else send me off with these goons instead of his best teams of Crimson Guards? Why else send us to this ghost town, where we haven't seen so much as a ghoul since our arrival, let alone a human being?

He expects me to fail? I'll show him how capable I really am.

"Caz is right," I blurt over their bickering. "You both are. We've been at it for hours today. We should reconvene and see if anyone's discovered anything, or at a bare minimum, gather the others and restate the importance of everything at stake. It's not just my neck on the line, and they may need a reminder of that."

"Is the blood oath still active?"

Before Caz can even finish asking the question, Renee has the lacey sleeve of her gown peeled back. She rotates her hand to reveal the tender underbelly of her pale wrist. In the very center, drawn in blood using the finest-tipped quills money can buy, is a gemstone.

We drew them on everyone this morning, as we have every morning since our search began.

"Still there," she says with a hint of annoyance.

She's been begging me for a permanent blood oath for years, just like the one Caz has. But every time she requests it, I find a new reason to say no. In the instance of our current predicament, I told her it would be quicker and perhaps safer if she had a temporary blood oath like everyone else. This way if she or any of them are captured by, say those responsible for the experimentations occurring around the realm, she can rub the blood stain away before they can learn anything about it. She won't be tied to me, nor the Devonshire family.

Besides, the last thing we need is for the humans to learn any more of our secrets than they already have.

"Very well," I say, exposing my own tattoo, the one that matches hers in design, but only Caz's in blood-threaded ink. "I'll send out word."

I raise the crimson tattoo to my mouth and whisper against the ink. "Rendezvous at the camp in one hour. Bring anyone you've caught."

Through the oath's bond, I sense Rhain's startled embarrassment as if I've just walked in to find him in some compromising position. His mate, my jovial and doting cousin, Ursulette, has a different reaction entirely, reminding me more of a rebellious teenager relishing every time she gets caught doing something improper. As expected, Harland's response is not much more than a grizzled grunt, while Davorin, his counterpart and Caz's and Renee's father, as well as the most trusted advisor to the king, bows—or whatever the equivalent of that is in mind-speak.

Neither Gregor nor Boris responds.

"Message received," Caz says with his usual crooked grin, and a dutiful salute that I'm sure many who don't know him easily mistake for anything but genuine.

"Let's get moving then," Renee says, waving us back toward the direction we came from. "It'll take us half a day to get back."

It's bordering an exaggeration. Although we covered a lot of ground since leaving camp this morning, we really haven't wandered too far. The roads of Gravenburg are tightly knitted things. They zig and zag around each other like a dense knot of canals that barely leave space for a cart or two to traverse down, even back when the town was alive and not covered in garbage. This would've been one of those places that reeked of urine and sweat, with flies buzzing around every open marketplace, and someone swearing, brawling, or both in front of every pub. Not a respectable city, but a bustling one.

Truth be told, it would've been exactly the kind of place I would've enjoyed escaping to. Somewhere far from aristocracy and wealth, where people lived their regular lives of indulgences. Somewhere Father and my royal obligations would've never found me. It's a place I imagine many of the noctis in my company would've found themselves at home, Harland and his brothers making the top of that list. It's possible that's part of the reason Gregor and Boris didn't respond. Perhaps they found some way to indulge themselves and are simply caught up in the moment.

That seems unlikely.

"Something's wrong."

Caz and Renee sober, glancing back at me.

"What is it?" Renee asks, her wide eyes flitting to every shadow around us.

Caz understands what I mean before I have to say it. As a long-standing member of the Crimson Guard, he's had more experience with blood oaths than his sister and knows there's only one reason I'd be alarmed when we're in the middle of such a quiet, uneventful street.

"Who didn't respond?" he asks.

"Harland's brothers," I tell them, my mind whirring, mulling over every piece of information I have at my disposal.

It would be one thing if it was just one of them that didn't reply. It happens sometimes. My communications come at inconvenient moments and every now and then somebody decides not to or simply can't respond.

But that's why they have counterparts. It's their partner's responsibility to reply for them, to make sure I know everything is okay.

To not hear anything from Gregor *and* Boris? It means with almost certainty that they're either unconscious or dead.

"Caz, you're with me. Renee, head back to camp and tell the others what's happened."

"Like hell, Malachi! I'm not just some lost pup you get to boss around."

Something flashes across Renee's expression, like she's just realized who she's talking to and that I do, in fact, have the authority to boss her around—even if I don't usually. She shifts tactics.

"Besides, you can't really expect me to just stay behind while you and my only brother stroll into danger."

Some days, she has a way of convincing me to give into her every whim. I think it's her voice. She can reach uncanny, shrill pitches or dulcet tones when she wants to.

Today is not that day.

"That's exactly what I expect you to do."

When her mouth pops wide in protest, I silence her through the oath bond. Without my lips close to the tattoo, I can't send her any direct commands, just sensations. And this time I make sure my frustrations are felt like a swarm of enraged wasps.

Just in case that's not enough, I grab her arms and pull her close. "I need you to tell the others where we went and why. Keep them in line while we're gone. You know how Harland and Ursulette can get. They're squirrely even on their good days. And Rhain will do whatever Ursulette tells him, and Ursulette will do whatever I say—if you're there to reinforce my message."

It's not the task itself that placates her, but the implication of it. I'm trusting in her to do this, and my trust is not something I dole out often. Especially not to Renee Vanderbilt.

But she is wildfire, and she's not ready to give up the fight.

"Are you listening to yourself? Your great plan is to go investigate on your own? It's too dangerous. Your father would have my fangs if he found out I let you go off on your own."

"We won't be alone," I tell her, releasing her and dragging my fingers through the thickness of my hair. "I'll have Caz. And I'm telling Davorin to meet us in the southern quadrant, where we sent Gregor and Boris. The three of us can handle it."

Her jaw sets. "Fine. For how long should I hold the others off? And what if you get hurt? What if you need our help, after all?"

"If we need help, I'll send word through the blood oath. Otherwise, I'll send word every hour, on the hour. If you don't hear from me, *do not* come chasing after us. You send for reinforcements."

She frowns, but I keep going. This is the most important part out of everything.

"If someone has incapacitated Gregor and Boris, if they do the same to Caz, Davorin, or I, none of you will be able to do anything that we couldn't. Not without more noctis in your ranks and not if you really intend on saving us."

Rolling her eyes, she throws her head back, thick waves of auburn hair tumbling off her shoulders and down her back. "You are such a hypocrite. The same thing could be said for our predicament right now! If someone was able to incapacitate

Gregor and Boris—and, need I remind you, one of whom could wrestle a bull, while the other could dodge it's every attempted ramming blow—then shouldn't we be sending for help already instead of sending more noctis into the slaughter?"

"They could still be alive, Renee." Unblinking, I hold her gaze. "You've heard what's been happening. Surely, you know that some of the noctis who've been found seemed to have been alive for much of what they endured. We can't wait to do something. We have to act now."

A gloss-like sheen polishes her eyes. I might not have seen any of the bodies, but with the reports my father has been receiving, we can't afford to pretend this isn't as dangerous as it could be. To take out Gregor and Boris would be no easy feat. We have to assume that whoever is responsible is formidable in their own nature.

Blowing through his pursed lips, Caz diffuses the seriousness of the conversation, as usual. "Not that she needs to worry about us needing saving. We know how to handle ourselves. These humans won't know what hit them. Right, *my prince?*"

Even if I know it's misplaced, his arrogance is contagious, and quite effective at bolstering my own.

A grin kicks up the side of my face, exposing one of my pearly white fangs, and I'm reminded of a mantra that's always put bravery in the hearts of noctis, for it reminds us of where we came from, and how we've always, *always* persevered.

"Blighted we suffered. Bloodied they'll fall."

6

THE MERCENARY LIFE

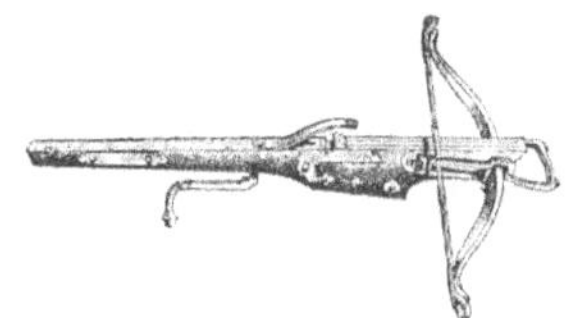

If I had known Boris' dead body would weigh so much, I might've taken Rowland up on his offer to help me carry him back to the compound. Not that it's really in me to let him, or anyone else for that matter, do something that I can do for myself. If anything, lugging Boris' deceivingly heavy body can be chalked up to the start of my new regimented training. After all, if I've learned anything today, it's that I could use it.

By the time Rowland leads us into his office, my thighs and arms are seconds away from falling off. I try not thinking about how Rowland has hefted Gregor's enormous body farther than I had to carry Boris, nor about how, despite his limp and the injury he sustained to his knee that never managed to heal, that every time I've glanced back at him, he barely even looks like he's struggling.

I'm practically dripping sweat and he still appears as divine as ever.

Typical.

It's not until we're inside his office that I realize he didn't take us to the laboratory he has stashed behind these walls somewhere, not that I should be surprised. Even after all these years, I'm still not permitted access to his lab. I'm lucky to even know it exists.

And although some people might be offended to have a secret like that exist between friends who have known each other for as long as we have, I get it. If anyone understands distrust, it's me. Besides, the fewer people who know Rowland has been studying ghouls and noctis he's been able to capture, the less likely the monsters are to discover his involvement, and therefore the safer his people will remain.

Before Rowland can finish crossing the threshold into his cluttered office, I drop Boris onto the first flat table-like surface I can find.

"Hey! Not on my desk!" Rowland barks.

A little too late. The damage is already done. The body is already draped over the scattered reports and discarded quills.

He groans, head shaking as he dumps Gregor and my crossbow off by the door, and then does the same with Boris. Together, sitting there all slouch-backed and unmoving, they could almost pass for two drunkards who have passed out after a night on a binge. One of them has even pissed himself.

"Sit," Rowland says, indicating to the chair in front of his desk. Stepping behind it to start tidying up the scattered paperwork, the stuff that Boris' blood has damaged beyond repair gets casts aside.

"I'll stand, thank you."

His sharp gaze cuts to mine. "Do what you will. But I, for one, am beat."

Rowland throws himself into the other chair, the leather worn from years of use, the legs creaky. He kicks off his muddy boots, propping the bloodstained things on the desk. For someone so concerned about me ruining whatever organization system he had going on at his desk, he sure doesn't seem bothered by disturbing the delicate system himself, but I keep my mouth shut about it. I'm in his domain now. He can do whatever he wants here.

"You've been busy since I last saw you," he says, breaking the silence and folding his hands over his stomach. "Did spending time with me really give you a death wish?"

My smile is tight. "It usually does."

Irritation flares behind his charcoal eyes. He never could handle my humor. Little does he know, it makes it all the more enjoyable for me.

"If you hate seeing me so much, then why do you come here?"

"I learned something today that I thought you should know."

"By all means then"—his arms spread wide—"tell me so I can get back to what I was doing. I'm a busy man. Believe it or not, I don't wait around all day hoping that I might need to save you from your own recklessness."

The way he says it, I'm almost not sure I believe he's lying. A lie is always best concealed in the truth, after all.

"Oh, I'm sorry, *Lord Rowland*. Did I come at an inconvenient time? Should I have scheduled an appointment?"

"Dammit, Charlotte!" His fists slam against the desk, loose sheets of papers flying into the air like dead leaves falling in autumn. "Not everything is a joke!"

Under normal circumstances, Rowland is well adept at diplomacy. When Hulbeck fell, it wasn't long before his mother established a new community, one that his mother raised him to assume leadership of after her passing, which she did a few years back. Since then, he's dealt with the usual conflicts that arise whenever people live under constant duress and fear of losing their lives. He's handled petty altercations as well as a near-uprising when they hadn't harvested enough food to feed everyone through the winter comfortably.

He's always handled such situations with a calm grace befitting his station.

But he has never quite learned how to handle me.

"Do you even care that you nearly died today?"

"Of course, I fucking care, Rowland! Don't act like you give more of a shit about whether I continue breathing than I do. It's *my* life. I want to keep it, and I definitely don't want to end up like a soulless ghoul eating everyone I come across."

Chest heaving, I stare into the pits of his dark, foreboding eyes.

The air is heady, rich and warm with the decadent scent of cloves and cinnamon. Being with him always reminds me of home, of the spice cakes my mother would bake for celebrations around the village, or of the early mornings he and I would spend together tucked under our mothers' skirts while they sipped their steaming teas and we nibbled on whatever breads his mother had left over from the bakery from the previous day.

If we have anything in common, it's our stubborn tempers, but mine has always been more persistent.

He breaks our gazes first, kicking his feet off the desk and rocking forward, head cradled in his hands.

I know he's just worried. He's always the maddest at me when my life is threatened. It makes me feel like an asshole, even when my own irritations are warranted.

Somehow, I find it within me to reel myself in. There are bigger things at play here, information he needs.

"I wasn't trying to stir up trouble today. I awoke this morning and discovered I was out of blood, so I went to check my traps—"

His eyes shoot up to mine. "Is that what's on your face? You know, my sentries almost shot you when they saw that. They thought you were one of them."

"That's kind of the point. It's not the best disguise, but it works in a pinch. And today was quite the pinch."

Disgust wrinkles his expression as he examines the dried blood on my chin. "What is it?"

"Pigeon blood."

"And they can't tell the difference?"

I shrug. "I don't think it matters to them if it's human blood or animal. They see something that looks human eating with blood smeared across their face, and they're going to assume I'm a noctis."

Understanding registers in his expression, the scientist in him being satiated. For now.

Instead of saying what's on his mind though, he turns his attention back to me, eyes scanning for what I'm guessing are signs of wear and tear. He won't find any though. My mother used to joke that my skin was made of obsidian, because it would take a hurricane of knives to cut through me. The worst injury I ever had was a sprained ankle from when my foot slipped while Rowland and I were climbing a tree, but according to my mother, even that injury healed as fast as the changing tide.

I might not be strong in muscle, but I am resilient in every meaning of the word.

Satisfied by what he finds—or rather, but what he doesn't—Rowland nods at me to continue.

"Go on. What happened after?"

His low tone is not too dissimilar from the way he sounds during our late-night rendezvous when he's whispering deliciously suggestive ideas into my ears.

Warmth settles in the pit of my belly. I'll be damned if I let it flare to the surface, to heat my pale cheeks.

"There was a ghoul at one of my traps, eating my catch. Before I could kill it or leave, those two showed up. They saw the trap, they knew a human had set it and therefore was likely nearby, and so I did what was necessary to survive. I pretended to be one of them. I couldn't take them on by myself. And I knew if I led them back here that your sentries could handle them. It was the only way."

Charcoal eyes burn into mine with the heat of the sun. Under the intensity of his gaze, my skin warms. It scorches. Most would kill to be beneath his glorious rays, but I prefer the safety of the shadows than the sunlight.

I turn around to head for the small table by the window where I know he keeps his spirits. It's not often I indulge in such things. It's not that I mind the flavor, nor the inhibited sensations that follow, but generally speaking, I can't afford to dull my senses with the stuff. You never know when you'll need your wits. More than anything, I just want to preoccupy my hands with something and to keep them from anxiously fumbling with the vials in my belt.

I open one of the decanters and pour a drink. By the time I finish, Rowland is hobbling across the room to make himself one as well.

"H-here," I stammer and thrust my glass at him. "You can take mine."

He looks confused but doesn't push the matter.

In one swig, he knocks the drink down his throat, then sets the glass back on the table.

It's then that I notice the distance between us has been swallowed.

No longer can I relish the comfort of knowing there's an entire desk between us to hold him, and myself, at bay. No longer can I rely on our spacing on opposite sides of the room to assuage those more intimate desires and impede our abilities to act on them.

The lack of space between us sends my heart into a frenzy.

It's not like when we're at my place, which is where our encounters usually occur. There, we can keep things between us private. No one knows he comes to visit me, and no one knows I host him.

But here?

His office is nestled in the middle of the compound; we easily passed a couple dozen people making our way here. Some of them I recognized. Others, not so much. But it still means that people know I'm here, and they know I'm with Rowland.

I don't know why, but the thought of them suspecting that he and I share a relationship that is anything beyond professional makes my stomach twist with knots.

This can't happen.

Not here.

Before he can get any ideas, I shield my face from his behind a veil of dark hair and shift my attention elsewhere.

Rowland's breathy laugh summons me back.

"What?" I snap, irritation pricking my skin. "Why are you laughing?"

"It's nothing," he says, shaking his head. "You just always do that."

"Do what exactly?"

After the question leaves my lips, I'm not sure I want him to respond.

Is it that I looked away the minute I started thinking about his full lips on mine? Or was it that I walked halfway across the room, in the hopes that putting some physical distance between us would stop me from wanting to lay him down flat on his back on his desk and ride him until the sun came up?

"That," he answers, and my heart skips a beat for fear I might've said the last part out loud. He points to where my hand rests against my shoulder, hair still caught between my fingers. "You tuck your hair behind your ear whenever you're —I don't know, uncomfortable or something."

The tight breath I'd been holding eases from my lungs. I

suppose I should be grateful that he's not the best sleuth in the realm. I can't have him knowing all my darkest desires.

"The thing you have yet to tell me—" he clarifies, leaning against the small liquor table— "I'm assuming it's pretty bad?"

"It is," I tell him, grateful for the change in topic. "Your people have been disappearing, right?"

"Yeah?" He inches closer. "What have you learned?"

The words aren't as easy to muster as I thought they would be. I know what these people—this community—means to Rowland. I don't want to hurt him more than he already is hurting. But he needs to know.

"I'm afraid it's worse than you imagined," I say honestly. "Those two noctis I was with today? They said they were hunting humans."

"So? Noctis are always hunting humans. That's just what they do. Ever since they were created. Even after the Magistrate tried brokering a peace with them, they still—"

There's no easy way to say this, so I just come out with it. "For the Hunt."

Slowly, Rowland's back straightens.

We're close enough in height that we practically see eye-to-eye, but there's something about the wariness in his gaze that makes me feel small right now.

He must assume I'm joking. That this is just another one of my exaggerations or paranoias.

The Hunt has always been a legend, a nightmarish bedtime story at best. *Leave it to Charlotte Thorn to turn everything into a joke*, he's probably thinking.

But to my surprise, the wariness wanes. In its place, concern creeps in.

"The Hunt. You're sure?" he asks.

All I can do is nod.

His voice is doing that aggravating thing again where the richness of it teases that strange ache deep in my belly.

Making matters worse, he actually sounds like he believes me, for once.

"So, it's true then. Exactly as we've been told." Again, I nod, only realizing after that I don't actually know. The stories we heard growing up might be true, but there might also be differences, nuances between what humans are privy to and what really happens. "But how? We've never experienced the disappearances like this before. If this has been going on for decades, wouldn't we have known?"

I do my best to alleviate the guilt strangling his tone. "They said the Hunt normally takes place in Neveridge, but this year they're doing it in the Shadowthorn. My guess is this is the first time they've poached people from Gravenburg."

"The Shadowthorn..."

"Apparently, they've depleted their resources. They said they had to travel farther and farther to find any humans. They haven't even been having great luck here, from the sounds of it."

He snorts. "Well, of course not. For the most part, people stay in Valor's Rest where they're safe."

"But I thought you said—"

"There *have* been disappearances. More than usual. Typically, I approve a handful of requests a week from folks who need to leave for whatever reason. Some are for business—the crews who tend to our wells, to go hunting and fishing. Others are for traders to visit the few communities remaining in the area. Some are mercenaries, like yourself. But the majority of those I allow to leave, return."

I already know the answer, but I ask anyway. "And lately?"

His voice takes on an ominous quality. "Lately, fewer have been returning. Just this morning I received word that another of our scouting parties hasn't come back yet, and they were due over twenty-four hours ago."

"Fuck."

It's the best I can do for him. Commiseration is far more honest and productive than me lying to him, filling him with false hope that everyone will be okay and they'll all be back safe and sound before he knows it.

That's not the world we live in.

"Fuck is right!" he bellows, alarmingly loud, even for our spats. Frustration rumbles through him like a tidal wave. "This is just what I needed to hear today."

Annoyance flickers inside me. "I'm sorry, are you actually mad at me right now—"

Before I can finish, his finger is in my face. "Don't start."

"Don't start?" The flames of annoyance that had flickered in me just moments before spew into a wave of molten anger. I ball my hands into fists. "I came here to warn you! To do my best to protect your people!"

"My people? Don't pretend to care about my people. All you've ever cared about is yourself!"

I stagger back, the blow striking me harder than I imagined anything he'd ever say to me could. That's what happens when you know someone for as long as Rowland and I have though. We know where the tender parts are, how to apply force with precision, and how to leave scars instead of just bruises.

And somehow despite the number of years we've known each other, Rowland still doesn't understand me. He never has, and at this point I'm not sure he ever will.

For him, sticking together is how he shows his love and loyalty, his devotion. When Hulbeck fell, he scoured the town until he found his mother, cornered and cowering before two noctis. He'd came across someone earlier too, someone who had been bitten but hadn't turned yet. They offered their life to help him, but he was determined to make sure they survived. When he charged the noctis with a rake, spearing one in the heart, he didn't know the human had taken their life and hastened their transformation until the newly-created ghoul was lunging for the other noctis. The way he tells the story, he even debated on bringing the ghoul with him and his mother as they fled, on the off chance that there could be a cure. Ultimately, his mother convinced him to put the poor thing out of its misery, a statement of loyalty and respect in its own way.

I've always been built different than he is. When the monsters came and destroyed our village, I learned that my survival was dependent on my silence, on remaining hidden, on my isolation.

That doesn't mean that I don't care. In fact, it's the opposite.

It's because I care so deeply that I stay away from him and the others. It's because I can't stand the thought of forming friendships just to watch them all die at the hands of monsters that I've chosen to live on my own. It's just easier this way. This way, I don't have to hurt whenever I find out that some of his people are missing. I don't have to know their names, or whether they had living relatives. I don't even have to see their faces later tonight when I lay down for bed.

If wanting to avoid all of that heartbreak makes me heartless, then so be it. It sure beats being foolish enough to think that living in a place like this will last long.

"You know what?" I say at last. "I don't know why I expected a thank you, but it doesn't matter. I came here to tell you what I'd heard, and I did. Do with that information what you will, but I've done my part."

Turning on my heels, I move toward the door, but his hand catches the crook of my elbow. He holds me in place, fingers twitching as if they'd like to do something more.

"Thank you."

Slowly, I turn to face him. I hadn't realized how close he was, but now I can feel the warmth of his breath against my lips.

I shouldn't want him. I never should.

Yet somehow, I always do.

Every time he touches me, my body sings a chorus as bright and breathtaking as an early-morning sunrise. When he's not near me, my chest is hollow and aching. But all it takes is one caress—and sometimes even just a glance—for that dark pit inside me to feel full again, as if the wide chasms are stitched back together, and my pieces are made whole.

It's not real though, I remind myself. This life he's carved out for himself, the life he tries promising me every time I'm with him, it's not real.

This community will fall.

He will fall.

And I can't be here when it happens.

"Rowland—"

The panic in his gaze stops me from finishing the half-formed thought. I almost regret it the moment he starts leaning forward, eyes closing, lips parting.

Not here. Not here. We shouldn't do this here—

Our lips meet and my mind stills. My breath hitches. I inhale the sweet taste of him and it's like no time has passed at all between us.

I know this is wrong. I know it can't work. But part of me wishes it could. Part of me wishes I could throw myself into him fully. Give him every part of me, even the parts that I've never seen myself. I'm tired of thinking about all the horrible things that could happen. We've fought so hard for so long, and at some point, we deserve the reward.

Desire and longing are strange things. They act as clouds that lift me away from my usual pessimism and into an enchanting place where only Rowland and I exist.

His hands find the small of my back and I arch into him, the cautious kiss deepening into something heady. Something dizzying.

I don't know who I am when I'm in his embrace. I'm not the girl who has been alone for years, defending herself against the monsters and surviving despite the odds. I'm someone fragile, vulnerable.

And I hate it.

I hate feeling so small and frail.

Gregor's voice is in my head.

Pathetic.

Useless.

Frightened.

Just as my fingers begin to weave through Rowland's dreadlocks, they stop. With a force that might split us both in two, I shove him away and stagger to where Gregor's and Boris' bodies lay. Mostly my eyes linger on the larger noctis. It's as if I need to make sure he's still dead, need to be certain we won, and that he won't *ever* hold so much power over me again.

There's no convincing me. I've seen too many humans reanimate into ghouls. And though I've never watched a noctis rise from the dead, I'm suddenly not sure it isn't possible.

The walls around us feel like they're closing in.

I can't stay in this room.

"When are you going to let go of the past, Char?"

It's the last thing I can handle right now.

"Maybe when people stop trying to convince me that it didn't happen and never will again!" I inhale sharply, tears stinging the back of my throat. "Just...just pay me for the noctis and I'll be on my way."

Half-expecting the fight to spark again, I brace myself for Rowland's ire. It doesn't come though.

"One second," he says.

Exhaustion ripples off him as he makes his way toward the door and summons a guard in from outside.

The man that enters is unlike any guard I've ever seen. He's inundated with adornment, but not of the chainmail or leather armor kind. Jewels of every color adorn his fingers, with at least half of the rainbow pierced in each ear. A simple, golden hoop loops through his nostril, and he wears charcoal around his eyes.

When he salutes Rowland, his hand almost gets lost in the voluminous cloud of curls framing his face.

"Sir?" the guard asks, but his eyes are on me.

He looks me up and down with the sort of judgmental grimace that makes me suddenly self-conscious about how long it's been since I bathed. Or combed my hair. Or even bothered to wipe the noctis guts from my blouse.

Rowland nods his respect to the man, either oblivious to the guard's judgment, or simply not caring.

"Charlotte here has brought us two noctis for our studies. Make sure she's given credits for the market."

The guard bows. "Of course."

"And I need you to put together a clean-up crew. Just a few men. No more." A new thought occurs to Rowland. "In fact, take the prisoners we grabbed from the tavern last night. If they're willing to work, if they can do this job well, I'll release them from the rest of their sentence."

The two of them talk a bit longer, Rowland telling the man about what happened with me and the noctis and what I overheard them saying about the Hunt. He tells him where to take the prisoners, where they'll find the locations of both Boris and Gregor's deaths.

Meanwhile, I wait impatiently, wondering if I should just tell him to put it on my tab and come back another time.

It's already dark. I should be back at my hovel by now.

"Make sure to leave no trace of noctis blood," Rowland instructs. "Or any signs of struggle, for that matter. If someone comes looking for these two, we need to make sure their trails don't lead back here."

"Consider it done," the guard says, clapping his decorated hands together.

"One more thing." Rowland stops the guard before he's out

the door. "Alert the people of Valor's Rest that we will be in a blackout for the remainder of the week, effective immediately."

The guard's friendly almost carefree expression folds like a bad hand of cards.

"A blackout? Sir, are you sure that's—"

"I'm quite sure. We need to keep a low profile until we're sure the noctis have passed through Gravenburg. Tell all the families with children to report to the underground shelter. Everyone else will remain inside their homes, shutters closed, noise kept down to no more than a mouse's whisper, until they receive further instruction or are summoned for essential duty."

Reluctantly, the guard nods, leaving not a moment later.

"He'll bring you your vouchers once the blackout has commenced. You should stay—"

"I'm good." I breeze past him, our shoulders almost knocking against each other, but I swerve at the last second, not wanting to start something up again. "When your guard returns, tell him to bring my vouchers to the fletcher. Elison has some bolts for me that I need to pay for, and since you guys will be in blackout, I suppose I should grab those before I get locked out for the week."

The look he casts at me is one I can't decipher. At first, I assume he's simply surprised at my knowing someone's name other than his in this place. Truth be told, I don't like that I do. It's too intimate. Better for them to remain faceless, nameless. But I suppose if I were to know anyone here it would be the master fletcher responsible for replenishing my crossbow bolts.

It's not until the surprise fades—giving way to sorrow—that I realize the sudden shift in the room. The very air stills, stiffening like hardened molasses.

It's a long, painful moment but neither of us speak.

I step closer.

Another of our scouting parties hasn't come back yet...

Hadn't Elison mentioned something about an excursion last time I saw her?

"Rowland, where's your fletcher?"

He rubs his temples and strides back to the liquor table to pour himself another drink. Swirling the amber liquid around in the glass, he can't look at me.

"Elison left two days ago. We haven't heard from her since."

The only word that seems to be in my current vocabulary is, "Fuck..."

Then again, what more is there to say? Come to think of it, *fuck* actually seems to sum it up quite nicely, given that if we had heard about the noctis using Gravenburg as their hunting grounds just two days earlier, she might still be here.

Instead, we have to face the reality that Elison is as good as dead.

There goes my high-quality bolts.

"You know, you might want to think about doing something other than a blackout. If the noctis have already been preying on your people, they might already know where you're located. Maybe you should take your people and run while you still can—"

His head all but thrashes. "I can't do that."

"Why not?"

He doesn't answer. The inside of his lip will soon be raw though, given how much he's gnawing on it. If his mother were here, she'd scold him and tell him that if he didn't stop, someday soon he'd find himself with no mouth at all.

But I'm not his mother. And although she always shrugged it off as some petulant pastime, I know better. Something worse than a missing fletcher is at stake here.

"You're not telling me something."

He startles as if he'd forgotten I was even here. But he just shakes his head more determinedly.

"Don't lie to me, Rowland. And quit playing games. What's going on?"

He tosses the drink down his throat and winces with a breathy burst of air against the astringent alcohol. I'm surprised when he moves for a third drink. We're similar in our abstention from alcohol, but where I don't drink because of how it dulls my senses, Rowland doesn't drink because he has a respectable reputation to maintain.

If he's indulging now, it must be bad.

Once he's done breathing fire, he summons me back over to his desk. Behind it, Rowland goes to a cabinet and pulls out an untidied stack of parchment, laying them out on his desk.

"What does this have to do with—"

"Look," he says, pointing.

Curiosity gets the best of me and I lean in, though with a healthy dose of skepticism. Black ink spreads across each sheet of parchment in a complicated system of veins.

I arch a brow at him. "Maps?"

He nods. "This is where we are—"

Scoffing, I fold my arms. "I know where we are, you prick. Just because I'm illiterate doesn't mean I don't know basic directions."

He's too immersed in his train of thought to pay me any mind, so he continues dragging his finger along a tightly knit system of corridors before stopping on a collection of buildings that I think might've been residential—back when Gravenburg still had residents.

There's a small, black dot underneath his finger.

"There," he says, the excitement in his tone causing me some concern. "That's where Elison went. To check the well for water and to make sure no ghouls or other creatures were rotting inside it."

"Gross." I blink down at the map, then up at him, waiting

for an explanation as to what this has to do with what he wasn't telling me. "And?"

"And—" He draws out the word, turning its single syllable into something closer to three. "I want to ask you for a favor."

No wonder he was acting so weird.

"In exchange for your bolts, and any other supplies you'll need for the next week, I'd like you to go check it out. See if you can find her."

My jaw unhinges. A week's worth of supplies isn't nothing, especially ones that come at no cost to me—at least in terms of credits. It might even have been a deal I would've taken from the job board myself if I'd seen it.

But the fact that it's coming from him directly ties my stomach in knots. I can't believe he's asking me to do this. Rowland, of all people, has always tried keeping me sheltered, keeping me safe inside these walls.

Now he's asking me to march straight into danger.

Thrusting my arm out, I gesture to the dead noctis near the door.

"Maybe you've forgotten but I've already paid for my bolts, and then some. You can count, right? I brought you *two* of them. *Two.*"

"Technically, I killed and carried one of them, and my sentries took care of the other."

My teeth grind into each other until I'm afraid I might break my jaw.

"If we're being technical, I never asked for your fucking help."

He sighs, itching his scalp. "Look, I need an archer for this job. None of mine know the city like you do, and even if they did, I need them to guard Valor's Rest while we're in the blackout. We're already down two thanks to the horde of ghouls that attacked a month ago."

"Oh," I balk, red the only thing in my vision. "And that's

supposed to make me feel better? Two have already died, Charlotte. Why not throw your life on the line now so that we can all stay safe and hidden behind these walls?"

His lips purse.

"You know what? I can't believe you. All your talk about loyalty and caring about people, and just like that you'd throw me to the wolves."

The restraint he's showing to bite down on his tongue begins to waver, but I storm on. I'm only getting started.

"And for what? To follow some dead girl's trail? Look, I know she was a good fletcher—a great one, even—but you've got two others here. There's no reason for me to chase after her when we both know she's already noctis meat—"

Finally, he loses it. "She's with child, Charlotte!"

The room stops breathing. Or rather, it's like it's inhaling, the four stout walls contracting and caving in on us.

I heard him wrong, surely. I don't trust what my ears are trying to tell me he said, but even more, I don't trust the protective, sentimental tone they think they detected.

"What...do you mean?" I dare ask.

I need him to say it. I need to hear the words come out of his mouth because until he does, I'm just a girl with a knife in her heart. Only once he removes it, once I'm bleeding and hollowed out, can I begin to heal.

"She's with..." He swallows, prolonging my agony, and this time the fingers that massage his temples make him look like the coward he is. "She's with *my* child."

My chest splinters.

The iceberg beneath my breast shatters.

A world of hurt comes crashing down around me with thundering and devastating might, encasing me in an icy shield until I barely even recognize myself or the man before me.

"What..." The word comes out in a fractured half-sob that I

also don't recognize. It's been so many years since I've cried that I wasn't even aware I knew how anymore.

Dizzy, my head rolls from one side to the other—or maybe it's my body that sways on the uneven, ever-shifting ground. My knees buckle. Bracing myself, I lean over the desk.

Rowland's quick to come beside me, but he knows better than to touch me. The hands hovering around my elbows sweep up to his head instead, sliding through the ropes of hair that I was just curling around my fingers not more than a couple of days ago.

Maybe once he left and returned here, *she* did the same.

"I didn't want this to happen, Char. I'm so sorry." Considering the lack of remorse in his tone, it's not a very believable apology. "You're not here though! I've begged you, a hundred times, to come live at Valor's Rest, but you don't want to be here. You don't want to be with me. And I can't just... I can't just spend my life sneaking off to share secrets nights with you in that—that—place. We're building something here—"

Fire roils inside me. "*We?*"

Eyes wide, his head shakes. "No, that's not what I meant. I was just trying to say that—this place, we can—*I* can have a life here. It's what I've been trying to tell you. If we can move on from the past, from Hulbeck, we could have a future here. You could too if you allowed yourself."

The flames melt through me, an inferno blazing, consuming me in a roar of fury.

My nails dig into the mahogany wood, and I shove myself upright.

"A life here? What? With you, your girlfriend, and your bouncing babe? And then what? You'd keep me locked in here with the rest of them, using me whenever you'd like, but only if I fit into the perfect life you're constructing for yourself?"

"It's not like that."

"Then what is it like, Rowland? Because that's certainly

what it sounds like." I feel the iron-hot poker of hot tears burning at the backs of my eyes, but I blink them away. "How long has this been going on? How long have you been seeing her while you're seeing me?"

Once Rowland and I found each other again—two teenagers ripe with trauma and brimming with hormones who needed some kind of release—it didn't take long before we discovered that there could be more than the friendship we'd grown up enjoying. Though I was loathe to admit it, I needed companionship, and Rowland needed a break from the pressures of preparing for leadership.

We needed an ounce of pleasure in this abysmal life, and uncoordinated and inexperienced as we were, we found it in each other.

But that was what? Three years ago? Maybe four? Was Elison already with their township then, or had she come later? How much of that time had I been unknowingly sharing him?

But instead of looking the part of a withering flower to a flame, Rowland's expression becomes incredulous.

"That's just it," he says, voice low. "I haven't been *seeing* you. Not in any real way. Or I just mean—" He shoves his face into his hands but recovers quickly. "You know what I mean. I've tried, Charlotte. I've tried to be there for you. I've tried to be there *with* you. I've tried to make you see that this place is nothing to fear, that I'm someone who will protect you and care for you no matter what."

I snort, pointing at the scattered maps beside us. "Oh, sure. You'll give me what I need as long as I'll run these errands for you. Bring you back noctis to experiment on. As long as I risk my life so that I can help you rescue your mistress. Your fucking damsel in distress!"

He slams his fists onto the table, maps flying everywhere.

"It could've been you!"

I stagger back.

"It's always been you, Charlotte… Why can't you see that? It could still be you."

Abruptly, he stands, striding over to me with a renewed sense of urgency. He takes my hands into his and I'm too numb to pull them away, too unfamiliar with the territory we've trudged into.

"Elison doesn't mean anything. She was—a distraction. I owe it to her and our unborn child to find her and make sure she's safe. But if you tell me that *this*"—he presses my hand to the warmth of his chest— "That *this* is what you want, then it's yours. It always has been. You have to know by now, after all of these years that I love—"

Before he can finish making this the second most miserable day of my life—although maybe he already has—I jerk my hands free and turn my back to him.

My face is so warm, I'm sure it looks like I've burned myself. It's a price I'm willing to pay to hold these tears back just a few moments longer, just until he's out of my sight.

I won't give him the satisfaction of seeing me break, of being the last person I cared about and trusted and to know that he ruined it all.

My hands fall to my sides, brushing against my belt. The jars at my fingertips are still mostly empty, and what little blood I'd gathered from the pigeon is already gone after everything I had to do earlier just to survive.

And that's just it.

I am a survivor.

And I've survived far worse than Rowland's betrayal.

But I need supplies to do so. I need my bolts. I need food and water, and maybe even some new boots.

Truthfully, I can't afford to turn him down. If he's really withholding my goods until he learns more about his precious missing cargo, then I have no other choice.

Turning around, I face him with the fierceness I've learned to face this cruel life with since I was eight.

I march to his desk and snatch the map off it.

"I'll find your girlfriend," I hiss, walking past him toward the door. I retrieve Sable from where he discarded her on the ground, grateful to have the comfort of my crossbow back in my arms.

"Now?" Rowland frets. "You can't go now. It's already dark. You should at least rest and wait until morning."

The brass doorknob is cool in my hand when I say over my shoulder, "No, I leave now. And once I return, hopefully it'll be the last you ever see of me."

7

OUT FOR BLOOD

When we see the ghoul's emaciated form lying sprawled atop a heap of sewage that reeks all the way across town, we know we're in the right spot.

Caz moves the dead creature with the toe of his boot. "Yep. It's dead."

I squat beside the ghoul, taking it's thin, grey arm into my hand and rotating it, examining every inch. "The blood's been drained. Not too long ago, judging from the lack of decay."

"You think it was Gregor and Boris?"

Releasing the arm, I shrug and stand. Next to most people, I'm a giant. But ever since our teenage years, Caz and I have rivaled in height. We take turns almost every year, one of us sprouting taller than the other, until the next year comes and the other person's growth spurt kicks in.

Standing beside him now, it would seem that this year, I am in the lead. Admittedly, not by much.

"It seems likely," I say, a watchful eye to the surrounding alleyways and empty streets. "The kill is too clean for a ghoul. And I don't know of any other noctis who are in the area."

I turn around and Caz and I exchange a glance, our expressions vastly different.

Worry has already begun to seep into my features. But if I didn't know any better, I'd say Caz almost looks intrigued, maybe even slightly entertained. I find his propensity for taking few things seriously reassuring. It tells me he doesn't believe us to be in any immediate danger because if we were, *then* he'd be someone else entirely. It's one of the many reasons I value his company. Too often do people jump to conclusions and instigate panic. They have unreliable senses of judgment, while Caz only shows concern when there is reason to be.

His judgment is reliable.

It doesn't remove the fact that this situation is still troublesome.

Two noctis are missing. The thought of returning home to report to my father that not only were we unsuccessful in finding humans for the Hunt, but we also managed to lose two of his Crimson Guards makes my chest feel like it's sinking in.

I can just imagine the tirade he'll be on, how much my ears will prefer bleeding over listening to his relentless hectoring.

Behind us, footsteps approach, an echo carrying down one of the many tight corridors. A heavy thud follows from the same direction, a sound that makes me think someone has just leapt from one of the rooftops and landed on the cobblestones before us.

Davorin and Harland appear in the shadows a moment later.

Though they are similar in age and are both of dark hair and dark eyes, time has worn on them differently.

Davorin has been a man of the court since its inception nearly twenty years ago. He has enjoyed the luxury of a catered lifestyle, even if he doesn't share as many of the riches as, say, a prince. He is cared for, provided for. His baths are always steaming and his access to blood always plentiful. He is a strategist, not a warrior, but the cunning in his eyes leaves the impression that he doesn't need brawn to win in a fight.

Harland, on the other hand, looks as if he was born on a mountain, punted off the cliffside, and then hit every rock on his way down, only to climb back up and repeat the process all over again. Scars cover more of his body than not, and the red mottled eyepatch he wears over his right eye is more a part of him than the prosthetic hand that he barely wears anymore because, as he claims, he's stronger without it.

They both have a large presence about them, and perhaps it's for that reason that it takes me a moment to realize...

They're not alone.

Two men trail behind them, one young with tussled blond hair, the other with a shaved head and a thin braid of facial hair dangling from his chin. Ropes bind their raw necks, wrists, and ankles, and they hobble behind Davorin who guides them toward us.

My glare pierces Harland's rugged face. "I thought I told you to head back to camp with the others."

His unflinching expression tells me he doesn't intend to deign me with a response. Fine. I'll deal with him later.

I turn my attention to Davorin. "What took you so long?"

Davorin's eyes flit to our grizzled friend, betraying his annoyance. But he recovers quickly, addressing me exclusively. "Regrettably, my prince, I've never had much of a poker face. When you summoned me away from the others, Harland suspected it had something to do with his brothers and insisted on accompanying me."

With a tremor of irritation, I reflect on how there are apparently times when I wish people obeyed my orders like they obeyed my father's, moments such as these when the last thing I need is someone who will fly off the handles at the drop of a dime when we're in the middle of what needs to be a stealthy investigation.

This isn't just about Gregor and Boris. It could be something bigger.

Before I can think of anything to say that won't make me sound like a princeling grappling at power he doesn't have or a petulant child, Davorin becomes distracted.

"Is that…the new cape you had commissioned?"

All thought of disobedience is washed away.

"Yes," I say, beaming. "Isn't it glorious?"

Out of the corner of my eyes, I see Caz roll his.

"Hmm." Davorin raises a single brow. "I'm afraid *glorious* isn't exactly the word I'd use for it."

"Oh?" I bristle, my pride wounded. "Then what would you call it?"

Davorin looks it over once more and says without feeling, "Ridiculous."

Laughter bubbles out of Caz. "That's what I said!"

One of the humans snorts, drawing everyone's attention to the bald man.

Grabbing the sides of my cape, I wrap them around my sides as I veer the conversation toward the two prisoners. "Yes, well, I'm glad someone's escapades through this town have proved fruitful."

Davorin bows his appreciation.

Harland, however, growls, his bearded sneer leaving little space for his fangs to show. "Not fruitful enough. Neither of them killed my brothers. That one there couldn't even keep his own piss in his cock." His head bobs to the young one, then he spits his disgust. "Should've killed them and kept looking."

"And wasted the opportunity to deliver two humans to the Hunt?" Davorin scoffs. "The king would've—"

"Fuck the fucking king!" The words are a mighty growl from a hibernating bear who's been prematurely awoken. "Those are my brothers out there!"

Beside me, Caz slips into his soldier-self. He stands taller, and whether consciously or not, he shifts his body closer to mine, coming between Harland and I to act as my shield, should he deem it necessary.

It won't be. For all Harland's ferocious exterior, I've battled him before. He's not nearly as skilled as he believes himself to be. Powerful, yes. But he lacks creativity, intuition, and clearly a sense of self-preservation.

"Tell me," I say, donning my princely mask just as well as Caz can don the mask of a soldier. "Did you find any trace of your brothers? Or are you simply suggesting we chase after them blindly and subject ourselves to the same foolish danger they stumbled upon?"

Harland's one eye becomes malignant, his coarse beard twitching. For what it's worth, whatever venom he wants to spew, he holds it back, even if the anger bashing about in his skull is so brutal that I can practically feel it.

It's Davorin who finally answers. "We only briefly found their scent. It led us to these two who were dutifully cleaning up what appeared to be quite a lot of blood."

"Noctis blood," Harland growls.

"Where was this?" I ask them.

Davorin gestures behind them. "Back that way a few blocks. One of them was holding this."

He hands me an arrow—No, not an arrow. It's much too short.

Caz leans over to me, a hand shielding his quirked mouth. "Crossbow bolt."

"Yes, thank you." I snatch the thing from Davorin's hands and turn it over. There's fresh blood on the tip. "Perhaps this is why Gregor and Boris didn't respond through the bond. Judging from the amount of blood, are you presuming them dead?"

Davorin nods.

"We don't know they're dead." Harland's words are like rabid dogs tethered by tenuous leashes.

If he were anyone else, I might try mustering more sympathy for the fear and pain he must be experiencing. I've never had a brother, not by blood, so I can't pretend to know what it must be like for your younger brothers to be missing, and very likely dead. But it's difficult to muster sympathy for someone who's never shown any to you, someone who looked me in the eyes after I watched my mother die—at his hands—and told me to *get over it*.

Even if I didn't harbor a seething hatred for the man, facts are facts, and the dead are the dead.

"They didn't send word through the bond, and when you traced them down, you found blood, and two humans cleaning it up. I know this might be difficult for you to hear—hell, it's the very reason you weren't invited—but here you are, so let's be honest. They seem to be dead."

Uttering the words out loud don't make me feel any better. And if he thinks he's the only one upset, he's wrong.

I didn't much care for Harland's brothers; if he had the civility of a wild and starved bear, his brothers behaved more like the impish fiends that once populated the Shadowthorn. But they were still men in *my* charge, and therefore I have failed them.

Failed the crown.

Even if we return with two humans as compensation, it won't be enough. I'm not even sure four would be enough. Or ten.

Although…maybe, it would be.

The thought gives me a flicker of an idea, but before it can fully form, Harland lunges for me.

Caz tries to leap between us, but I shove him back.

Harland doesn't scare me. Let him start something he can't finish. It's about time I put him in his place and remind him who is a full-blooded Devonshire noctis, and who was raised in the gutters on rat blood and filth.

Before a good brawl can even begin, Harland stops short, teeth bared and snarling mere inch away from mine. "They can't get away with this. I won't let them."

"They won't," I promise.

Though I'm loathed to agree with him, he's right. We can't let them take two of ours and return with only two of theirs. It's hardly an even trade. Not in the eyes of the king anyway.

I examine the two humans, neither of whom appear to be struggling by any means. The younger of the two has almost definitely bathed recently, given the sheen of his golden wheat hair, and I'm willing to wager that the other, a grouch of a man with the figure of someone who's not accustomed to food scarcity, has a home somewhere—perhaps nearby—where the missus is preparing his next warm meal.

Just yesterday, Ursulette captured a human—a woman who also seemed to be in fine health.

It could be a coincidence, to find three humans in the same city all within a day of each other. But that seems unlikely. These aren't just folks wandering aimlessly around the same abandoned city. They came from the same place.

"Davorin," I call to my father's adviser. "Ursulette found a human woman yesterday at a well. Do you remember where she said it was located?"

Davorin pulls out his map and unravels it for me. "The east side of town, I believe. Near the forest, there. Why?"

My eyes scan the sketches of roads, an idea forming. "Three people... They've lost three people so far..."

"What's your point, Malachi?" Harland huffs.

This time, I let the informality slip.

"My point is, the girl Ursulette found and these men here? They're all from the same community. Ursulette said the human she found was repairing a well, perhaps cleaning it. If we could find that well—"

"Then we find their source of water," Davorin finishes for me.

"That there? That could be a well." Caz points over my shoulder to a black speck on the map. "Or it could be some other kind of ominously deep hole in the ground."

"Then that's where we'll go," I say.

"It could be a trap," Davorin warns, stroking his thick beard. "It could be guarded."

Caz's fangs flash and he gestures to the human men behind us. "Let's find out then, shall we?"

We turn around to stare expectantly at our human prisoners, hoping that the answers will come pouring from their tongue. But we only find them doing what prisoners do best: fighting imprisonment.

The younger one has managed to procure himself a nail—presumably taken from one of the plentiful dilapidated buildings in this dungheep of a city—and is frantically scratching away at the ropes bound around the bald one's wrists.

No wonder they've been so silent.

Harland marches forward with steam rising from his ears, but I stop him with a hand to the chest. I'm curious to see how long it takes for them to notice that our conversation has died, and all eyes are on them.

It doesn't take long.

The bald one nudges his friend to stop sawing away at the ropes, and with frightened, guilty eyes, the young man drops the nail.

"I'm s-sorry. We didn't m-mean to—"

"Doesn't matter." I stride forward, finger marked on the map. "What do you know of this well?"

The bald one squints, leans closer. "It looks like a well, alright. What do you want with us about it?"

"The girl we captured. She was taken from here. You know her?"

He scratches at where the rope chafes his neck and winces. "Can't say that I do, and even if I could, I can't say that I know what's in it for me."

Harland snarls like a wild boar. Soon my bracing hand won't be enough to stop him from lunging for their throats.

I look to Davorin. "You were there when Ursulette brought the woman back. You saw what she looks like. Jog his memory."

"I don't know," Davorin says, dragging an apprehensive hand through his smooth, dark hair. "Red hair? Freckles?"

"Someone who doesn't go down without a fight," I add, remembering the struggle Ursulette had described trying to secure the scrappy woman.

Caz seems delighted by this new, unexpected turn of events. Or maybe he's just proud. He always prefers a fight.

I turn my glower on the humans.

The younger one cowers behind the bald one, who makes every attempt not to look frightened. Of course he is though. What human wouldn't be? He is bound and standing before his apex predator.

It is admirable, however, that he hasn't pissed himself, I'll give him that. This close, I'd be able to smell it. But instead, all I scent is their blood.

My mouth waters for the taste of it, my hungry stare lingering on their raw throats.

Over the years, I've learned how to tell a delicious feed from a mediocre one—and these two will likely fall somewhere in the less-than-mediocre territory, tasting downright vile, although given the young man's age and fair complexion, it's possible he could surprise me.

The thought makes my eyes hone in with more precision on the veins snaking down his throbbing throat, just a taste away.

That's when I see the disturbance. The puncture in his flesh. One black hole is pierced through his otherwise flawless skin.

I grab the other man by the back of the neck and tilt his head back to confirm my suspicions, ignoring his frightened whimpers

My glare slams full force into Harland. "They've been fed upon?"

Harland glares back at me, unflinching. "Just be grateful I didn't kill them."

"You—"

"No, I didn't bite them." I breathe a sigh of relief. "I'm not a complete idiot. Your father would have my fucking head. I just pricked them and had a little taste."

It takes all my restraint to hold back my temper, but I guess I owe him that much for him holding back his hunger. Still, the order was not to feed on anyone. The participants of the Hunt prefer their kills to be fresh, fully vital, with not a single drop of blood missing. Harland is long overdue for being reminded of his place, but we have more important matters to attend.

I have men missing and I need answers.

"I'm only going to ask you this once," I say, turning to the humans again and releasing my grip on the young man's neck. "You know the woman we took, yes? That well belongs to a community and the three of you live there together, correct?"

Nervously, they stare at each other, but eventually the young one cracks.

"Not together in *that* sense of the meaning. Huh, Lewis?" He giggles, somehow managing to make himself seem even younger, though I had him pegged for at least eighteen. When his friend remains straight-faced, he clears his throat. "Um, yes. S-sir. We live in Valor's Rest. Just right over near—"

With both hands bound together, the man named Lewis still manages to thwomp the younger man upside the head, practically knocking them both over in the process.

"Shut it, Dunce! Or you'll give away our only bargaining chip, you idiot!" But when he glances up and realizes the damage is already done, he shifts gears. "Fuck it. I'm not dying just to save their sorry asses. You guys said you're looking for people to bring to the Hunt? Dunce and I here could tell you where to find your fill and then some. There's all sorts of humans where we come from. Hundreds."

"Interesting." I shift my weight to one hip and idly stroke the bloodred amulet around my neck.

Lewis seems pleased with himself. He thinks he has us figured out. Like all the other humans, he sees us as nothing more than senseless, ravenous beasts, who would stop at nothing to get a quick bite in. That's how the ghouls are. That's how the demons of the Shadowthorn were. So why would the noctis be any different?

In his defense, many aren't. Like Harland, Ursulette, and Rhain, some noctis only think about satiating their hunger for a day.

I'm not like most noctis.

I think about the future.

Slaughtering an entire community would be one means to an end in terms of survival, but then we would have depleted an entire food source. We don't need mass genocide, nor do I think any sane noctis would want it. We need the human population to replenish.

As if he can sense my disinterest in his proposition, Lewis shifts uncomfortably. "Y-you can even keep Dunce."

"What?" His blond friend blanches, but Lewis ignores him.

"He's useless alive anyway. Can't even stop wheezing long enough for that fella there to walk by without noticing us." He gestures to Harland who presumably found them hiding somewhere. "I'm sure he'd make a fine meal. Let *me* go though, and I'll tell you everything. I'll tell you exactly where you can find Valor's Rest. You could have the feast of a lifetime."

"I don't need the feast of a lifetime," I snap at him.

Beside me, Caz whispers, "I wouldn't mind one."

"What we need is a few more captives to contribute to the Hunt," I say to him as much as the others, Harland most of all. I don't need him getting any ideas. "And although the information you claim to have would be valuable in procuring them, I'm afraid it would be too risky, and a little reckless, for the four of us to waltz into a community of a hundred armed humans."

"They're not armed," Lewis insists. Desperation has turned his face as red as an heirloom tomato that's ripened too long in the hot summer sun. "Most of them have forgotten what it was like to fear you. They've lived in comfort too long and barely know how to make a closed fist, let alone how to hold a knife."

His statement piques my interest.

With the crossbow bolt still clenched in my fist, I hold it high. Although the sun has mostly set, the sharp tip—still wet with either Gregor's or Boris' blood—glistens in the dim dusk glow.

"Someone knows how to wield a crossbow. In fact, they're capable enough with one that they appear to have taken out a two-hundred-pound noctis."

"It wasn't the crossbow girl who killed them." He shakes his head. "She almost got herself killed after bringing them to our doorstep. Rowland had to step in and handle things."

An expletive that sounds like an earthquake bellows from Harland's mighty lungs. He storms across the courtyard, fists punching, legs kicking anything in his path. Better the littered streets than our human confidants though.

"H-he had to!" Nervous, Lewis glances between the rest of us. "He couldn't just let the noctis leave knowing where we were. It's his job to protect the town"—wryly, he snorts— "A lot of good that's doing us, if his little mercenary bitch keeps drawing attention to our doorstep."

My smile grows increasingly more and more wicked the longer he speaks. I'm learning so many interesting things about this place that they call Valor's Rest, a town that, before a few moments ago, I don't think any of us knew existed.

I tuck the name *Rowland* away, someone who appears to be in a leadership role in this town, and save it for another day, but I'm most curious about this *mercenary bitch*. He said she *led* them to their front gates. She didn't flee to their doorstep with two noctis chomping on her heels. Hell, it doesn't even sound like she captured them and dragged them there. She *led* them. They came willing, of their own accord.

How curious.

Before I can follow any line of questioning, Harland stomps back toward the group, seething.

"Harland."

But my warning isn't enough. The bull has been released.

Caz and I lunge for him, gripping his broad shoulders and pressing into him. It holds him in place, which is good enough for now, but it won't hold long.

"Harland, you need to hold on just a minute. We don't even—"

"The fuck you mean *hold on?*" he growls, smacking both of our arms off him in a pinwheel motion. "You heard them. They killed my brothers! I'm not letting them get away with this!"

"We'll handle this," I promise, trying to force him to meet my gaze, but his hurt and angered eye is unwavering from his targets. He glares past me. "Harland, please. You need to calm down."

That seems to get his attention.

"Don't fucking tell me to calm down! I'll calm down when every last one of those human bloodbags' heads are on spikes!"

When he advances again, this time Cazimir has no choice but to put more effort into his bodyguarding. He gives Harland a hearty shove, sending the large noctis back a few staggering paces. "Back off, Harland. Last warning."

The two of them square off, ready to bash fists to skulls to burn off some of the tension and grief of the day. I'm inclined to let them. Harland might be able to think more clearly once he's let his aggression out on someone, and Caz is always invigorated by a good duel.

"Prince Malachi?" Davorin's quiet, but commanding voice summons me. "What would you like us to do?"

"Hmm?" I barely hear him, too wrapped up in watching the noctis in my ranks regress into animals. We can't even treat each other with respect. Why would the humans ever have any reason to expect anything less than monstruous from us?

"Our next move," Davorin says. "Are we chasing after justice for Gregor and Boris? Are we considering an ambush on Valor's Rest or are we returning to camp to meet back up with the others and reconvene?"

Idly, I tap the red amulet on my sternum. "Do you think Harland will be able to let it go?"

"We did capture three of their humans. Perhaps that's good enough, knowing that we didn't risk more of our own in the process."

He sounds less convinced than I am.

"Mmm."

"Hey." The young prisoner—Dunce, I believe his friend called him—whistles through his teeth like he has a secret meant for only our ears. "You want justice for your dead friends?"

I look at him, disbelieving. "Wouldn't you?"

He thinks for a moment, then nods the way an overly honest small child would. "I can't give you Rowland—he's always tucked safely behind those walls. But I can give you the next best thing?"

"And what's that?"

"The mercenary he works with—the woman with a cross-bow? She's the reason your friends were at Valor's Rest, yeah?"

"It would appear so," I say, still curious about how that came to be. "And?"

Lewis gives an exasperated sigh. "Oh, take your time, Dunce. It's not like our lives depend on it or anything."

The boy looks sheepish, swallows, and then says, "I over-heard him talking to one of his guards after she left. He sent her back to the well to look for the girl you took."

The grin that creeps up my face is more malicious than joyful.

"You hear that, Harland?" I shout over my shoulder and over their grunting. "It looks like we'll get you your justice yet."

He releases the headlock he has Caz stuck in. I've never seen him stand so eager, so willing to listen. At least not to me.

I speak loud enough so that everyone can hear. I want them all to understand the plan without me having to explain it, in case there are listening-ears nearby. "We head to the well."

8

SPIDERS AND THEIR WEBS

As we begin our trek across town, Davorin adjusts his black chest plate and leans in close, his words meant only for my ears. "Should we summon the others to join us? In case the prisoners are being less than forthcoming."

Contorting my features, I give Lewis a once over. "I doubt he's trying to deceive us. But if it'll make you feel better…"

I raise my wrist up, my lips lightly dusting the blood oath tattoo where I whisper the instructions to our team. Ahead of us, Caz jolts for half of a second, startled when the message reaches him. Harland, too, tilts his head as if there's an annoying bug buzzing around him.

Davorin tugs on my arm. "And perhaps have Ursulette retrieve The Fox."

I stiffen, my cool demeanor falling, if only for a fraction of a moment. I recover too slowly for Davorin not to see.

"This is the way it has to be. It's not your fault, Malachi. And she won't be harmed."

I give him a derisive scoff. "Yeah, not today."

He quiets, but his beseeching, dark eyes don't leave mine until I acquiesce and raise my wrist to my lips again. Though the message is meant for Ursulette only and I am plenty capable of sending it directly to her, I allow it to permeate into the other's minds. It'll save me having to explain the plan later.

Within an hour, we've located the well.

Within another, Ursulette and Renee arrive with The Fox, though I can hardly recognize her with the burlap sack tied over her head. Her hands though, the fingers that were hacked off at awful angles and left to heal horribly on their own, those I recognize. A twinge of guilt settles in my belly the way it always does when I lay eyes on her or remember she's in our possession. For all the talk my father shares of the importance of family, he has shown no such loyalty or respect for my aunt.

"Good," I say, summoning the calm and cold tone of my prince facade. "Get her into position."

Ursulette jerks Fox steady when her knees go weak, nothing even close to resembling empathy reflecting in her pale gray eyes, the eyes of a Devonshire.

"And then what?" she asks with a voice as pleasant as a honeycomb, but as dangerous as the horde of hornets guarding it. "How long will we be sitting here waiting for one measly human to wander by?"

As if on cue, Caz's voice reverberates in my skull.

"Not long," I tell her. "I think our mark has just been spotted.

* * *

From my vantage point atop the roof, I'm impressed to say that the place still looks and feels deserted, despite the half dozen noctis hiding about.

I suppose I shouldn't be worried. With the moon high, we're in our element. The night makes us deadly.

As we wait for the girl to make her way through the narrow Gravenburg streets, I let my mind drift to what our welcoming will be like when we reach Nigh with—not one, not two, not even three, but—four human donations for the Hunt. I find it highly unlikely that any of the other teams scouring the lands right now will find their efforts half as fruitful, and my father will have no choice but to commend our efforts—for once in his life—and praise *me* for a job well done.

"Do I dare ask what's brought that terrifying grin to your face?" Caz asks, nudging my shoulder with his own.

My smile collapses so that I can glare at him instead.

"Ah, that's better." He moves to give me a hearty pat to my back but seeing the sharp points of my cape and remembering the pain they caused him last time, he settles for a faltering tap of my shoulder. "There's the brooding prince I know and love. Why don't you leave the random acts of smiling to me, yeah?"

"Keep it down, Caz," I say casually, not a hint of the royal power I could muster anywhere in my tone. "We don't know when the girl will arrive, and it would be a huge disappointment to give away our location prematurely."

He blows through his nose, but his grumbling is in my mind only. "'Cause the estimate I provided is *so* unreliable."

"You said *ten minutes* over twenty minutes ago," I remind him.

"It only took me seven minutes to get back here, so bite me."

We both chuckle, our laughter suppressed behind the inner walls of our minds. The blood oath is strongest with him. Since our tattoos are permanent, we can feel each other's joy as if it's our own. Other emotions too, if we allow them.

I, for one, try to keep Caz safe from any of my more regrettable thoughts, and I believe he does the same for me.

Once the laughter has faded, I think more about what he said. Although I don't think he was truly offended, I also think part of him could be. Like me, he's spent most of his life in shadow, trying to live up to someone else's unreasonable expectations of him. I never want that to be the way he feels around me.

"Unlike you, the human girl has to take a more cautious approach when it comes to meandering through a city like this," I offer and the slightest breeze of appreciation flutters through the oath. It's almost overwhelmed, though, by the rumbling of Harland's impatience. "I hope she gets here soon. I don't know how much longer I can keep Harland on a leash."

"You call him leashed?" Caz snorts, this time audibly. "That man is an active volcano that erupts every few months, and that's on a good day. With his brothers gone? Us capturing this human girl isn't going to do much to calm him."

"Fair enough."

With a wary glance my direction, he changes the subject. "Is Fox in position?"

"Yeah," I sigh. "But she's not too happy about it."

He's quiet for a moment. "It's not your fault, you know. You didn't capture and torture her into servitude. The king did."

"You know, your father said almost the exact same thing."

He beams. "I guess intelligence runs in the family, despite what Renee would have you think." Rolling his eyes, he glances back over the rooftop ledge, searching the streets for any signs of the human and finding none. "All I'm trying to say is don't beat yourself up about it. Your...aunt? Is that what she'd be to you—You know what? It doesn't even matter. Whoever she is, whatever relation she might have to you and your twisted family, she is in far better company by being here with us than she would ever be with your father."

There's a truth to that, one that makes my bones chill.

My father has already caused her so much pain and suffering, it's hard to imagine he could do more. But I know him at his core. I know how ruthless his imagination can be. He will always find a way to make the people around him suffer.

Even family.

Especially family.

And maybe Caz is right. Maybe since she only married my father's cousin, she's only *family* in the loosest sense. But when you have so little family members in your life already, and the ones who are around are miserable tyrants bent on spreading misery, the kind ones, the innocent ones, they're worth protecting.

"I'll make it up to her soon," I think to myself, forgetting that the blood oath is active and open.

The words might not seem treasonous, perhaps nothing more than a harmlessly mindless declaration. But in thought form Caz understands their full intent.

Wide-eyed and choking on air, he whirls on me. "What do you mean *you'll make it up to her soon?* Not that I'm usually against recklessness, but I hope you don't mean what it sounds like you mean."

Heaving a sigh, I rub my face, realizing it's too late to deny my intent now. Not to Caz. Besides, I think in time I would've told him anyway. The only reason I hadn't yet was because the idea had only just come to mind a few days ago.

For almost two full years, my father has held Fox's sons prisoner. He meant to use them to draw my uncle Alphonse, the former Magistrate of Arcathain, out of hiding, but instead, my aunt came for her children, was captured, and thrown into a dungeon. In all this time, there have been no reports of Alphonse, not since the day the Capital fell eighteen years ago, and my father claimed regency. Not even when we captured Fox did she mention any word of her husband, despite endless hours of torture and threat on her children's—my nephew's— lives. And she's never made an attempt on his life, or mine. Every time she's broken out of her cell—the cunning spitfire that she is—her only goal has been to find her two boys, but to no avail. My father always recaptures her, and the punishment is always the same.

"A thief will always be a thief," my father said the first time he enacted her punishment. "Until they lose the means of being one."

The last time I saw her, she was down to just six fingers, but not even that could tamper her feisty spirit.

It wasn't until we left Neveridge and I saw my aunt, filthy and bound, glaring from the back of one of our prison carts, that I realized there was no end in sight for her. She would continue to fight for her sons. My father would continue to torture and torment her even though she knows nothing, even though her husband clearly is uninterested or unable to come for her.

She serves no purpose in captivity. Neither do her boys.

And yet, my father refuses to release her or end her suffering. To him, my uncle is unfinished business. A loose end that needs to be tied off. And currently, she is his only connection to him.

I'm not even sure my idea to free her is even fully formed yet, only that I know I can't let her live as our prisoner forever. She and her boys deserve a life outside of my father's cruelty.

"I don't know what I mean," I admit to him, nervous in my confession.

Despite us being brothers, a secret as big as this, a direct act of rebellion, is not something we've shared so openly before. I've griped about my father, certainly, but this is different. This is treason.

"It sure felt like you did," he says. "It felt like you were considering throwing your life away to save that woman."

I stare down at the black, empty street. "Maybe I am. Maybe I'm tired of all of this."

Silence settles over us, amplified only by the darkness, and the death that took over these parts of the country years ago. My stomach coils, my unease deepening the longer we wait for something—for him to respond, for this human girl to arrive, for Harland to fly off the walls, anything.

"Well," Caz says at last, a little more cheerful than I anticipate, and immediately putting me at ease. "If you need anything from me, let me know."

I stare at him, agape, entirely at a loss for words.

"What? You think it's so shocking to find out that you want to disobey your father's orders, release his most prized prisoners, and embrace a life of exile in the name of your own freedom?" He gives me a mockingly dubious look. "Please. You've been talking about giving him the middle finger as you ride off into the sunset for years. It was only a matter of time, really."

As a smirk begins to grow, I thank him through the blood oath.

Jarring us from our private—bordering criminal—conversation, a smooth, rich voice coats the inside of my mind.

"Tell the others to look alive," Rhain says, sounding as if he's on the edge of ecstasy. "I just spotted our bleeder heading your way. And ooo, if she doesn't look like a treat."

"They're coming," I tell everyone through the bond, grateful that we decided to refresh our marks before we split up again. Most of the others managed to keep their oaths safe from the rain earlier, but this way I knew they could be relied upon. I turn to Caz, who's expectant and waiting. "It was Rhain."

"So, she's coming from the west then," he says, and then pauses to think, expression contorting. "He only mentioned the one?"

I nod. "I guess Lewis was telling the truth."

Caz still looks unconvinced. "I guess. It just feels...like a trap. Or about the dumbest decision I've ever heard. Why would you send one mercenary to a spot where you know your people have already been preyed upon?"

He's right. It doesn't make sense. To send a single human into danger would be a fool's errand.

Unless, like he said, it's a trap.

"Be on guard," I say into the bond. "We've spotted just the one girl thus far, but there could be others following behind her. Keep your eyes and ears open. And report anything suspicious—and I mean *anything*."

Beside me, Caz dons his soldier's mask and presses lower, taking cover behind the short wall before us. But if Rhain was the one to spot her, given our position south of the well, we likely won't even be able to see her approaching.

"Come on," I say to Caz through the bond. "Let's get closer. I want to be there when she arrives."

"You mean you want to make sure Harland doesn't do anything foolish."

"Precisely."

We climb down from the rooftop and make our way closer to the well. My jaw sets in a firm line at the sight of my aunt huddled there, but I try steeling myself against whatever empathy I might be experiencing for her. I can figure out how to save her later. For now, I need my focus.

* * *

We see the human girl before we hear her, which is more than can be said for most humans. In my experience, they're loud and careless. The heavy breathing. The sniffling. The clunky footsteps as they struggle to meander across uneven terrain. They don't give a second thought to how much noise their bodies make as they move about the world despite their very survival depending on it.

But the young woman who approaches is as silent as the moon rising into the night sky, and just a mesmerizing. The sharp angles of her high cheekbones, the slender curve of her neck, and the way her honeyed eyes glow in the night are strik-ing. But even more so is the way that she moves, as if the night is as much a part of her, as she is it.

Most humans steer clear of the dark maw of shadows as if they might bite them. She, however, gives herself over to them. When she slinks from one to another, I notice the dried stream of half-cleaned blood crusted on her chin and down her neck. It's not an unusual sight for a noctis—feeding can get messy sometimes. But for a human? I find myself suddenly entranced and curious to know more about her.

But first things first.

Concealed in the shadows, Caz and I hang back, awaiting the spring of our trap.

9

THE FOX

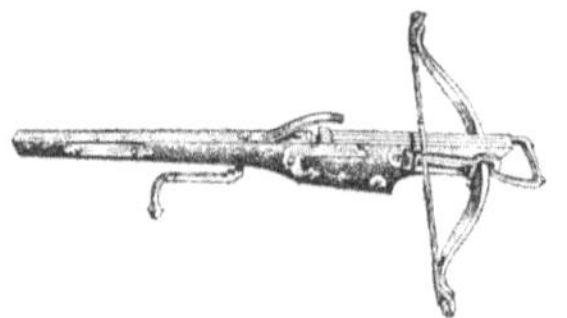

No matter how much distance I put between me and Rowland, I can't seem to shake the feel of him. The weight of his expectations. Of his betrayal.

But it's not really a betrayal, is it? Not by the truest meaning of the word. And that's the part that hurts the most. Because if it was just him that I could be mad with this would all be easier, but unfortunately, he's not the person I fault most.

Everything he said was true. I've kept him at a distance our entire lives. What did I expect to happen? That he'd be content with our arrangement for the rest of his life? He's the leader of an ever-growing community. He has big dreams about the possibilities of the future, he has endless hope for mankind and optimism for his research.

He doesn't just want to survive.

Rowland wants to live.

I have no doubt he wants to take a wife someday, make a family. And I don't fit into that vision for his future. I never have. I've never wanted to.

So then why does it feel as if someone has taken a chisel to my heart and pounded it straight through?

I do my best not to think too hard about it. The last thing I need is to be distracted.

Night has fallen and these streets will be more dangerous than they were before. I already almost lost my life once today; I don't plan on tempting fate again.

I probably should've taken Rowland up on his offer and waited out the moon, but I needed to get out of that compound. I needed fresh air and for the walls to stop pressing in on me.

"That's not the life I want," I whisper to myself, the words barely making it past my lips, I utter them so softly. "This is where I belong."

Steeling myself to the terrors that roam about, I pause at an undisturbed doorstep and hold one of my ears up.

The streets are quiet, vacant as usual. There's something about it that's soothing, as if I'm the only soul left alive in this forsaken place. Like it's just me, the rubble of a society long-since destroyed, and the glowing half-halo of light that I can just barely make out over the tops of the buildings.

I move forward, making my way to the well again, careful to avoid the rubble cluttering my path. Rowland has clearly instructed his people to leave this area untampered with, a wise choice to ensure that any noctis who venture this way will be less inclined to think that anyone lives here, let alone frequents it enough that it would be a worthy stake-out location.

The state of the place reminds me of all that the humans have lost. Our ancestors ended demonkind and reclaimed their Arcathainian territories, only for a new monster to bring them to their ruin.

They should've killed them all when they had a chance.

While magic still existed, the once-celebrated *Hero of Arcathain*, Halira Devonshire, should've used the druid magic she still had at her disposal to conjure her powerful cyclones and blow each and every one of the bloodsuckers back into the bowels from which they came.

Instead, she let the monsters live.

Instead, she let the usurper king—her *brother*—live and condemned us all.

That's where I channel my energy. Not to Rowland and the news of his unborn child. Not to Elison, my own fletcher, and the fact that I'm risking my life to save hers right now. I channel all of my anger, all of my frustration, toward the Devonshires.

After all, it was King Tor himself who laid waste to Hulbeck. It was on his orders that the Crimson Guard were in Hulbeck that day. I might not have seen him do it, but I know it was his sharp incisors that ripped through Agnes' throat and laughed while she choked and gurgled on her own blood.

Just as the molten rage is beginning to harden like an impenetrable shield around my aching heart, a cry cuts through the air from somewhere up ahead.

"Help…" A hoarse voice, possibly female, whimpers from the dark. "Is anyone there? Please."

I don't have to glance around to know where the safest, closest hiding spot is because I've been making note of that with every step I've taken since I left Hulbeck ten years ago.

Currently, it's the building at the end of this corner, through a doorless doorway on my right.

Shit. Shit. Shit.

In one swift motion, I leap through the doorway, Sable drawn. I crouch low, slinking across the dark room, acutely aware of the lack of crashing coming from inside. If a ghoul had been in here, it would've leapt into action. Even a noctis or another human would startle at my sudden entrance, so at least I can breathe a sigh of relief knowing that at least I'm not in danger in here.

But whoever's screaming, they could already know I'm here.

I creep my way to the that window faces out toward the raucous. Only once I'm certain I won't be spotted do I chance taking a peek.

On the other side of the wall, I spot the figure of a woman hunched on the ground. She looks like she's trying to move something heavy, but I can't tell what with her back to me. She cries out in pain again when she fails.

"Please!" the woman yells louder than before, sounding more desperate. She sniffles. "I—I'm bleeding. I don't want them to smell it, and…"

I should leave.

I learned long ago that it is never safe to follow a strangers' cries for help and therefore there is no reason for me to stay. Either she is a fraud who will turn on me the moment that I find mercy in my heart to aid her, or she's right, and the noctis will soon be swarming these streets, and neither she, nor I, will stand a chance against them if the scent of blood is in the air.

But the crack in her voice sounds so much like the pleas I heard in Hulbeck, the cries for mercy from my friends and neighbors, that I can't help but think what could've come of our town if there had just been someone there to rescue us. Or what could've happened if monsters never existed.

Abandoning someone in need is a monstruous act… I know this.

Guilt tightening my chest, I dare another peek through the window to get a better look.

Against Gravenburg's backdrop of slate grey and obsidian black, the woman's red hair stands out like a bloodstain on white. From this distance, I still can't see the thing she's fumbling with at her feet, but I can make an educated guess all the same, considering how she winces every time she tugs on her ankle.

A trap. One of a different making than the nefarious intent I'd originally expected from her.

Worst of all, I think it might be one of mine. Rowland stopped having his people set traps in the city awhile ago. He has farmers and hunters to provide food for them now. But I, on the other hand, couldn't pass up the opportunity to capture any of the critters that come lurking this way—on occasion, I've seen deer, even boars wandering these parts—and I couldn't risk them fidgeting their way out of a basic snare either.

The trap I set out here is one of sharp, metal fangs.

She won't be able to walk for weeks, and that's only *if* she takes care. If she has to run from a horde of noctis? Well, she wouldn't live long enough to heal anyway.

I try shaking away the guilt. This isn't my fault. I might've set the damn thing, but I didn't shove her into it. She should've been watching where she was stepping, everyone who's survived this long knows that.

In another effort to pry the metal jaws away from her ankle, her grip slips. Her hands smack to the wet ground with a splash. Defeated and becoming more frantic, the red-haired woman brings her hands up, dragging them over her face as she sobs into them.

It's only then that I notice the reason she hasn't been able to free herself from such a simple contraption yet.

The hand closest to me, the one I can see from this angle, it seems to be missing fingers.

Fuck me.

I'm not sure she can muster the strength to pry open one of my traps if the other hand is in any kind of similar position. If I leave her now, I can almost say with certainty that she will remain here until someone far worse than me finds her.

She's not my problem! I don't even know who she is, and I wouldn't even be out this way if Rowland hadn't—

That sentence has too many endings for me to think any of them through coherently.

I have to focus on what's here before me. My task is to search for Elison, or signs of her. But…

As much as I'd like to turn a blind eye and keep a safe distance, I can't very well search for Elison out here with this woman screaming, beckoning forth every vile creature in the area.

If a ghoul finds her shackled, they'll just eat her and be done with it. But if it's a noctis to come, they'll see the trap, and just like Gregor and Boris, they'll know to come searching for me or anyone else.

Too much attention has been drawn to *Barret Town* today already.

I don't have to take her under my wing, or anything, but at the very least, I have no choice but to free her.

Before I can convince myself out of it, I'm catapulting through the window and charging toward her. I keep my senses about me as I approach, of course, my eyes darting to the darkest corners of the streets, assessing whether the monsters have found her yet.

I detect nothing.

"Oh," the woman says when she sees me. "Someone actually came…"

She sounds neither relieved nor grateful, causing me some alarm. Then again, she might just be in shock, both from the metal jaws clamped around her ankle and at someone coming to her aid in a world that's shown us nothing but cruelty.

I set my crossbow down as I take a knee beside her.

"Believe me," I mutter. "I'm just as stupefied as you are."

Everything about her is dull, from the film in her eyes that suggests she's hardly had a single night's rest in maybe a decade, to the grey sheen of her skin. Even her red hair is streaked with a cloudy shade of white that mutes the color from what I'm sure was once a vibrant shade.

She looks as if she's been living on the road for some time, the layers of grime caked into her pores hardly even fazed by the rainfall from earlier, let alone the tears streaking her cheeks.

"Now let's take a look at—"

As I reach for her trapped foot, the stillness in the air makes my spine stiffen.

I take another look into the woman's eyes, replaying her voice and the words she said to me in my head until I realize it wasn't relief or gratitude in her tone, but sorrow and guilt.

She wasn't helpless.

She was baiting me.

At the same time I grasp the imminent danger I've put myself in and reach for Sable, I hear my crossbow clatter across the cobblestone street as the woman shoves it away.

I whirl on her, but not a second later, something cool closes around my wrist.

"I'm sorry," she says softly, and I can't tell if I believe the sincerity I find in her parched voice or not. "I had to do it. I was given no other choice."

Frantic, I paw at the metal cuff clamped around my wrist.

As the woman stands, her foot free and without injury, I realize it wasn't my trap she'd been clutching onto and acting like it had caught her. It was this. This heavy iron band that's now clasped around my arm and chaining me in place to where it's bolted to an impossibly large and heavy lump of cement.

Mouth agape and tongue like charcoal against the back of my throat, I can't do anything but stand there and gawk and struggle as she disappears down some dark alleyway, her head low.

If I don't find a way out of this, I'll be lucky to die of starvation before any monsters find me.

Sable's black shadowood glistens out of the corner of my eye like a night sky dazzling with a thousand stars. I throw myself at her. My free arm outstretched, I strain to reach her smooth frame, to wrap my fingers around the dark wood that had belonged to my mother, to defend myself in this very spot with the same weapon that should've defended her in our home all those years ago.

But the crossbow is too far out of reach, my shackle bound too tight.

I twist my arm, the metal grinding atop my flesh while my hand squeezes into the iron cuff.

My palm is too fleshy though, and no matter how much I crane myself, I can't seem to slip free.

"Stupid." At first, I curse under my breath, but what's the point in whispering anymore? "So fucking stupid!"

I knew better than to fall for this. If there's one truth I've always understood, even as a small child, long before Hulbeck fell, it's that far more people are undeserving of trust than those who are. If it were anyone else but me in this predicament, I'd say that they deserved the death coming their way. But I've fought so hard for so long. I've earned a better, more honorable death, than being chained in one place until starvation or a diseased throng of cannibals claims me.

Panicking isn't going to help me much. As far as I can tell, I have two options: do nothing and die, or think about what I know and try to find a way out of this mess. Dying sounds pretty unappealing, so I focus on the facts. The woman clearly wanted to bait me out into the open, but I don't know why. What was her goal? It's not uncommon for people who live on the road to rob, rape, or cannibalize humans they come across —sometimes all three—but the woman I encountered had done none of those things. She left Sable. She left my belt of supplies. She didn't so much as even glance back at me or my belongings as she walked away.

I had to do it. I was given no other choice.

At the time she said it, I just assumed she meant she was doing it for survival, but it's becoming increasingly more obvious that assumption was wrong.

I was given no other choice.

Someone forced her to do this, to trap me here. But who?

Nothing about the circumstances make it seem like an accidental trap set by cannibals. It was too staged, her placement too perfectly aligned with the path I had to take to get to the well where Elison had last been seen. But the only person who knew I was coming here was Rowland, and no matter how much we bickered, he would never have reason to capture me —okay, *reason*, perhaps. But he'd never act on it. Of that, I am sure. As much as he's begged me to join him in his community, he has always wanted me to make that choice of my own free will, I think because he knows it's the only way I'd ever stay.

If it wasn't him who set this trap, and it wasn't some crazed lunatic...

It could be whoever took Elison. If they knew she belonged to a larger community and thought that someone might come looking for her, they might try snagging the next person who comes.

Which means it's only a matter of time before they return for me.

I can't pick the lock.

I can't very well just stay here and wait for them to kill me either.

I only have one choice.

I fumble for the hunting knife strapped to my belt. The blade is thin, but sharp. I've used it to cut through squirrel bones and to decapitate pigeons. I'm not sure how it will hold up against a human bone. Truth be told, I'm not sure how well I'll hold up either, but it's the only option I have left.

The human body can only sustain so much blood loss

before failing. The distance back to Rowland's town isn't too great. If I staunch the bleeding, maybe I could make it back there before drawing too much attention…

There'd be a trail of blood leading straight back to him and his people. He wouldn't be too pleased about that, but if I die now, it's not like I can come back. At least they can relocate, rebuild.

They might not have the time though.

There's no telling who set this trap, how fast they'd follow me back to Rowland, and how deadly they could be.

The knife's tip stops short just between the cuff and my skin. I'm not sure I can do this, to myself, to him, or to any of the innocent people in Hulbeck—

Not Hulbeck… Though, if I lead a gang a vicious ruffians to their doorstep, the town could find itself in much the same predicament. What if that's exactly what happened with my home? Someone was out wandering, they stumbled upon trouble, and instead of dying with honor, they ran like a coward and brought upon the devastation of our entire home?

I can't do that to someone…

"Careful now," a rich, silken voice croons from the shadows, making me jolt and drop my knife. I scramble to retrieve it as the man continues. "You might give yourself a nasty cut. And all that blood? You wouldn't want to draw the attention of the monsters I have waiting in the shadows now, would you?"

10

THE BLOOD PRINCE

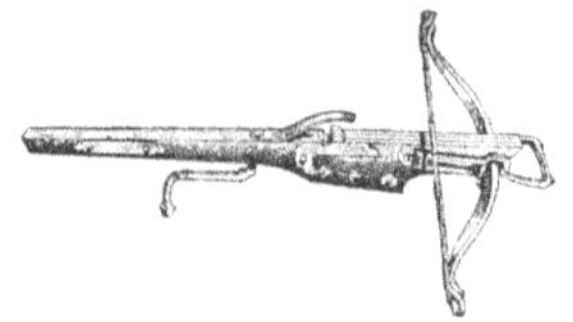

His tone says it all. Evil has arrived. Not the kind that robs someone blind either. I can tell just from his ghastly inflection—and perhaps from his disturbing choice of words—that this is the kind of monster that takes pleasure in lapping up blood.

Noctis.

Many of them, if I'm to believe him anyway.

My blood runs ice cold and I stiffen. With my blade still hovering over the tender underbelly of my wrist, I can't help but wonder if I should just plunge it into my flesh and be done with it. Bleeding out here in the middle of this grimy street would surely be better than whatever torment they have planned for me.

But what if there's still hope? Rowland knows I came out here to see if I could find anything about what happened to Elison. Surely, if neither of us show back up, he'll send others to come looking for us.

Maybe death isn't yet inevitable.

Deciding it best to see how this plays out, I lower my knife and get a better sense of my bearings. As I glance around the courtyard, the well where Elison reportedly disappeared from just a few feet away, an envoy of noctis descends upon the previously deserted streets. They circle me like a pack of wild hounds, ravenous and antsy.

My neck snaps wildly to keep a wary eye on them all, trying to assess which of the monsters prowling toward me will be the biggest threat. The unfortunate truth is that as long as I'm chained in place and without my crossbow, I won't stand a chance against any of them. Only one of them doesn't frighten me, a young noctis male with a complexion not quite as dark as Rowland's, and that's only because the hunger in his eyes is duller than that of his counterparts, his fangs tinged pink from a recent feed.

The others though—the female noctis with hair as fiery as her temperament; a deranged-looking, middle-aged male noctis with a lifetime of war reflected in his eyes and etched in the scars marring his body; the smirking noctis who seems all too pleased with himself at finding me so helplessly snared—all of them make my bones rattle with fear. Their hollowed eyes scream of a hunger that's been gnawing away at them for days.

But it's the white-haired noctis that petrifies me in place.

In the blink of an eye, I'm back in Hulbeck, peering through the front window at the noctis king as he storms into town.

They look so similar that it takes me a long moment to convince myself that the male marching toward me, snuffing out the safe distance that's cast between us, isn't King Tor. It couldn't be.

The noctis king was in his early twenties when he overthrew the Magistrate to claim the throne. He'd have to be nearing forty by now, but the noctis headed for me looks far younger, perhaps even close to my own age.

With startling clarity, I realize I'm staring at the noctis prince.

King Tor's son and only heir.

The one and only Prince Malachi.

I know, as sure as day turns to night, that he was the one who called out to me from the shadows.

He carries himself just as I wield Sable: with precision, and the power to make any kill he sets his sights on. Dark shadows spill off him like liquid night pooling at his feet. The others clear a path for him, and the more he comes forward and into the moonlight, the easier it is to study him.

He is not like most of them. Of the noctis gathering into the courtyard, he's the only one who holds my gaze, his icy blue eyes burning into mine instead of fixating on the throbbing vein in my throat.

Unsurprisingly, he wears garments fit for royalty. The lavish, form-fitting outfit does little to protect his body and more to accentuate his impossibly flawless physique.

My treacherous eyes drift to the unbuttoned jerkin, only momentarily snagging on the red amulet resting there before a new distraction catches my attention. There's nothing beneath that black silk. No padded doublet. No shirt or tunic to speak of. Just firm, alabaster skin as pale as sugar, and seemingly just as sweet.

Of its own accord, my gaze drives deeper, languid as it travels over the deep grooves of muscles of his abdomen that are still visible beneath his garment. Men and women alike would gravel for a chance to behold such a beautiful creature. Hell, who wouldn't when everything else in this world is so hollowed and monstruous looking. Hunger, fear, and a constant need to run have made emaciated shells of much of humankind, some of us even looking more like monsters than people.

Rowland has always been one of the exceptions, but even the noctis prince puts his disciplined muscles to shame.

But I suppose that's one of the many ways you can spot a

noctis from the rest of us. Especially those of wealth and prestige.

His brilliance doesn't make him any less of a predator. He's one of the deadliest.

I've heard the rumors. The carnage that has befallen The United Realm at his behest—never by his own hands though. Gods forbid he gets those pristinely clean fingers dirty. No, he sends his servants out to the poorest regions with the sole purpose of capturing young men and women to take back to his lair, never to be heard from or seen again.

I can't even begin to fathom the number of people who have died in his jaws.

And if that wasn't enough to tarnish the tantalizing thoughts I had about his near-perfect physique, the spattering of red that dusts the plane of his chest is.

Blood. Fresh, from the looks of it.

He may be handsome, but he is still dangerous. A vibrant, alluring flower with petals that are poisonous to the touch.

I snap my glaring gaze back to his, determined to show no fear—or any of the other feelings I'd been experiencing moments before.

Relaxing into the trap I so foolishly walked into, I sit taller on my heels, and feign calmness. "Great. A *royal* bloodsucker. As if this day couldn't get any worse, now I have to deal with the ego of a prince."

Glee flashes behind his bright eyes. "Ah, I see my reputation precedes me."

I shrug, casually glancing to the opposite end of the street, though on the inside I am anything but. There are more noctis here than I would think necessary to trap one, meager human. But these are desperate times, I suppose.

"If it does," I say, the epitome of apathy. "Your reputation has falsely glorified you."

The prince's stride falters. "Oh? Do tell. What it is you expected of me, human?"

Human.

He spits the word like someone might say *maggot* or *carcass.* We are grotesque to him, a fungus needing to be wiped clean from the realm.

Still, I remain as neutral as dirt. If he's attempting to goad me, it won't work. I can't let him see how much I loathe when they call us *human.* I can't give him, or the others standing nearby, that satisfaction.

With any luck, the egos of noctis men are just as frail as human men, like dry autumn leaves, a mere breath of wind can crumple them.

I muster a smug grin. "Rumors said you were devastating, both in beauty and brutality. And yet, here I am. Alive, despite being woefully outnumbered. And there you are, nothing more than a cocky prince who can't even afford proper clothes."

He glances down at his exposed chest. His crooked smile tells me it's more obligatory than anything. This is a game to him as much as it is to me. See who can outlast the longest. See who will bring the other to their knees. As much as I'd love to believe I'll be the one proclaiming checkmate, the cuff around my wrist has me doubting myself.

But I have to try.

As much as I hate the noctis, I hate him even more.

His family is the reason mine is gone.

Slowly, he brings one of his fingers to the exposed, rigid muscles of his chest and wipes one of the droplets of blood away, bringing it to his mouth. No one has ever looked more sated as he laps at it.

His eyes open dazedly, and they take their time flitting up to mine almost as if he'd forgotten I was here. It's all for show though, of course. For his kind, everything is play.

Licking his finger, he finally answers. "Why bother with shirts when I'd just dirty them anyway?"

Malachi takes another taste and my eyes snag on the red design on his wrist. It reminds me of the smears I saw on Gregor's wrist too, only the one on the prince's arm is much more define, possibly even permanent.

I want to get a better look at what the marking might be, but he notices me staring before I can and lowers his hand, the cloying nature of his saccharine smile returning.

"So sweet. But not as sweet as you will be, I imagine."

"As sweet as a bolt to the heart," I reply, nodding to the crossbow across the street. One of the gathered noctis, a woman with hair just as white as the prince's is eyeing it with too much interest. I don't recognize her, but her bone-white hair is indication enough of what family she belongs to, and I find myself wanting to kill the both of them. "Release me, and maybe you'll find out just how *sweet* I can be."

Prince Malachi chuckles, revealing a dazzling smile that has no right to be as gleaming as it is. He drinks blood, for pity's sake. Shouldn't his sharp fangs be stained red? Shouldn't they be the serrated blades of my darkest nightmares?

"Oh," he says, licking the front of his teeth and slowly circling me. Each calculated step he takes makes one more hair on my body stand straight, each one standing guard, haplessly waiting to defend me from his attack. Their sacrifice will, of course, be in vain. "You mistake me," he says, flashing that wicked smile of his. "The more venomous the creature, the sweeter the blood."

This time, I do flinch. *Creature* is an even lower station than human. And I'll never be able to understand how they can speak of us as if we are no more than beasts.

Then again, I suppose to his kind, we are just that. Nothing more than flesh and blood and sustenance.

He must notice the way his taunt impacts me because the

corner of his mouth quirks up in a devious grin. "What's wrong? Don't appreciate being called *creature*? What about *pet*? Would you find that more suiting?"

I deny him any response, which only makes his devilish smirk deepen.

"Tell me, what's the word you used to describe me? *Bloodsucker*, I believe you called me?"

My teeth aren't nearly as sharp as his, but I bare them all the same. "That's what you do, isn't it? You suck the life from the living?"

"Sometimes from the dead, as well."

"You're disgusting," I scoff.

"No, I'm Malachi," he corrects in that infuriatingly confident and condescending tone. "I thought you said you knew me."

"I know *of* you."

I'm not sure why I feel the need to correct him. Perhaps because of the way he hasn't stopped smiling in that predatorial way since we started talking. Not to mention the fact that, aside from the noctis I was forced to endure earlier today, this is the longest conversation I've held with anyone other than Rowland in a decade, let alone a conversation that—dare I say —I've actually...enjoyed.

That acknowledgment makes me bristle, and I feel the need to remind myself of who he really is, what his family is capable of.

"You're a Devonshire."

"One of the many." He spreads his arms wide, the heavy black cape expanding with them. "The best, if I do say so myself."

"Can't be difficult to be the best in a lineage that's done nothing but kill."

His father, Tor Devonshire, comes to mind. The first of the

druids to embrace his noctis nature after Halira freed them from their demonic forms.

Malachi recoils, almost imperceptibly. A chink in the mask that I don't think he meant for me to see. However, he's quick to recover. "Perhaps that's the very reason why I'm the best."

"What do you want with me?" I ask at last. This game has gone on long enough.

He gazes upon me for an uncomfortable moment before turning to the noctis male beside him, the one who's dark hair is tied back at the base of his neck.

Just as the prince opens his mouth to speak, another noctis barges through the crowd.

"What the fuck is this?"

Of the noctis who descended upon me, he was the one I feared most.

The scars slicing across his face and arms tells a harrowing story of violence and brutality that I can't even imagine. Judging from the way he glares at me as if his single eye could make me my heart implode in my chest, I can only fathom just how much he despises humankind, and just how many of his war wounds were given to him at the hands of innocent humans who were likely just defending their lives.

With Malachi turned away from him, the disgruntled noctis doesn't see the prince roll his eyes. The dark-haired friend smirks as well, his amusement seeming misplaced but maybe that's just because I can't seem to find anything comical about the way the new noctis is looking at me.

"Well, Harland," the prince answers, pivoting to face him. "I'd say it looks like a girl."

"I know it's a fucking girl," Harland sneers from behind a thick beard as black as lichen. His one exposed eye cuts to the prince. "What are we doing just standing around talking to it? Let's kill the bitch and be done with it!"

Harland's fists bulge like boulders colliding into each other, the noctis preparing to come forward and apparently handle my death himself. This seems personal, but I can't yet figure out why.

Thankfully, the prince catches him before he can make it very far.

"No."

"No?" The rage in Harland's voice makes the very blood in my veins shudder. "What the fuck do you mean *no*? You can't deny me this, Malachi!"

"Actually, I believe I can."

"He can," whispers the smug dark-haired friend.

Harland vibrates with rage, but at the sound of the white-haired noctis' voice, he stills.

"Come on, Malachi," she says sweetly. "You don't really mean that. She murdered his brothers, after all. Surely, he's earned himself a taste, if not the entire meal?"

His brothers?

Shit.

Ice chills my veins. My death suddenly seems so much more imminent than I was allowing myself to believe.

She must mean the two noctis I encountered earlier today, Gregor and Boris. After everything I've been through today, I almost forgot about them. Looking at Harland now though, I can see the resemblance in their rugged natures, and that broken-shaped nose they all seem to share.

Shared.

What dumb luck that I'd run into the brutish brother of a noctis I'd aided in killing.

What dumb luck that they even *have* a brutish brother.

Unless our crossing of paths is no accident at all. But how could it not be? If they knew I'd been involved in his brothers' deaths, then they had to know about Rowland's community. Shouldn't they be ambushing them instead of trapping one measly *creature*?

Maybe the ambush will happen later. Maybe first they needed bait.

They'd be better off using someone that anyone gives two shits about.

Someone like Elison…

The prince waves them both off.

"Your brothers will be avenged. We came here to secure more donations for the Hunt."

Double shit…

This day just keeps getting better and better.

Why couldn't I have been trapped by a normal crazy human instead of one working with a bunch of noctis to fuel their annual bloody games?

Come to think of it, who the fuck works with the noctis? If I ever see that woman again, I'll—

"If you want her throat, you'll have to bite it fair and square like everyone else participating. Until then"—the prince turns to his friend— "throw her in the back with the other prisoners. The king will be pleased to know we're bringing such a feisty *creature* to Nigh."

11

A VOW OF TREASON

Davorin exchanges the cuff around the human woman's wrist for one around her neck and guides her toward the prisoner carriages. I suppose calling them *carriages* is perhaps a bit misleading. They're more like oversized crates on wheels with hardly enough space inside to stand. They're hardly anything compared to the luxury the rest of us have been fortunate to travel by.

I feel a twinge of shame for the way we transport them, what little comforts we provide. But, with less than a fortnight to live, my father finds no sense in exerting his resources on frivolous matters such as affording humans better accommodations.

Davorin tosses the young woman in with the other prisoners—all except Fox.

At my father's orders, she has a cart all to herself. I think he fears what she'd be capable of accomplishing if she had the ears of her fellow prisoners to whisper into.

If only he knew it wasn't the other prisoners that he needed to worry about.

Once I'm sure Davorin is far away from here, and Caz and

the others are still preoccupied with dismantling our camp and readying the horses for travel, I slink to my aunt's cart and rap on the shuddering door.

Her weary voice answers from the darkness. "What do you want?"

It's a simple question with a very straight-forward response. I've come to tell her I mean to help her escape, and yet I struggle to articulate it. I'm suddenly acutely aware that I am a noctis prince, one of the most powerful beings in the realm, and she is a prisoner we've left crippled behind bars.

"I…was hoping I might have a word."

A derisive sound huffs past her lips. "I'm hardly in a position to deny anyone, let alone a *prince*." The sting of her words cuts surprisingly deep. "Spit it out. What do you want from me now?"

All at once, a surge of heat and ice bubbles through me. The seething hatred in her tone, the palpable distrust. I hadn't been expecting it, though I realize now that I should've.

"N-nothing. I want nothing from you," I tell her, taking a seat on the topmost stair leading into the wobbling cart. "You've done far more than you should've ever had to."

I think I hear her lift her head, her attention piqued, but she doesn't utter a word. She waits for me to speak.

"You will likely not believe me," I say, searching the surrounding darkness for any signs of someone listening, and finding none. I keep my voice to a low whisper, regardless. "But I wanted you to know that I'm done letting him treat you the way he does."

"Letting who?" she asks, a challenge sharpening her words.

I glance around yet again. We are alone. Not even the other prisoners are within earshot, their cart resting a safe distance away, much closer to the circle of rocks where we warmed ourselves around a fire last night. Meanwhile, my aunt had been in her own cart all the way over here, far from the fire's heat, likely shivering herself to sleep.

"The king." Despite my resolute tone, my words make me shift uncomfortably where I sit. But sensing that her doubt has not yet been remedied, I continue. "It's gone on long enough—it should have never even begun, and I'm—I mean...what I'm trying to say is—"

Nothing is coming out quite the way I mean for it to. I have no clear plan yet, and so the gust of a whim I'm riding as I contemplate my aunt's freedom is a wild and blustering tempest of fear and doubt and agony that is impossible to see through.

I still have much to figure out: when to free her, how to get her away unseen, where to take her so that she'll be safe. Most importantly to her: how to also save her sons, for I know that without them, I cannot grant her freedom, not in any true sense of the word.

And then there's the matter of how I can do all of it without jeopardizing my own life.

Somehow, I eventually manage to find some semblance of coherency, the only promise I know I can make. "You and your sons won't be our prisoners forever."

"I'm well aware of that, *prince*." She uses my title like a swordsman uses a blade, jabbing into my gut with a swiftness and being just as quick to withdraw so that the wound is as painful and deadly as it can be. "Why else do you think the great *King Tor* has decided to bring us to this year's Hunt?"

My brow creases. I hadn't yet truly wondered. Or at least, if I had, I simply assumed it was because he was too vain and paranoid to leave his precious cargo unattended in Neveridge while he was so far away.

Sensing my grappling, or perhaps simply lamenting in her own forthcoming demise, my aunt sighs. "No, I imagine we won't be your prisoners for much longer at all."

I want to tell her that she's wrong. That my father would never stoop to something so low as butchering his own family. But deep down, I know she's right. My father toyed with them long enough and to no avail. In time, overseeing her torture will lose its rush. Maybe it has already.

And just like that, I have my timeline.

"Before the Hunt," I say, unwavering in my defiance now. "I will find a way to free you and your sons before the Hunt begins."

Fox breathes another humorless laugh. "Forgive me if I don't hold my breath."

Before I can attempt to convince her of my word, and remind her that I, of all people, am aware of my father's cruel wrath and that I am motivated best by thwarting him, Caz's voice sneaks up on me.

"Hey, Malachi? Do you have a minute?"

I bolt upright and shove myself away from Fox's cart. She doesn't call after me or beg me to stay. She's grown used to the solitude. It might even be the only time she relishes, if any time a noctis is near it means either acting on our behalf or facing the consequences.

My mind can hardly think about her now though, not while I follow Caz to wherever he's leading me.

"You alright?" he asks, gesturing to Fox's cart behind us.

"I'm fine," I tell him, my clammy hands grateful for my brisk pace and the cool night air that slips between my fingers like a mountain spring. "What's on your mind? Is everything alright?"

"With packing up camp? Sure," he says casually. But then his face bunches in consternation. "But it's not looking too good out there."

"How do you mean?"

He scans the darkness around us, making sure Davorin or Harland haven't snuck up on us—or worse, his own sister who has a tendency of finding us whenever we're seeking a private conversation. Deeming the area safe, he brings his attention back to me. His gaze catches on my exposed chest. "Well, for starters, it doesn't help that you fed while the rest of us have been starving ourselves for days."

My worried eyes jerk down to the blood. "This? This wasn't even a feed. When I pricked my finger to repaint the blood oaths on everyone, some of it must've dribbled on me."

The human woman had believed it was from a kill too, and I'd let her. After all, she already thinks us monsters. Might as well use that to our advantage.

"I know that," he says, pointing back toward camp. "But the others don't. You put on a pretty convincing display, Malachi. Some of them are starting to wonder if they should follow your orders about leaving the prisoners alone."

"They're not even my orders!" I bark, the rumble of my anger seeming to rustle the very earth beneath my feet. Remembering Caz's quiet tone, and his desire to have this conversation privately, I clench my jaw, furiously wiping away at the blood. "If Harland is hungry, we'll catch him a squirrel or something. He is hardly a problem worth fretting over."

"I think he is," Caz insists, the seriousness of his tone causing me to pause. "Besides, it's not just Harland."

I meet his gaze then, and for the first time, I feel the heavy weight of his concern.

The others…who? I can hardly imagine Davorin struggling with the concept of self-control. He's one of the most disciplined noctis I know, and he past that trait down to his own children, even if they abide by it with their own rules.

Though I could see her bemoaning our predicament and complaining if she thought I'd eaten while the others hadn't, Renee wouldn't dream of crossing my father or I, so I doubt she's the one causing Caz concern.

Which just leaves…

"Ursulette and Rhain, then?"

Caz nods.

Neither are known for their hot tempers, not in the way Harland is. But coming between them and a feed is much like jumping into a pit of writhing, striking snakes.

I know how difficult it can be to endure the hunger. More than anyone. It was me, after all, who lived among the humans until I was a young adolescent. It was me who learned how to ignore my appetite in favor of the scraps my mother would procure for me from the butcher.

If I could go years without drinking a single drop of human blood, then my companions, my own friends and family, could endure a few short weeks. Especially my own cousin. She's the only one among them who has any inkling of the kind of restraint it takes, for she is the only one to have lived among the humans as I did. At least for a time. Back when she was an adolescent herself and she'd wanted to find her human mother. My aunt. Halira Devonshire.

I forget how long Ursulette was away—half a year? Maybe longer? And in all the time that she scoured the realm for a mother she'd never had the chance to meet, she never fed upon a single human.

Not until she had to save a young noctis who'd found himself trapped by a mob of them.

My cousin saved Rhain from his own foolish demise that night, and she said that when she'd tasted human blood again, it was like an awakening. She'd made a vow to never return to that slumber again.

Still, I expected better from her, from all of them—with Harland maybe being the one exception.

"I'll set things straight tonight," I grumble, disheartened by the entire thing, but largely by my own high expectations. They're noctis, after all. They're hungry. They're tired. And if they truly believed I'd fed without them, then it's no wonder they're upset. "We'll be in Nigh soon. Surely, they know what sort of a feast awaits us after such a successful expedition. There will be plenty of time to indulge before the Hunt."

"Not for all of us," Caz says, a bit morose compared to his usual tone.

It's not meant as an argument. I can tell he's parroting back whatever conversations from the others he's overheard. But I have no patience for it.

"And what do you mean by that?"

His lips become a tight line. It's rare for him to struggle with honesty, at least with me. But sometimes I forget that before we became brothers, he'd been raised to become a dutiful, obedient soldier.

If his father's teachings about respecting the crown hadn't done it, Harland's training beat most of the free will out of him. For a time. Until our paths crossed, and I taught him that true loyalty meant complete honesty and trust. Caz never has to shirk away from telling me what's on his mind, or what's on the mind of those around us.

Sometimes, however, he reverts back to those early years of his training, the ones that molded him into someone mindlessly compliant, spineless, and bland.

"Caz," I say softly, reaching for his shoulder. "Whatever it is, you can tell me. We might disagree, but we'll always be brothers."

The reassurance is enough to snap him out of whatever past memory he'd fallen into.

"Some of us aren't returning. We might be bringing back more humans than any other envoy, but we've lost two of our own. Your father won't overlook that, and he won't be pleased."

"He's never pleased," I retort.

But Caz continues, unhindered. "There's one way we might please him."

"Oh? And what's that?"

"That prisoner," he says. "Lewis or whatever. He said that

there's more humans nearby. An entire community of them we could collect—"

A ragged sigh billows from my lungs.

He doesn't stop, mistaking my disagreement for an invitation to attempt to convince me otherwise.

"King Tor needs bodies for the Hunt, right? He over-promised. We know this. He misjudged how many noctis would pay to participate this year and now we don't have enough humans. They've been impossible to find."

I know where he's heading with this. I know the point he's trying to make, and I already have my counter for it. But I fold my arms and try to listen regardless, try to be better than my father.

"We have four humans to bring back. It's not bad, but it's nothing that would save the Hunt, let alone our people from civil unrest." He paces now, the excitement and urgency in his voice unmistakable. "Between the seven of us, I'm sure we could handle it. Lewis could tell us where their weak points are. We could take out their guards, turn them into ghouls to aid in our infiltration—or not that last part. Only if we needed the numbers, which who knows if we do. Most of the large communities have fallen by now, your father saw to that."

Exactly.

My father did.

My fangs pierce the inside of my lip. He, out of everyone, should know better than to suggest such a thing to me.

After what I witnessed when my own home was ambushed, my people and my mother slaughtered, all so the great King Tor could reclaim his only heir?

I will never lead an invasion on a human town. Especially not for a pompous source of entertainment like the Hunt.

How could Caz ever suggest such a thing? Does he even know me at all?

For all my best intentions, I can listen to my friend no longer.

"No."

The word is an axe, cleaving his proposition in half.

The expression it leaves on his face makes me wince. It's the kind of way I look at my father whenever one of my suggestions are silenced before I can even reach my main point. It's not the way I ever dreamed of making anyone feel, let alone Caz. But hearing mention of the monster of a man who claims the title of my father makes me lose my patience.

"I appreciate the advice," I say, trying to smooth things over between us. But the damage might already have been done. "It's out of the question though."

He doesn't say a word. His gaze is fixed on the dark ground at our feet like a scolded child.

"We are two days behind schedule already," I continue. "Our carts might not be as full as we'd hoped, we might've lost two of our own, and we might not have solved my father's problem of having an underfed Hunt, but our team's efforts have been more than fruitful. We have enough humans to head for Nigh. Besides, it's a bit senseless to listen to the ramblings of a prisoner. He could be leading us straight into a trap."

"We can be vigilant," Caz insists, grasping for a chance to convince me otherwise. "If the humans are planning an ambush, we can plan for that. Just think of it! If we returned with a dozen humans, your father would—"

"My father has nothing to do with this!"

I don't know what's gotten into him, or what's gotten into me either. This conversation is over though.

"I think we've lost enough noctis for one night. Don't you? Or would you feel differently if next time it was your father they slaughtered? Perhaps your sister?"

Finally, Caz's jaw clamps tight, the muscles pulled so taut

that, even in the dim glow of the moonlight I can see where his fangs poke at the bottom of his lip.

I start to march back to camp to check on the progress, but his voice, edged and strained, startles me.

"What about Harland?"

"What about him?"

"The girl killed his brothers, Malachi. After everything he's been through, he'll do anything to claim the vengeance he's owed."

"After everything *he's* been through?" I bellow, unable to stop myself.

My chest is heaving, a heavy weight pressing down on it as I recall the first terrible moment I laid eyes on Harland.

Every scar that's etched into his skin is only a fraction of a representation of the pain that he's inflicted upon me and others over the years. Harland might've lost an eye and a hand during the raids, but that's nothing compared to the life he took from me.

My father spent years searching for his possible bastard children, but most of the mother's had their babes butchered the moment they'd discovered their thirst for blood.

Mine had cherished me too much to bring herself to do it though.

For years, she kept me and my true nature hidden. She'd made a deal with the butcher so that we had constant access to the blood of the animals he slaughtered. She kept my Devonshire lineage hidden by rubbing berries and plant roots into my hair every day.

Despite her profound efforts, however, eventually we were found.

By none other than Harland.

Before the raids began, I had a family. One far more loving and tender than anything my father had tried building with me at Neveridge. I had a mother. A half-brother. I even had a first love—as best as youth are capable of such a thing.

Of course, it was the girl who betrayed me. It was the love of my life who led Harland to me and my family.

Annabel had been her name, not that she had it for much longer because Harland did exactly as Caz is suggesting now. He used her to get exactly what he wanted, and then once her life no longer held any more meaning to him, he killed her. Right in front of me. Then he killed every other person in Drayfil Shore, sparing me only because he had instructions to retrieve me for King Tor.

And Caz knows all of it.

He had been too young to participate in the raids, but he'd been at the castle awaiting Harland's and his father's return. He'd been there when I arrived. He'd been there for me when we were just two small children struggling to discover who we'd become.

Caz knows better to sympathize with Harland in my presence. And he's remembering it too.

In a sheepish gesture, one of his hands reaches for the back of his neck. "I—I'm sorry. I didn't mean it like that."

I hold up my hand, my voice calm but tight enough to restrict my breathing. "I know. It's…it's fine. Let's just—we should catch up with the others."

Almost too keenly, he nods.

To keep my mind from returning to that dreadful day, I think about what's next.

"Have your father send word to mine—" Davorin is, after all, the only one among us with a permanent blood oath with the king— "Get him to pass on that we were delayed but we'll be arriving shortly. Don't tell him about our gathering efforts. I want it to be a pleasant surprise when we arrive with triple the number of humans as any other search party."

"Consider it done."

12

BEHIND BARS

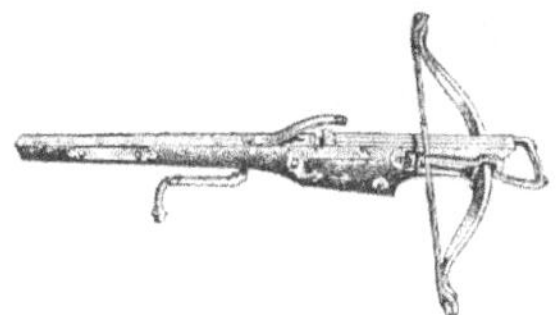

For two days I know nothing but the crunching of wheels as we travel down cobblestone streets of Gravenburg, and then the wet squelching as we make our way through the muddy fields between here and Nigh.

Rarely do the noctis stop for rest, and when they do, we're only given a respite from the cramped cart to relieve our bladders. I've been hunched for so long that my bones crack whenever I'm yanked outside, my spine screaming and threatening to break every time I'm forced back into my prison.

No one speaks.

Not the prisoners.

We barely even cast wary glances at one another during the entire trip. Mostly because I think we're all a bit too preoccupied lamenting over the actions and choices that got us into this mess.

Also because it's too dark to see anyone anyway.

I do think I saw a flash of red hair before the scarred noctis closed us in darkness though. I think I found Elison.

At the end of the second day, the carriage stops.

The noctis guard draws open the door and the four of us

are grabbed by our chains and pulled outside into the crisp evening air.

As my stiff spine adjusts to the idea of standing again, I realize we've arrived. Beyond the decrepit ruins and fallen pillars of a demolished courtyard, stands an immense and dark castle.

Legend has it that when the Shadowthorn fell, demons ravaged the Castle of Nigh, laying waste to the very place where the Crusaders had trained, the place that represented the demise of demonkind.

Of course, seeing it now, it seems that not all legends are true, or if it is, this place must've been as large as Gravenburg at one point.

"Come," Malachi says. With a wave of his hand, the guards holding our chains pull us to follow. "We'll drop them off in the dungeon with the rest of the prisoners and then, with any luck, we dine."

My knees buckle and clack together as we're led through the splattering of bricks and statues littered throughout the courtyard. With me in front, I try to glimpse the prisoners behind me to see if it really was Elison who'd been held prisoner with me all this time, but I can barely keep up as is, let alone not fall on the uneven and unkempt grass. After spending the last few days sitting in the carriage, my legs have already become weak and unaccustomed to the idea of brisk walking.

Judging from the moans and groans coming from behind me, I'm not the only one to struggle.

They lead us through winding halls, up and down flights of stairs, and finally into a dimly lit hall lined with cells on either side. Dozens of dirty faces cram up against the bars to get a look at us, and I feel each and every one of them imprinting into my mind. I can already see their deaths. I can already smell their blood.

The Hunt will be kind to none of us.

At the end of the hall, Malachi's hand presses against my back, ushering me into another dark and cramped space.

"In you go."

Only once I'm behind the iron bars does he unlatch the cuff around my neck.

I turn around, scrutinizing him as I rub the raw skin where my cuff had been. It seems strange that the noctis prince himself would personally deliver us to the dingy dungeon. Surely, he has more important things to do. Maybe he's just as controlling as the rumors say his father is. Or maybe he doesn't trust his guards to do it correctly, a possibility that I take note of.

If there's any hope of escape, maybe it's in the unreliability of his guards.

Or maybe it's something else.

Whatever it is, I plan on learning everything I can about this place, studying its every movement and every noctis until I can figure out how to get the fuck out of here.

No matter the cost, I will not be in the Hunt. If it's anything like the stories we were told in our youth to scare each other, it will be a place worse than anything I've ever encountered. Even worse than what happened at Hulbeck. The Hunt is more than a way to feed for them. It's a game. A source of entertainment. And I can only imagine the numerous ways in which they make it *entertaining*…

As Malachi shoves another prisoner in behind me, and another guard shoves two others into the cell next to us, I note that there is already someone in this cell with us.

In one corner of the room, she sits on the cold stone floor with her knees cradled against her chest. Thick curtains of hair drape over her shoulders and down her scratched and trembling legs.

Someone with a bigger heart than mine might try to comfort her. But I see no point in lying to the scared girl.

Instead, I scope out our surroundings. There isn't much by way of furniture, except for a single bench.

The woman with hair the color of autumn storms toward it and slumps down, her hands gripping the bottom edge as she stares past to the noctis guards finishing up. Even tucked away from the torchlight, I can finally make out the familiar face of my fletcher.

"Elison," I say softly, hoping none of the guards will hear me.

Startled and a bit confused, the woman's deadly glare falters and flits to me. "Ch-Charlotte? What are you doing here?"

"Funny you should ask—"

Before I can tell her, Malachi's voice echoes in the corridor.

"Rest up, everyone." His voice is alarmingly resonate compared to the casual way I'd heard him talking with his companions for the past few days. Maybe it's just the echo of the dungeons though, making him sound intimidating. "King Tor will arrive in another day or so."

As he speaks, I glance around the rest of the dungeon. As far as I can tell, the cells are segregated, the men and women kept apart from each other—at least there's that to be grateful for. Most of them have a dozen or more people each, which leaves me to wonder if ours will continue filling until the start of the Hunt.

"It won't be long now until you're released in the Hunt," Malachi continues, addressing us all with his condescending nose held high. "If you're wise, you'll rest while you're able."

With the constant bobbing and jerking of the carriage, the last decent night's rest I had was one of the nights Rowland came over, and I'll be damned if the last good night's rest I get before the Hunt will be one where I was in Rowland's arms.

I saunter over to an unoccupied corner in our cell, the one connecting to the empty cell beside us instead of the male cell on the other side, and plop down to the ground a little too rough.

No matter how far I bury my face in my hands, I can feel Elison's gaze upon me. I wonder if she's pieced it together yet that I know. I wonder if she even knew Rowland and I were… whatever we were. Can I be mad at her if she didn't? Can I even be mad at her if she did?

It's even harder to drown out the sounds of our prison. The constant hacking and coughing. The sobbing. The imprudent shrieking for our release. The petty bickering.

In the cell beside ours, the men haven't stopped quarreling since the new members arrived—one of them is quite young, perhaps my age if not a year or two younger, while the other is at least a decade my senior. I think I recognize him. We haven't spoken much, if ever, but I'm almost certain I've seen him around *Barretville*, and always with that same sour look on his face.

When he notices me staring, the look in his eyes turns malicious. "This is all your fault, you bitch!"

"Lewis, no!" The young man who'd been captured with us grabs for his arms, but he's no match for the belligerent bull. He's flung backward, landing into a group of miserable prisoners and knocking everyone down.

Lewis charges for our cell—our cage—and clutches the bars. His cheeks dig into the bars, and for a moment I fear he might actually try squeezing through them.

"If you hadn't brought those noctis to Valor's Rest, we wouldn't be here!"

The noctis he's referring to must be Gregor and Boris, and I can't imagine many people knew about my encounter with them, outside of Rowland, his archers, and the guard he spoke to about cleaning up the mess. As best as I can gauge, Lewis doesn't have the discipline for archery, so I doubt he was one of the archers who helped guard the gates. Rowland had asked the guard to send a few men to clean up after the bodies, and suggested they use the men they'd arrested after some incident at a tavern the previous night. Lewis certainly looked like someone who could fit that description. Had he been cleaning up her mess when he was captured by the noctis prince?

He spits through the bars. Thankfully he's a terrible shot because even standing still he misses me.

"You're gonna have to do better than that," I snarl, exhausted and with no patience to deal with the likes of him.

He just shakes his head, slowly backing away. "You better hope they kill you in the Hunt. You don't want it to be me who finds you first."

Every muscle in his shoulders is clenched when he returns to the young man he knocked over and hoists him to his feet.

"Th-this is it, then?" the kid stammers. "We just sit here and w-wait to die?"

The noctis guards who brought us down here haven't quite finished vacating though, and the prince's ear twitches at his sniveling. He turns around.

"Well, yes. I'm afraid so. And if you're having trouble understanding what that entails, there are others you can look to for an example."

The prince points to the woman in my cell, the one cowering in the corner.

Lewis scoffs. "Another worthless, whimpering bitch."

"Leave her alone," I hear myself say in a tone far deadlier than anything I've ever wielded.

"Oh yeah? Or what?" Scalding heat flickers behind his bright eyes when he returns his gaze to me. He crosses the small cell again, coming back to the thick bars that keep us separated. "What are you going to do about it?"

I'm on my feet and across the cell in an instant. We live in a world where human-like beings bite into our flesh and feast on our blood. He doesn't scare me.

I grab the thin, pathetic braid dangling from his chin that he calls a beard and I yank it forward, his cheekbones slamming against the bars. "I'll rip this pathetic excuse of a beard off your face, for starters."

"Oh, come now." Distantly, I hear Malachi groan. "Do I really need to come in there and break this up? I can promise you; it won't be pretty. Let's not forget, we've traveled a long way. Barely eaten, barely rested. And you're exactly the kind of meal my brethren and I wouldn't mind sinking our teeth into."

Lewis and I glare into each other's eyes, neither one of us backing down.

Behind me, I hear Elison growl from where she sits. "You wouldn't though. You can't. You need us for your precious Hunt."

Malachi is quiet for a long moment. "You're not wrong. We did, indeed, bring you here for the Hunt. But make no mistake, if anyone proves to be a greater hassle than they're worth, I'll let my guards feast. So keep that in mind whenever your cellmates are being belligerent. Keep them in check and you'll all get to live a few days longer. And who knows? Maybe you'll get the opportunity to escape."

My eyes flick to his, hope brimming in my chest like an overflowing river.

The prince winks at me and I realize how foolish I am to believe anything he says. It's the same false hope Rowland and all the humans feed each other.

"Any argument?" he asks, his menacing gaze leering at Lewis and me. Finally, begrudgingly, Lewis releases the bars and I release his facial hair. Malachi grins. "Good. Now, if you'll excuse us, we've *all* had a long journey and if we don't leave you now, I'm afraid someone here is going to get eaten."

"Fucking bullshit," Elison grumbles to herself.

It warrants a smile from me. It's one of the reasons I've always liked her. We're similar, the two of us. Whenever we'd talk about what she'd do if the *Rowlandia* ever fell, she always said she'd join me and that the two of us would kill every last noctis in the realm. I believed her. It was so easy to see: the two of us who had lost everything banding together and going on a suicide mission to fight and destroy all noctis.

I still need that to be true.

Despite everything.

Despite Rowland.

I need her on my side if I'm going to survive this.

Before he leaves, Malachi sinks to his knees to talk to a woman in another cell. The fire-haired woman responsible for my capture. They're too far away to hear what they're saying, but I'm sure it has something to do with plotting their next plan for tricking more humans into capture.

Once all the noctis have left, I join Elison on the bench.

She looks up at me with glossy eyes. "Charlotte, there's something I need to tell you."

So, she did know then…

I'm not sure it changes anything though. Not now that we're both trapped and facing imminent death anyway.

"I know," I tell her, inching closer so that no one else can hear us. "Rowland told me about the baby. It's why I came looking for you."

Confusion wrinkles her forehead, but why, I'm not sure. I don't want to think about it, honestly. We have one purpose now.

"I'm going to get you out of here," I whisper with lethal quiet. "You and I won't be caught dead in the Hunt."

THE BONDS OF WOMEN

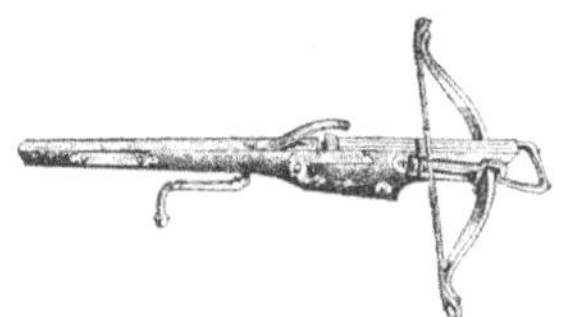

"What's the plan then?" Elison asks the next day, after we've all had some rest. She uses one of her nails to scrape away the dirt from her thumbnail, trying not to look suspicious by paying me too much attention or speaking too loudly. "You said you had one, but you haven't shared any of the specifics."

"That's because I don't have any yet."

Irritation lingers behind the eyes that briefly flit to mine.

I shrug. "What? You just expect me to know exactly how to break out of here before I've ever even set foot in the place?"

"Yes!" she whispers emphatically. "You said you came looking for me to help me. I assumed you did it with an escape plan in mind!"

"I didn't exactly plan on being captured!" I growl, my voice carrying farther than I intended and capturing the attention of our fellow prisoners in the neighboring cell.

If we're too loud, the guards who meander down this way periodically might learn of our plan of escaping, and that would be one additional hurdle that I can't afford.

Closing my eyes, I breathe in through my nose and exhale

slowly before continuing with a quieter, calmer tone. "Whether I planned it or not, I'm here now, and if we don't get ourselves out of this, we will die. So, I suggest we learn what we can about this place and the noctis residing here as quickly as we can, so that we *can* form a viable plan."

With a long, impatient sigh, Elison returns to cleaning her fingernails. "What is it we need to know?"

Before admitting it out loud that I don't actually know, I take a look around the place first. From our cell at the end of the block, it's difficult to see all the way down the corridor to count how many humans they've got stashed here, but we were dragged past them when we arrived, and from my memory, I'd estimate that there are at least fifty people down here with us.

Beyond that? My knowledge of this place is extremely limited.

"Anything," I say at last. "Everything we can learn. Like where all of these people came from. How long they've been here. What they were doing when they were captured."

Bitterness puckers my tongue as I remember my own actions that led me here. If we survive this, I'm still not sure I'll ever let myself live down my own stupidity for falling for the oldest trick in the book.

"I can see if any of them remember the path we were dragged down here," she suggests.

But I'm barely listening. A memory has directed my attention back to the mystery woman in the cell diagonal to ours.

"What's her deal?" I ask, the jerk of my chin pointing to where the lonely woman sits in the middle of her cell, her back turned to the rest of us. "She's the reason I'm here, you know? She was calling for help in the street and foolishly I came to her aid."

"You, of all people, fell for that?" Elison snorts, her attention never once peeling away from her fingernails and the grime she's cleaning from under them. "That was foolish, especially for you."

"That's what I said." There's a bite of irritation on my tongue that I can't stifle.

But Elison doesn't react. She just laughs, a short and airy sound that feels too bright for this dark place. "Well, I guess we all make mistakes."

I bite back the urge to argue with her. Mistakes are for the weak and for those who don't value their lives. This mistake was avoidable. I shouldn't be here.

"It's funny you should ask about her," she continues. "You won't believe this because I had a hard time believing it myself when I first heard the guards and the prince talking about her. But apparently, that's Fox Devonshire. She's the former Magistrate's wife."

I nearly choke on my words. "His wife? But wouldn't that make her—"

"The prince's aunt? His own family? I think it does. But she's not a noctis, so I guess that makes her relationship with the Devonshires inconsequential."

"My gods…"

My eyes bulge at the thought. My family was taken from me when I was still young enough that many of my memories of them have faded, but I still remember the love and loyalty for which we had for each other. I can't even fathom what it would be like to have them turn on me.

Then again, thanks to Rowland, I've recently discovered the sting of betrayal. I imagine her predicament might feel similar, having the people you trust obliterate that allegiance, that relationship.

Looking at her now, her misery is beginning to make sense.

"What happened to her?" I ask. "Why is she here? And why is she…missing so many fingers?"

Elison shrugs. "Apparently it's what happens every time she

tries breaking out of this place." When she finishes cleaning her second hand, she leans back against the cold wall. "You know she used to be a thief. At least that's what all the legends about her say. She had a good sleight of hand. She was exceptional with lockpicks. That sort of stuff."

I'd almost forgotten that part of our history lessons. Most of the stories regarding the abolishment of the mages and demon-kind revolved around Halira and Ryven, the druid heroes of Arcathain. But there are few that detail the Magistrate Alphonse's contributions to our nation's victory—if you can call it that—as well as some recordings of the assistances made by his then soon-to-be wife, Foxlynn Abigail.

Hers was a true rags-to-riches story. A homeless orphan who was left with no choice but to join the Shadow Crusade, only instead of joining the ranks, she met her true love when General Alphonse Reid Graham started her training.

"So, tell me, Charlotte," Elison continues, glancing at me from the corner of her eyes. "If someone as skilled as her can't break out of here, how do you propose the two of us can? Mind you, I'd like to keep my fingers, preferably."

"And you will," I say, my attention drifting over to Fox.

I swear she's perked up since we began talking about her, even though I know we're being too quiet for her to hear us from this distance.

If she could hear our plotting, maybe that wouldn't be so bad. The secrets she could tell us about this place...

I file that possibility away for now, still unwilling to trust her farther than I can throw her. She was, after all, working with the noctis. Maybe she still is. Maybe she's down here to spy on us all and report what she sees and hear.

Until I know her motives, it would be best to keep her in the dark.

There is plenty else to study and learn about in the meantime, like how frequently the guards venture down here and when they rotate, what opportunities we have for stealing their keys, or other items that might be fashioned into lockpicks, how astute are they, and most importantly, what the layout of the castle is like.

First and foremost, however, I'd like to get to know our other cellmate.

The girl in the corner hasn't moved or spoken in a full day, which both concerns and intrigues me. Someone like that has either been broken beyond repair, or she understands the way this place works and knows how to survive. I intend to find out which.

"Okay," Elison replies, clearly losing her patience for my vague responses. "Then how?"

Without a word, I gesture toward the girl's lowered head. Elison watches me with confusion as I stand from the bench and approach our cellmate.

"Hi," I say awkwardly. "What's your name?"

She flinches at the sound of my voice, curling deeper into herself like she can just shrink and shrink until there's nothing of her left.

Under normal circumstances, I'd take the hint. But right now, I have nothing else to occupy my mind with. Sliding my back along the stone wall, I crouch beside her and take a seat.

"I just figured, since we'll be stuck in here together, we might as well get to know each other a little." My throat is dry, my conversational muscle woefully out of practice. I sound harsh and intimidating, even to my own ears, and I can't blame her for the silence that falls between us.

And I startle when she breaks it.

"M-Mira," she says hesitantly. "My name is Mira."

"It's nice to meet you, Mira. I'm Charlotte. That's Elison—" Elison waves when I gesture toward her. "How long have you been here, Mira?"

The girl, who can't be more than sixteen, pulls the weight of her hair over her shoulder and begins curling sections of it around her finger. "Mmm. I don't know. A couple of weeks, I think. It's hard to keep track of time down here."

"I imagine it is." Nodding, I pause, allowing time to pass so that hopefully the girl won't feel like I'm interrogating her. Now that we've started talking though, she seems to warm up quickly; already her arms are unfolding from around herself. "Do they give you regular meals? You know, that's one way we could keep track of that days."

Her head shakes, her miserable eyes lowering. Her only response is a strangled sound, so I try a different approach.

"Have you eaten since you were brought here?"

"A few times." She bites her lip. "I'm one of the lucky ones."

"Lucky ones?" I glance to Elison but try not to appear too suspicious and uncaring. "How?"

She's hesitant again, and it dawns on me that she was alone in here for quite some time before the two of us showed up. Maybe, like me, she'd been alone even longer.

Or worse, maybe she hadn't.

"They—they have us on different diets. They'll tell you yours soon."

"Tell us ours?" Elison interjects, body shifting forward with sudden interest. "What does that even mean?"

Mira shrugs and, stroking her thick, almost-matted hair, glances nervously between the two of us. "I know. I'm sorry. It's...troubling to hear. But I don't think they want us to starve. You know, because they're going to..." When her lip begins to quiver, she turns away again, retreating back into the silence that she's held onto so strongly for the past day, if not longer.

There can be comfort in silence. This I know. But right now, I find none. It seems she finds none as well.

"Please, Mira," I say, trying to spin my usually harsh voice into silken threads of gold. At best, I think I manage to make a slightly more malleable steel than what I usually wield. "Please tell us what they have you eating—"

The blacks of her pupils become as expansive as the dungeon.

"Oh, no! It's nothing like…like what you're thinking. They feed us normal food. Food fit for humans. Soup and bread, mostly. Sometimes an occasional vegetable. But we don't all get to eat at the same time. I get three meals a day, but some of the others…" With a cautious glance around the cell block, Mira leans closer and lowers her voice. "They're lucky to eat once a day. Some of them—mostly the men who look like they could pull a cart of hay without needing an ox to help—they're only given a meal every couple of days."

The worrying information hits me like a deep-sea wave might collide with a ship full of drunken sailors. My head lolls back, and for a moment, I feel my world swaying all around me. The noctis already have the upper hand. Mankind is already half-starved and weak. And they want to take away any advantage we might have once we're in the Hunt. They want us as weak as we can be just to ensure that their kind can kill us.

It's no wonder no one has ever escaped.

"I think the noctis want to keep us weak," Mira continues in her hushed tone, and I realize I was right about her. She's been watching, listening, learning. She might prove a great asset. "Since some of us have already done a good job of making ourselves feeble, we're not a threat. Or at least, I think that's why some of us get to eat more."

I can almost guarantee she's right.

If Elison and I are going to get out of here, we'll need our strength. We'll need to appear weak enough that they won't want to limit our rations.

"They can't do this!" Elison's teeth are clenched as she stands from the bench. "We need food. We need—"

It's not until her words falter that I realize the placement of her hands, the way they're clawed over her belly like a wild mother bear defending her cubs.

Her choice of words had seemed innocuous before. Not *I*. But *we*. Not in the collective sense that I'd mistaken them for earlier. Not referring to those of us who find ourselves prisoner down here. But *we* as in her and her unborn child.

Rowland's unborn child.

My stomach writhes like a nest of coiling, hissing snakes.

Elison's instinct is to protect and defend.

Mine is to strike with lethal precision.

Venom has always been in my blood. My mother used to tell me that I should be careful with my sharp tongue, or I might just cut myself. In truth, she always seemed more worried for everyone else. Some parents teach their young that words cannot hurt. Mine seemed to understand the opposite, and she seemed to believe that my tongue could become my deadliest weapon.

Second to having Sable locked and loaded in my arms, she would've been right.

I have always had an eye for weakness. Elison makes it easy.

Her fears exude from her like black smoke billowing from a pyre. A young mistress-turned-mother. Someone who is imprisoned in a noctis lair and knows their days are numbered. If she is sacrificed to the Hunt, she will never get to meet her unborn child, nor will she return to the arms of the man who's apparently been keeping her bed warm at night. All her hopes for the future, gone before they can even come to fruition.

My vipers are hungry.

They want blood for the way they've been treated.

But even as my lip begins to curl back, venomous tongue ready to strike, something stops me from releasing my viper. All I can think about is how I lost my own mother too young. How I never got to see her again. How all our hopes and dreams were torn away from us in one terrible instant.

For all my anger toward Elison, toward Rowland, I know that's all it is. Anger. Not hatred. Not malice. Just heartbreak over a bitter betrayal that I don't want to admit because that would imply that I actually cared about something outside of myself.

Uncoiling the snakes in my belly, and digging my nails out of my palms, I take a shaky step toward her and press my clammy hand over her belly.

"I won't let you starve," I tell her, staring straight into her eyes to make sure she knows I'm telling the truth. I wonder if she can see the jagged rocks lodged in my throat when I swallow and amend my statement. "*Either* of you. I'm going to get us out of here."

And I'm not sure what possesses me to say what I say next. Perhaps I'm just pissed off and determined to make the noctis rue the day they trapped me in this nightmarish place.

Whatever the reason, I turn to where the meek Mira is crouched and say, "All four of us are escaping."

14

A CASTLE AND IT'S KING

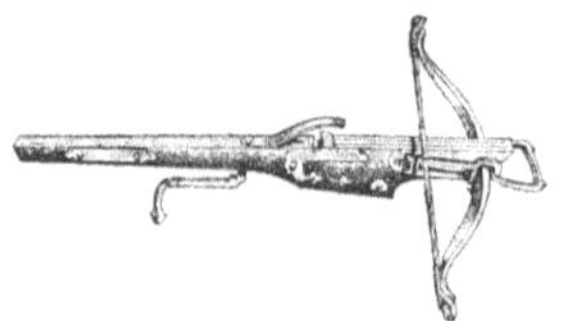

When we lay down that night, something has changed between the three of us. We don't lay in our separate corners like we did the night before, but lined up beside one another, finding comfort in each other's presence and warmth.

It's strange to think that other than Rowland, this is the first time I've slept next to someone in ten years. Stranger still that one of the people beside me now is a girl who has also shared his bed. But honestly, strangest of all, is how quickly this arrangement feels…natural. When they'd gathered up next to me, I hadn't even thought twice about it. I hadn't wondered if it was a bad idea to allow myself to feel close to them. I certainly hadn't thought about what it would be like to lose them.

Of course, in the dark, silent hours of the night, those thoughts assault my restless mind now.

The longer we stay here, the closer the Hunt approaches. But it's not the Hunt I'm worried about. I've escaped worse nightmares than this place. If I survived Hulbeck, I can survive the Castle of Nigh.

But that's the problem.

We might be relatively safe while we're here, but once we escape, once we return to a world where we have to run for our lives from a predator that fills their bellies with our blood, then we return to a world where I can't afford to care for anyone but myself. The bond that might be forming while we're here? It's only temporary. Once we escape, Elison will return to Rowland, Mira will return to wherever she came from—or perhaps she, too, will seek out the safety that Rowland's people can provide—and I will return to my life of solitude, and be all the wiser for isolating myself for another decade.

That's the way it has to be.

"Charlotte?" Elison's voice, heavy and ominous, fills the quiet cell like a storm cloud.

I keep my eyes pressed shut and try desperately to focus on anything but the pressure of her lingering, anticipating question hovering over me.

"I know you're awake," she says, annoyed. "Your eyes twitched."

I release the breath I'd been holding, my favorite curse exhaling along with it as I finally look at her. "What?"

But she's not looking at me. Her gaze is fixed upward, as if she's searching the black ceiling for something other than the nothingness above us.

My annoyance dissipates.

"I…" She takes a moment, struggling to find the words. "I didn't know he told you."

Of everything that could've come out of her mouth, this was farthest from my mind, for once. And I wish she'd have kept it like that. I don't want to do this. To talk about *him and her*.

"When did he tell—"

I cut her off before the concern in her tone can ooze with too much pity.

"The day I was caught." This time when I roll over, flipping onto my side so I don't have to look at her, I can't close my eyes. They sting too much. They need to stop. I am not some weeping waterfall of human emotion. I am a steel sword, hardened and cold.

"He sent me to look for you," I tell her, fixing my voice with as much indifference as I can muster.

Silence returns to the room again, but it bears with it the same tone as her earlier question. For too long, I lay there, wondering if the tension filled clouds are going to pass without incident, or if they will flood us.

Finally, just when I'm about to close my eyes and try to get some sleep, Elison speaks.

"I'm sorry. I didn't know he was going to tell you. And I didn't know that he'd send you after me once he did. That… isn't a great place to put you in—"

"Stop."

The word is barely more than a whisper at first, but it carries with it a threat as deadly as any storm.

Elison's mouth makes an audible snap shut.

"Just stop." Propping myself up on one elbow, I whip back around to face her. "We don't need to talk about this. We don't need to talk about the fucked up mess that the three of us have found ourselves in. You two are having a baby. I know what that means, and I'll be fine—I *am* fine." I pinch the brim of my nose, and exhale until I'm laying back down, the cold stone floor pressed against my skin. "Let's just focus on getting out of this place. That's all that matters right now."

Silence again.

"Okay," she says after a while. "Not another word from me about it unless you ask. Good night, Charlotte. And thank you…for coming for me."

Tonight, sleep comes just about as naturally as breathing while underwater. My chest won't stop aching and my mind won't calm itself. If I'm not lamenting over the ways I practically pushed Rowland into Elison's arms, I'm mulling over our options and our very abysmal odds for escape.

In time, I do finally succumb and darkness blankets me…

Until the blanket is torn away. A small legion of noctis storm into the dungeon what feels like only moments after I've just shut my eyes. The prince leads them forward, key in hand when he stops before our cell.

He smiles through the bars. "Rise and shine. Your presence is being requested." When the three of us start to stir, he holds his hand up to Mira. "Not you."

Elison and I exchange a wary look first with each other and then back at her.

Leaving her alone in this place just seems wrong. There's something childlike about her, something innocent and pure that makes the idea of abandoning her in such a dark and corrupt place seem evil.

Seeming far less worried about it than we are, she simply mouths the word, *"Diet."*

It's not as settling as I think she hopes it will be, partially because at first it looks like she's saying the word *die*. But then it registers, and my stomach growls as if accentuating her meaning, and I remember what she said the other day about being assigned a meal regiment.

I suddenly find myself wide awake.

Not only am I dying for something to eat, but more importantly I want to make sure that I am fully conscious for the act that myself and Elison are about to put on. We need it to be convincing, beyond a doubt. It'll be easier for Elison. Being with child has already taken its toll, and she's awoken today with a tinge of green about her freckled skin.

I'll have to work harder not to be too intimidating, too threatening, to prove to the noctis king that he has no reason to fear us.

It shouldn't be too hard.

If I know anything about the arrogance of men—apex predators, at that—it'll be his instinct to overlook us.

With the guards dragging us from our cells, our charade begins.

I hunch my shoulders, trying to appear small and frail as they jerk us down the corridor. It's probably just in my own head, but I swear I detect a hint of suspicion behind the prince's gaze when it sweeps over me. But in the next moment, he's stopping the group before the next cell.

"Just that one," the prince barks, pointing through the bars. I notice the red tattoo on his wrist again before dipping my head to hide my alertness before he can sense it like he seems to sense everything else. "We'll retrieve another batch after these ones are done."

Before I can see who they grab, the prince takes my arm from one of his guards and ushers me forward.

Days without food have made me weak and a bit light-headed. Even starved, under normal circumstances, I would attempt to rip from his grasp and run. But with so many of them around us, that would do me no good just yet. Until I can get a better lay of the land, until I know where we'll run once we escape, playing docile is the best plan I have.

My belly rumbles and I lean into my hunger like it's a crutch. I let myself wobble as the prince takes us through the weaving crypt corridors, guiding us down hallways lined top to bottom with shelves of skulls, bones, and decay.

I can't believe I didn't notice them on our way down here. Then again, the path we're taking feels different than the one we took when we first arrived. I would know, seeing as I was searching for any possible opportunity to flee and found none.

Hopefully my efforts will prove more fruitful today.

Long after my nose has desensitized itself to the musty stench of long-forgotten dust, we ascend into a dark room lit only by a crackling fire that seems to burn all memory of the dead below us away.

The Castle of Nigh is far more expansive and elaborate on the inside than it had looked while standing among the shattered ruins of the courtyard. We walk its twisting halls and traverse its dimly lit chambers for so long that on more than one occasion I forget I'm among wicked creatures, I forget who's walking beside me.

One glance at the tall noctis prince though, and I remember. All too clearly.

Two white fangs peek out beneath his lip, and the image of him licking the blood from his finger suddenly consumes my mind.

These are the monsters who stole our world, who carved out its essence and vivacity, and took away our homes.

I hate them.

I hate them all.

But I especially loathe him, and every other Devonshire who's ever lived.

We reach a set of ornate double doors, the doorknobs gilded with thin accents of red decorating their surfaces.

The prince makes his grand entrance by shoving them both wide, and without even needing to beckon us in, we follow.

There's a chill in the dimly-lit room we enter, one that reminds me of walking through a forest at night. The ceiling-to-floor stained-glass windows on one side of the room have been shattered, colorful shards still littering the ground like confetti, and yet, even the sunlight still can't seem to permeate the darkness that's contained inside this room.

I shudder the farther in we submerge ourselves.

The prince looks down at me and I realize in my chill I've inadvertently pulled him closer.

I jerk back, glowering up at him and the smirk I expect to

find. But there isn't a hint of amusement in the expression that lingers on me.

Shaking away whatever emotion had crossed him, the prince continues leading us into the dark grey abyss.

Each candelabra we pass only lights up the small area surrounding it, but I still manage to catch glimpses of the décor around the room. The velvet runner beneath our feet is as dark as blood. The stone columns lining the long room are as rigid and cold as the rest of this castle, and they disappear somewhere high above.

Most notably, of course, is the throne at the end of the long runner.

The throne and the king sitting on it.

If the rest of the room is dark and cold, King Tor is practically luminescent. White hair tumbles over his shoulders like sheets of snow beneath a full moon's light. He wears enough gold to make him sink to the bottom of the Varenholm Ocean, and yet even in the shadows his jewels manage to shine. But it's the irritation in his eyes that makes him glow the most. His eyes are like two roaring bonfires in the middle of the night, their scorching beauty daring every moth to chance getting closer, only for his wild flames to engulf them.

He looks as deadly as he did the day I first laid eyes on him, all those years ago.

The prince and his guards give us a forceful shove until all three of us are clambering at the bottom of the stairs before the king. The guards stand somewhere behind us, out of sight but surely not too far away to intervene in case one of us gets a wild idea. But the prince continues his graceful stride up, never once glancing at us as he takes his place beside the throne.

He doesn't glance at his father either, I notice.

"I've been waiting over an hour," the king mutters, idle fingers drilling against the obsidian armrest.

The prince folds his arms behind his back, gaze fixed

forward. Although I don't hear a response from where I'm standing, his father's head jerks, and I know that whatever the prince has said beneath his breath isn't something that most people would get away with saying to a king.

King Tor's glare burns into the prince's face for a long, long moment, before he finally returns his attention to us.

Beside me, the young man they'd grabbed from the other cell, the one who'd been traveling with us to Nigh in the cart, cowers under the king's brutal glare. On my other side, Elison, too, bows her head. It's so unlike her that I'm left dumbfounded for a moment. She is normally as sharp and as lethal as any of the bolts she ever made for me. She's always possessed the bold spirit of an undefeated bull, a woman who would stand her ground and fight whomever—even if the odds were stacked against her.

To see her cower before anyone leaves me unsettled.

From behind her lowered lashes, those sky-blue eyes cut in my direction. A warning that takes me only a moment to remember.

I follow her lead—albeit a bit delayed—and throw my head forward like I'm chucking an anchor overboard at sea. I can all but hear the hollow sound of my failure as it plummets into the dark depths. Already, I've failed my task. I entered this room with the confidence of someone who is capable rather than someone who's fearing for their life.

But I can still try.

I owe myself that much.

"This is all?" the king asks, the disappointment in his tone palpable.

"No. There are others in the dungeons. But I wanted to deliver a sampling of them to you first, knowing that the other hunting parties were nowhere near as successful as ours was." The arrogance in his voice, the pride, it makes me sick. "Allow me, Father."

My curious gaze can't help but wander up as their footsteps flit down the stairs to examine us. Like we're cattle being brought to the slaughter.

"This one, they call Dunce." The prince gives the young man beside me a hearty pat on the shoulder that makes his knees tremble. "Though, I hardly say that's a fair assessment of his character. Of all the heartbeats we gathered from Gravenburg, he's the only one who's been wise enough not to undermine authority. Of any kind. Even between his cell brethren."

"Mmm."

The sound the king makes could either be one of agreement or one of contempt. It's difficult to tell with him.

But the prince seems to register it as something positive—or at least the closest thing to approving that he'll get—and moves on.

They slide over to me. My heart thrums like a wild beast trapped beneath my bones.

But to my torture, the prince keeps walking.

"We'll come back to you later." He winks at me as the king and him slide over to Elison instead. "I present to you, Elison Wade. It's not often we learn their surnames, but, for such a feisty thing, she was quite willing to divulge an unthinkable amount of information about herself when we found her." Leaning closer into his father, he cups one hand over the king's ear, but I wouldn't call what he does with his voice anything close to whispering. "She's with child."

The king's pale flesh takes on an eerie glow. His eyes shine and I quiver to think of what vile kind of hunger has just sparked him back to life.

"Or at least"—the prince continues with a carefree shrug—"that's the impression we've been given. Holding her belly when she sleeps. Vomiting in the mornings, even when she hasn't eaten for days."

"Is this true?" the king asks her.

When his crooked finger reaches out and coils around one of Elison's bright and wild curls, the façade of the scared, placid girl she'd so perfectly crafted shatters. Elison jerks her head and her hair out of the king's grasp, baring her teeth.

"Don't touch me."

His eyes become alight again. "It's true then. You have the fight of two inside you."

Her lip trembles, but it's more like she's biting her tongue than about to burst into tears.

"I told you," the prince says as he meanders back up the stairs. "She was feisty. Took a swing at Ursulette and gave Rhain a black eye when he tried wrangling her. Not that the man couldn't afford a little imperfection."

He reaches for something behind the throne and a moment later pulls out a goblet of gods know what. My imagination doesn't have to run wild for long. He takes a drink, and when he lowers the golden chalice, his lips are stained red.

"You think you're impressed with Elison, Father?" Swirling the red liquid around in his chalice, he points it at me. "Just wait until you meet *her*."

A wave of ice washes over me. My body knows I have to escape to survive, but none of my limbs are working. They're too cold to move; frozen in place no matter how much I scream at myself to run.

"Elison might've been feisty," the prince continues, pausing to take another drink and walks back down the steps. He stops before me, bright eyes burning into mine. "But this one here? She's fierce. She means to survive. She means to fight. I could see it in her eyes then as clear as I can see it here now."

Fuck.

Of course the prince would weigh in on these decisions and give the king insight that he would otherwise not have. What did I think would happen? That he'd take one glance at us and make a random decision based on appearance alone?

Just like that, my chances of eating a full meal for as long as I'm here are ruined.

But that doesn't mean Elison's have to be.

Slowly, I exhale away my panic, my fear. I whip my dark hair over my shoulder just to show him how little I care, and how little he intimidates me, no matter how much I have to crane my neck just to glare up into his piercing eyes.

"You think *she's* feisty?" A mocking snort escapes me. "An expectant mother who hasn't been able to stomach food for weeks? If you ask me, that says more about your incompetence of handling prisoners than it says about her."

Heat flashes behind those icy eyes, but none of it reaches his carefree tone. "Oh, well my incompetence should most definitely be addressed. And promptly. Please, I implore you. Tell me the ways in which I should have handled my prisoners more to their liking."

Embarrassment burns through me. Embarrassment, and something else...

"In fact," he continues, and with the speed of a spider snatching its prey, his hand is tangled in my hair, my head jerked back. His sharp fangs hover over my exposed neck as the hot air of his panting breaths burns my skin. "Perhaps I should practice on you first. Make sure my *handling* is to your liking."

"That's enough." King Tor waves him away as if he's bored. I've never been so relieved by anything he's ever done in his life, nor will I again. "There will be no sampling of the livestock before the Hunt. I thought I taught you better than that, although it would seem I was wrong."

The king gestures to the young man with straw hair besides me who began whimpering the moment the prince lunged for me. As if it were his neck on the line.

Begrudgingly the prince releases the back of my skull and

tosses me aside. "You can blame Harland for that. He bled two of the prisoners before we arrived."

"Mmm. Yes," the king says, wryly. "Because why fault an incompetent leader when we can blame those simply following orders."

A muscle in the prince's jaw tightens.

Before whatever vicious words are brewing on his tongue can spew out, the king turns his back to us and makes the short climb up to his throne. His knees tremble with every step, quaking so hard that they almost topple him.

I could be wrong, but he seems to be in worse of a condition than Elison.

I wonder what ails him.

I wonder if it's terminal.

Once he's finally settled, one of his hands flicks up to Dunce.

"Give the boy and whoever else was fed upon an extra ration today. Something hearty to replenish what was taken. Beginning tomorrow, he'll receive one meal daily."

Like the coward he seems to be, called Dunce nods vigorously, almost appreciatively. My lip curls in disgust.

"For the mother-who-never-will-be," King Tor continues. "Fatten her up. As much as she'll eat, and anything she'll keep down. Our constituents will be ravenous knowing that one of them will have the honor of hunting and feasting upon a woman with two heartbeats and increased blood volume."

The image he's painting attempts to take hold of my imagination, but it won't work. Elison and I will be long gone before the Hunt ever begins, and before any vile monster will be able to sink its teeth into her belly.

I've done my job. At least she will be well-fed. Even if they will be treating her like a prized hog.

"Now," King Tor says, leaning to one side of the chair to prop his face on his palm. "What to do with her?"

The guards take the other prisoners away. Elison's pleading gaze meets mine, but I shake my head. Whatever fight she thought we should consider, now is not the time. Besides, the king has already proven that they won't do anything to me.

Yet. Not until the Hunt.

When the doors slam shut behind me, I'm acutely aware that I am standing in a room with the two most powerful noctis in all the realm.

"She doesn't look like much," the king says to the prince. "She's so…thin."

The prince folds his arms, and I'm relieved that he's at long last covered that ridiculously plunging neckline of his and the hard plane of muscles beneath it. "I wouldn't underestimate her, Tor. She's the reason Gregor and Boris are dead."

If the king had intended on reprimanding his son for addressing him so casually, he loses his drive at the mention of the dead.

Fuck me. Of all the noctis I could've crossed paths with, who'd have known that those two lowlife scum would cause me so much trouble?

"Is this true?" he asks, regal voice echoing all the way down the empty hall as he settles back against the throne. "You've slain two of our Crimson Guards?"

As much as I'd love to argue semantics and protest that technically speaking, I didn't kill either of them, I don't see it mattering to either of them. Their minds have been made up.

I opt for a slightly misguided, more confrontational approach.

"I'd do it again too, if given the chance."

The king's eyebrows arch. "Hmm."

I can't tell what I'm supposed to make of that, but the lack of response unnerves me. *Yell at me. Scold me. Threaten me. Do something,* I want to scream.

The prince, off a short distance beside him, reaches for an

amulet around his neck. The garnet stone might as well be a vial full of blood for how deep and rich the color is, catching in what little light the room provides like a burning ember floating away from a fire. The way he clutches it reminds me of the way I hold onto Sable.

Sable…my mother's crossbow, lost to the hands of some foul noctis. I wish I believed that I would ever see her again, but it's a hope I can't afford to harbor, or it might cloud my judgment during our escape.

"She will prove a challenge," the prince reassures his father, fingers idly stroking the sharp edges of the gold-encrusted garnet. "Perhaps we can even proclaim her some sort of delicatessen."

The king considers. "It's not a bad idea. What's your name, girl?"

Names are precious, special things. These two monsters haven't earned the right to know mine.

My mother gave me my name. She named me after her late grandmother who she'd always said was the rock that kept their family grounded any time tragedy struck.

I've shared my name openly with so few, that I don't even know how to respond.

The king sees to it to help me. "Unless you'd prefer that we continue referring to you as *the prisoner*, or something even more dehumanizing. The choice is yours."

"Charlotte," I say firmly, turning my name into two bitter syllables.

The king's fingers tap a brief melody on his armrest. "Charlotte," he repeats. "And tell me, Charlotte, how much of a problem do you intend to be?"

"Why? You scared that I might be too strong for the legion of noctis you plan to unleash upon us if I'm kept too well-fed? I'll tell you a secret: us humans are more acquainted with starvation than you've ever experienced."

A scoff of a laugh eases from the prince's quirked mouth. But the king remains unmoving.

"My dear," he says, eyes lowered. "You fail to understand the point of it all. The noctis who have chosen to participate in this year's Hunt pay well for the opportunity we provide. They expect a good chase—a bit of sport, if you will—but they are no more interested in the hassle and uncertainty of a life-threatening fight than you or I. They fought for years merely to exist."

Anger buzzes around me, alive and churning like a tornado of angry hornets.

He paints them as victims, rather than the killers they are. Maybe at one point that was true. Maybe for the first few months or so. But they've been slaughtering humans for years now. Almost two decades.

They're no victims. They're evil incarnate.

He continues before I can mold my rage into anything coherent to launch at him.

"I will not have you, or anyone else for that matter, causing more problems than you're worth. So I will ask you again, one final time. And do consider your answer thoroughly before blurting the first caustic thought that comes to mind."

My teeth grind together. I know that my pride isn't worth my life, but I can't make myself agree to his terms. The best I can do is bite my tongue and hope my silence is good enough for him.

But I do it for me. For Elison and Mira.

Not for him.

"How much of a problem do you intend to be, Charlotte? Should I dispose of you now, call back my guards and let them drain you until you're nothing but a shriveled vessel? Or should I allow my son's contribution to the Hunt and send you back to the dungeon to await the big day?"

My entire body revolts against my will to keep my mouth shut.

It might save me now to tell the corrupt king what he wants to hear, and it might buy me the time I need to figure out how to break out of here, but the choice he's giving me is absurd. Die now or die later. That's what he's proposing. Saying it as if it's some gods given grace that I might be among those poor souls released in the Hunt.

How many before me has he given the same ultimatum?

How many after?

"It's like I told your incompetent son," I hear myself saying, the tremble in my throat somehow nowhere to be heard in the strength of my projected voice. "Give me back my crossbow and I'll show you just how much of a *problem* I can be."

I brace myself for them to lunge, jaws unhinging as they knock me to the ground and drink their fill from my dying body.

Fuck it. I mean, really, what was I thinking? That I stood any chance once they had ensnared me? Once they threw me down into their dungeon? No one before me has ever escaped. Not a single person. Every one of them has bled and died in the Hunt, and I'd rather die here, in this icy chamber than out there on a bloody battlefield. At least here I won't have to watch as Mira is killed slowly. I won't have to listen to Elison's cries as a noctis feasts on the unborn child in her belly while she's still alive. I won't have to suffer knowing that the few people I care about are once again dying at the hands of monsters.

So, fuck it.

Let them kill me here and now and be done with it. Knowing how badly they need to populate the Hunt, it's about the best *fuck you* I could hope for anyway. Really, it's a wonder I hadn't considered this option sooner.

As I await the pressure of their fangs on my neck, to my surprise, it never comes.

The king simply takes his face into his hand with a long, ragged sigh.

"She is permitted one meal the night before the Hunt. Not a single crumb more," he tells the prince. Glancing at him sideways, he adds, "And should she prove anything less than docile and obedient during the remainder of her time here, deliver her to Harland and let him do with her what he will."

Suddenly, it's like I can't breathe.

How can he do this? How can he deny me a dignified death? One that I was already coming to terms with.

"What?" My voice cracks beneath the pressure piling atop my chest. "No… You can't—you can't do this."

The prince is already trotting down the stairs, obediently following his father's commands while my head swims in a vast and churning sea of all my greatest fears.

We can't escape.

I can't watch them all die.

The blood…

I can't go through that again.

The prince takes my arm into his iron-clad grasp and drags me away, back the way we came. As I thrash, I kick and grab at anything I can reach, the candelabras passing in hazy hues of gold and grey but standing firm no matter the contact I make. Frantic, I jerk and pull harder, my body flailing to break free from his relentless grip, but he might as well be hauling a bag of rice for how effortless he makes it look.

And that enrages me all the more.

The Hunt is an unnecessary source of entertainment. Given the ever-growing ghoul population, they outnumber us. They overpower us. They don't need a Hunt to feed. They need it to fuel their egos. To satiate a sick and twisted part of themselves that I'll never understand.

Mira's and Elison's screams already echo in my ears over and over again. Their soon-to-be mangled and bloodied corpses engulf my vision. And then so does my mother's. And then all of the people in Hulbeck. My vision is a red massacre of torn heads and gutted bodies.

I can't do this again.

I don't want to.

"Just kill me already."

I hear the fragile whimper in my voice as it cracks through my center. It just might be the most brittle I've ever allowed anyone to see me. My face is slick, but I have no idea when the tears started to fall. They've been buried so deep for so long they feel foreign against my cheeks. The taste of salt grows more bitter on my tongue the deeper my embarrassment and disappointment clenches my heart.

I didn't mean for those words to leave my mouth. I swore that thought would never cross my mind again. But there are dark days when it won't leave. There always have been. Like the clouds themselves cast a shadow upon me, and in their darkness, I know nothing but doubt, fear, and complete hopelessness.

Hearing my pathetic cry, the prince finally halts. His broad shoulders become a tight board of muscle.

Lethargy consumes me, crumbling my strength until I feel like nothing more than a pitiful puddle. I can hardly stand. My shoulders hunch, my knees buckling as the prince turns ever so slowly on the crimson runner to face me.

His cold gaze reaches mine, chilling the tears streaming down my face.

I want to wipe them away. Now that the initial moment of weakness has passed, now that I've regained some of my common sense, I don't want him—let alone anyone—to see me like this. So raw. So vulnerable.

But *he* sees me.

With eyes that seem to be capable of seeing everything, Prince Malachi watches me with a sort of empathetic familiarity that makes me forget momentarily that we're on opposite sides.

I feel his grief like a thousand swords to my heart. He's lost people he's loved before. I'm not sure who, but I can see the scar it dug into his heart. Perhaps like me, it was his own mother—after all, there was only one throne behind us, and I've never once heard any mention of Tor's queen.

In this moment, we're more alike than we are different. My despair greets his grief like two long-lost friends, and suddenly the shame I felt, the rawness that had wrapped itself around my heart like a rope of serrated blades, loosens. It falls away, leaving behind wounds that are still there, no doubt, fresh and dripping with blood. They'll leave new scars that'll color every choice I make from here forward, for the rest of my life. But at least the pressure is fading. My lungs don't have to strain so much for every breath I try taking. The fog that had filled the dark forest of my mind is starting to fade, allowing not quite sunlight to filter in, but something a little brighter than what had been there just moments before.

People are resilient when they want to be. And I want to be. I am a survivor. Always will be, even if I have to remind myself every so often when I'm veering down a dark path.

My life may be dire. The world may be dark and seem completely hopeless. But I want to live for as long as I am able.

I will fight for that right.

Almost as soon as our eyes meet, our souls speaking to one another in a way that I've never spoken to anyone before, Malachi turns back around.

"You don't want death," he says so softly that I almost don't hear him. "You want release. Freedom." His voice is restrained, like he's gripping onto the reins of bucking bulls and he's trying to keep them contained. It would be a fool's errand for anyone without the aptitude and strength, and he appears to have plenty of both. "So, fight for it. Don't...don't let the monsters win."

Without another word, he tugs my arm, this time with less urgency and something close to—dare I say—sincerity, as he guides me back to the dungeons.

15

LIKE FATHER, UNLIKE SON

Not soon after I've locked Charlotte back into her cell do I feel her absence.

The way she'd looked at me when we were in the throne room has left a lingering ache somewhere deep in my soul. I've never seen that look on anyone else before. That despair. That sense of utter helplessness to the life that you want but for some reason can't seem to attain. Even the humans I've fed upon have never shared such a glimpse of their misery with me. Not a single one has ever begged me for death.

What does it say about Charlotte and what she's endured that she was the first?

Despite never having seen someone look so miserable and lost and broken, I recognized it all the same. Because I've been there. I've felt that way myself, on more occasions than I'd like to admit.

Hiding behind the tall, sharp edges of my cape, I leave her inside her cell and go to the one beside it. I give my guards instructions to grab the next group of new arrivals for my father's inspection before turning for the exit. I need to get away from her, to clear my head—

"Psst. Prince Malachi? A word?"

Down the corridor, I find my Aunt Fox with her head pressed against the bars.

This is the last thing I need right now, but she catches me in a bad mood and so, rather than ignoring her and continuing out the dungeon, I signal for Crimson Guards to leave with the prisoners without me and I storm to Fox's cell.

Seeing what's left of her hacked fingers wrapped around the iron makes me grateful for the empty stomach, and I avert my attention to her slightly-less miserable face.

"What is it?" I growl. "You know I shouldn't be seen speaking to you. Not here."

A shadow cuts across her face. "Fine. Forget it. I knew I was being foolish anyway."

She whips around and slams her back on the bars, sliding all the way down until she's sitting.

I groan, rubbing my face. I *really* don't have time for this. But she was right in her anger toward me. My curtness was uncalled for.

"I'm sorry," I whisper, hunching down so my voice has less distance to travel, well aware that we've already drawn the attention of everyone and that a prince bowing to a prisoner is likely only making it worse. "What is it you wanted to say?"

"Nothing," she says, arms folding. "I was being stupid. Like always."

I wince, wondering what she means by that. "I don't think you're stupid. I think you're…exhausted and desperate."

She huffs a humorless laugh. "You have no idea."

I can feel every prisoners' eyes upon us, making my hair stand on end. There's no telling who among them could slip to my father of our rendezvous. I have to keep up an act that I inherited but never even wanted.

"You'll eat when we deem you worthy of a meal!" My voice rumbles like thunder rattling every cell in this wing. I resist the urge to glance over my shoulder to make sure everyone overheard, and instead direct a soft whisper to my aunt. "I'm sorry I snapped at you. And I'm sorry I haven't checked in on you. The king has returned, and it took me awhile to find—"

Her neck snaps, eyes flicking to mine. "That abomination will never be anything close to resembling a *king*, and if saying as such costs me another finger, then so be it."

I frown. "I wouldn't—" Seeing her unconvinced expression, I realize my words will do me no good. They mean very little to a woman behind bars who's been promised her release. "I didn't want to speak to you until I learned where he was keeping your boys."

She blanches. In the blink of an eye, all signs of the warrior she once was disappears and her face softens with the tenderness of a hopeful mother.

"What of my sons? Are they with him? Are they...please tell me, are they alive?"

A gaping fissure cracks my chest. I want to tell her everything, but her increasing volume is becoming problematic.

I slam my palms against the bars for a show of theatrics and shout, "You are in the presence of your prince, and you will be silent, prisoner!" While the bars still reverberate through the room, and the hushed whispers of the other prisoners fill the air like smoke, I murmur hurriedly, "They're alive."

She keeps her face hidden from the others, keeps her tone low now. "How do you know? Have you seen them?"

"Not yet. But I promise you, my intel is good. I know where they're being held. And soon you'll be reunited. Just...try to be patient, for just a little longer."

"Patient?" I can hear the disdain oozing in her voice. "Don't talk to me about being patient. You promised days ago that you'd get me and my sons out of here before the Hunt, but that's only what? A few days away? What good is patience when all it earns me is broken promises?"

"My promise hasn't been broken. I just understand the importance of timing."

Her head shifts, not quite looking up at me, but I can tell I've gotten her attention.

I would lose my cool if I wasn't so painfully familiar with being misunderstood by everyone.

Fox doesn't know me. She doesn't know that I spent the first thirteen years of my life in a small human community until the noctis came and slaughtered everyone, including my own mother.

When my aunt looks at me, all she sees is my wicked nature and thirst for blood. I can't prove to her I'm any different with my words alone.

"The morning of the Hunt," I say softly. "That's when I'll come. After they've taken all the others to the Shadowthorn, I'll come for you and then we'll grab your boys and run." Her head jerks, her eyes searching mine as if she's waiting for me to tell her more. But we've drawn too much attention already. "I can't say anything else, and we can't talk like this again."

When I turn around, leaving her spinning to clutch the iron bars as she watches me walk away, every eye in the room is upon me.

Just to be sure that no one misconstrues what's happened here, I remind them who is in charge and who they should fear. "The next person I find staring my way will lose their eyes and be forced to eat them."

It does the trick. Almost every prisoner turns their back to me so quickly that their collective movements summon a gust of wind.

That is, everyone except Charlotte—a woman who already

knows me more than I'd like. A woman who has already seen farther into my soul than I'm comfortable with.

I almost don't even see her at first, tucked away in the shadows of her dark cell. But I feel her amber gaze, bright and warm like a late-spring sun, searing into my own. It had felt the same way when we were in the throne room.

She's leaning against the wall with her slender arms crossed. At first glance, she seems frail. And perhaps some would classify her momentary breakdown earlier as something akin to weakness, but I know better.

I've seen the strength in her eyes. The sheer determination of will.

She might not possess physical prowess, but she is certainly someone who shouldn't be underestimated.

It's one thing for me to understand her, but the way she watches me now as if she's trying to figure me out, is not something I can abide by.

"Don't tempt me," I hiss at her as I storm by her dark cell.

"Wouldn't dream of it," she mutters, voice heavy with derision.

There is no kowtowing her. She isn't perturbed or dissuaded by the usual sorts of threats. And yet, she'd begged for death rather than enter the Hunt. Why? As much as I can relate to her pain, to her desire to make the endless misery stop, I don't think I fully understand its source. It's deeper than the usual misery of life. If it wasn't, she'd be begging for death now still, or she likely would've brought it about herself long ago.

No, it's something beyond just the Hunt that made her falter, but what?

It's foolish to dwell on it. What is she but one more human who will soon face her death, and then none of her secrets will carry any meaning any longer.

I stride forward, my head down as I try to focus on

anything other than the pressure of her eyes tracking my every movement.

The walk back to the throne room is laborious, but only because I make it so. Being in my father's company is not exactly at the top of my list of ways I'd like to spend my afternoon, and more than once I contemplate retreating to my quarters and disappearing for the rest of the day.

Caz talks me out of it when I run the option by him through the blood oath.

"Then what do you say we endure my father's company together? Just like old times."

"Tempting, but I think I'll sit this one out," he says. "I'll join you for drowning your sorrows later though, if you'd like?"

I don't have time to respond before I come upon the grand double doors of the throne room. With a fortifying breath, I shove them ajar.

"Pathetic," my father is grumbling inside, his thumbs rubbing his temples as the last of the prisoners are taken away from him to be returned to their cells.

It appears I've missed most of the showing. I'm supposed to feel guilty, but I can't bring myself to feel even a hint of shame when all I can think about is that maybe this means I don't have to stomach his company for much longer. In fact, I can duck out with the rest of them now and pretend I was never even here.

Unfortunately, the king catches sight of me before I can.

"Ah. How nice of you to join us." With a sweeping of his arms, he gestures me forward.

For a moment, I consider leaving still anyway. That was the last group of prisoners he needed to see today, all of the others having been assessed and given their diets already, and if we're done with the prisoners then my royal obligations here are finished as well.

Then I think of my aunt and the treason I'm going to commit in a few days.

It might be best to stay on his good side until I'm free of him forever.

I continue down the crimson runner until I meet the base of the stair where I await further instructions.

He looks at me with weary eyes. "Not a single child among them?"

I scoff. I can't believe him. He hasn't uttered one word of praise or gratitude for the haul me and my team brought him.

Realizing there's no way I can survive this conversation sober, I go for another glass of wine.

"Excuse me if humans aren't exactly repopulating the realm right now. I'm not sure many of them see the point of bearing children when they're being slaughtered by the hundreds every day."

He glares at me. "You speak as if you're on their side."

I make him wait for my response, savoring each pull of the cabernet as it slides down my throat. Food might've lost its appeal to my kind, but at least wine remains as decadent as I imagine strawberries or chocolate might be.

When my glass is empty, I consider returning it to the table. Knowing how much it will grind against my father's nerves to see me down another drink though makes me decide to pour another.

"I'm not on their side," I tell him, bringing the full glass at eye-height and twirling its ruby contents so he can see. "It's about survival. If we deplete them as a resource, if they die out, where do you think that leaves us?"

He waves me away. "Blighted we suffered. Bloodied they'll fall."

"You're so hell-bent on revenge that you can no longer think clearly. We don't have to kill the humans to feed—"

He slams his fists against the armrests of his throne. "And

you just expect them to give us their blood willingly?" Spit flies from his mouth when he screams.

With a shrug of my shoulder, I open my mouth to elaborate. Whether he believes me or not, I've actually thought this through quite a bit. There are humans who are willing to provide blood to us in exchange for resources. Humans who are exhausted by having to look over their back their entire lives and ready for a change, for peace. Rebuilding trust will take time, but we can do it if we're willing to try.

Not that I have a chance to tell him any part of my vision for the future. For whatever reason, the words we've briefly exchanged have already pushed him over the edge.

"You think we didn't try that?" A vein bulges from his temple as his yelling intensifies. "You think we were so hasty to kill in the beginning? After everything we'd been through? We were just grateful to have our lives back! We wanted nothing more but to live! And those self-righteous simpletons were too hateful to ever give us a chance!"

I'm stunned into silence.

This is more than he's ever shared about what that time in history was like.

I knew that humans had feared us, so much so that their Magistrate declared all noctis dangerous and orchestrated a manhunt for all those who didn't willingly turn themselves over to the Capital.

But could what my father's saying be true? Did the noctis really first try to live in peace?

I fumble to find something to say, and like a bumbling idiot I settle on, "I-I'm sorry. I never knew—"

"Of course you never knew," my father sneers, making me regret my empathy. "Like the humans you were raised by, you've ever only seen us—seen *me*—as the monster they painted us as."

"That's not true," I protest. "I didn't fully understand what our kind were capable of until the day you unleashed Harland upon my family."

"Your *family*." He spits the word out like poison. "If they were family, why did they hide who you were? Why did they let you feed from the butcher's floor instead of honoring your true nature as a hunter?"

My fists become so clenched that I fear I might tear through my palms. "My mother was protecting me from *you*."

"She was protecting you from the very humans who would've seen you executed!"

I stagger backward, his words striking deeper than I anticipate.

I'm used to his tongue-lashings. After years of disappointing him, I've developed a tough skin to the many ways in which he'll verbally assault me: I'm not good enough, not trying hard enough, not taking things seriously enough—I've heard it all a hundred times before.

But this time it's different.

This time, I hear the truth for what it is.

My mother did many things to conceal me from my father, of that I am sure, but perhaps her motives weren't exclusively about him. How many times did she sneak me away from our neighbors so I could feed somewhere no one would accidentally stumble upon us? How many times did she whisper into my ear reminding me to pretend to eat human food whenever company was around? How many times did she warn me not to let them see me salivate at the sight of blood?

I always assumed it was all part of keeping my existence a secret from a father who had abandoned her well before he even knew she was with child. I assumed it was meant to keep us both safe.

But now...

Perhaps he's right. Maybe she was hiding me out of fear of

what our friends would do to me if they discovered I was a noctis.

Could it be true that both of my parents were so ashamed of me?

"The only human who ever cared for our kind was your aunt."

Despite my fugue, he still manages to catch my attention. "You mean Aunt Fox?"

Scorn contorts his regal features, his eyes heating as they narrow in on mine. "Not that wench. She's no family to you."

"She married your cousin."

"On my father's side," he snaps. And then, as if he's just swallowed a bug, he adds, "On the *human* side."

Slowly, he shakes his head, and I can't tell at what. At me and my perceived stupidity? At himself for something that was beyond his control like having a human father?

With a sigh, he rubs at his temples again, the same way he had been when I first entered the room. "If you hate me for the rest of your days and believe nothing I tell you, so be it, but trust me when I say you can never trust a human, and you can never trust someone who isn't of your blood. Even then, there will likely come a time when they turn on you as well."

I realize all too late that the *aunt* he was speaking of was one of his sisters, either Kalli or Ursulette's mother, Halira. But it doesn't matter. Just like the former Magistrate Alphonse, no one knows where they are either. But I'd venture a guess that they didn't just turn on their brother out of nowhere.

Even if they had, my father is wrong.

I've experienced firsthand what it's like to form a family without blood connecting you. Sometimes all you need is to understand each other's misery.

Like me and Caz, desperate to be accepted for who we are instead of molded into something we despise.

Like me and Ursulette, who lost our mothers too young and wish every night for just one final interaction.

Like me and—

I shake the thought away before it can fully form. Charlotte does *not* belong on that list and I'm not sure why my mind even considered her for a moment. We've only known each other a few days, not the years that Caz, Ursulette, and I have had together.

And yet…looking into her eyes earlier, I feel like I've known her a lot longer. Like I understood her, and she me. But that is a falsehood that will never happen. Soon I'll be fleeing the castle and turning to a life on the run, and she'll be released to the Hunt to die.

My aunt or a stranger. I can only save one. And I have to choose family.

My father startles me out of my misery and guilt.

"We've received reports that the Shadow Crusade have been active again."

My brow furrows. It's been years since anyone's heard from them. They disappeared shortly after my father claimed the realm, but I always just assumed that was because they were slaughtered.

"Are they the ones responsible for the mangled noctis we've been finding all over the realm?" I ask him.

"I'm afraid we don't know yet. But it does seem to align with their handiwork, what with their obsession with dismantling the dead." I don't know what he means by that, but I decide against asking him, especially considering the dark shadows that spill over him next. "It must be. This seems far too personal."

Not trusting the simmering rage in his eyes, I do what I can to shift his focus back to the facts. "What are these reports you've been receiving? What do we know?"

The smile that splits his face is humorless, unsettling. "Why, we know they're planning an attack, of course. I wouldn't be surprised if that regrettable cousin of mine was leading at the helm, intent on earning back his throne."

He must be talking of the former Magistrate and Fox's husband, Alphonse, but the last thing I want to talk about is my aunt.

"An attack?" I ask instead. "When? Where?"

The hard set of his brow lifts as his gaze meets mine. "Since when are you so curious about our political warfare, son?"

I scoff. He acts as if I flit about the realm without a care outside of myself, never mind that I have friends and family whom I care for deeply, and that an attack on us puts their lives in danger, as well.

Let him think me selfish. I've been done trying to change his opinion of me for years now.

"Since my own livelihood might very well be at stake, depending on what they're planning, *Father*."

It's so rare that I call him by that title. Only in moments like these when I want him to hurt as greatly as I have. It's a fool's goal though. Noctis like him are incapable of feeling anything so profound.

Instead of dismissing me with his usual annoyance at this point in our conversation, the king watches me the way a scholar might observe a newly discovered poisonous plant.

My indifference to him, mingled with the few glasses of wine I've had by now, do their best to numb my desire to care what's on his mind and what he thinks of me. But the longer he stares, the more I start to wonder just what it is he's seeing. Not the perfect heir he's always hoped I'd become, that much is sure.

So what is it then that he finds so interesting now?

He doesn't say and I don't ask.

At long last, he turns his back to me and begins his regal departure down the royal carpet. "In time, you'll understand there's more to concern yourself with than your own longevity," he says from halfway down the hall. "It won't be long now that it'll be you on that throne deciding the fate of us all."

With an inaudible groan, I try to suck down another hearty pull, but find my glass empty.

"Let the day come, then," I sneer. "I look forward to denouncing my crown and giving the title to the first noctis who asks me for it."

My father becomes as stiff as a sword. There's something so satisfying about knowing how easily I can get under his skin.

With my glass still in hand, I uncurl one finger and tap it thoughtfully to my chin. "I wonder who it will be. Perhaps Renee? She certainly has proven her dedication. Or maybe it'll be Ursulette? Can you imagine? She would prove an interesting leader, no doubt. I wonder how she'd balance her devotion to Rhain, while leading our people. I half expect she wouldn't do it very well. The noctis would sooner rather break into factions than follow the lustful commands of those two—"

My father whips around so fast that the candelabras on either side of him blow out. "You are a fool if you think anyone but a Devonshire is fit to lead our people."

"And why is that, *Father?*" I cross my arms, daring to walk closer. "We weren't always in power, you know? And even if we had been, have you met us? Go down the list and you'll find that your options of adequate Devonshires are limited. Halira might've been a doting sister at one point in your life, but she all but renounced you the day you took your throne from Alphonse—a cousin who, from what I've been told, has always been a bit pompous and yellow-bellied, so he's not much of a contender either—"

"We don't need a contender when we have you," he growls, clearly dismayed by his only option.

"I told you years ago," I roar. "I don't want it."

"That's too bad, because it's yours, whether you want it or not."

He spins on his heels, storming the rest of the way down the corridor in a matter of seconds before I can fix my hanging jaw.

He thinks he can just tell me how to live my life forever? Well, he's wrong. He might've held power over me all these years, and he might hold power over me still because I'm the prince and I'm stuck here under his command, but that will all be over soon.

For now, I'll let him think he's won, but I feel immense satisfaction at knowing the truth. Come the Hunt, he'll no longer rule over me.

However, before he reaches the doors to leave me in my solitude, a guard bursts into the room.

"My king. You must come quickly. We need to hide you."

"Hide me?" My father jerks his arm away from the guard before he can get a good hold. I glide across the room to listen. "Hide me from what? What's going on?"

"It's humans," the guard says, glancing between the both of us. "They've infiltrated the castle."

"Where are they?" I demand, thinking only of Caz and my friends. But his answer shocks me more than I anticipate.

"The eastern wall," he says. "They've broken into the dungeons."

16

FOOLS RUSH IN

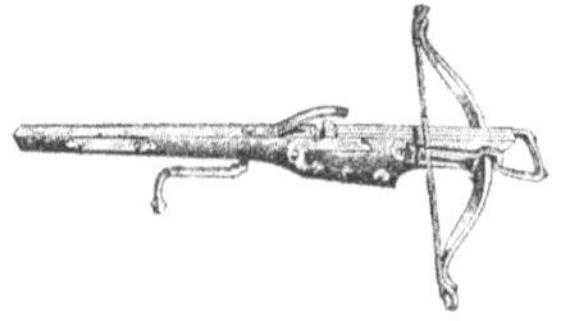

Most of the other prisoners are asleep.

Not me.

As much as I wish I could pretend the reason I'm so restless is because I'm trapped in a castle under guard by who knows how many monsters, only one of the noctis is on my mind tonight.

Normally when I'm within spitting range of a noctis, I have to resist the urge not to plunge a bolt straight through their neck and watch them bleed out.

Only, that didn't happen today.

For all my recoiling as Malachi—as *the prince*, I correct myself—guided me through the dark corridors of Nigh, not once did I imagine myself relieving him or one of the other guards of the daggers in their belts and burying it into their hearts.

I tell myself it's because it wasn't the right time, but I would've at least expected myself to consider it as an option. Instead, I passively followed them along, not a murderous thought in my mind. And for the life of me, I can't seem to figure out why.

This place is changing me.

I need fresh air to right myself. But all I have are these dank walls.

I redirect my focus to anything but the prince, and instead try remembering the paths we were led to and from the dungeon. We'd been taken through such winding routes that none of my memory of the layout of the castle is very reliable, but it's still our best chance out of here. And now that I have a better sense of the guards' rotations, the times in which meals and water are provided, if we can figure out the fastest route aboveground, we just might survive this imprisonment yet.

I'll have Malachi rue the day he ever let his guard down around me—I mean, *Prince Malachi. The prince.* Whatever the fuck I'm calling him.

A thud echoes from down the hall.

My back stiffens against the cold stone wall, but I'm the only one who seems to startle. The sound was so muffled, it didn't rouse anyone else, which is almost more concerning. Who would be coming down here at this hour? And why are they trying to be so quiet? The dungeon door alone is usually a deafening and whining thing.

On the soft feet of someone who has traversed a treacherous, noctis-filled realm on her lonesome for a decade, I slink toward the cell door, keeping to the shadows that the torches cast my way.

I try angling myself to get a better look. The dungeon hall is too narrow to see much farther than a few cells down though. I can't hear anything either, so I can't say for certain if someone approaches.

Not at first.

I trust my instincts more than my senses though, and right now I have the distinct feeling that someone's coming. The air thickens with the heat of their breaths. The quiet of the dungeon livens in that subtle, eerie way it does whenever someone is nearby but out of sight.

Whoever they are, they are skillfully silent, which is both impressive and terrifying.

I'm tempted to call out. At best, one of the guards will yell at me to shut my trap. And at worst? I'm not even sure what could be worse than being locked away in a noctis stronghold. Death, I suppose…

Just when I decide nothing quite so dire could be headed my way and that I have nothing to lose by calling out, I see someone's silhouette in the dim torchlight.

Thanks to the hood that shrouds one of their faces in shadows, the other man comes into clearer view first. I recognize him instantly. His buoyant, curly hair. The colorful rings decorating his fingers and ears.

But even before I recognize him as one of the guards from Valor's Rest, I don't need to see the cloaked person's face to know who's leading this infiltration. I would've recognized him even if he'd waltzed in without a head. That uneven gait. The way he clutches the hilt of his sword as he walks like he's prepared to draw it at any second. The dark, dreaded locks peeking out from his hood.

"Rowland?" I whisper, pressing up against the bars.

He rushes to the cell, my name a harsh breath on his lips. "Charlotte! I can't believe it. We actually found you."

His hood falls back when he reaches me, revealing the only face left in the realm that I've known my entire life. If I were the sentimental type, I'd confess that in the mere seconds it takes him to reach me, our whole lives flash before my eyes. Watching the sunsets on Hulbeck's beaches. Finding each other after our village fell. The many nights we've spent together in my hovel.

His hand closes around mine and my heart becomes as full and serene as a calm blue lake.

"You have no idea..." he begins, but he isn't able to bring himself to say more.

His head hangs and he presses his forehead against the bars. When his fingers squeeze tight against mine, I wish he could hold me like he has on so many nights, his fingers idly caressing my every curve as I drift off to sleep.

But Elison stirs behind us—a smooth stone across my calm surface—shifting onto her other side like she does every thirty minutes or so thanks to her softening hips. Thanks to the baby Rowland put in her belly.

My hands drop to my sides, and he stares up at me.

"What are you doing here?" I whisper, glancing to his accomplice, the colorful guard who Rowland summoned when we were speaking in his office. I can't say that I would've pegged him as the breaking-into-a-noctis-stronghold type. Then again, the dark charcoal lining his eyes does make him more menacing than before.

As if remembering what he's holding, Rowland shoves himself back from the door and begins fumbling with a ring of keys that belonged to one of the guards.

"You're not the only clever one," he says, a hint of pride twisting into a smirk as he crams the first key into the hole. It doesn't turn. He tries the next. "Besides, you'd be surprised how unguarded this place is. We were expecting a challenge, but there was no one patrolling the perimeter, and only one guard down here."

"Cocky sons of bitches," his friend says.

Cocky as they may be, they're also paranoid. I can't imagine that they just left the perimeter unguarded, especially not days before their precious Hunt. Noctis are gathering from all over the realm. Surely, they have some kind of security. If not to help newly-arriving noctis to find their way once they arrive, to at least deter any non-participating noctis from breaking into the dungeons and eating us for themselves.

Something about this isn't right.

Rowland tries another key.

"Still clear?" he grumbles over his shoulder, frustrated by yet another failed attempt.

"No signs of trouble yet," the man replies. With one hand padding his buoyant and curly hair, he mumbles under his breath, "Unless you count the trouble we've made for ourselves by wandering into a bloodsucker-infested castle."

"I don't want to hear it, Julian," Rowland growls, moving onto his sixth or seventh key.

Julian holds up his bedazzled hands.

"Your friend is right though," I say to Rowland. "This place is trouble, and you've managed to put yourself right in the center of it."

"We're fine," he insists. "Everything is going to be fine. I just need to find the right key."

"It's not fine!" The people in the nearby cages stir at the sound of my shrill voice. "The noctis were crawling all over the grounds when we arrived here, and more were supposed to come every day. You shouldn't have found the grounds empty unless..."

"Unless it's a trap," he breathes, hands stilling on the lock.

"They're coming!" A third member of their party comes stampeding through the darkness. "It looks like the prince is with them."

My breath catches. For Rowland and his impending doom? Because I'm not ready to face Malachi yet? I don't know. But Rowland notices, and the way he fixes his gaze upon me makes me think he knows better than I do.

Then, right before my eyes, the boy I grew up with, the one I might've even fallen in love with, disappears as the leader he's become steps into place.

Rowland draws his sword and uses it to command Julian and their other accomplice to his side.

I shove my hands through the bars. "Give me the keys!"

Without taking his eyes off the dark corridor, he tosses them to me. I lose sight of them as they fly through the shadows cast by the torches and land at my feet with a clash, rousing Mira and Elison.

As I fumble to retrieve them, I see Elison's sleepy eyes blinking over at me. "What's going—"

The dungeon door bursts open. I spin around, fumbling with the first key I can grip onto as Rowland and the others bunch together, weapons readied. I shove my hand through the bars, my wrist bending to get the right angle with the keyhole, but it's harder than I imagined it being, the angle unnatural and the keyhole sticking.

The stomping of soldiers in leather armor rings throughout the dungeon, making many of the sleeping prisoners stir.

Finally, I get the first key in place, but the lock won't turn.

Behind me, I hear my cellmates livening, Elison pushing herself off the cold ground while Mira scuttles back to the corner where she'd been when we first met.

"Are those the keys?" Elison asks over my shoulder. A gasp escapes her when she reaches my side. I don't realize why until she finds her voice again. "Rowland? You…you're here?"

His head might twitch in her direction, but he doesn't break focus. He can't afford to. Noctis emerge from the dark hall, Prince Malachi at the helm.

"Well, well. What a pleasant surprise," he says with unnerving calm and arrogance. There's a dark allure to his voice that feels like slender claws tracing my spine. "Never had I dreamed that humans would be delivering themselves to us and aiding our efforts."

Rowland doesn't flinch. But the fist he has clutched around his sword tightens. A warning.

"Stand aside," he says. "And none of your guardsmen have to die."

The prince rolls his shoulders, his cape rippling like the quiet, distant thunder at the onset of a storm. He doesn't speak as he assesses the three-man party before him. Based on physique alone, Rowland is the only one among them who looks like he can hold his own in a fight, and Malachi seems to be drawing the same conclusion.

At least, that's what I assume he's thinking, until his bright eyes, as sharp as steel, land on me. I don't flinch as his gaze drifts down to the key I have wedged unsuccessfully into the lock and then back up to me.

Something changes in his expression then. Hope? But for what?

He glances to Fox's cell opposite mine and closes his eyes. When they open, his expression has shifted again.

"Tell you what," he says. "I'll agree to your terms, no one has to die today as long as she returns the keys. You three may leave with your lives."

It's the challenge in his gaze that makes my hand falter.

What is the noctis prince up to? He can't afford to let Rowland and his company leave. They need more humans for the Hunt. Besides, there's no reason to agree to his terms when the noctis clearly have them outnumbered.

It's a test, but I'm not sure what for.

"No. They're leaving with us," Rowland says, every muscle in his back flexing. For the first time since they became under threat, he averts his gaze, bowing his head as he considers his next words, a choice weighing heavily upon him. "Keep the rest. But Charlotte and Elison are coming with me."

When I notice that he said my name first, my heart skips a beat. When given an opportunity to save the both of us, he thought of me first. *Me.*

One glance at Elison and I can tell she's noticed too.

For what it's worth, she steels herself well against whatever pain his words might've caused. She might be focused on the same thing we all are: our freedom.

Just the two of us though? He can't be serious. We can't just leave everyone else behind. We'd be condemning them all to their brutal deaths.

What about Mira? What of the other prisoners? Or the woman named Fox who is watching everything unfold like a wolf stalking prey in the night. It hasn't gone unnoticed by me that she is acutely aware of the keys in the lock of my cell door, and I think even from where she's locked away behind iron bars, she's plotting how to snag them away from me.

"Interesting," the prince purrs, one hand stroking his smooth chin. "Not your feeble attempt at a proposition after I was already presenting you with a more than generous offer, but that you'd condemn everyone else in this prison for these two women."

The noctis beside him, the one I believe they called Caz the day I was captured, chuckles. "It'll be even more interesting to see what the other prisoners think of him now that he's sacrificed everyone in this dungeon for the sake of saving his women."

Mine isn't the only neck to almost snap.

Malachi, Rowland, Elison, and I all jerk in different directions, my friends and I gawking at Caz while Malachi's inquisitive gaze pins me in place. I don't trust the way he watches me, assessing every movement, every flicker of emotion that crosses my generally impassive expression.

Why? Why is he so interested in figuring me out?

Rowland struggles to regain his composure, his face flushing and his tongue tripping over his every word.

"They're not my—that's not what I—" Exasperated, he scratches at the tight braids, the same ones he used to despise so much when we were children. When they had once irritated him, they serve to calm him now, the braids a symbol for his mother and the comfort she'd once provided him. Calm and collected, Rowland glares up at Malachi, unintimidated by his size, or the sharp fangs glistening from beneath his lip. "They're members of my community and that's where they belong."

"So defensive," Caz utters from the side of his quirked lips to the smirking Devonshire woman who stole Sable.

Despite my keen eye, I don't spy my crossbow anywhere on her, and my heart sinks. I'm not sure what would be worse, a noctis using her to torture and kill humans or having her abandoned in Gravenburg.

Maybe Rowland found her? That could make sense. Maybe he went searching for me and stumbled upon Sable, discarded in the gutter, and brought her back to his people before setting out to come to our rescue.

If that's the truth, it's too bad he didn't bring her here. I would feel much safer with her at my side once again. Especially considering the sudden turn of events. Some rescue this is shaping out to be.

"We came prepared to fight," Rowland barks, unaffected by Caz's taunt.

"Sure," the prince says, unconvinced and nodding in mine and Elison's direction. "But did they?"

The answer that rushes to my forethought, armed to the teeth and hungry for blood is *fuck yeah, we did.*

But as I stare out from my cell at the boy I grew up with, the boy so stupidly heroic and dependable that he broke into a noctis stronghold just to free us, I realize what I say next won't just impact me, but the one person left in this world that I care about.

For whatever reason, Malachi is giving them a chance to leave here with their lives. I don't know why, and I'm worried about whatever twisted angle he might be playing, but whatever his reasoning may be, it's not an offer we can pass on lightly.

The whole room watches me.

If they were in my position, they might make a different choice than the one I'm about to make. Fox likely would've already broken out of this cell and somehow fled the dungeons without anyone noticing. Elison and the bold men, like Lewis, also would waste no time breaking free, but they'd stand to fight, and almost certainly die fighting, deciding that a death down here would be far more merciful than one on the battle-field of the Hunt. There are others, though, like Mira and Dunce, who have become complacent in their capture. I can't imagine them doing anything but freezing until the noctis retrieved the keys themselves, and then they'd spend the rest of their enslavement sobbing in the shadows, much like they're both doing now.

Then there's me. The person the choice has been left to.

If I try to escape now with every noctis eye upon me, Rowland dies. More than likely, so do we.

Without breaking eye contact with Prince Malachi, I jerk the keys from where they're wedged awkwardly into the lock in my cell door and toss them at his feet. "There. You have your keys back. We're still trapped in here. Now let them go."

His lip twitches, a half-kick of a smile appearing only for a breath before curiosity returns to his expression. Was that all this was to him? An experiment to see how I'd react?

"Char, don't—"

Rowland starts to make a move for the keys, but Malachi shifts his foot atop them.

Everyone in the dungeon stills. The prince bends to retrieve them.

Keys dangling loosely in hand, Malachi crosses the room with the ethereal grace of a peacock basking in the sun. He comes before our cell, his eyes locked with mine the entire time.

Behind me, I hear Elison backing away the closer he

approaches. But I remain where I stand. Unflinching. Unblinking. Heart pounding in my chest.

As if he can hear my rapid heartbeat—and I'm not entirely sure he can't—his gaze flickers briefly to the space above my breast.

"Scared?" he asks so quietly that I'm sure only I can hear him.

"Of a spoiled boy in a crown?" I lean closer, heart thundering louder and louder. "Never."

Without another word, Malachi tugs my cell door. I jump at the loud and sudden clang of it holding itself in place, the lock not budging, and a deep sense of self-loathing washes over me.

Seeing my reaction, a faint smile dusts his face. "Of course not. The brave *Char* isn't afraid of anything. Not even death itself."

He tucks the keys into a pocket in his jacket and behind him I see Rowland squirming to remain where he stands.

"I think I understand now," he says, causing my stomach to dip. Understand what? I don't want him understanding anything about me. "You're afraid of nothing—except the Hunt. That's not unusual, of course. Most humans aren't too keen on it—for all that's wicked in the realm, even noctis like me aren't strong proponents of it."

He realizes his divulgence at the same moment I do, regret flashing across his face.

Not a strong proponent of it? How can that be possible? He helped capture me and brought me to the castle, after all, so it's a little difficult to imagine that he doesn't support the Hunt. But then why else does he look like he's just accidentally told me his deepest, darkest secret?

He recovers quickly, picking up precisely where he left off, his focus still on understanding me.

Maybe two can play that game.

"It wasn't that you wanted to escape the death that awaited

you in the Hunt, just like it's not your own death that you fear now. You're afraid to watch the others die."

There it is.

My greatest fear.

My greatest weakness.

The secret that I've worked hard to conceal for years.

And now the son of my greatest enemy knows it.

I do what I can to stop it from showing in my face, but at this proximity, there's no denying how much his revelation pains me.

With something almost akin to remorse, the prince lowers his head.

"I understand that fear." I have half a mind to punch his pale, flawless face for having the audacity to try to commiserate with me—an actual prisoner who is days away from being served up on a platter for hundreds of starved monsters —but before I can, he adds, "Watching the people you care about…die? Seeing them torn to shreds right before your eyes? It's…it's…"

"Malachi," Caz calls in an attempt to draw the prince out of the dark recesses of his mind and back to the guards he left squared off with Rowland and his feeble rescue party. He succeeds, the prince blinking furiously before meeting the dark-haired noctis' hard gaze. "You know what we have to do."

Slowly, Malachi turns again, this time his gaze veering to the cell diagonal of ours. Hair disheveled, Fox draws nearer, mangled fingers wrapping around the iron bars of her cell as she awaits his next move.

Whatever inaudible communication is shared between the two of them, I can tell by the pained expression he turns on me that it doesn't bode well. His lips move in a motion that I almost think looks like an apology, but that can't be right considering what he says next.

"Throw them in the cells with the others."

"No," I breathe the word.

Rowland stiffens, just as dumbfounded as I am.

"Keep them spread out," the prince continues, spinning on his heels and marching toward his men. "They were bold enough to attempt this botched rescue mission. There's no telling what they'll try to do if they're allowed to strategize."

Rowland braces for the swarming noctis, but they snatch him and the others swiftly. I watch helplessly as he struggles against their clutches, but they outnumber and overpower him, and there is nothing neither him nor I can do now.

"You—you said we'd go free if she returned the keys!" Rowland bellows, a last-ditch effort to appeal to the prince.

Malachi doesn't heed him. He continues marching down the dark corridor, cape billowing behind him as he leaves his guards to do their work. "I am the prince. I can do whatever I please."

17

A HEART'S BETRAYAL

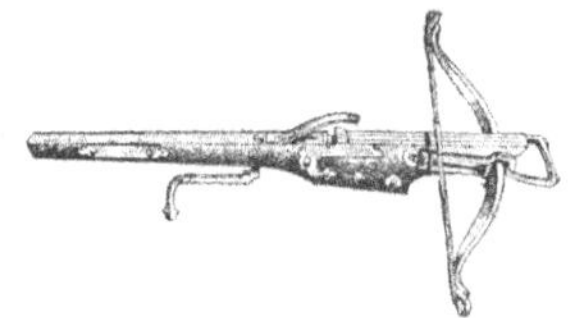

Whatever insight Malachi gleaned into my relationship with Rowland had apparently been lost on his guards, for when they divvy up his crew into separate cells, they place him in the one beside mine.

He waits until they leave before coming to check on Elison and I.

"Genius plan," I tell him. "Now you're stuck here too."

"I was trying to help," he growls.

"By getting yourself caught and leaving your community leaderless?" I fold my arms and turn around to slam my back against the bars. "You didn't think anything was off when there was no noctis standing between you and the humans they've captured for the Hunt?"

"We scoped them out all night!" he insists. "They've only had a few noctis on patrol. I figured they were just busy preparing."

He did everything correctly. Even if he hadn't, I should be grateful he came after us.

But I can find no such appreciation for him condemning himself and making our escape all but impossible now. They'll be on high alert if they weren't already. And now instead of needing to get Elison, Mira, and I out, our numbers have doubled.

"You shouldn't have come."

Even without watching him, I know the look on his face. The quiet indignation.

My heart puckers at the bitter sting of retribution that settles there. He thinks he's mad? He knows nothing of it. I didn't betray him by sleeping with his only friend. I didn't send him off on a suicide mission to search for said friend, ultimately leading in his capture. And I didn't come traipsing after the both of them, getting myself caught and alerting the guards to the weaknesses in their watch.

We stand there in a familiarly charged silence, one that feels oddly comforting considering the rest of the gloom around us.

Until Elison joins us

With one hand on her nearly-flat belly, she approaches Rowland as if I'm not even here. Even from the corner of my eye, I can see his hand reach for hers. It's so tender. So caring.

It makes my heart bleed anew.

I wonder if I've ever seen them interacting before, or if this is the first time? If I had, how could I have missed the way they behold each other? The gentleness with which they take each other in and relish the company?

There's a tear in her eye when Elison says to him, "Thank you for trying to rescue us. It means a lot, Rowland."

"We're in this together. All of us," he says, turning to me almost as if he thinks I need a reminder about being a team player. He doesn't give me enough credit. The only reason I'm even in here is because, against my better judgment, I was *being a team player*. "Now we just have to figure out how to get out of here."

Elison looks curious. "Until you arrived, we weren't sure there was a way out. How did even you get in?"

"It wasn't anything special," he says. "We came in through the main entrance."

Despite wanting to put as much distance between me and them and bolt to the opposite corner of this cage, my curiosity piques, as does my desire to get the fuck out of here before it's too late.

"Did you see any other ways in?" I ask begrudgingly. I don't want him to think he was right in coming here, but maybe he's gleaned some new intel that might be of use to us. "Was there another door, or are there any windows leading into this place that you think we could sneak out of?"

I glance over my shoulder and find Rowland shaking his head. "No, nothing like that. But...on our way down here, we might've found a passage that led from the dungeon into the castle."

"What do you mean? Like a secret corridor?"

"Something like that. We didn't know which way to go so we followed every hallway we came by. One of them led us so far astray that I was pretty sure we were beneath the castle at one point. But we kept going. We needed to be sure they weren't keeping you down that way. We reached a dead end and were about to turn around before Julian noticed a dim light that was bleeding from the bottom of the wall. I gave the wall a shove and it opened into a room colder than even the dungeon, but it was furnished and carpeted with fancy rugs. It seemed like the kind of place that might be inside a castle."

"And then what?" I press him. "Where did it lead?"

"How would I know? We didn't follow it. We didn't come here to infiltrate the castle. We came here to find you two."

I suppose that makes sense. The three of them would've only gotten themselves killed considering how many noctis are supposed to be here.

"You did the right thing," Elison says reassuringly, and I have to refrain from rolling my eyes. It's no wonder he likes her. She's so agreeable. Far from me. "And now we know something that the noctis didn't want us to know. We can use that information to our advantage."

It takes me a moment to figure out what she's insinuating. "Hang on. Are you suggesting that when we break out of these cages that instead of finding the closest exit outside, we wander into a noctis stronghold? No thanks."

"What else can we do?" Rowland asks, voice stern but as quiet as mist in a meadow. "I'm not willing to sit around and wait to die."

"Neither am I!" I counter.

"I'm sorry to interrupt but—" a meek voice calls from our cell, and the three of us spin to find Mira rubbing her arms, unsure where to settle her gaze. "But I'm afraid Charlotte is right. That plan is awful. No offense. And, well, it doesn't matter if there's a way out now, anyway. I'm afraid you already missed your window of opportunity."

Rowland leans closer. "How so?"

Elison pinches the brim of her nose. "It's the Hunt, isn't it? We're too late. It's here."

"That can't be right," I say, my thoughts racing. They just assigned us our meal designations. If the Hunt was so soon upon us, why even bother? There must be something else. "What is it, Mira? What do you know?"

"It's not the Hunt," Mira says, and the tightness in my chest temporarily loosens. "Not yet. That's still a few days away. But...it's the king. *He's* here now. And I overheard the guards. They said they'd been waiting to commence the celebration until his arrival, and now it seems that they'll begin."

"Begin what exactly?" Rowland asks.

Mira swallows, tucking a chunk of dark hair behind her ear. "I—I don't know, exactly. But the way they talked about it, it sounded big. Like the grounds would be crawling with noctis for the rest of the week as they...indulged themselves in their vices."

Soothing herself, Mira's begins rubbing her arms.

"That's actually perfect!" Rowland pushes off the bars with excitement. He paces. "That means they'll be distracted. Maybe drunk if we're lucky."

Elison winces. "Do they drink anything other than..."

Her unfinished question turns my thoughts to Malachi. I do what I can to ignore the burning sensation that consumes me from the inside out, but it refuses to go away. It's like he's still here, watching me in that far-too-intimate way that Rowland sometimes does when he's figuring out more about me and the walls I've put up.

Only, with Rowland it's taken him a decade to fully understand those secret parts of me. Malachi's barely known me a week.

"Maybe," I say, trying to stay focused on the present conversation and getting us out of here as soon as possible. "Prince Malachi was drinking something earlier. It could've been wine."

Rowland's expression sours. "Prince *Malachi?* You're calling him by name, as well as title now?"

The heat in my chest burns hotter, but I roll my eyes and ignore his very perceptive questioning.

Fuck me for even opening my mouth.

"Whatever was in that glass," Elison interjects, and the way she looks at me makes me wonder if she isn't intentionally saving me from his accusations. "They're a bunch of brutes a few nights away from an expedition. If I were them, I'd drink."

The smile Rowland flashes her way makes my heart ache. On second thought, maybe she didn't interject for me, but for Rowland. Maybe her goal had been to alleviate his frustration, to give him a reprieve from the chaos of the night by granting him the simplest yet most profound things: an opportunity to smile.

Suddenly, I become all too aware again of their close proximity and the way I feel like a weed trying to sprout between two lilies.

"It's getting late," I say abruptly.

"So?" Rowland laughs. "Got somewhere else important to be?"

I cross the small cell to where Mira was cradled earlier and slide to the floor. "It's been a long night is all. We should rest. We can talk more tomorrow."

I don't glance their way again, though I think if I had I might've caught Rowland watching me, slack-jawed, and trying to work up the words to say. If I had looked a moment later, I would've seen Elison step into his line of sight, blocking me from view, and leaning her forehead toward his.

As I curl up on the stone floor, I'm acutely aware of their conversation. Their caring whispers and hushed giggles.

I force myself to be okay with it. They deserve each other far more than I ever did. They deserve whatever few tender moments they can have before the end.

18

BOOZE, BLOOD, & DEBAUCHERY

The blood that drips onto my tongue should be sweet, decadent.

Instead, it coats my tongue like ash.

I hand-selected the beauty before me, as well as two others, to join me in Nigh specifically for the nectar that I've known to pour forth whenever they break their skin for me. My father has never approved that I keep a selection of humans on standby, largely because he abhors the idea of having to keep them fed and housed under his dime, and because of the political discourse it can arouse when other noctis discover that the prince doesn't kill his meals and has his own personal selection of blood. Those conversations can get particularly heated, especially around the Hunt when so many are thirsting for blood.

However, what he despises most is their mere presence.

Since the day they turned on him, he's never trusted humans.

Only because I am a prince—and only because I threatened once that I would only eat the blood of pigs if he didn't permit me this—does he allow me to shelter a small entourage of humans.

They traveled with my father, his journey far safer and more suitable for humans than the gathering party I headed. And I am eternally grateful they're here. Given the events of the past few days, I've been thirsty. Only, no matter what I drink, I can't quench my thirst.

Gently, I shove the young woman back. "This isn't working."

It's been like this for days now. Ever since those humans broke into the dungeon, I can't seem to enjoy anything. Their arrival has struck a match to my father's paranoia, which had already been scorching after the reports he received of the Shadow Crusade. Now he's tightened security even more.

How am I to uphold my promise to my aunt with the grounds crawling with noctis on strict orders to attack anyone behaving suspiciously? I knew it would be challenging to break her and her sons out, but it seems impossible now. Already my father's guards have apprehended two of our own, one man who was simply too drunk and had accidentally stumbled into one of my father's personal quarters—an act punishable by flogging under even normal circumstances—while the other was a girl, barely outside of her youth, who had giggled at the expense of the king when she was among her friends. A harmless jest a few eves before the Hunt, and now her screams ring throughout these halls as my father delivers her punishment himself.

I fear I won't be able to succeed in my task, but I worry I can't ignore it either. How much longer until my father loses interest in Fox, in her children? How long before he kills them all? Could she be right? Is that what he planned for her so soon?

For Fox's sake, I've resorted to locking myself in my room. It's best that I stay out of my father's eye. It's the only way I'm guaranteed not to rouse his suspicions or bother him, lest I find myself prematurely sent back to Neveridge.

"Leave me," I tell the woman, throwing my legs over the armrest.

"But...sir?" She wraps a handkerchief around the incision on her bleeding arm and I am grateful to have the scent alleviated from the air. I just need to focus, clear my head. "Sir, y-you haven't finished. If you'd like, I can—"

For a moment, my tongue pricks with anticipation, but there's no appetite to back it. I wave her away. "That's quite alright. I'm finished for now. If I need more, I'll summon you."

For a moment, she looks as if she might try convincing me otherwise. I don't know whether to feel guilty that she feels so responsible for my well-being or touched by her concern. I'd like to think she stays here of her own volition, that I've provided such a fulfilling life for her and the others in my entourage that I've earned their trust and loyalty.

Her meek bow tells me otherwise.

I suppose I can't blame her. Although I've promised she will have my protection for as long as she is in my care, I imagine it wasn't much of a choice. It's as my father said, the humans don't want to give us their blood willingly, and it's likely she's only agreed to it out of fear of what might happen if she ever denied me.

Gathering the hem of her skirts, she scurries across the room to a table by the door. A freshly washed linen rests beside a basin, filled to the brim with red, glistening fluid.

My blood.

She dips her fingers into it without hesitation and hastily smears it down her neck, making sure that her most prominent veins are concealed. It's the only way the others won't feed upon her, the only way I can mark my—for lack of a better word—territory.

When she's finished, she wipes her hand on the cloth and

throws the door wide. She gasps, drawing my attention to the figure standing just outside my bed chamber.

"Come on," Caz purrs, a wicked grin curling up his cheeks. "I'm not that horrendous, now, am I?"

The young woman whimpers. I feel the need to intervene to put her at ease.

"Shows what you know," I tease him. And then to her I say, "Thank you for your generous offer today, Nadine. Rest easy knowing that with my blood on you, none will give you any trouble."

She gives me a curt nod before disappearing into the hallway. Only once she's gone do I realize that I'm not sure what will happen to her once my aunt and I are free from here. She and the others I keep on hand will likely be descended upon, maybe even tortured for intel they are not privy to.

Watching Caz casually enter my room, I'm tempted to ask him to take care of them and help them escape once I'm gone, but even that would put him at risk. I'm afraid the humans I've promised to keep safe are on their own.

"Another unfinished meal?"

"Concerned about my figure?" The wry smile I flash him is only half-hearted, my mind still preoccupied elsewhere. "Or were you hoping for my sloppy seconds?"

Caz doesn't miss a beat. "Both, of course."

As he enters, he glances about the bedchamber as if he hasn't seen it a dozen times already. Or perhaps he's as equally disturbed by it as I am.

Every time I enter this room, I feel like I'm willingly walking into my father's suffocating, domineering gaze. Everything is so uptight, so stuffy, it makes it difficult to breathe. And no matter how much dishevelment I attempt to incur during the time I spend here, the room is always returned to the same pristine tidiness as it was when I first entered, as if my father himself oversees the cleanliness of this room. My discarded garments tossed haplessly about the floor are always returned to my wardrobe, cleaned and pressed—sometimes within hours of me discarding them. The two Devonshire banners that hang from ceiling to floor—the golden *Ds* embroidered on them unoriginal and unimposing by nature—are kept well dusted, the crimson fabric relentlessly bright against a backdrop of grey stones. And no matter how many times I open windows that overlook the Shadowthorn and give this room its magnificent view, I always find them closed, locked, and the curtains drawn. As if it's a crime for this room to not only breathe, but also see the light of day. As if this room is as much of a prisoner as the rest of us are.

Often, I wonder if he did it on purpose. If my father oversaw the design of this room just so it would feel as if he was always watching, always disapproving, and controlling my every move.

And yet, I find myself here often.

Where else am I to go when the castle is crawling with boisterous, excitable noctis and all I want is a little privacy.

I watch Caz cross the room with increasing concern. He didn't have to come all the way up here. He could've easily called to me through the blood oath. And although he heads straight for the liquor table near my desk, surely, he didn't come all this way for a casual drink.

He pours two glasses and delivers one to me where I lounge.

"What are we drinking to?"

"You tell me," he says, tossing the drink down his throat before I can even answer. "What's got you locked away in your tower while the rest of us are down in the lounge celebrating like gods? Guilt? Fear?"

Then he stares at me, holding out his empty goblet with a look that says *what are you waiting for? Drink.*

I don't protest.

My tongue puckers as the tartness fills my mouth, and I'm ashamed to admit that I feel more anticipation for the way it'll warm my belly than I did while drinking Nadine's blood. It makes me pull even deeper, draining the goblet of its every drop before looking back up at Caz.

With a smack of my lips, I hand him my empty cup. "You think I'm so rudimentary that I'm just up here sulking like a child?"

"Of course not." He takes it and hastily refills both of our drinks. "But something has you hiding up here. As your friend —and most impeccable guardsmen—I came to figure out what. You can either tell me now of your own accord or"—he shoves another full goblet into my empty hand— "or I'll get you drunk enough that the truth finds its way out anyway. Your choice."

"You say that like I don't enjoy having a good drink or two."

"Oh, believe me, I'm hoping you'll pick the latter," he says, that crooked smile of his becoming even more askew as he folds his arms and watches me take another drink. "Besides, we've been waiting for you to join us all day. I figure a little booze might loosen you up so you will."

My mood shifts in an instant, the goblet halting on my lips. "I'm not going down there."

"And why not? Too preoccupied with your sulking?" When the only response he gets from me is me finishing my drink and nestling back into my chair to get some rest, he tries another tactic. "We're playing your favorite game."

"Oh yeah?" I chuckle at his ludicrous attempt to goad me. "And what game is that?"

"How-Drunk-Can-You-Get-Off-Drunk-Humans."

One eye opening, I give him a scathing look. "That's *your* favorite game."

He laughs to himself. "Oh right. I suppose it is. Oh well. So when are you coming?"

My patience starts to wane to the point where I can't even get comfortable where I lounge anymore. "I already told you—"

"Yeah, yeah. I heard you. Mr. Important Prince is trying to think himself out of whatever problem is ailing him. He thinks himself undeserving of fun until he's figured out every angle and every option of the troubles on his mind—and even then, is he ever truly deserving of fun?"

Groaning, I shove myself out of the chair. A headache is beginning to throb at the base of my skull, and as much as I know it is most likely because I haven't had a decent meal in over a week, the more Caz pesters me, the more I'm tempted to blame it on him.

Anything to avoid the truth.

Anything to avoid having to tell him that I'll be leaving soon when I'm not ready to say my farewells.

"You're wasting your time, Cazimir." I knead at the dull ache at the back of my skull. "I'm fine. I just have no interest in going down there."

"Why not?"

"I just want to be alone."

"Bullshit. You're lying." He strides toward me so fast that I jolt where I stand, his eyes searching mine with scary determination. "What's got you so freaked out that you'd rather stay in this depressing ass room than come be among friends?"

Finally, I can hold back no longer.

"Because I just can't!"

My voice booms, startling him into silence. But it's not out of fear that he falls quiet. No, there's a knowing in his eyes as he's beginning to understand, or perhaps admit to himself what he might've already suspected.

"Soon?" he asks.

My throat doesn't feel strong enough to speak, so I merely nod.

"What's the—"

Someone groans from the doorway, cutting him off before he can finish his question, and a woman enters my room. A waterfall of white hair flows around her face and down past her shoulders.

Ursulette plants one hand on the curve of her hip and watches us with an air of disapproval that must be a perfected Devonshire trait. "You're still up here, Caz? How long does it take to convince someone to join their friends for a drink?"

"Not all of us have your womanly wiles," he says, falling back into his casual, boyishly amused demeanor so easily that I almost question whether the past few moments even occurred.

She tosses her hair over her shoulder. "You've got that right."

Unlike my brother, it takes me longer to transition. "So, Ursulette, uh. What brings you here?"

"Did you not just hear me? We've been expecting your company."

"Like I told Caz, not tonight."

"Or last night, or the night before." She counts the days on her fingers. "So tell me, if not tonight, then when? Honestly, I'm surprised you're not racing down there after what Caz had to tell you about your father—"

That catches my attention. "What about my father?"

"He didn't tell you?" Ursulette's silver eyes stray from me to Caz, pinning him in place. He shrugs, warranting an irritated huff from her. "Your father's been looking for you. He stopped by the lounge not too long ago and…someone told him you'd be up here."

"She conveniently left out who," Caz interjects.

Ursulette silences him with a glare. "Fine. It was Rhain. But he is rather…inebriated. He wasn't thinking clearly."

"When isn't he inebriated," Caz adds. "Or thinking."

Unamused, Ursulette returns her focus to me. "The point is, you can remain up doing whatever it is that you're doing and await your father's imminent arrival, or you can come down to the lounge for a drink and...berate my lover for being a drunken buffoon."

Even on a normal night when I don't have a legitimate reason to avoid my father, they know I'd do just about anything to avoid being subjected to his presence.

It's no choice at all, and they both know it.

Besides, it's not as if I didn't want to see my friends before the Hunt begins tomorrow anyway, before my life changes forever.

I decide it's time for me to make the most of the evening.

Snatching Caz's goblet from him and handing him my empty one, I chug the contents in one gulp and flash them a smile that's all teeth. "Berating Rhain? Now, that seems like a good time."

We leave my bedchamber, taking a less-traveled route to the lounge in an effort to avoid bumping into my father. Thankfully, our efforts are rewarded, and we make it to the lounge a few stories below without so much as catching a whiff of him.

The air is thick and hoarse here, plumes of smoke from the cigars coat everything in a dreamy haze. The moment we enter, I'm overcome by the warmth of the place, a blazing fire in the hearth only accounting for half of it, as the rest seems to ripple in hearty waves of laughter from my friends at the bar.

Rhain is hunched over the counter, one hand holding him upright as the rest of him animates what appears to be a hilarious and daring story of one of his many tantalizing escapades. Everyone around him smiles and gasps. There are a few unfamiliar faces among them, other noctis who have traveled far for a chance to participate in the Hunt, but a red-haired woman sits directly before him, and I halt before we go any farther.

"You failed to mention Renee would be here."

"You failed to ask," Ursulette says flippantly before leaving me where I stand and waving excitedly at Rhain.

He stops in the middle of his story just to greet her properly —and to shove his tongue down her throat. Caz practically has to tear them apart before they can start ripping each other's clothes off. When he does, there's a moment when it looks like Rhain might rip his throat out—after all, coming between two mated noctis is a risky endeavor, especially two who are so early in their devotion to one another.

Fortunately for us all, no one has seen me for almost an entire day, and the moment Rhain catches sight of me across the room, his hatred is replaced with eager enthusiasm.

"Malachi!" he hollers, fists pumping overhead.

He pulls me in for a hug, one that nearly cracks my ribs and makes me lose my breath. As I pat his back and try to dislodge myself, I notice Renee watching. There is a fury in her eyes that outmatches any rabid beast. Or perhaps it's lust. The two are often easily confused when I catch her staring at me. Sometimes they're both present, warring with one another, and on occasion I've wondered if it would be easier if we just had the encounter she keeps propositioning me with. It's not as if Caz would care. He's told me as much, himself, though I have wondered if it wasn't at her behest.

The only problem is, I'm not sure I've ever truly wanted her. I admire her fire, the fierceness with which she approaches everything. And she is of course beautiful, no doubt. I imagine between the two of us, we have enough experience in the bedchamber to keep one another entertained for a millennium. But I'm afraid that's where our opportunity for connection would end. And what's the point in tampering with a decade-long friendship for a few nights of fun?

Renee's lips quirk, suggesting she's still willing to find out.

Clearing my throat, I give Rhain one final, hearty pat on the back and gently shove him away from me. My hands are the only stability he has until Ursulette slides back under his arms, holding the lanky weight of him. His eyes shine like gold amidst his bronze complexion as he gazes up at her.

That look. I thought I'd had that once. Of course, I'd been wrong. However, I can't help but still chase that feeling of being so utterly enamored with someone that anytime I'd gaze upon them I'd be oblivious to a tornado heading straight toward me.

Suddenly, Rhain sobers as if he's remembered something horrible. "Malachi! Fuck me 'til world's end. I didn't mean to tell him anything. It just slipped. You know? The man has that effect on a room, and I'd already drank an entire barrel of"—he glances up to Ursulette, brow wrinkling— "What have we been drinking?"

"You"—she says, reaching across him to shake the empty glass in his hand— "haven't been drinking a thing since dinner. I told them to cut you off. How is it you seem more drunk than when I left you?"

With a squiggly grin, he gestures to a room of people who erupt with a chant of his name.

Ursulette rolls her eyes despite herself and disappears into the crowd, leaving Rhain to battle with his balance on his own, though he seems confident he can handle it.

Now that I'm down here, I can see why Caz insisted I come. When I think of the Hunt, I think of the old noctis set in their ways and stuck living in a past that never worked for them or anyone. Like badges of honor, they wear the scars of being trapped inside the Shadowthorn no matter how long it's been since they were freed. They carry the weight of the soon-after noctis rebellion and the disdain the humans had for them in a time when they were as equally frightened and unsure of the future. They're a bitter, fearful, sordid lot that only ever talks about their prowess in battle and their plans for dominating the realm—with Tor Devonshire at the helm, of course.

But those congregated here, in our lounge, in our safe haven, they are of the newer breed.

We didn't choose this life. We were the bastard sons and unwanted daughters who were born into bloodshed. We know our nature, of course, but we are closer to our humanity than our elders ever can be again.

Whatever they endured in the Shadowthorn, it changed them for life, and what I endured as a small child changed me too. Sometimes I don't notice myself slipping into the darkness, the isolation. But Caz does. Just like I do when it happens to him. And when it comes, it's best to be in good company and not locked away in a room somewhere dwelling on the things that could've been and never will be.

I glance at Caz and send him a word of gratitude through the blood oath.

He nods and nothing more needs to be said between the two of us. Tonight isn't about gloating. Tonight is about friends, family.

Before Rhain can launch into another drunken apology and waste what little time we have left of the evening, I grip his shoulder.

"All is forgiven, Rhain." Turning to Caz, I cock my head. "Now, you dragged me down here and I still don't have a drink."

"Oh, but don't you?"

Ursulette appears, somehow managing to hold four different glasses in her hands, and making it look effortless. She hands one to each of the boys, keeping the last for herself.

"To answer your question," she says to Rhain, hoisting her drink into the air by the thin stem. The red liquid dazzles in the firelight's glow. "*You've* been drinking shit wine that was likely made by the grotesque feet of peasants. But *this*—this is a new kind of drink. One fermented in oak barrels full of human hearts and veins and decadence."

My tongue pricks at the thought.

My mind, however, knows I should be repulsed. Normal humans would be. This is evolution though. This is our nature. That is the mantra that has guided us all through our guilt and to a place of self-acceptance, anyway. I'm not sure it applies to indulgences, such as wine, just like I'm not sure it applies to extravagant events like the Hunt.

But when my friends raise their glasses, I join them without showing my hesitation, anticipation heady in the air.

The invitation to drink comes in the way Ursulette tilts her head, a smirk flirting at the edges of her mouth. We bring our glasses to our lips.

"They call it," she continues. "Sangwine."

Just as we tilt our glasses back, Caz bursts out in laughter. A fountain of red spews from his mouth, drenching Ursulette and splattering her hair. She looks like she's just walked out of a massacre, red wine dripping everywhere.

This, of course, turns Rhain into a cackling hyena.

I, however, find myself too impressed by the eruption of flavors filling my mouth to use it for anything other than savoring every second. As a noctis, there's very little that tantalizes our tastebuds. For some, even blood can be an acquired taste. For most though, it's one of the few substances that our bodies don't find repulsive. For whatever reason, one of only a few others is wine and the garnishing flavors the winemakers add to it. The rich berries, the bitter nuttiness, and the floral notes can oftentimes quench our thirst and satiate our appetite when we have no one to feed upon, or simply when we're in need of a change of flavor. Coffee is another. And I know from some experience that we can even stomach raw meat, not just the blood.

It should be no shock to me that this sangwine would make the short list of acceptable things that I can ingest. Wine and blood, what better possible combination could there be?

More surprising, however, is that I think I might like it even more than fresh, warm human blood.

I wonder if I'm the only one, if it's because of the way I was raised.

Disgusted and drenched, Ursulette wipes away at what she can of the drippage. "Wasteful," she mutters, returning to the bar for a towel.

Caz and Rhain are still howling as we join her, and the laughter doesn't stop for most of the evening.

It's rare that we're all together like this. Not only do Ursulette and Rhain live outside of Neveridge Castle these days, but generally when we do all come together, it's for business—discussing updates and intel they've gleaned from their travels, organizing the rest of the Crimson Guard, training new recruits, and the odd task like finding humans for the Hunt.

We might've spent a couple of weeks scouring the land together, but we rarely had a night to just enjoy each other's company.

And enjoy it, we do.

"Laugh if you want," Renee says hours later, crossing her arms over the deep neckline of her scarlet dress. The dying fire casts glowing shadows across her skin, making her more ravishing than ever, even in the middle of her indignation. "It doesn't make it any less true."

"I'm not saying it isn't!" Ursulette chuckles, one hand idly combing through Rhain's dark, curls where his head rests in her lap. "It's not that I doubt you, I'm just having trouble picturing it is all. You—you said that to *the king?*"

"Of course she did," Caz bellows. "Have you ever met my sister? She would've said the same thing to the gods if they'd have listened."

Renee rolls her eyes. "Requesting a private room so I no longer had to share quarters with my animal-of-a-brother hardly seems the kind of thing to worry the gods about."

"Hey!" Caz barks, seeming wounded. He sniffs his underarms. "I bathe...occasionally. Besides, like you're one to talk. You know, when we were kids, it was like wrestling water to get her to wash weekly. She'd kick and scream any time the maids would try. After a while, our father stopped insisting on it. He said if she wanted to smell like a pigpen and scare everyone away, that was up to her. She was about a month in of a no bathing period when she met you, Mala—"

"That's enough of that." Renee flicks one hand at her brother, the other straightening her skirt over her crossed legs. "We were children. Don't act like we didn't *all* do it."

I've never seen her cheeks a deeper shade of red, which is saying a lot since Caz is quite adept at embarrassing her.

Disagreement breaks out among my inebriated friends.

Though I've heard many a story of Ursulette, Caz, and Renee in their childhoods, how they grew up together, taking turns stressing out the king and Davorin, the stories they've been sharing tonight are ones I've never heard before.

There are many of those, the lives they led before I was brought to the castle a robust and endless supply of entertainment. Although I wouldn't trade what little time I had with my late mother for the world, I often find myself wishing I'd known them all back then, back when we had few cares in the world, before we really understood our roles and our responsibility to the noctis.

While the two siblings start to bicker, Ursulette mutters something to Rhain, inspiring a robust bout of laughter from his belly before he nuzzles back into her lap with an expression that says he's about three seconds away from whisking her up to their room. Renee seems moments away from fleeing, as well.

However, I'm not quite ready for the night to end yet.

In a few days' time, we'll be separated again, set on our

different paths of duty, honor—and at least one of us —rebellion.

It could be years before we see each other again.

For all I know, this could be our last night together.

When there's a pause in the heated argument, I seize an opportunity to intervene, to continue the bantering and reminiscing so that the others might stay. Just a little longer.

"Is that really how you got your room at Neveridge? You just…told the king to give you one?"

Renee takes on an air of indignant satisfaction. "It wasn't so hard."

I watch her incredulously. "I beg to differ. Do you know how many simple requests I've sent that man, only to be denied for the most random of reasons? When Caz and I ripped my cloak, I asked him to summon the tailor for a fitting. He denied my request on the grounds that cloaks were no longer deemed *suitable*. What does that even mean?"

They encourage me with their bemusement.

"Or, when I asked to finally start training with the rest of you. You remember what he told me then?"

When Caz nods, there's an exhausted quality to the movement. "Don't I."

"I'd been at Neveridge for months, and that whole time all he kept telling me was to make the most out of my new home. I didn't think I could, but then I met you all, and thought maybe I had finally found some semblance of belonging and family, and just when I thought I could see myself in the Crimson Guard and was finally warming up to the idea of my new life he told me—"

"He said he couldn't trust you to be trained and not turn around and murder him in his sleep." My head jerks to Renee, surprised by her near-perfect memory. From behind lowered lashes, she adds, "He was afraid of you."

"How do you kn—" I eye her warily, catching the meaning

behind her words and in the subtle ways that she shifts in her seat. "Don't tell me... Do I have *you* to thank for his reconsidering?"

This time, there is no flushing to her cheeks. No embarrassment. No frustration. Only resounding pride.

Caz's mouth is unhinged beside me. Even Ursulette looks surprised, if not impressed.

Part of me always knew I had someone to thank, I just never knew who. At the time, outside of Caz and Ursulette, I hadn't made many friends at Neveridge. Renee and I had met and periodically interacted at one social gathering or another, but I wouldn't have expected it to have been her to speak on my behalf.

"How did you do it?"

Foolishly, I make no attempt to mask my wonderment, and in so doing, I spark a small flame of hope, the same one she always has at the ready, just in case of moments like these when I seem truly awestruck by her.

She is a lioness ready to pounce. "I can be very persuasive when I want to be. And I almost always get what I want."

The tension between us builds in the extended silence that drops like a fallen column in the room.

"Well," Caz says with an exaggerated sigh. Both hands slap on his knees as he hoists himself up. "I need another drink. Anyone else?"

Grateful for the interruption, I raise a finger. Renee does the same, but she stares only at me. When Ursulette shakes her head, Caz doesn't insist or wait for deliberation before continuing to the bar.

"I guess we should call it," Ursulette says, gently ushering Rhain up from her lap. "I think that's a night for us. As always, it's been fun."

"Some of the most fun we've had in ages," Rhain agrees, sitting upright. He takes her hand from his shoulder, dusting each knuckle with a kiss. "Let's not wait as long before the next convening, yeah?"

"Wouldn't dream of it," I say before the guilt can set in.

While the two of them stand, stretching limbs that have gone numb from lounging for too long, Caz returns with a fresh round of the sangwine, and the faintest hint of red tingeing the fangs poking out from his lips.

"I know you passed up on my offer, but I'm a stubborn ass so I brought you each a drink and I expect it not to go to waste."

Rhain takes his without a second thought.

Ursulette, however, has never been so easily manipulated. In fact, of the few who I know to have tried, they're all maimed or dead now.

With childlike impatience, Caz groans. "Ugh, please? Do it, for me? This could be our last taste of blood as a family before we make our way back to Neveridge."

Ursulette considers him, but ultimately takes a drink in one hand, smacking him upside the head with the other.

"Hey!" He winces, the remaining glass of sangwine almost lost.

"Don't you ever try to strong-arm me into doing something I said I wasn't interested in doing again. Understood?" He nods, and just like that, her ire is gone. She loops her weaponized arm through Rhain's, sheets of white hair tumbling over his shoulder like an avalanche when she rests her head. "He's so unnecessarily dramatic. We'll be hunting together tomorrow."

A haughty snort escapes Renee at her brother's demise.

"Not all of us." Caz gives me the side-eye, utterly oblivious of his grave mistake until it's too late.

And just like that, the lighthearted conversation ends.

With widening eyes, Caz blanches as the realization hits him. He tries saving himself from the slip, but the girls are too clever, too astute to let a simple implication like that go unnoticed.

Even Rhain is sober enough to catch it. "What do you mean? Who won't be participating in the Hunt this year? It's tradition."

Ursulette groans. "Oh, do you even need to ask?"

But no one is nearly as irritated by the news as Renee. Her gaze burns into me like a midsummer wildfire. "What does Cazimir mean? Why won't you be participating in the Hunt this year?"

I don't answer her. I can't.

The truth is something that must be kept secret, even with their suspicions aroused, it'll surely make pulling off what I need to do tomorrow morning all the more difficult. Now all of my closest friends will be on their guard, suspicious and waiting.

"For all that is wicked in the realm, haven't we been through this already, Malachi?" Only Ursulette, niece to a king and daughter to a disgraced but historical hero, could roll her eyes with such entitlement and aristocracy. "Yes, it's an unnecessarily extravagant event that serves no real purpose but to entertain the elite and the bored. But you're the *prince*. You're expected to be there, regardless of how you feel about it."

Audibly, I groan, plopping back down to the leather armchair and sinking into the deflated cushion. She sounds like my father, but maybe with a little more care in her tone.

I bury my face into my hands and try to conjure up some acceptable excuse. But she's right. We *have* been through this before, and she's already succeeded in persuading me in the past. In fact, it's why I'm even here this year. For a long time, I refused to show my support. But Ursulette reminded me that when the noctis don't have their entertainment, their killings become sloppy. Reckless. Senseless. It's why we have such an infestation of the ghouls now. They bite just to feel powerful. The Hunt gives them purpose.

The official start tomorrow morning will be the best time to free my nephews and aunt. Only Caz is aware of those plans, and only vaguely since we haven't had a chance to truly discuss it. I didn't want him involved, but more importantly, I want the rest of my friends to remain completely oblivious. It's the only way to protect them from my father's wrath.

Whatever false reason I conjure will have to be ironclad.

The sheepish grin Caz wears only partially exonerates him from my wrath, and only because it reminds me of how frequently he mucks things up and therefore how little faith people are willing to give him.

And *that* gives me a way out of this mess.

"For the hundredth time, Cazimir," I groan, fingers still rubbing my temples. "I said I would be arriving late, not that I wasn't coming at all." I peer up from where I'm stooped. Only Rhain's suspicion seems to be put at ease by my lie, so I go on. "Look, Tor thought it was about time I assisted with the logistics of the Hunt. I'll be transporting prisoners from their cells to the Shadowthorn all morning, until the horns sound."

"And then?" There's a bite in Renee's tone that suggests she's still far from convinced. "I highly doubt that there's a task your father wants you completing that is more important to him than making the first kill and proving yourself worthy of the crown."

"That's not—" Irritation bubbles up in me like the once boiling, caustic waters of the Pits of Bagamore. This event, this *Hunt*, isn't even as important as anyone makes it out to be. Making the first kill doesn't mark the future king, only the king does that. And my claim to the throne has never been contingent upon whether I make the first kill or not. My father has no qualms with nepotism. He just wants me to work for it. To earn my allegiance and devotion.

Unfortunately for him, I will remain to be a disappointment.

But if I am to be convincing and assuage their lingering suspicions, I have to remain focused.

"And then—" I finally answer, focusing on Renee's former question, instead of her latter points "—I'm assisting with readying this place for the concluding events. Once they've made their kill, the noctis will need a place to stay while they await the rest of the Hunt to conclude. They'll likely prefer it if the castle was primed and ready for them."

"That's what you have servants for." Renee's wit is sharp, but her tongue sharper. "What do you take us for? Fools? You can't expect us to believe that he has you on clean-up duty like some common-street peasant?"

It's a blessing that everyone's eyes are on me and not Caz, for his demeanor is wound tightly, the guilt he feels for causing all of this seeming like it's about to eat clean through him, digest his skin and bones, and leave him a liquified puddle on the ancient rug.

Without seeming too obvious, I try to tell him with nothing more than the briefest glance that everything will be alright, that I have this under control.

"No, not clean-up duty. I'll be directing the grounds staff this year. I'll be orchestrating the post-Hunt festivities and entertainment. Blood and booze and debauchery. I'll be responsible for ensuring that everyone is safe, comfortable, and well-fed."

The shield of skepticism that Renee's wielding is tough to crack, and always has been, but I can see her starting to lower it.

Not quickly enough though.

The longer they ponder whether I'm telling the truth, the less likely they will be to believe the lies I feed them. And I *need* them to believe. I can't have any of them caught up in what transpires tomorrow.

There is one strategy I've seen my father use with her that has worked in the past when he hasn't wanted to budge. It makes her feel small, worthless. It reminds her that he is powerful and all-knowing—at least in his mind—and that she will never measure up to him.

I hate myself for even considering using it. But right now I'm desperate.

I muster a saccharine tone that churns even my own stomach and paint a smile across my face like a thin, poisonous spiderweb.

"And this is why my father is always so insistent on the Devonshires continuing to rule. You're being simple-minded, Ms. Vanderbilt. Don't you worry that pretty little head of yours." The knife cuts deep. I can see it in her swelling eyes. But I push forward. "I know what I'm doing, and everything will be well-prepared for you and the others upon their return. In fact, I'll have things running so smoothly here, that I'll likely be joining the rest of the Hunt before lunch, and before any of you can make your first kill."

Caz catches on, notices his opportunity, and seizes it. "Did I just hear a challenge? The Vanderbilts versus the Devonshires?"

The possibility of a competition has all but wiped clean the worry he'd been feeling before, as if the conversation hadn't even occurred.

"Hey!" Rhain turns his outraged but pleading eyes on Ursulette. "What about me? I'm neither Vanderbilt nor Devonshire. Whose team will I be on?"

"Don't worry, my love," she reassures him, a long, pointed nail tracing the curve of his perfect jawline. "I'll take no part in any game if you're not by my side. This is between the three of them."

"Aww," he whines. "But I love a good challenge."

She pats his head. "Not as much as you love a good chase, which you'll still get."

His grin becomes predatorial. "The best part of the Hunt is the chase."

"Two versus one, then?" Caz says, his smile just as wicked. "This keeps getting better and better."

I ease into the light-hearted nature of the conversation like I'm scaling a cliffside over a chasm full of spears. It's difficult to muster an adequate laugh, but I manage what I can and hope no one notices.

"Could just make it four on one," I say. "Might even the odds out."

Caz's robust laughter buckles him while Ursulette rolls her silver eyes. But she and Rhain consider the challenge silently, the math seeming too much in their favor to turn down.

"I feel like you're going to regret this," Rhain says, laughing.

"Regret? I'm not sure I'm familiar with the word."

He gives my shoulder a shove. "Soon, my friend. Soon."

"Fine." Renee's sharp voice cleaves through the heart of our collective laughter. "It's a deal. We'll see if any of us can claim a kill before you wrap up your princely duties and return to the Shadowthorn. You said you'd be joining us midday, correct? Where should we meet? At the border or—"

"No." The word splurges out of me like the first drain of a tapped wine barrel, and when it does, it makes one of Renee's eyebrows stand ready. "I mean," I try sounding more casual, "That won't give me any time to try to get my kill. You'd be meeting me right when I entered the Hunt. That's hardly fair."

"What about at that abandoned camp that used to belong to the—whoever they were?" Caz suggests. His youthful enthusiasm has returned so completely that I'm beginning to wonder if he's already forgotten that this conversation only started because I needed to cover up his accidental slip.

Regardless, I'm grateful for his ability to bounce back. It makes all of this that much more convincing.

"The Warden's Camp," Renee corrects him, cunning eyes not leaving mine. "What do you say, Malachi? Does that work for you and your busy schedule?"

"Yeah." I swallow, throat as dry as a desert. "That should work."

"Alright then, it's settled." There's no toast when Renee lifts her glass, nor are there any words. Before any of us can follow suit, she's already dumping the sangwine into her mouth.

The whole time, she watches me, and I'm too afraid to move for fear of making the mask of casual arrogance that I've plastered over my panic fall or shift, even in the slightest. It's like I'm balancing on a tightrope with a bucket of sand on either shoulder. The slightest breeze could make me lose it all.

"Good," she says, tongue tasting the last droplet of sangwine from the rim of her glass. "I'll see you at the Hunt then."

19

THE HUNT

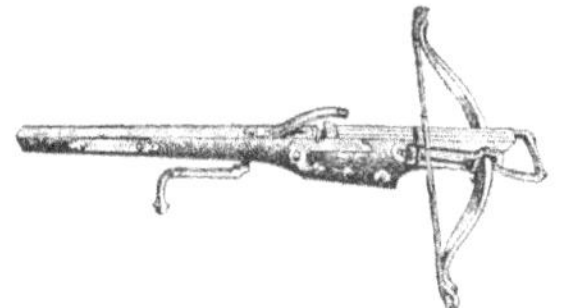

By Mira's calculations, today marks the Hunt.

How anyone was able to sleep last night is beyond me. Not a single one of them tossed and turned for more than an hour, except Elison who only made it up that long because she was feeling sick to her stomach.

Once she finally fell asleep, it was just me.

I lay there awake, frightened. No matter how much we analyzed, no matter how many times we watched the guards and reviewed our options, no other opportunity had presented itself for escape.

And now, once the sun rises, we face death. Worse than death, some of us will be forced to watch as the others are torn to pieces, as noctis devour the only people I have left in the realm.

The thought has my hands trembling like the last crispy leaves dangling precariously from branches at the start of a blustery winter.

The only thing that's been able to soothe me are the songs my mother would sing. Trapped down here in these cells, I can hum their tunes freely without fear of ghouls or noctis hearing me. It's ironic, really. For years I fought the urge to let her songs live through me because uttering a single note would mean my death, but now here, in the early morning hours of the day I die, I can finally breathe life into her songs.

And the one I hear her singing in my thoughts most often is the same one she was humming the morning I left her in her garden so I could find Rowland and Agnes:

Leaves and sprigs
Herbs and twigs

Let them grow, grow, grow
Let them grow, grow, grow

In dirt, I dig
With water, seeds swig

Let life flow, flow, flow
Let life flow, flow, flow

A somber chuckle from the cell beside ours makes me jump.

"You sound just like her, you know?"

I glance over to find Rowland propped up on one of his arms, his shirt discarded beside him.

I avert my gaze from his rippling muscles before my treacherous eyes can betray me.

"I know," I tell him, my heart pinching.

Suddenly, the dungeon door heaves open. A loud, cavernous sound gnaws its way through the dark corridors, and I feel the jaws of death pressing down around us, the sharp teeth of fear puncturing my lungs.

Beside me, Elison and Mira stir, sleepy-eyed and unperturbed for the handful of blinks it takes them to remember what's coming for us today. Then Mira's eyes fill with tears. Elison's hands clutch the belly that she will never get to see grow.

In the cell next to ours, Rowland is scrambling to get his shirt on while his cellmates start to rouse. When our lines of sight catch there's an apology and a promise warring within the shadows of his eyes.

He wishes he could've saved us.

He still plans to try.

Not knowing what he's up to, I focus instead on the noctis scurrying into the dungeon like spiders. Even the shuffling of their feet against the hard stone floor makes my skin crawl as if a thousand ants are writhing beneath it.

There are plenty of cells to stop at—at least ten, maybe more. But as luck would have it, they come before Rowland's first. Once they have the door unlocked, noctis barge into his cell by the dozen.

"What's going on?" Lewis barks in the face of the two cornering him.

He's not the only one to show his frantic frustration. As noctis surround the male prisoners, outnumbering them two-to-one at a minimum, and in some cases more, the men become alive. They yell. They fight. They scream and kick. It's the most action I've seen from any of them since my arrival and I almost want to scream at them for waiting for so long. But for some, there is no better time to fight than when death has finally come.

It's almost inspiring, especially to see them working together. Not all of them, of course. Most are too stunned or depressed by their imminent demise to be able to do much of anything but flail. But there are a few who stand with their backs together, fists raised.

For the briefest of moments, I actually feel hope.

They might outnumber us, but maybe we can fight back? Maybe that's been our problem all along. Humankind has been too content with kowtowing, with being shoved to underground communities and remote villages disguised as ghost towns instead of taking action.

Rowland, is of course, among those rallying. The man behind him, his face is unrecognizable to me, looks like the kind of man anyone would trust having at their back. He has an honest face, an abled body. But most of all, it's his eyes. They tell a story of a lifetime of pain that he's tired of running from. They show a man who's ready to fight and reclaim what he's owed.

Their efforts are futile though.

Rowland's compatriot is one of the first to be snatched and chained, Rowland following soon after.

Terror is something I'm familiar with. It painted my world in black ink the day Hulbeck was taken, and I could never wash away its stain. This terror is no different. Knowing that they're taking Rowland to his death instead of slaughtering him in front of me almost makes it worse. As I watch them drag him and the others away, I feel even more helpless. Against the noctis, I suppose we all are and always will be.

Dragging a dozen or more men in tow, the noctis leave the dungeon in stunned silence.

Elison holds Mira in her arms and rocks her as she sobs while I'm still planted in place like a petrified stump hacked off at the base.

They took him.

Rowland is really gone.

The next hour is an endless cycle of a noctis militia barging into the dungeon, seizing an entire cell of people, disappearing, and then returning for more.

It's my own personal nightmare that our cage is left for last. I had to watch each and every one of these people be dragged out of here and taken to their demise, and although I didn't know all of these poor souls, I still felt for every one of them.

And I fucking hate it.

I hate this wretched thing they call a heart that still, despite all these years, actually cares about this doomed race, actually wants to save them, even when I know I can't.

I can't afford those feelings today. If I allow my heart to open, that's when the real death will come.

So I numb myself to the sensation. I let ice flow into my veins and into my heart until I can feel nothing.

Mira and Elison flinch and hold onto each other tighter when the door opens a final time, but I don't even blink. I barely breathe. I am braced for the atrocity that is about to befall us.

But the carefully crafted internal shield I've strapped to myself cracks the moment Prince Malachi's face appears in our doorway. His presence catches me off guard. He hadn't been down here for any of the other retrievals. I would've recognized him, if not immediately, his birch white hair would've eventually snagged my attention. So what's he doing down here now? In fact, why has he ever come down here? He's a prince. It seems odd that someone of his station would even bother venturing into a filthy place like this unless they were forced against their will like the rest of us. Maybe his father's making him? But if so, why now? Where was he for all of the others?

"That's the last of them?" he asks as the guards filter into our cell.

One of the noctis behind him grunts in agreement. "Just the three."

"Don't underestimate that one," the prince tells him, pointing straight at me.

My body become as taught as Sable's bowstring, ready to snap into action at a moment's notice. But when the guards seize Elison, and then Mira, I have no fight left in me. I realize, every ounce of energy I have left has to be reserved for the Hunt now.

With a careless wave of his hand, the prince—the bastard—sends four guards in for me. This time, I don't fight. It will do me no good now. I simply stand there, arms extended, and let them shackle my wrists and drag me from my cell.

"See you in the Shadowthorn," I sneer from gritted teeth as I'm jerked past him.

The words come from somewhere dark inside me, a place I almost don't recognize as my own, which is fitting because I don't recognize him either. Not today. Where did the gentle man go who I met in his father's throne room just days earlier? There seems to be no sign of him now.

Maybe there never was.

Maybe it was all just an act, a way to get me to cooperate and head back to my cell. And like a bloody fool, I played along.

Surprising me out of my tumbling thoughts, I hear him utter, "I doubt it," before I'm dragged out of sight.

What does that mean?

The door slams shut, and with the dungeon behind me, my attention converges on my surroundings and on our worsening predicament. The three of us are taken aboveground, shuffled like bleating sheep through a crowd of monsters salivating like street dogs.

I'm surprised any of them have the restraint to let us through. The way their hungry eyes follow us, it's as if they're already imagining the feel of their fangs puncturing our necks, the taste of sweat and blood as their tongues lap up the fountain of life that pours from our gaping wounds.

Only one other time in my life have I been surrounded by so many ravenous beasts.

Only one other time have I been so frightened.

I survived it then. Will I be capable of surviving now?

We only stop once we've breached the masses. I glance to Mira and Elison, register the fear in their black, hollowed eyes, and quickly divert my gaze to something far worse. Down the fields, dozens of insatiable, rapacious noctis have gathered. There's another bundle an acre away from them. And another. There must be hundreds of them, spread out into clusters as far as my eyes can see.

If I strain hard enough though, I think I can count at least ten.

Ten cells.

Ten clusters.

We're the farthest group north... Does that mean Rowland is the farthest south?

Before the dread can twist its knife deeper into my watery belly, my eyes are drawn east to the looming Shadowthorn forest.

Even without the Blight hanging over it to cast the canopy and everything underneath in a foreboding sort of darkness, evil still looms over the dead woods. Even from this distance, the earth looks withered, like one footstep would shatter the ground beneath. The trees hang heavily, their bare branches seeming impossibly heavy for the puckered trunks to hold onto any longer.

Long ago, this place was cursed by a Primordial's wrath. It was turned into a haven for demons until the mages stopped tampering with the land's magic. The histories say that when Halira restored the magic they'd stolen, the forest began to thrive once more. Verdant trees and vibrant foliage. It became a beacon of hope for the people, a symbol that their lives could improve despite the darkest of omens.

Then magic disappeared, and everything withered again.

With how much blood has likely been spilled beyond its borders, I wouldn't be surprised if the entire place is cursed.

Hoofbeats pound atop the flat grass, and I spy a trio of horsemen galloping our way. In the center, sitting ramrod straight with a mane of white hair whipping behind him as he leads them forward, is the noctis I loathe most.

"Greetings fellow Hunters." King Tor Devonshire addresses his people with a tight smile and a subtle tilt of his head, one that suggests he knows it's expected of him to bow, but he despises lowering himself to anyone. "We are honored to host you today in commemoration of our most glorious moment in history. The day when we stood up against tyrants and their prejudices. The day we reclaimed our place in the realm."

They all cheer, a sound like a thousand crashing waves on the shoreline. It's been years since I've heard anything so loud, but it's the lie of it that makes my nerves splinter.

He paints them as victims when they slaughtered thousands.

King Tor's hand moves with the grace of a gentle breeze, but I know better than anyone to believe him capable of anything but brutality.

"The humans told us we were monstrous. They told us we were better off dead. They tried to murder us, but what was our crime? Surviving our imprisonment in the Shadowthorn and merely wanting to exist and return home to our families? Today we celebrate who we are in our truest nature and honor our vow to never be anything but ourselves ever again."

A bitterness fills my mouth and upturns my lip. They're hanging on his every word like he's some pariah instead of the monster responsible for the downfall and near-extinction of an entire civilization.

"A few reminders before we release you to your hunting." Pausing for effect, he takes them all in. "You paid for an experience, but this year only the strongest will reap their rewards. The human-to-noctis ratio is admittedly more unfavorable than in year's past, but I'm sure you can appreciate the circumstances we're all facing. It's why this year, we're instilling a one-kill decree—you've all been briefed, so consider this your final warning. Anyone greedy enough to kill more than one human will be imprisoned until the Hunt is over, used as a source of entertainment in the celebration that follows, and ultimately exiled to the Unresting Mountains."

A murmur ripples throughout the group. Even Elison, Mira, and I exchange glances.

The Unresting Mountains is one of the most feared places in the realm, second only to the Shadowthorn.

Now I know why.

King Tor continues. "You have three days to hunt. If you make a kill before the final day, feast upon your prize and then join us back here in the Castle of Nigh, where you'll wait in luxury for the arrival of the rest of your brethren. If you have not been successful in your hunt by the third and final day, you are expected to return to the castle as well. We will celebrate the victories of our people regardless of your individual gains, enjoy entertainment, and of course, round up all of the remaining humans to provide as refreshments for the final days of festivities."

It's no wonder no one has ever survived. Even those skillful enough to last three days in the noctis-infested Shadowthorn are still doomed to be served up on a platter in their banquet hall.

A new thought occurs to my ever-churning mind.

If he thinks he can round us up, that must mean the borders are guarded. Maybe even blocked. Or perhaps he has another failsafe in place to prevent anyone from leaving the forest once they enter.

If he was smart, this sort of information should've been

shared with the participants ahead of time, outside of earshot of those of us with the will to strategize, fight, and live another day. Although admittedly, as of now, I'm not sure how to utilize such intel.

Unless he's doing it on purpose. Unless he's telling them now—telling *us*—because he wants to snuff out all the hope we might have for escape.

"As you can see," he continues. "You have been separated into groups. I hope we've done well enough matching your particular tastes with suitable candidates."

I glance around at their nodding heads, and then to my former cellmates.

It hadn't occurred to me before that there had been a reason why we'd been placed in a cell together, or why the prisoners were retrieved in batches. I wonder what similarities they found between us to decide, anything to give me an advantage when I face them in the Shadowthorn. All I can come up with is our gender. But could it be something else? Something more?

This time, when the king opens his mouth to address his following, he's so close that his poised voice reverberates through my body.

"Those of you in this group requested something out of the ordinary. Something spectacular. A challenge, perhaps. A delicatessen."

Spectacular?

I glance between the sorry faces of the women I've been imprisoned with for the past week. There's nothing spectacular about any of us, unless you count being starved and plucked from our homes by ravenous monsters spectacular.

"At first glance," the king says, gesturing down to us. "The three humans before you might not seem like much. But I assure you, you will not be disappointed. I am delighted to present to you the greatest prizes in the entire Hunt, and they're all yours for the taking."

The king hops down from his horse, leather boots thudding in a patch of dirt where he lands. With the presence of a prowling predator, he strides toward us, snatches our chains, and pulls each of us forward, one at a time, into his darkness.

Elison is first.

"May I present to you a woman with child. Two heartbeats for the price of one."

He shoves her back in line.

Next, he grabs Mira. Spinning her around with pale fingernails that dig into her shoulders, King Tor parades the frightened girl before the hungry mob.

"An innocent twice-over." He explains further, "A virgin who has not yet bled on her moon. The blood you feast from her will be the first she's ever given."

Another careless shove, Mira stumbling over the hem of her long skirts as she crashes into Elison. Her sun-kissed complexion burns with embarrassment as she withers into herself, and I grow to hate the king all the more.

Then King Tor stands before me.

He's just as tall and as looming as his son is. But there's something far more vicious in his cold gaze. Something detached. In the dark depths of his eyes, thousands of the dead cry out for justice. I can see the limbs he's severed without a hint of remorse. The gallons upon gallons of blood he's spilled out of anger, not even bothering to lap at it.

This isn't just about survival for him. It's about power.

Whatever happened to him in the Shadowthorn, it made him snap. He lost his humanity long before he became a noctis.

When he reaches for me, it's like the dead guide me, their vengeance becoming my own.

My bound hands ball into fists and I take a swing at the king.

With a muffled curse, he dodges, my hands flying past his shoulder. I stumble forward, off-balance. He catches me by the back of my neck and steadies me, his sickening smile slithering into place as he addresses the crowd and their roar of laughter.

"And let's not forget those of you who requested a challenge. Dare I say that this one has just proven that she will not disappoint." He glares down at me as if in warning, the sickening stench of copper wafting from his every breath. "She killed two of our own during the expedition. She'll make for a delicious kill." He leans low, mouth pressed to my ear so that I alone can hear his threats. "I hope they make you suffer."

This time, instead of tossing me back in line with my cellmates like a discarded piece of trash, I'm flung forward.

Toward the Shadowthorn.

With a hammering heart, I realize my wrists are no longer bound either.

My wide eyes meet the king's. He shoves the remaining prisoners forward and utters one final word.

"Run."

20

AN ACT OF TREASON

From the window in my stone tower, I watch the noctis assemble. We're doing things differently this year, thanks to the humans my team and I procured, and a half-hearted suggestion from yours truly. The prisoners are retrieved and sent to clusters of noctis, instead of the usual free-for-all-frenzy. I told my father that giving the Hunt an element of elitism might make up for the fact that we're short on humans this year.

To my surprise, he liked the idea.

How ironic that it's taken this long from him to agree with me now that it matters the least.

I almost wish I could stick around to see how well it plays out. Then again, I'm not so sure the noctis who return empty-handed will be anything less than antagonistic, and that is not something I mind missing.

Especially for my aunt and her sons.

As far as I can tell, things are running smoothly down below. The noctis are sticking to their groups and no one has prematurely devoured any of the prisoners yet.

I make a mediocre attempt at searching for any of my

friends, but I can't find anyone. Not even Ursulette, thanks to her new hooded cloak that is likely shielding her iconic hair.

"We can't have you being the only fashionable one around here," she'd said to me when she showed off the brocaded velvet garment this morning.

I don't allow myself to look for the someone else. Besides, I already know she's not on the field yet. Her cell will be saved for last. She's nothing more than a walking corpse waiting to expire now.

Nothing more.

She *can't* be more.

As more prisoners are retrieved from the dungeons and stationed before the Shadowthorn, I know my time has come. My father will give the signal soon, and then the Hunt begins.

I have to go now.

Turning my back to the open window, I leave my room, my cape snapping at my heels as I stride out of my bedchamber and through the nearly vacant halls. Everyone is either participating or has found themselves a nice vantage point to perch in and watch as the spectacle begins.

Still, I don't want to linger about too long. My father regularly participates in the Hunt, but this year with so few sacrifices, he's opted to observe instead, as well as to greet everyone upon their return. It means I don't have long before he's back inside these castle walls, asking every servant for information on my whereabouts.

Surely, if he hasn't noticed my absence yet, he will soon.

For now, he'll remain distracted by his duty—a distraction I can't afford to squander.

My bed chamber is decidedly closer to both of the rooms where the boys are being held—which, consequently, took me days to discover their exact whereabouts. Two secret rooms that aren't even on any of the blueprints of this ancient place. I had to bribe one of the guards just to find out what floor they were being held on, and then bribe two more to learn of each location.

I'd wanted to free them first, but thanks to the Hunt, the dungeon will soon be all but vacant and unguarded, at least for a window of time. It'll be easier to free my aunt now before activity around the castle resumes to normalcy, and the guards return to their usual posts.

I take the most direct path I know, sacrificing some of the stealth I had hoped to utilize today and inadvertently running into more than a handful of servants who I'm surprised to see aren't hanging out of windows or standing in the courtyard to watch. Maybe I'm not the only one who finds this entire ordeal distasteful.

Being a prince, and a mostly beloved one at that, has its perks, so none of the servants show me much concern. The ones who do look at me with that question in their eyes, I ignore. By the time my father speaks to them and discovers where I was heading, we'll all be long gone.

The heavy dungeon doors swing open with a deafening creak. I stride into their dimly lit halls like I have so many times before, but this time far more on edge, when a group of noctis appear behind me.

"P-prince Malachi." The man leading the charge stands at attention. "We weren't expecting you here. Shouldn't you be—"

I think quickly. "I know, I know. I'm supposed to be enjoying the Hunt like everyone else up there. But I think my father's anal retentiveness is finally rubbing off on me. I couldn't rest until I verified for myself that everything was running smoothly down here."

I'm not even sure where the lie comes from, but the effect it has on the guardsman—someone I recognize by face, but not name—is more than favorable.

"Yes, sir. Of course, sir. Everything is going as planned.

We're on schedule to begin the Hunt before midday. We were just retrieving the last prisoners."

"Good, good," I say, stroking my chin thoughtfully, only to find that my palm is drenched with sweat. "Well, since I'm here, let me help."

I lead the guardsmen into the stifling darkness. With most of the prisoners gone, the place feels gutted. The doors hang ajar. The air is lighter, more breathable now that there is barely anyone vying for an ounce of what little fresh air seeps its way underground.

Aside from the few stragglers nearly hyperventilating at the very end.

Fox rises at the sight of me, a heaviness weighing down her expression more than usual at the sight of the guards I'm with. As subtle as I can, I shake my head at her, a plea to be calm until I can handle the predicament I've walked into.

I'm not surprised to find that the only other cell with a locked door is the one holding Charlotte and the two other women. My father's most prized catches.

He'll make a spectacle of them. It's likely why they're not aboveground already, even though I waited ample time for the dungeons to clear-out. He wants everyone to notice their grand entrance.

He wants the noctis to crave hunting them.

I signal for the lead guard to give me the keys and he obeys. As I open Charlotte's cell door, her gaze snares mine. I can't tell what I find there. I expect the usual: the fear of death, fear of pain, denial of both, and crazed desperation for anyone to change the circumstances. Oftentimes, when I've stared into the eyes of someone who's life I hold in my hands, there is an absurd amount of pleading and bartering, as if that has ever saved anyone.

But she bears no such things.

Whatever anguish she'd felt in the throne room, it's all but iced over, like winter's first snowfall in the northern regions. There's nothing but darkness in those amber eyes, a nothing as dark as a barrel of ale laced with hemlock.

And I want nothing more than to stare into those poisonous depths for days.

There she is.

The fighter.

The survivor.

I send the guards in, telling them to keep an extra eye on her.

"See you in the Shadowthorn," she says as she's shoved out of the cell and down the hall.

Despite myself, I smile. A true genuine smile that makes me forget just about everything—what today signifies for the noctis, what I'm about to do—and for the briefest of moments, I have no cares in the world.

For the smallest of moments, I actually look forward to what she's suggesting. I actually wonder what it will be like to meet her outside of these prison walls, unbound, amid the trees.

Then I remember who I am. A noctis prince. A monster, in her eyes, forevermore, just as she will forever be food in mine. Not to mention the fact that I won't be seeing her in the Shadowthorn because I won't be there.

My aunt clears her throat, reminding me of her presence and the reason I've come down here today.

A forlorn breath of a laugh eases from my lungs, and though I know Charlotte can no longer hear or see me, I find myself responding to her anyway, wishing I had done so sooner.

"I doubt it," I utter just before the door shuts us in darkness. "But wouldn't that be interesting."

"Are you just going to stand there talking to yourself, or are you going to let me out?"

Like snapping out of a trance, I glance to the keys in my hand and then to Fox's locked cell.

"What happened?" she asks, her auburn hair sitting surprisingly flat and groomed atop her head. "Why didn't you wait for them to be gone?"

Her tone makes me uncomfortable.

"I misjudged them, is all. It doesn't matter. It all worked out. I got the keys, didn't I?"

Her nostrils flare almost as wide as her eyes bulge. "You didn't have keys? What was your half-brained plan if you didn't have keys? Jiggle the bars until they broke free? Trust me. I've tried that. Doesn't work."

"You're in quite the shit mood for someone who's about to have their and see their children for the first time in months."

Fox hangs her head. "I know. I'm—I'm sorry. I don't know— I'm nervous. Hope is a dangerous thing, Malachi. When I saw you with those guards—"

Finally, the right key fits. The lock makes a metallic clang as it turns and the door opens.

Cautiously, almost in disbelief, Fox steps across the threshold and toward freedom, toward her family.

"You thought it had all been a lie," I say softly. With the door open, no more bars between us, and the heartfelt admission she's just made, I'm tempted to offer her an embrace. But I remember myself. I remember who I am to the humans, and my arms stay cemented to my sides. "I made a promise. I wasn't going to break it. We should get moving though. We don't have much time before the Hunt begins."

"Do you know where he's keeping them?" she asks, a glow already returning to her dull skin. "Do you know where my boys are?"

A gentle smile lifts my face, and for the second time that day, I feel light. Weightless.

"Come on," I tell her, ushering the both of us out of these dingy halls and into fresh air. "Let's go save your sons."

We open the dungeon door to find a woman with marmalade hair and pointy, upturned nose, blocking our way.

"R-Renee! What are you doing here—"

She peers behind me, spies Fox and the lack of chains around her wrists. "I could ask you the same. You mentioned being busy today and having *so* many responsibilities to tend to. I thought you might need some help, so I followed you here."

She's lying. I should've known the night we were all drinking that none of my lies had placated her suspicions. Nothing can get past her. At least not when it comes to me and her brother, the two people she knows best in this world.

"My turn for a question." Arms folding, she stares me down. "What are you doing with *her*?"

The words congeal in my throat like curdled blood.

"Here, you appear to be struggling with that answer. Let me help you. You've come to release your aunt, and presumably the children she bore, as well. Does that sound about right to you?"

There's no point in arguing now. Not with her, and not when the truth is so glaringly obvious.

"You don't understand, Renee—"

Her hand shoots up to block anything else I might've said. "Oh, no. I do. You've always been a softy, Malachi. And despite what your father might have you believe, it's not a weakness. It's one of your strengths. One of the things that makes you so much better than any of us."

I must not be hearing her correctly.

"So…you're not going to try to stop us?"

A look of incredulity wrinkles her expression. "That *would* be a nice thing for me to do for you, but unfortunately, I'm not as soft as you. There are things I want."

"For fuck's sake, Renee. I don't exactly have the time to be playing your games right now. What is it that you want?"

"You know what I want."

Of course, I do. She's been practically screaming it at me for years. I just didn't think it would come to this. Not here. And certainly not now.

"You...you want *me*? That's what this is about?"

She huffs her impatience. "Have I been anything but obvious with my intentions all these years? Consistent in my pursuit of you? Of course that's what I'm demanding as my price—and don't you dare try to tell me it's unfair. What you're doing, is so far beyond treason, your father could have us both killed if he deemed it a suitable punishment."

He wouldn't though. Not with me being his only heir.

But that's a protection only I possess. Now that Renee knows what I'm doing, she's at risk of the most severe of punishments. It's why I didn't want any of them knowing.

"I've tried patiently winning your heart fair and square, but you're too stubborn to know what's good for you. And—" she inches closer. I'm still too shocked by her arrival and stunned by how swiftly events have devolved into blackmail, that I can't even bring myself to blink, let alone move. I just stand here, stiff as the metal door cracked open beside us, as she presses herself against me. She looks up through her long lashes. Blinks them slowly. "If this is how I secure our union, so be it. You'll grow to forgive me in time. I think you'll even—"

"Our *union*?"

I shove her away and stagger a step back myself. I bump into my aunt behind me but it's almost worth it, just to put some distance between me and the succubus of a woman before me.

There have been times in our lives when I've referred to her as a sister. That was a long time ago, when we were much younger, but *still*.

I've never quite been able to make myself see her in the romantic light she wants me to. Not even for a single, drunken night of passion, let alone for the remainder of our lives in matrimony.

"I thought you meant a kiss! Or—or perhaps a romp in one of the more luxurious bedchambers once we finished the Hunt! But marriage? Marriage? You're blackmailing me for a betrothal?"

"You thought I'd settle for a kiss?" A haughty laugh escapes her. "You think too small, Malachi. This is what I'm talking about. You *need* me."

My jaw creaks like an unhinged door as I'm left utterly stunned. But it's more than that. Stunned is looking up at the clouds and swearing that your mother's face is among them. Stunned is watching a young doe enjoy a peaceful graze and not noticing the cougar as it bursts from the trees, killing the creature with one clean chomp to the neck.

I'm more than stunned by Renee's proposition.

I'm scandalized.

I'm infuriated.

With the coyness of a viper, she advances. "But I have the rest of our lives to prove to you that we could be good for each other. *You*, however, are on a tight schedule. Are you not?"

My shoulders feel like heavy, craggy boulders as they roll back, chest heaving. I glance at Fox. All she does is shrug, seeming irritated and quite impatient about our many setbacks so far, and possibly, what it foreshadows for the rest of our endeavors.

Renee, however, waits with the patience of a high-noon sun.

She thinks she's winning this ultimatum.

She has no clue how little she's holding over me.

"Stand aside, Renee." Snatching one of Fox's hands into my own, the nubs of her fingers crooked in my palm only fortifying my resolve, I press forward. My shoulder knocks into Renee and she staggers back.

"Hey!" she wails, catching herself on the doorknob and averting crashing to the floor completely. "Where are you going?"

"Do what you want, Renee," I call over my shoulder, not deigning to turn back toward her. "Tell my father, or don't. He'll find out soon enough and I'll receive whatever punishment he sees fit, or I won't. Regardless, you have bigger problems."

Outside the dingy dungeon, the first breath of fresh air aches in my lungs. I take a cautionary look around the courtyard. Still empty, thank the gods.

"What problem?" Renee asks, and I can hear her scrambling to her feet to stand tall, to pretend that my rejection wasn't a complete blow to her ever-growing ego.

"My father." Behind me, she falls silent. "He's rather observant, you know. Especially of the ones he keeps tabs on. By now, I'm sure he's noted my absence and he's beginning to wonder where I am. It'll prompt questions, and once his mind begins, it won't stop until it has answers."

Glancing over my shoulder, I see Renee rolls her eyes. "I'm not really sure what you're trying to imply, but—"

"I'm implying nothing. I speak factually. My father has already started looking for clues regarding my absence. He'll notice *you're* missing too. And once he discovers my aunt has been freed, he'll put two and two together. He'll assume I was behind it and that you were involved, and whatever punishment he bestows upon me, I'm sure yours will be tenfold."

Finally, her porcelain mask cracks. Horrified eyes blink back at me as she tucks a strand of orange hair behind her ear.

With nothing left to say, Fox and I leave her. Before we're even out of earshot, I hear her scurrying back to the frontlines to rejoin the others.

I just hope her delay won't be held against her…but I can't clutter my mind with that concern now.

Once we're back inside the castle, I feel the pressure of our dwindling seconds. The Hunt is about to begin. There is only a limited time before my father shifts his attention to me, and it won't take him long to figure out where to find me.

In the interest of avoiding running into any servants, we take the longest, most untraveled route. It was one thing to be spotted earlier when I was still alone, but now that I'm gallivanting around with a woman draped in burlap who reeks of her own urine, there would be no avoiding their questions. Half of them have likely already seen or heard of Fox. They'd know I'd broken free a prisoner.

Fortunately, thanks to the festivities taking place outside, most of the servants are preoccupied and therefore our journey through the narrow, twisting halls goes uninterrupted.

We reach the first room without incident. Using the secret compartment in the wall that I was told about to twist the lock on the hidden door handle and enter.

It's only been a few months since I last saw my…I'm not sure whether they'd be my nephews or my cousins, but the last time I saw them was the day they were brought into my father's possession.

They'd been thin, of course. Which human struggling to survive in this realm wasn't? But they'd also been bright-eyed and healthy, even as terrified as they were to be led through the castle in Neveridge, even after being taken away from their mother, I could see the life in both of them. They had felt true joy.

Until my father crumbled their world to pieces.

The blond boy we find inside the room, curled into a ball like a cat desperate to clutch onto what little body heat it can produce, can no longer be described as thin. He is barely more than bones. The joints of his body are gnarled, the skin stretched over them unnaturally taut, like someone took him apart, stole all of his meat, and then pieced him back together again.

He's so weak, he can hardly lift his head up to see us. But he's so frightened that he musters the strength.

How many times has my father come in here to bleed him? Or sent one of his other guards to have a taste? And to what gain? Just to torment him and their mother? Under most circumstances, my father doesn't allow to keep humans around for their blood. He doesn't think it's worth the risk of creating more ghouls, and doesn't trust the Crimson Guard not to sink their fangs into human flesh if it's kept around. So why change his rules to torture little boys?

Rage is a small flame compared to the hatred that roils within me. But I stand guard at the door as Fox races to the small boy's side, arms spread wide.

It takes the child a moment to register us, eyes heavy-lidded, perception skewed by bloodloss.

"Eirrick, sweet boy," his mother coos, offering him her embrace.

I remember the name, but the face before us hardly matches it.

I remember more too. Eirrick was her eldest, and I shudder to think of the state of his younger brother. He's only younger by a year or two, but two years might as well be decades considering the suffering these boys have likely endured.

With what little strength he has in him, Eirrick recoils from the gentle tenor of his mother. His bony limbs scrape like nails against the floor as he clambers back.

"Eirrick, it's me," Fox says, voice quivering like a rippling brook. "It's your mother. I'm here. I'm going to get you out of this...this place."

Recognition slams into him. He throws his arms around the mother he hasn't seen in months, the mother he's likely called out for hundreds of times, and sobs tear out of him as he buries his face in her shoulder.

When Fox's arms envelop him, I have the distinct feeling that she's never letting go again. Not if her remaining fingers are snapped off. Not if her arms are hacked from her body. She'll still cling to him, and likely tear out the throats of anyone who dares to separate them again.

Rubbing his back, she turns to me. Both of us notice the thick, heavy chain around his neck at the same time. She looks at me as if I have the answer for that, but no one told me we'd find him in chains. I suppose I should've known though. Like my father would ever let his prisoners roam freely. He likes having control too much for that.

It's because of that need for control that I already know we won't find a key anywhere in this room.

I shake my head at my aunt, but she waves it off. "Check over there. That table looks…busy. See if you can find anything long and thin for me to pick the locks with."

I cross the room as I'm told and head for the table with an assortment of gleaming metal instruments that I'm sure have sliced and punctured his skin in numerous places. Quickly, before my aunt can see them, before they can carve through her heart any more than the sight of this room already has, I slide my body between her and the table so she can't see them.

It seems the kind thing to do, but she snaps at me. "Move so I can see."

My lips part, ready to protest, but who am I to decide what she can or can't handle? She's already endured far more than I ever have in my lifetime.

I step aside and her sharp eyes roll over the instruments.

"That one. Bring it here." She points to a thin metal rod that's sharp enough on one end to skewer an eyeball clean from the socket, and I oblige her eagerly.

She makes quick use of the weapon. Even missing half of

her fingers has no hindrance on the skillful way with which she slides the thin tip into the locking mechanism and begins her work.

"Hold still," she whispers into Eirrick's ear. "Try to be quiet so I can listen for the sound. Just like I taught you."

To my surprise, the child who can't be any older than twelve stops whimpering instantly. I try not thinking about whether he's always been able to understand the severity of situations such as these, or if his obedience is something that's been trained into him since his capture.

When the lock makes a noise that I can't hear, he looks up to his mother. "That?"

Pride flashes in her eyes when she nods at him, and then she calls back to me, "I need something for the second chamber. Something thin, long enough to fit inside. Is there anything over there that could fit?"

Time is running out quickly.

We still need to find the second room and likely pick the lock of yet another chained boy we find there.

My eyes devour the small table again, but as they scan the small knives and curved blades, they don't find anything matching the description she's given.

"Nothing," I tell her.

I feel pathetic. Useless. Here I am, a powerful prince who can't even save a child in need.

In a moment of defeat, I reach up to stroke my mother's amulet around my neck. The last piece of her in this realm.

When I give the heirloom a squeeze, my thumb pricks on a decorative rod that extends from the bottom of the garnet. It's thin. It just might be long enough to work.

"What about this?" Unclasping the chain from behind my neck, I hand the relic to Fox.

She snatches it from my grasp. "It's perfect!"

Fox wedges it into the lock and within seconds the metal

cuff around Eirrick's neck is unhinged. He lunges from his chains, crashing into his mother with another aching sob.

I collapse to the floor, as well, fingers frantic as I grab my mother's amulet from the lock and make sure it's not broken. To my immense relief, it comes out whole and undamaged.

"We should keep moving," I say, fastening the amulet back in place and then retrieving the other tool—the skewer—from the tampered lock.

Gathering the boy who is almost too grown to be carried into her arms, Fox stands. "Lead the way, Malachi."

2 1

DEATH TO THE NOCTIS

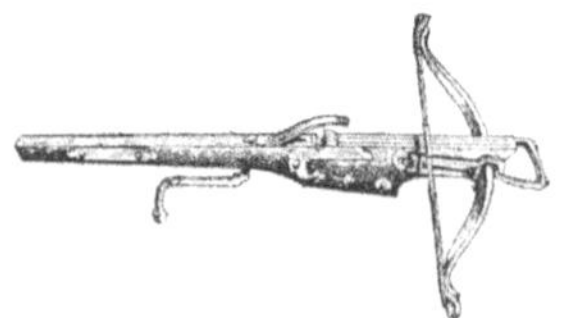

Years of survival and instinct have led me to this moment.

Running is what I've always done best.

And so, without a second thought, I do as the king says.

I run.

A decade of solitude makes me forget the past week I've spent with the others, the vow we've made to help each other. All I think about is my survival. It's in my nature. Fuck the odds stacked against me, I will do whatever it takes to live another day, as I always have.

It's not until I'm buried a few hundred feet into the black forest that I remember the people I've left behind.

Just when the guilt is settling in, I remember Rowland too. I can't leave without him. And I know he won't leave without me either. Without *us*, I remind myself. He'll want to find Elison too. This whole predicament only started because he wanted to find her.

And now she has quite the target on her back. So does Mira.

"Fuck."

I should've never abandoned them. I don't know what came over me.

I should double-back, but the ground already quakes with the stampeding of hungry noctis. They're coming for us, and whatever minuscule head start we were given, it won't matter if I sacrifice the ground I've already gained. Forward is the only option at this point. Even if it's a shit one.

The king said that after the third day, those remaining alive are rounded up and brought back to the castle to be fed upon anyway, so it seems like even if I run farther into the Shadowthorn there's no feasible escape. For all I know, the entire place is fenced-in. I could get all the way to the edge of the forest, safety just within my reach, only to find that there's a blockade standing in my way.

Or worse, an even larger army of noctis just waiting to snatch me up again.

I can't risk it.

But I can't stand here either.

There is only one exit that I am assured is open, and that's the way we came in.

And there's my plan. Find Elison. Find Rowland. Should probably find Mira too, if she's still alive. And instead of running deeper into the Shadowthorn like the rest of the fools, the four of us will instead retrace our steps back to the border of Nigh.

Just as my racing heart begins to soothe with the comfort of having a plan, a scream cleaves it in two. The scream of a young woman.

* * *

Branches whip my face, the constant lashings drawing blood as I race through the blackened forest toward the terrified cries. My mind runs wild with possibilities. I imagine Mira, cornered and terrified, curling-up like a young girl who still relies on her parents to protect her. I imagine Elison, and the numerous horrific ways that any of the noctis who find her will feed upon her, shredding through her just for a taste of the unborn speck-of-a-child in her belly.

And as my feet pound against the hard soil, my hatred for the Devonshires erupts.

This is all the fucking king's fault.

He declared us *delicatessens*.

He made us desirable, and convinced his regime that we were prizes worth winning, worth sinking their teeth into.

I'm so sick of him having the upper hand. I'm so sick of our only option being to run.

I'm ready to fight.

With deafening silence, the scream stops. My feet drag and stumble to a halt. That was the cry of the dying. That was the last sound that person is ever going to make.

Numbly, I blink ahead through the trees, toward death. Whoever it was, Mira or Elison, they're gone now. I couldn't get there in time. No one ever can. The noctis always win. And even if I had arrived soon enough to stop the agony, to intervene before the noctis made their killing blow, it wouldn't have mattered. Once bitten, you're doomed. Death is a mercy compared to living out one's days as a ghoul.

I just wish—whoever it had been—didn't have to die alone.

Like dense smoke, slowly my awareness rises. My body is left where it's standing in the dark, creepy woods, and now that I'm not focused on running, the distant cries of all of the others ring in my skull. But the numbness has already begun to take over. I can no longer afford to feel for them. For anyone. I am the jagged cliff of rocks on Hulbeck's shore, pummeled by wave after wave every day, and still left unmoved. Unchanged. Cold and impassive. Their cries for help, for their loved ones, they simply become noise. Evidence. Fact. Removed so far from something living, something with a lifetime of memories and hopes and dreams that I ignore them with ease.

The fear they would've instilled in me dissipates like smoke on the wind. They're all lost now and there's nothing I can do. Except to keep moving forward. Keep to the plan.

Then a new sound yanks on my attention. Feet stampeding. Limbs tearing through branches.

Scrambling to catch my bearings, I fling myself behind the tree, putting it between me and whoever is running closer. The rumble grows louder, the footsteps drawing nearer. At least two sets of them, maybe more.

With my head cocked at an angle, I watch the runners pass by. In the lead is a young woman with long, black hair that whips at her back like a horse's mane.

Recognition soothes the hot blade of grief that had been wrenched into my stomach.

Mira is alive.

Which means…Elison isn't. The mother of Rowland's would've-been child, and the babe along with her—gone. My heart aches for the pain he will feel when I have to tell him the news.

If I get to tell him the news.

The way Mira runs, black dirt and crunchy leaves kicking up with each leaping, uncoordinated bound, she reminds me of one of the tills Rowland has at their farm. She's all protruding, jagged limbs in a cyclone of desperation. There's a reason for her incoherent movements. I realize what just before she disappears through the trees.

Her arm is soaked red. She cradles it with the other as she barges through the forest.

Was she bitten? Am I already too late to save her?

A noctis barrels after her, cutting me from my wonderings, a crazed look in his charcoal eyes. He scents the air, making me swallow my heartbeat like a bag of rocks. I've never known for certain if they can smell us, whether by sweat or blood, but I've always suspected.

"Come out, come out, wherever you are," the male noctis croons. "I have a bet to win."

My back presses harder against the trunk of the tree. I don't want him to follow Mira, but I also am in no position to face him myself.

The tenor of his voice changes, a playful smirk poisoning the inflection. "Better yet, keep on running. The best part of the Hunt is *always* the chase."

He bounds in the direction Mira fled and the breath whooshes from my lungs.

That was too close for my liking. But I have a feeling that things are only going to get worse. Especially for Mira if I don't help her. Because he didn't stop to get a better sense of where she'd gone. Even someone who knew nothing about tracking could've followed the blatant trail of broken branches and disturbed underbrush that she left in her wake. And it wasn't like he had stopped to catch his breath either. Someone as young as him? In the prime of his life?

He's toying with her, I realize. Making the chase last as long as possible.

And he's getting off on it.

His kind are the ones that I fear most. The ones who delight in our torment more than the ones who simply feed to survive.

I suppose that's likely all of the noctis participating in the Hunt though. They've come for entertainment. To exert their power. To brutalize their prey.

I have to stop him before he finds her. I don't know how she was injured and if her days are already numbered, but I can't let her die alone like Elison did, like so many others have, and especially not at the hands of a crazed lunatic of a creature like him.

Despite knowing that I'm much safer if I stay where I am, I charge after them, deeper into the Shadowthorn.

When did I become such a bleeding heart who would risk her life for a stranger? It goes against every rule I've ever had about surviving in this world. But maybe it's time for the rules of survival to change. Maybe we're ready for the pendulum to swing in our favor. Or maybe I'm just sick and tired of all of us being so helpless to a fate that has almost always felt impossible to change. My parents deserved better than what they got. Elison deserved better than what she got. Me, Mira, Rowland, everyone—we all deserve better.

Whatever the reason, my gut is telling me to protect Mira and I don't make it a habit to question my gut. I won't leave her alone to die the way so many others have.

I won't abandon her.

I won't run.

Ahead of me, I hear Mira shriek. Not the kind of sound one might make when being bitten, but the kind heavy with defeat, a yelp that says it is only a matter of time before the noctis have their teeth around her neck.

As silently as I can, I push harder through the dead woods, and when I see movement ahead, only then do I slow.

Through the thick undergrowth, I see Mira. Then I notice the noctis advancing on her in slow, deliberate steps that make her quiver. Her back thumps against the base of an old, blackened tree.

"End of the line," the noctis says, sharp teeth exposed through his sickening grin.

Mira's hands reach blindly behind her, grasping at leaves and twigs. She snaps one off from the bush next to her and thrusts it between the two of them.

The male noctis erupts with belly-aching laughter. "My, oh my. What a terrifying twig you found yourself there. What do you plan to do with it? Brush me to death?"

He's not wrong. She isn't going to swat a fly with that thing.

Heart racing, I scour the area around me. Maybe I can find something better? Something that might actually injure him or slow him down long enough for us to get away. My options seem just as limited as Mira's though.

She swats at the young noctis as he takes a step closer. "St-stay back! I'm warning you."

Her voice is about as menacing as the limp stick in her grasp, but this is a new side of Mira that I haven't had the pleasure of seeing before, and I think I like it. Survival. Doing everything in our power to breathe another day, another second. That's all we have. Her weapon might be meager, her circumstances dire, but I admire the fight in her bones, and wonder where it's been hiding these past few days. Hibernating and conserving energy for this very moment, I suppose.

Her bravery emboldens me, and I come crashing through the bushes. The noctis barely has a chance to register me. Or he assumes I'm one of them, another crazed monster ready to feast. Whatever is going on in that unperturbed skull of his, I use it to my advantage.

Before his full attention can spring upon me, I lunge. My arms wrap around his torso and Mira's eyes go wide.

"What in the Shadowthorn—"

The noctis thrashes, trying to knock me down and assess the situation. But unlike the last noctis I faced on my own, whose body was a mountain of muscle, this one is slim, delicate in a way that I am not.

"Ch-Charlotte?" Mira stutters, finally catching a glimpse of my face as the noctis bends forward and I with him.

"Find something"—I grit out; he might not be strong, but

even a bucking horse can toss down the most skilled rider if they have reason—"to kill him with."

Understanding illuminates her features despite the dark wood around us. She springs into action, zipping around the surrounding area while my battle with the noctis continues. His fangs are bared now, and every time he jerks my grip slips, my arms rising closer and closer to his snapping jaws. One prick is all it would take. One puncture. One drop of whatever toxin is in his saliva to infuse with my blood, and I'll be doomed like the rest of the sorry, vicious husks that haunt the realm.

Mira bellows in a panicked frenzy, "I—I can't find anything!"

"Get the fuck off me," the noctis growls. He swings his body into the tree Mira had been pressed up against.

I'm able to dodge the first blow, leaning in the opposite direction so as to protect my head, but I can't save my shoulder. It slams into the tree trunk. Hot pain bursts from my shoulder, ricocheting against the raw nerves in my elbow, and turning my fingers numb.

My grip loosens and the noctis seizes his moment, throwing an elbow into my ribs and, arms wide like a bird in flight, bursts free from my grasp.

I stagger to my feet, barely catching myself as he whirls around on me.

The corners of his mouth curl like dying ferns. "Well, isn't it my lucky day?"

Mira stills when she sees him free. Part of me expects her to run now that his attention is fully on me. It would be the wise thing to do. There are hundreds of noctis infesting these woods as we speak, and the more distance she can put between her and the rest of them, the better.

For whatever reason, she stays.

The noctis drags his tongue over the point of one fang.

"Here I was, prepared to settle for the boring prize because eating anything is better than eating nothing. But then you come along and serve yourself up on a platter."

"Go fuck yourself," I spit.

But he only delights more. "Feisty, feisty!"

Mira's eyes jerk suspiciously, but only I see them. I follow to where they're pointing and find that something is cradled in her arms. Something heavy and jagged.

A rock. But she's too far away to do anything with it.

We need a distraction.

Predators expect their prey to cower or to flee. They don't expect them to fight back.

"The king wasn't exaggerating," the noctis says, hands tucked into the waist of his trousers. "You are the prize of the Hunt."

"You have no idea."

Before his appetite is too far piqued, I bolt forward, cutting the space between us in the blink of an eye. He has no time to react. My shoulder collides with his sternum and the two of us tumble to the ground. He hisses, muscles straining to kick me off him.

"Now!" I yell at Mira, who's still petrified in place but watching wide-eyed. "The head! Hit him in the head!"

As if she's possessed, she shuffles closer and thrusts the rock out from her body. The noctis thrashes so much that I fear my own head might be struck, caught between the two of them, but I manage to hold myself away. Then Mira's knees buckle. She drives her heavy weapon down.

The rock slams into the noctis' face with a squelch that makes my stomach flip. His body twitches on impact and it reminds me too much of the day I saw a noctis feasting upon my mother. I jolt away, releasing him in time to watch the boulder roll beside his bleeding skull.

He gurgles on his own blood and shattered teeth, his nose

concaved and already making him nearly unrecognizable. If he were anyone else, the sight of him would sicken me. It would enrage me. But that's because I've only seen such brutality at the hands of *them*.

We didn't ask to be captured and released like a bunch of helpless piglets waiting for slaughter. This was self-defense. And what I do next is too.

My arms drag across the earth when I lean closer to retrieve the heavy rock. I struggle with the weight of it for a moment and try not to think about how it's the same size as a head and therefore might weigh as much as the heads the noctis put on spikes just outside of Hulbeck.

Weakly, the noctis before me raises a hand. A plea. It'll go unheard just like ours would've if he had pinned us down and feasted.

He watches me through bloody slits of eyes and I wonder if this is the first time he's tasted his own blood. His own evil.

Without a second thought, I grit my teeth to prevent the furious scream from spilling like lava from my throat, and I bury the rock into his skull. Once. Twice. I beat his face until there is nothing left, not of him, nor of the memories that haunt and enrage me.

It's only Mira's gentle hands cupping my shoulders that finally makes me stop.

Using the hand she offers, I stand, equally relieved and surprised that she doesn't shirk away from the blood dripping from my fingertips.

Apparently reading my thoughts, she musters a smile. "You don't make it this far without having to do things you don't want to do."

I can't tell if she's talking about me or herself. In all likeliness, it's probably both.

In the wake of my monstrous actions, I can feel myself slipping back into the hollow darkness that has been most of my life. I can feel the chill of ice as it recasts itself around my heart, encasing it and keeping me protected from the world.

The noctis' body is still warm at my feet, and I can't turn away from it. From what I've done. From what I'm capable of doing.

I'm not a normal girl.

I grew up cold and alone and that's the only way I know how to live.

I shouldn't have come here.

But I'm here now.

"Thank you," she says. "For coming back for me. For saving me."

It shatters my heart in two. I don't deserve her kindness, her appreciation. I almost left her. I *did* leave her. Her and Elison both.

"Yeah, well," I say, voice hoarse and hollow. "It looks like you can handle yourself.."

This makes her blush, and she folds her arms over herself as if to hide it. The action makes her wince and I remember the blood drenching her arms.

"What happened?" I ask. "Did he…"

Her eyes bulge. "No! I wasn't bitten. It's embarrassing but… I fell. I was trying to lose him, and I jumped over a stream and fell onto some rocks."

"Are…are you okay?"

"I think so," she says, and then a little firmer, "I will be."

I hope she's right, but only time will tell how much of a lie we're telling ourselves.

We look at each other, silence stretching thin around us, punctured only by the intermittent shrieks of those less fortunate than us in their noctis encounters. I nod for her to follow me, and without a word, we leave the dead noctis behind us.

I've never set out with someone else before, and the idea of *needing* anyone other than myself to make it in this world sends my heart lurching. I can't rely on her and she can't rely on me. No one can rely on anyone but themselves because that's the way the noctis have made the world.

Slamming my face into my hands, I try to set myself straight, to think beyond the bombardment of doubt and fear and horror. But I don't know how to do this! I don't know how to work with someone else.

Mira stops too.

"Th-they..." she hesitates, but her timid voice has already summoned my every focus. "I think they took Elison."

Clarity returns to me, everything else fading as I think about Rowland and what Elison meant to him. I wanted to save her. I did. But I never had the chance.

Mira's voice breaks on a sob. "I don't want to—to die like she did. I don't want you to die, either."

"No one does." And then thinking back to how I've seen Rowland comfort his people, I add awkwardly, "We're not going to."

"What are we going to do then?"

"We're going to find Rowland. I think he'll already be making his way north to find us, so we shouldn't have to scour the entire forest. Hopefully we'll meet him somewhere halfway. Once we do, then we double back to the border. It'll be far safer than going anywhere deeper into the Shadowthorn, and the noctis won't expect it."

"But the king is back that way," she protests, one nervous finger twisting around a lock of dark hair. "And so is the castle, with all of his guards."

Irritation tightens my chest. Not at her, but at our predicament. "We have no choice. The king made it obvious: there is no exiting the Shadowthorn. Other than the way we came in."

Mira bites on the inside of her lip, but eventually she nods. "Okay. I believe you. And thank you—"

"You don't have to keep thanking me for—"

"Not for saving my life. Not this time. For telling me the plan. For trusting me."

An uncomfortable airiness bubbles up in my chest. I scowl at her, spinning on my heels and heading south. "Just...stop thanking me for everything. Let's find Rowland and—"

Before I can finish the thought, another scream shreds through the forest from maybe forty or fifty feet behind us. It belongs to a woman. To her shattering heartbreak. And then to her smoldering rage.

Whoever we just killed, the noctis we left smashed into a pulp not too far back, he's been found. And he meant a great deal to the woman who's found him.

DECISIONS

Finding and freeing Fox's second son, Bastion, proves a much smoother endeavor. We're not surprised to find him chained and bound, much the same way as his older brother had been, and we don't need to waste time searching for a way to remove them, since we come wielding a makeshift lockpick that worked just fine on his brother's chains.

We're in and out of Bastion's room before my father even releases the noctis to hunt.

Of course, we hear their battle cries the moment we reenter the hallway, and my aunt and I share a look of understanding.

Our time is up.

With Bastion cradled in her arms and Eirrick clinging to one of her hands, they follow me through the twisting corridors of the ancient castle. I'm not sure how, but miraculously we make it through without any incident, even with two sniffling children in tow.

It's a rarity that I'm ever grateful for the Hunt, but today is one of those days. Without it, we wouldn't have ever made it outside undetected.

We exit the castle on the west side of the building, just as I'd planned.

Fox barrels past me, examining the distance. "W-what's this?"

"Your...freedom?"

I'm taken aback by the sharp cut of her tone. It almost makes me forget to ease the door shut behind me, so as not to alert any guards who might be wandering the area. Almost.

Instead of barking at the ungrateful display, I remind myself what's at stake here, what she's survived already, and the fears that have to be weighing heavily upon her shoulders.

"We're on the west side of the castle. The Capital is that way. I just assumed that's where you'd—"

A horrifying scream cleaves the air.

It shouldn't be any different than the others. The Shadowthorn is an eruption of agony and fear today. But this cry stands out. This one I recognize.

This one belongs to Ursulette.

Every impulse in my body tells me to run to her, to race into the Shadowthorn, find my friends, and figure out what could cause her so much anguish and ire. But I'm on a new life path now. I made my choice and I have to stick to it.

"The Capital?" Fox wails, drawing my attention back to her and our nearly-complete escape. She whips around like a flame bursting from a bonfire. "What are we going to do at the Capital? The gods-forsaken place fell nearly two decades ago." Shaking her head, she marches past me, adjusting Bastion on her hip. "I'm taking them east."

"East?" I grab her arm, but quickly let go when she tenses. "Into the Shadowthorn? Have you lost your mind? You know what's happening out there right now, right?"

"Of course I know. I'm no fool."

"I might beg to differ." My fingers scrape against my scalp as I drag my hand through the length of my white hair. "The Hunt has started. The Shadowthorn will be teeming with noctis by now."

She tips her head back. "I said I'm well aware."

I'm too frustrated to think. For a moment, I can't even seem to make the words tumbling around in my head form coherent sentences. I just risked everything for her, for the two children clutching onto her like trembling leaves. And her plan, all along, has been to walk them into another bloody fiasco.

"You only just narrowly escaped the worst experiences of your lives, and now you want to drag your family through another gauntlet of terror? I—I can't let you."

A mother bear protecting her cubs would be put to shame by the ferocity that sparks behind Fox's blue eyes. "You don't get to *let* us do anything. You're not our keeper. Isn't that what all of this was about? Giving us our freedom? Or do you no longer care if you're just as controlling as your tyrannical father?"

"Stop trying to rile me up," I say just in time to prevent my anger from rising. "Why would anyone in their right mind— any *human,* to be more specific—willingly enter the Shadowthorn on today of all days, knowing full-well the carnage awaiting them once they're inside?"

"We don't have a choice, Malachi!" Just as quick as her fury bubbles and rises to the surface, it fizzles out again. A lifelong battle of survival has left her wearier than ever. "Or haven't you noticed? There is nowhere left for us to go. Your father controls the realm. He's bled the continent dry, quite literally. Village after village have fallen. Entire cities—the Capital! My own home was infiltrated and obliterated, all before you were even a toddler ambling about with that crown askew on your big toddler head."

If she were anyone else, I'd be compelled by my pride to inform her that as a boy I barely had any possessions, let alone a crown among them. My mother and I lived a simple life, one that I was quite fond of and wouldn't have changed for the world. Most of the people in my life forget that. They forget that I, too, was robbed of a peaceful adolescence, that my home was decimated, and my friends and family murdered.

At least she doesn't have to blame herself for the fall of her home. But my mother's blood will forever stain my hands. If I hadn't been born, if I hadn't been a noctis, if I hadn't fallen for the neighbor girl, my mother and our entire village might still be standing.

"I'm not saying you'll live a prosperous life out in the wasteland of a country you've been left with," I tell her, trying to sound reasonable. "I'm saying that you should at least go hide somewhere and wait for the Hunt to end before you even think about entering those woods. The noctis will eat you alive if you go in there now. We could..."

I trail off, hearing my words before I even registered that I was saying them.

We.

I haven't talked to her about where I'll go after all of this. Part of me had been assuming I would be on my own after we left the castle, even though it's far from what I want.

I don't think she realized that I was leaving—the castle, my crown, all of it—until just now. But she's a quick woman. She understands that now that I've aided in her escape, after today, I'll not be welcomed in the company of any noctis.

Tor Devonshire will finally give me what I've always wanted from him: disownment. My only regret is that it comes at the cost of losing my friends.

"I could keep us protected," I begin, sensing her understanding, and hoping I'll find her compassion as well. "But only if we leave the castle, and we leave all notions of traveling through the Shadowthorn until the Hunt ends."

I can hardly swallow, barely breathe as I await her response.

What human would want a noctis around them though?

Someone who serves as a constant reminder of the fear and suffering they've had to endure their entire lives. Especially a Devonshire noctis, at that.

She blinks back her surprise. "You're...you're not staying here?"

I shrug, the sharp shoulders of my cape rising behind me like black, ominous mountains and making Bastion jolt in his mother's arms. "There's nothing here for me. Besides, you really think my father would allow me to stay after what I've done?"

"You're his heir."

"He can't afford to have an heir if it's one who can't be controlled, let alone one who sympathizes with humans."

She smirks, lost somewhere in her own memories. "Must be a Devonshire trait to go rebel against the status quo." At first, I don't understand her meaning, but then she clarifies. "Halira was the same way."

Sometimes I forget that they knew each other, and that together they saved the realm from darkness. For a time being.

"Well, not all Devonshires." Forlorn, Fox looks back out across the Shadowthorn. "I appreciate the offer, Malachi. Truly. And I can't express my gratitude enough for what you've done for me and my boys today. But, where I'm going, I'm afraid you're not welcomed either."

"Where you're going?" I say, taken aback by how certain she sounds, like she already has a place in mind.

As far as I knew, there was nothing beyond the Shadowthorn though. Once the realm lost its magic, the Eyve—home of the druids—was ransacked and then abandoned.

But my gaze falls upon the dark forest before us, a horizon of black branches that stretches as far as the eye can see, and I remember something my father said not a few days earlier.

"You're returning to the Shadow Crusade."

She looks stunned that I've pieced it together so quickly,

and maybe even wonders if she should deny it. Instead, she fixes her expression with steel.

"Something like that," she says. "The boys and I will be fine."

Curiosity has always been a weakness of mine. As I boy, I'd ask my mother a hundred questions a day about why plants grew at different rates, why the seasons changed, how fire was made. On days when I'd exhausted her with my inquiry before it was even lunch time, she'd tell me that sometimes curiosities are best to be left unasked and unanswered.

Despite wanting to ask Fox a dozen questions—such as where the Shadow Crusade has been hiding all this time, how they've been communicating with her, and how they plan to ensure her safety once she enters the woods—I let my imagination conjure as many answers as it can. Like many other communities, they have likely gone underground, making it more difficult for the noctis to find them. I doubt they've been able to communicate with her since she's been in captivity, but we've had plenty of prisoners brought into the cells since then. It's possible that some of them might've been involved with the Shadow Crusade as well and that they fed her intel of an escape plan. As for her safety in the Shadowthorn, that'll have to remain a mystery.

"I understand," I say after a time, not because I have all the answers I want but because I'm sure she'll give me none. "I suppose this is where we part ways then."

"I suppose so."

There's a bittersweetness on my tongue. It seems I may never know the meaning of family again.

Fox lowers Bastion to the ground and ushers him to his older brother.

Surprising me thoroughly, she throws her arms around my back, my neck too high up to reach.

"Thank you again, Malachi. For everything." And then, she jerks me lower, my ear coming within reach of her mouth as she whispers so quietly that even the boys can't hear. "You underestimate your father's need of an heir. The man struggles to trust anyone but his kin, even if they stab him in the back. He wants a Devonshire on the throne, and you're all he's got."

I pull away to stare down at her, but she pulls me back in.

"If you want my advice," she adds, guilt edging her tone for even considering giving a noctis a piece of advice. "He'll forgive you if you show him you're still on his side. Go participate in the Hunt. Bring back a kill. Gods, impress him by being among the few to kill one of his prized possessions. You have nothing to fear from him. He was raised to be loyal to his family, no matter what, and I believe that still rings true."

A humorless laugh escapes me. "Oh yeah? He sure didn't seem to show you any loyalty."

"I don't count. I don't have Devonshire blood in me. Neither did Alphonse. Wrong side of the family."

Fox gives my back a pat before returning to her children. She hoists Bastion back into her arms and settles him on her hip. To Eirrick, she hands something silver, the blade catching on the sunlight shining high overhead.

I chuckle to myself when I feel the empty sheath on my belt. My father might've beaten her, maimed her even, but he was never able to kill her spirit and cunning.

As I watch the three of them enter the dark woods, I wonder if I should follow after them. It's more than wanting to keep them safe. I'm so curious to see where they'll go. But I get the impression that she's more acquainted with those woods than I am, and she'd lose me the moment she noticed me tailing her.

I think about what she said. How I could enter the Shadowthorn to hunt like she suggested, but I'm not sure she's right in her assessment of my father and his ability to hold grudges. Especially of late. With everything going on, from managing the Hunt, to capturing the humans who infiltrated our dungeon, to hearing about the possibility of an attack from the Shadow Crusade, he's been even more prickly than—

The Shadow Crusade.

When I mentioned the Shadow Crusade, Fox didn't confirm their presence in the Shadowthorn, but she didn't deny it either. Who else could possibly be able to aid her once she entered the forest? After all, it was the Crusaders who trained in Nigh to enter that very same forest back when it was overrun with demons and plagued by the Blight.

And now hundreds of noctis roam those woods, and not a single one of them know that Crusaders could be lurking about.

Not even my friends.

Ursulette's scream rings in my thoughts again. It might already be too late.

I have to warn them.

Tugging my sleeve up, I expose the red tattoo on my wrist. "Caz! Caz! The woods aren't safe! You have to get yourself and the others out of there."

With my breath hitched in my lungs, I stare at my blood oath and await his response.

"I know," he says at long last. "They already killed Rhain."

PISSED OFF NOCTIS

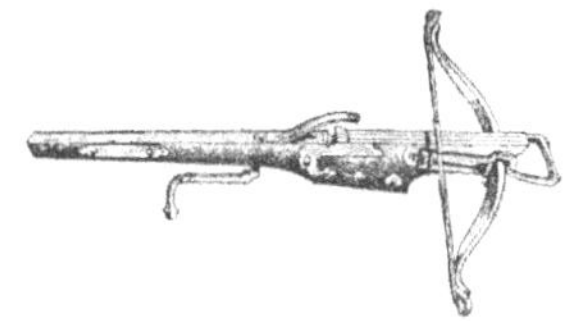

"**R**hain!"

The noctis behind us shrieks, her voice as sharp as a thousand crystal glasses shattering, the shrapnel flying through the air. There's an unspoken promise in her agony. A vow of vengeance that makes my skin clammy and cold.

"Who did this! Who did this!"

With one glance at each other, Mira and I start running. We set out once more, racing through the doomed forest, eager to put as much distance between us and the scene of our crime as we can.

But it's not enough.

In a matter of seconds, the female noctis is charging after us. I can hear her gaining speed as she thrashes, twigs snapping beneath her feet as loud as bones popping.

"I'll find you, you worthless wretch! I'll kill you for this!"

Whipping through the trees, I glance behind me and spy her. A silhouette of black with a snow-white river streaming down her head and back. Another Devonshire. *Of fucking course it is.* As if the realm didn't have enough of them.

She's carrying something heavy, the black thing dangling from her grip as she bursts through the forest. Something silver glints from one side of it and it takes me a moment to remember I saw her the day I was captured. She was the one who took Sable from me. And she's holding onto her now.

My feet stagger, the temptation to face her and fight for my crossbow strong in my blood. The victory under my wing emboldens me. We've already defeated one noctis. Between the two of us, I'm sure we can take her down too.

But Mira crashes into my shoulder, nearly toppling the both of us over.

"Mira! What are you—"

I cut myself off when I see the mountain of a man barreling at us from the other direction. If the patchwork of jagged scars or the peppered beard that hasn't been groomed in a decade wasn't enough for me to recognize him, the rust-colored eyepatch is unmistakable.

He's the noctis I remember most from that day. His menacing glare. The seething hatred that exuded from him like noxious gas. I even recall his name because how could I ever forget the name of a man who glared at me like he was imagining ripping my entire fucking head from my spine.

Harland.

And Mira had every right to throw us out of his path because he is like a raging bull that can only see red.

Catching our footing, we dart deeper into the Shadowthorn—against my better judgment, but for now we have no choice. Engaging either of them would be suicide. A grieving brother and I'm assuming a grieving widow, and I've had a hand in causing both of their pains. They'd eat us alive, quite literally.

But we can't just keep running either. Even if we could, I have to get Sable back.

A whistle, high-pitched but wavering, whips through the air

behind us. Mira doesn't seem to register it, but my ears have been fine-tuned to that sound for a decade.

The shot is amateurish, and thankfully gives just enough warning for me to dodge the bolt that whizzes past my head and thumps into a tree in front of me.

Mira gasps.

"Just keep going," I tell her, my breaths ragged and harsh. Before my chase through Gravenburg with Gregor, it had been a while since I'd run like this, and even longer since I've had to do it on such an empty stomach. "Don't run straight. Zigzag."

We break apart, weaving in and out of the trees as we trudge forward.

My mind is a pendulum of activity, one thought of possible escape swinging into the next. We could climb up a tree and wait for them to pass—but they're too close and they'd see us scaling the branches. We could turn around and try to fight— but with what? Our bare hands? They'd break our knuckles and use our splintered bones as straws to bleed us dry. We could separate, one of us heading north while the other heads south—but we'd just be running into more danger, considering there are noctis all over these woods, and then we'd have to face it alone.

Suddenly it dawns on me that the female noctis won't be able to nock another bolt. Not while we're all scrambling through the forest. Our sporadic movement is all but meaningless, only costing us valuable seconds and distance.

I check beside me for signs of Mira and notice our paths are much wider apart than I'd like them to be. I cut a hard left and try to devour the space between us, yet the way she darts between the trees has no rhyme or reason—it would've served her well, if there was any threat of another projectile coming our way. But even when I look behind me, I can see that neither noctis is taking aim.

"Mira!" I shout, hoping that my volume won't draw the

attention of even more noctis who might be nearby. "Stay close!"

Running full-speed, she turns her head toward me at the same moment she collides into someone else.

Just our fucking luck.

"Mira!"

I forget about the others chasing us. I forget about needing to run as far away from them as possible. My feet skid in the dirt as I course-direct, charging after the moans and groans of Mira and the male noctis she's run into.

But as I barrel through a particularly dense thicket of bushes, I find not a noctis, but more humans. Four additional figures register in my sight, but it's just the one that I hone in on.

"Rowland!"

My arms are around his sweat-slicked neck before he can answer and he's burying his face into my hair.

"Charlotte! Thank the gods. I was worried I wouldn't find you."

Beside us, I'm deftly aware of Mira and Lewis gathering themselves off the ground.

"Watch where you're going!" he snaps, hands busy dusting off the dirt from his already-stained and worn clothes.

His lack of urgency makes me remember my own. "We're being followed," I blurt between panted breaths.

"By who?" Rowland asks, eyes scanning the forest behind us.

Mira is panting as well. "There are two of them. A male and a female. I think we...I think we killed—"

"He was going to kill us," I remind her before guilt can cloud her judgment. "We're in the Hunt. It was either be eaten or fight back."

"I don't see anything," Rowland says, his attention still locked behind us. "I don't hear anything either."

Tilting my head so my hair falls away from my ear, I strain

to listen, but I realize he's right. There's no sign of them barreling through the woods any longer. Only the unnatural quiet of a forest that should be heavy with screams and bloodshed.

There are two other people amid Rowland's company, the man who I believe Lewis has so affectionately called Dunce, and the man who aided Rowland the night he tried breaking us out of the prison—Julian, if I remember correctly.

Julian speaks now. "How far behind you did you say they were?"

Between the four of them, he looks the most uneasy, despite trying to hide half of his face in the sheer, lavender scarf draped around his neck.

"They should be—" My head snaps around in a desperate search of the deadly noctis. But I find none. It's as if they just disappeared. Which is far more unsettling than it would be to see them crashing through the foliage. "That's...impossible. They were right behind us. The girl has bone-white hair; she shouldn't be difficult to spot."

"The Devonshire bitch?" Lewis sneers, smacking his knuckles into his palms. "I've been waiting for this."

"Maybe they saw how many of us there were, and they decided to retreat?"

I give Mira a dubious look. "Doubtful. We killed her...whoever he was. And the big guy? He lost two brothers, thanks to Rowland and me."

Eyes wide and assessing, Rowland looks to me for confirmation of what he thinks I'm saying. When I give him a what-do-you-think-I-just-said sort of look, he blinks his surprise.

"They wouldn't just stop chasing you then," he says. "This is personal."

I try to contain my irritation, but the moment is too charged, and I'm too depleted. "I already fucking know that. The question is, where did they go? We can't just sit here, waiting for them to attack. We need to know what they're doing."

The longer we stand here waiting for them to attack, the more I devolve into a common field mouse that flinches at every gust of wind.

They wouldn't have just given up, which means they're still here, somewhere, plotting the perfect opportunity to attack. But what could that be? Why not charge after us like they had been? It's not like any of us are armed—

A moment too late, I remember that the female noctis, on the other hand, was.

Another bolt rips through the air like a knife tearing through flesh. It strikes Julian and he's flung backward by the powerful blow. Shoulder-first, he crashes to the ground with an agonizing wail that almost reminds me of a distressed wolf calling to its pack.

Before most of the others can make sense of what's happened and why Julian is suddenly writhing on his back, thunder rumbles through the earth.

Harland is coming for us.

FOREST OF DEATH

My heavy legs slow when I find Rhain's body—or at least, what I think is his body. The face is so badly brutalized that it's honestly difficult to say and I have to identify him by complexion and fashion alone. The figure on the ground is dressed in a jade doublet, the same one Rhain was wearing just last night.

He's difficult to look at for too long though, and any time I do, I can't not look at the carnage. The place where his head should be is far too distracting, too upsetting. Where is his face? His head? Something more closely resembling a mashed-up pumpkin rests there instead and my stomach can't take it.

I'd expected to find him dead, but I didn't expect *this*.

"Who did this to you?"

I almost expect him to answer. Like any second now he'll pull the pumpkin guts off from his shoulders, his head tucked safely behind the mess, and he'll explode with laughter and tell us all that we should see our faces.

Only, I realize, there's only me to tell.

Where is Caz?

These woods are more dangerous than I imagined they

would be and suddenly I find myself worried—truly worried—about my friends.

"We're here," Caz says, emerging from a dense bundle of trees just before I can send word through the blood oath. "Sorry to make you wait. We wanted to see if Ursulette left any tracks. And let me tell you, yes she did."

Renee appears behind him, spine and shoulders drawn in an effort to ignore the awkwardness between us after my dismissal of her earlier. Or perhaps she's so stiff because of the disturbing sight at our feet. Maybe both.

Her bottom lip trembles, but not once does she allow her gaze to brush over Rhain.

"You found her tracks?" I ask them, trying to keep us focused on finding Ursulette. There's nothing we can do for Rhain now anyway. But if she's chasing the Shadow Crusade, we have to stop her before it's too late.

"Yeah," Caz confirms. "Thought we'd circle back for you before we went after her though."

"Thank you."

He nods, but his expression is pained. "I'm not sure we would've been able to get through to her if we found her anyway. Not without you."

Wiping the tears away, Renee scoffs, a sound that says he puts way too much faith in me and too little in his own sister.

On this matter, I might agree with her.

"I'm not even sure I'll be able to get through to her. Ursulette without Rhain is just..."

"She'll survive," Renee says sharply. "She was somebody before him, somebody with him, and she'll be somebody without him. But she needs her friends right now to help guide her back. Finding Rhain—like this? Anyone would become unhinged for a time."

Taking his cue, Caz gestures to the disturbed earth and scattered leaves.

"Judging from the tracks, it looks like two people did it. I think they were gone by the time Ursulette found him though, or there would likely be two more bodies here. The effort and time it would've taken to do that to him...she wouldn't have just stood by and watched. But she either saw them finish him off, or suddenly learned how to track better and is chasing after them. Either way, there's about to be bloodshed, which could be bad for the Hunt—" before I can glower too hard at him for having his priorities out of line, he adds emphatically— "and therefore bad for the realm. I know your father's rule is questionable, but he keeps the noctis in line. If they start to question his leadership...there could be anarchy, another rebellion, even."

I almost laugh. He has no idea how close to chaos we already are. Which is when I remember that neither of them knows what my aunt told me.

"I'm afraid we have bigger problems."

Caz shoots me a look that says he's both a little scared and kind of intrigued.

Renee steps closer. "Worse than Ursulette disobeying the king during the most sacred event of the year?"

I nod. "Whoever did this, it wasn't an accident. And it wasn't some frightened prisoner trying to fight back. This person had strength. They bested Rhain, a member of the Crimson Guard, and then bashed his skull in until he was unrecognizable."

"You...think his death was done...professionally?" Renee asks. "By who?"

I rub my eyes, dreading what I have to say next, the implication it has on me and my involvement in Rhain's death. But they need to know what's out there. They need to know we're not the only dangerous ones in this forest.

"When I released my aunt, she didn't confirm this, but I think she was returning to the Shadow Crusade. My father received intel that they've been seen about the realm again, and

Fox made it seem like they were somewhere in the forest, ensuring that she had safe passage to regroup to wherever it is that they're posted."

It's silent for a long moment. Then Renee punches me in both shoulders.

"And you just let her go?"

"I had no choice!" I argue, stumbling backward, almost tripping over Rhain's cold carcass. When Renee aims to strike me again, I catch her wrists and shove her back. "They would've killed me—or worse, taken me prisoner and used me as a bargaining chip to blackmail my father. Neither of those options are preferable, if you ask me, so I came to find you two instead."

A haughty, viperous laugh escapes her. "Right. Us *two*."

While we bicker, Caz is left reeling. "Just...hang on a second, guys. Can we go back to the part where the Shadow Crusade is reforming? For all that's wicked in the realm, they've been disbanded for...for...who knows how long! I'm not sure I've heard mention of them outside of historical context since I was seven. Didn't they all die?"

"Apparently not," Renee chirps.

"Maybe most of them did," I say. "Or maybe they went into hiding after the last battle."

"What are they planning?" Renee asks. "They must be here now because of the Hunt. Are they going to attack the castle while we're all out here? Make an assassination attempt on the king?"

Feeling the heat of her demanding and borderline accusatory tone, I feel the need to defend myself. "I know as much as you."

"Oh I doubt that," she says, fangs glistening behind a smile as cold as ice. "I haven't been buddied up to an aunt who's working with them for the last few months."

"Renee, cool it," Caz tries interjecting.

"No, I think I won't! We're just supposed to believe that this wasn't part of his plan all along? We're just supposed to believe that he's on our side and here to protect us?"

Caz's voice becomes deadly. "Yes."

It's not enough for her though.

It's not enough for me either. For all our strife, Renee is still family. It niggles at me that she feels like she can't trust me anymore after what she witnessed earlier.

"Renee," I say softly, gently, trying to shrink down from my oftentimes threatening size. I start to reach out my hand, but at the scalding look she flashes me, I let it drop back to my side. "The only reason I released my aunt today was because she's family and we were holding her and her sons—my nephews—for no reason other than torture."

"So? They're humans. What does it matter to you if humans are tortured?"

Disappointment inches into my heart, but I try one last effort to get her to understand. "They're *family*. I don't know about you, but that's not how I treat mine, and that's not how I'll rule—"

The statement catches us all by surprise, but me most of all. Hadn't my plan just this morning been to leave this life behind? And here I am talking as if my reign is still inevitable.

I shake the worrying notion aside. My royal status and my intentions to claim it hardly matter right now.

Renee's stony disposition is resilient, but eventually my words reach her. By her standards, she softens, and with a roll of her eyes she stands down. "Fine. I believe you. So the Shadow Crusade is back, they killed Rhain, and now Ursulette is chasing after two of their Crusaders. Do we think they're leading her into a trap?"

"Maybe," I reply.

"Well," Caz adds, "If their goal is to take down the king, they couldn't have asked for a better bargaining chip than his beloved niece—no offense," he says to me.

"None taken."

With a smirk, Caz raises his hand. "All in favor of running after her to try to stop her from doing anything reckless?"

Each of us puts one hand in the air.

"I'm impressed." Renee flashes him a condescending smile. "Suggesting we avoid recklessness? How very mature of you."

The mischief in Caz's eyes dazzles. "Oh, I didn't say it wouldn't be reckless."

2 5

BITTEN

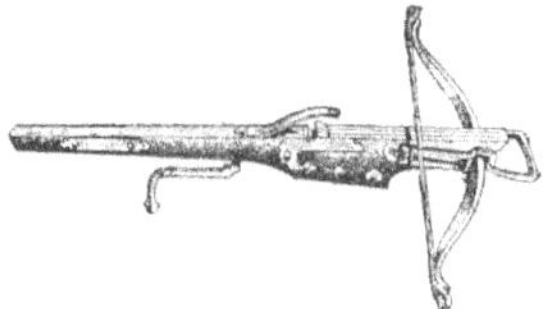

"She's got Sable!" I tell Rowland, even though the information hardly comes at a surprise. I have something more useful though. I point in the distance, to a village that I can just barely make out through the trees. "There! The shot came from over there."

What I don't tell him is that either she lucked out with that shot or her aim is either as good as mine.

"She has to be somewhere in that town, in a tower or something."

Even though I still can't actually see her, I know my way around a crossbow. I know that if Julian had been hit straight-on, given where the quarrel struck him in the shoulder, his body would've spun more. But instead of being tossed around like a rag-doll, he fell backward, as hard as a sack of rocks. The force that an arbalest puts into her nocked bolt can of course make the difference between her prey stumbling slightly or falling all the way back on their ass. But Sable was designed for a petite woman who'd never had to fight a day in her life. My father had it made as a precaution, and he carefully instructed the bowyer to make the string easy enough to work with that even my mother could do it. Gods, it was even manageable for me, an eight-year-old girl at the time when I first drew back the string—not easy, but manageable. Elison always said she thought it was because it was made from shadowood.

Thinking of Elison, one of the few women I've ever been close to, reignites a fire inside me.

It would be so easy to run. Running is what I've done all of my life. When the female noctis started chasing after us, it was common sense to try to run for our lives, just like it was common sense to run from the bull-of-a-male-noctis. Surviving to see another day. That's always been the goal.

But now?

Harland pushes his way through the bushes, pinning us in between him and the village.

I've lost most of my sense of direction, but I think we've gone farther north than I ever intended. How far, I'm not sure, but the air feels crisper, fresher here than it had when we'd first entered the Shadowthorn.

Perhaps we're near the edge of the forest already—I have no idea how deep this place goes.

"Don't kill any of them just yet, Harland!" the female noctis hollers in the distance.

She keeps herself concealed, but I can tell from the sound of her voice that my previous estimation was correct. She's somewhere high, hidden in one of the buildings.

If I could just get a better look...

Harland scoffs, his scarred lip tugging up to yell back, "Tell me how to enjoy my Hunt again, and it'll be your throat I rip out next."

Without another word, Harland advances. Each corded muscle ripples and bulges, his menacing gaze fixed upon all of us with a look that says he could kill everyone here with the flick of his pinky finger.

I look around at the people beside me.

To Rowland, a man who has, for his entire life, committed himself to protecting others.

To Mira, who's shown more strength and resilience than I thought most ordinary people capable of.

To the others—admittedly, Lewis isn't the best person I've ever met, but he's not the worst either? And not him, nor Julian, nor Dunce, deserve to be yanked from their lives and used as human fodder to be hunted down like game.

We might not have any weapons. We might not be as strong as the noctis closing in on us. But we have each other.

If we work together, we might be able to survive this yet.

I know Sable and, more importantly, I know the distinct curve of her shots.

I can find *the Devonshire bitch*—as Lewis so eloquently called her. If I can focus, I know I can.

"One of them killed Rhain!" she screams.

"What do you want? A confession?" The mammoth noctis grumbles but fixes his attention on us. With the nub of one of his arms, he scratches a branch-like scar below his only eye. "Which one of you maggots here has the balls to confess?" There's no sincerity in his tone, and no time given for anyone to answer because he already knows no one will. "No? Just as I figured. No one's confessing, Ursy," he yells to the female. "They all look guilty to me though. Might as well kill them all just to be safe."

"Y-you can't do that," Dunce stammers. "Your king said the rules were—"

"Fuck the rules," Harland says.

"Fine!" shouts the female, and seconds later another bolt is loosed. It impales Lewis in the thigh, jutting all the way through the other side. Over his wailing, I almost miss her maniacal laughter when she says, "But I'm going to make them suffer first."

My eyes meet Rowland's.

No words are exchanged.

There's no time.

But he knows as well as I do that Ursulette is a threat we need to deal with, and with Sable in her possession, there's no one else I'd let go in my stead.

When Rowland lunges for Harland, I pivot in the opposite direction, the female noctis the only target in my sight. After firing three bolts, she should still have two left—if she hasn't lost any since the last time I had Sable. Letting her get two more free shots could mean the end of us.

Guilt heavy in my heart, I leave Mira, but at least she's in capable hands. Her odds are better with the group than with me now anyway.

Before I can take my first stride toward the hidden village, something snags my arm. I'm ripped backward and a mountain of a monster erupts into view.

Out of the corner of my eyes, I find Rowland scrambling to his feet on the ground, a gash in his head where he was tossed into a tree.

My eyes return to Harland's, untampered rage gathering in a dark cyclone behind their dark depths.

"Where do you think you're going?"

He doesn't give me an opportunity for smartass banter, nor adequate time to escape. Fingers as rough as tree bark and as hairy as a rat's hide wrap under my jaw and jerk me closer.

A horrendous sound shreds Rowland's throat. "No!"

And then Harland's fangs sink into my neck.

The pain is piercing. Molten. Like someone's learned how to forge flames into teeth and their brand is coursing through my veins.

I'm skewered in his grasp. Unable to move. Unable to voice my terror in a scream or cry or anything. My torment remains trapped in my mind alone. A prison of fear that I am all too familiar with.

I might've begged Malachi to kill me days ago, but I knew then that I wasn't ready to die. I've never truly wanted to cease living; I just wanted the pain to end. I wanted a better life, to stop having to run. But I never wanted my life to come to an end, especially not at the hands of a noctis, one who looks like he's killed half of the United Realm single-handedly.

Like a rabid dog, Harland locks his jaws around my flesh and gives my entire body a jerk. Warm blood pools from the wound and drips down my neck, a waterfall of warmth down my chest. He laps it up, savors the sweet revenge on his tongue.

I suppose I should be grateful that I won't have to watch the others meet their fates now.

Even though that might be true, my body refuses to give up. Once the initial shock of pain has passed, the rest of my senses reawaken.

I pound against his chest for release. I kick. I roar, a sound so horrific and guttural that it scares even me to hear it.

Suddenly, I'm flung to the ground, my skull smacking into the thick roots of a blackened tree nearby.

I don't know why he's stopped. I don't feel nearly as weak as I expected I would, but I think that's because I still have so much blood left within me. He didn't finish. For whatever reason, I'm not dead yet, let alone even close.

The wound on my neck will be the death of me soon if I don't staunch the bleeding.

Harland spits blood to the ground. "What the fuck is this?"

Before anyone can answer or I can make sense of what's happening, Rowland barrels into the heavy noctis, and the two of them are a clash of fists and flesh.

Mira is in front of me a moment later, blocking my view of them.

"What's happening?" I try asking through gurgles of blood.

"Let me see." She peels my hand back and winces at the

sight. She presses my hand back to the wound before tearing a strip of cloth from her skirt. "Here, this will help—"

When she removes my hand, she gasps.

My first thought is one steeped in a lifetime of fear, and I'm certain that the transition has already begun. Soon I'll be a ghoul, and no one will be safe around me. Someone better kill me first.

But as she gapes at my exposed neck, I realize it's not sorrow or terror etched in her face, but shock. Amazement.

And I'm no longer gagging on blood.

I swallow thickly, testing my throat and the horrid taste of metal I expect to find. To my surprise, the pain is nearly gone, and there's only a hint of blood left.

Pawing at my bloodied—if not smooth and punctureless—throat, I mimic her look of surprise.

"How is that possible?" she whispers, touching the tender flesh where a wound should be.

"I—I don't know," I say. Using the tree for support, I sit straighter, but within moments I realize I don't need the support at all. I feel fine. Better than fine, if not for my lingering questions and worrisome thoughts, but those can be addressed later. "It doesn't matter right now."

As I shove myself to my feet, I find Rowland ahead. A sword shines in his hand like the gods summoned it down just for him —and maybe they did, since I'm not sure where else he would've found one. Julian, hunched over with a broken bolt jutting from his shoulder, wields a knife in his good hand, and the two of them corner Harland together.

I don't know Julian's skills, but I trust Rowland's. If he has Harland handled, then I have to take care of the remaining threat.

"What are you doing!?" Mira calls after me as I run.

But I don't respond.

There is no more time to waste. And now that I know I'm

impervious to the bite of a noctis, I have nothing left to fear.

The village pops into view as I burst into the clearing, but I hardly see it, my gaze fixated on the only two buildings tall enough to give her a vantage point: a guard post on the west side, and a bell tower in the cathedral just ahead.

Only the bell tower gives her the angle she needed for that shot.

A bolt whizzes by my ear. Thankfully, I saw Sable appear in the window just a second before, so I knew when to dodge, narrowly escaping with only a nick on my cheek instead of a quarrel through the eye.

As I bound across the field for the cathedral, I can't help but wonder if it would've even mattered. Maybe I'm puncture-proof as well as noctis-proof.

Or maybe that's a fool's way of thinking.

Another bolt whizzes by me, but it's wide and careless.

Using my shoulder, I crash through the main entrance. One of the stained-glass windows lays shattered amid the debris inside, and I gather the longest shard I can find among them before bounding up the stairs. A noctis bite might not kill me but I still need a weapon to fight her with, to put an end to her life.

Up the stairs I run, until I come to a closed door. When I kick it down *the Devonshire bitch* is waiting for me on the other side, Sable aimed at my chest.

"Don't you fucking move, or I'll kill you!" The female noctis tosses the black hood from her voluptuous white hair to reveal her beautiful, enraged face. Tears have made the charcoal around her eyes run, but I doubt if she's ever looked more menacing. "Was it you? Did you take my Rhain from me?"

My jaw snaps shut, anger pulsing through me.

Her family has killed thousands. They're responsible for the entire fall of our once great nation. And she has the audacity to cry for the death of one demented noctis male?

A decade of running. A decade of forcing myself to be alone so that I wouldn't ever have to feel the pain of losing a loved one again. All of it has culminated today. A day when the humans fight back and the noctis get what they're owed.

I am fortified and I am bold.

And I just fucking survived and healed a noctis bite.

Fuck this bitch and her grief.

I lunge, claws outstretched, and teeth bared like I'm the fucking teeth of the realm sent to claim its justice.

She staggers back, the crossbow becoming limp in her grasp. As it clatters to the dusty floor, I realize there's no bolt nocked, and I remember she wasted her final two shots while I was running here.

She was bluffing.

That still doesn't mean she's defenseless.

Before my eyes, the vile beast inside her—inside them all—awakens. A monster trapped in human skin. Her eyes glow red with the blood she's thrived on. Her fangs seem to glint with anticipation of more.

We collide in the middle of the room, fists to bones, vengeance for justice.

Neither of us are fighters. Being a royal Devonshire, I doubt she's had to spend any of her time learning to fend for herself, trying to overpower her prey. They're probably bled for her into crystal decanters, and then poured into wine glasses that probably cost more than this entire village did. She's lived a life of luxury and doesn't even know how little she means in the grand scheme of things.

I'm no fighter either, but the two of us are well-matched. We trade blows and blocks. We trade blood for blood.

One of her fists slams into my gut. I counter with a crack to her back.

Before she loses balance, she uses the momentum to roll,

nearly sweeping me off my feet, but giving us both time to recover.

But we're never apart for long. This fight has been brewing for decades. She represents everything I've ever hated, everything I've ever wanted to fix.

When my right jab misses and she snatches my arm out of thin air, I let her. I let her latch onto me and drink. I let her think that she's bested me.

The same look of confusion that crossed Harland after he drank from me crosses her now.

Her face sours and she releases my arm. "You don't taste right—"

Before she has time to recover, I bury the shard of glass I still have tucked away in my non-dominant hand into her belly, all the way up to my fist. She splutters, my blood and hers spraying from her lips. The sight of it reminds me of my mother, and the way the noctis killed her slowly, making each pull of blood agonizing.

I bring *the Devonshire bitch* close and look dead into her eyes. "It was me." My voice is husky, steady in a way I didn't think possible. "I killed him. I took your Rhain away from you."

I prepare for her to unleash her fury upon me.

I brace myself for her fist or her fangs.

But I did nothing to brace myself for her tears. They pool in the depths of her grieving eyes like my mother's blood had pooled on the floor.

She looks at me the same way I looked at the noctis that day. Like I am a monster. And like she just lost her entire world. "Blighted we suffered," she splutters. "Bloodied you'll fall."

Unprepared to deal with the assault of guilt and remorse and disturbed by the way her words sound like a vow of vengeance, I jerk the shard of glass out of her stomach and give her a swift death with another slash across her throat.

CHASING URSULETTE

Tracking has never been my forte. I'm more adept at reading for endless hours and retaining almost all of the words that my eyes have skimmed, so much so that when we were boys, Caz would quiz me by flipping to a random page in a book I'd just put down, read half a sentence, and ask me to finish it from memory alone. I was almost always correct.

I can't read the underbrush like Cazimir can, and so when he says we're getting near, I'm inclined to believe him.

We slow at a clearing, a body visible between the trees as we approach. Not Ursulette's though, not unless the morning of the Hunt she spiraled her hair in the tightest of curls and died them a muddy clay color.

The three of us proceed with caution.

"Is that a Crusader?" Renee asks.

Caz taps the body with a foot before looking at me. "Isn't this one of the prisoners?"

I forget the dead man's name, but he made enough of an impression that I remember his face.

"He was one of the ones who broke into the dungeon to free

Char"—I catch myself, even if they both already noticed my slip— "To free some of the prisoners."

Renee's look of annoyance only intensifies, while Caz flashes me one of his bemused grins before resuming his inspection of the man. Most of his neck has been torn from his spine as if a beast was interrupted while mauling him, or perhaps just bored and wanted to play. I suppose that's all the Hunt is, bored beasts looking for some excitement.

The man's entire tunic is soaked through with blood, but Caz zones in on the dark spot on his shoulder. He nudges the body onto the man's stomach to reveal a wound on the back of his shoulder.

"Someone shot him," Caz tuts, breathing through his teeth. "It's not what killed him, but I doubt it felt good."

My first thought is of my cousin, and the black crossbow she pilfered while we were in Gravenburg. Then I remember, she might not be the only one in these woods with a weapon. Then again, it's not like the Shadow Crusade would have any reason to put a bolt through a human.

"Ursulette had a crossbow," Renee says, drawing the same conclusion I have. "It had to have been her shot."

Caz rolls his shoulders like he's not convinced. "It could've been the Shadow Crusade." Crouching beside the body, he gestures to the gaping wound on the side of the dead man's neck. "Maybe they were aiming for whatever was feeding off him."

I hadn't considered that.

"Could be." My gaze falls to the ground. The dirt here is visibly disturbed, almost like someone tilled it, but I can't make much sense of what the different patterns might mean. "What do you see in all of this, Caz?"

"It's hard to say, it's so busy. Something definitely went down here, that I can say without a doubt. I'm guessing there were four—maybe five of them? Looks like it was a pretty big brawl."

"Well, this is the Hunt," Renee says, taking a step back to get a better view of the area. She might not be as good as Caz with tracking, but even she knows a little. After all, knowledge is power, and power is a weapon she enjoys wielding. "A couple of noctis probably fought for this human. There are fewer this year, so I wouldn't be surprised if that meant more physical altercations."

Although her scenario seems likely enough, something won't let me believe it. We're in the northernmost region, the place where the prized female prisoners were released. And yet this fellow here should've been sent to the south with the prized males. What was he doing all the way up here?

"Or," I say at long last. "Maybe there were multiple humans and multiple noctis fighting each other. Maybe this one here and his buddies came back up here to try to save their women."

Something primal and territorial within me snarls when I say it, but I try not to let it show.

"Those weak males? Fighting back?" Renee's laughter is rife with condescension. "What would they even have to defend themselves with?"

The color drains from Caz's face. "Ursulette's crossbow."

Cold sweat beads along my spine. I hadn't even considered that someone might've taken it from her. That she might've stormed headfirst into trouble and lost.

No, that can't be right. The dead man was fed upon after he was shot. For whatever reason, Ursulette shot him first and then—

I lean down to examine the body and take a closer look at the bite marks on his throat. The windpipe is completely gone. Ripped from sternum to skull. Another noctis did this, not Ursulette. I don't think she'd have the strength. Then again, I forgot what we're dealing with: a heartbroken, vengeful creature who probably barely even resembles the woman we know and cherish.

When I move the body, blood continues to drip from the wound.

"Whoever fed upon him didn't finish the job," I say, doing nothing to mask my confusion, nor disgust. "None of this is adding up."

"You're right about that," Caz replies, taking a knee beside me. Frowning at the neck that looks more like a cavernous, bloodied maw, he shrugs. "This is good for us though. We should eat."

I jump to my feet. "You're suggesting we feed... Now?"

His shoulders bob. "Whoever was here, they fought, and they fought hard. You said the Shadow Crusade are active in these woods. Maybe it was them. Maybe it was someone else. Or maybe it was a combination of the two."

That's too terrifying of a thought to even consider. Some unknown source working alongside the Shadow Crusade? It almost makes too much sense for it not to be true though, especially given my conversation with Fox earlier. Someone had to have been communicating with her. Or maybe *someones*. What if all the time we spent collecting prisoners for the Hunt, they were actually willing participants? What if some of them had been members of the Shadow Crusade who planned their imprisonment just so they could be released in the Hunt where they'd ambush the noctis?

We could be even more doomed than we realize.

"We need our strength for whoever we're chasing," Caz concludes.

With a begrudging sigh, Renee steps beside him. "Cazimir's right. This is uncharted territory. We can't afford anything less than our best right now. If the body still has any blood in its veins, we should use it to fortify our strength."

Without another word, she bends down, retrieves one of

the man's arms, and bites into the flesh. She shivers as the cooling blood pools into her mouth, but she drinks all the same.

"They could be watching," I say, shooting a cautionary glance over my shoulder. "If the Shadow Crusade are here to trick us, this is exactly the kind of—"

"Just drink, Malachi!" Renee whirls on me, the blood on her lips too thick to dribble. "You are who you are. You need blood for sustenance, and I didn't see you at the dining hall this morning, nor were there any of your weird human blood-bags wandering the halls near your bed chamber, which means you haven't eaten all day. He's already dead. You don't have to feel guilty about it. It's not like you're killing him. You just have to drink."

I can tell from her savage tone that this is not up for debate. Not this time. She has turned a blind eye to my lifestyle on numerous occasions, but one of those occasions will not be right now.

She gestures for me to take the man's arm from her grasp, and I oblige. I lift the dead weight of it to my mouth.

Blood isn't meant to be cold and congealed. It's meant to have a life of its own as its silken smoothness slides onto the tongue, sweet as chocolate with the tangy allure of one's forbidden desires.

I gag against the acrid taste and before I can pull away, Renee presses my head down harder, urging me to pull deeper. I can barely stand another gulp, but I take it in, thinking only of Ursulette and the strength I may need to protect her.

Only when Caz calls to us does Renee finally release me. "You guys? I think I found a trail of blood."

"Where does it lead?" I ask, wiping my mouth on the back of my sleeve and standing to join him.

Together, the three of us follow the trail of blood that's really more like a geyser in some spots.

"It's how you can tell they were struck," Caz answers when I ask why the sporadic changes in splatter. "Likely from a sword or some other big blade. Once back there, now here. They covered a lot of ground in their fight, and someone got quite a few good blows in."

Other than his periodic teachings, we're silent otherwise, our hearts in our throats as we anticipate stumbling upon Ursulette's dead body next.

We step between two trees, the bloody imprint of a body slammed into one of them, and we stop before a puddle of red damn near large enough to swim in.

"Something died here." Caz sounds amazed the way he says it.

"Was it...was it her?" Renee asks.

He's slow to respond, that sharp sight of his taking in every detail of the scene that neither of us are privy to. "I don't think so," he says at long last. "Look at the size of the footprints around here. None of them are as small as hers. And where the body crashed into that tree back there, and then down to the ground here? Ursulette might be a curvy woman, but she's not this big. Whatever died here was huge."

Renee plants one hand on her hip. "You keep saying died, but I don't see a body."

"Better yet," I interject. "And correct me if I'm wrong here, but it doesn't look like one was dragged away either. It's like whoever died—"

"Shrugged it off, jumped back up to their feet, and walked away?" Caz flashes me a bewildered grin. "Yeah, that's exactly what happened. There's his tracks."

We follow his extended finger, and I can just barely make out the slightly more disturbed ground compared to the rest of the uneven mess.

Renee scowls. "So, he's not dead then."

In disbelief, Caz shakes his head. "He should be. This is a lot of blood. A whole body's worth. We should know. We survive off draining people of the stuff."

Great. As if worrying about Ursulette and the Shadow Crusade wasn't enough, now we have to worry about the dead coming back to life and going for strolls.

We're focusing on the wrong thing though.

"Dead or alive, it doesn't matter. We still need to find Ursulette."

Caz angles an eyebrow at me. "Who's to say this fellow isn't looking for her too?"

I think about it for a moment, dread sinking in. It couldn't be though. A noctis had definitely been here. They'd eaten that other human's throat. If another human had fallen here, there'd be no blood left because every last drop would've been lapped up.

Which means that whoever fell here was one of us, perhaps even fighting alongside Ursulette.

Maybe they were ambushed by the Shadow Crusade, and she took the higher ground to cover him. The prisoner we saw back there could've just as easily been caught in the crossfire, in the wrong place at the wrong time. Or maybe they'd been hunting him when they were attacked.

Suddenly, I remember who else had been eager to be stationed with the northernmost group of the Hunt, and he fits the build of the man Caz is describing now.

"Harland."

Caz whistles, an exaggerated sound of impending doom. "Well, I'd hate to be on his shit list right about now. Judging from the way he's marching, he's out for blood."

"What a pair," Renee chimes in. "Ursulette and Harland, out on a suicide mission for revenge."

That sinking feeling of dread unspools in my chest.

Charlotte had been on Harland's *shit list,* as Caz would put it. For murdering his two brothers. Could she have been the one who murdered Rhain as well? A confliction of emotions rises up inside me at the thought. But with no time to address them, I'm forced to ignore them. We are on a mission.

"Then let's follow after them, before they get themselves killed. Again."

ARISEN

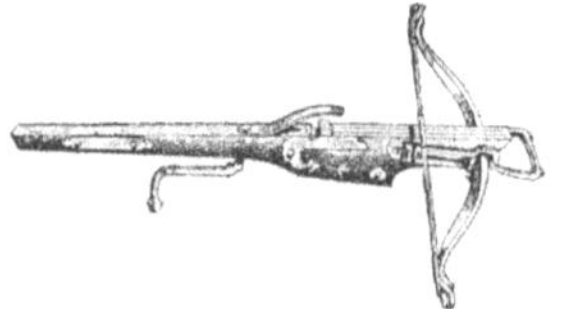

Sable feels strangely heavy where she rests atop my lap, my knees bent and back pressed up against a column near the middle of the room. It was the only place in the entire downstairs that wasn't covered in broken glass.

I don't know how long I've been sitting here, but the sun is starting to set, a suffocating sort of darkness seeping into the cathedral like my own personal demons have finally found me.

I can't shake the look in her eyes out of my head. The horror that cleaved her in two at my callous words.

"She would've killed me," is something I've uttered repeatedly to my black weapon as the minutes have ticked by. "I had to kill her."

There's no absolution in those words though. Because, despite them being true, despite all of the hardship I've experienced, all the towns I've fled while an army of ghouls or a pack of noctis were hot on my heels and I barely had the will to survive, despite being held prisoner and then hunted like a terrified doe, I might've had to kill her, but I didn't have to tell her I killed the man she loved. I didn't have to show her the same malice they've shown us for decades.

I'm no longer sure I can tell the difference between the monsters and myself. Maybe it's been that way for a while now. Maybe it's why I've always kept my distance, all these years.

Maybe deep down I knew the truth: that we're not so different from them.

The heavy double doors swing open, casting me in a ray of dying sunlight. It's all that the day has left to offer as the moon fights for her turn in the sky.

"Charlotte." Rowland breathes my name like it's both a prayer and a pinch to his arm.

I barely lift my head to greet him. The dark chasm of remorse and self-loathing that I've fallen into is going to be difficult to climb out of. But I register the figures following behind him—one, two, three of them—as they enter the cathedral and close the door behind them.

I'm only dimly aware that there's one fewer than there had been before, but I'm grateful to find that it's not Rowland or Mira.

Rowland takes his time making his way to me. With a sword readied in his grasp, he checks behind every column, around every bench to make sure the space is empty except for five of us. He doesn't bother checking upstairs. I'm relieved for that.

"Hey, I almost forgot," he says, appearing beside me. "I found these outside." Two bolts plop on my lap. I glance up at Rowland in disbelief. "They were in the pasture. I'm guessing she shot them at you on your way here?"

I nod and fasten the bolts into their holding bracket. I would ask him about the two that struck Lewis and Julian, but I'm guessing that they had to break the one in Lewis' leg to get it out, and Julian—well, I'm guessing they let Julian rest where he fell.

"You okay?"

He moves to sheath his sword, but stops himself, thinking

better of it. Finally, I'm able to crawl out of my fugue long enough to glance up and see why. Blood drips from the curve of his blade and I wonder how many other noctis he had to kill on his way over here.

We exchange a somber look and I know he's thinking the same thing that I am. It's the same thing everyone's thought since the day the realm fell to the noctis: when will this nightmare end?

Breaking eye contacting, Rowland wipes his sword on his trousers before stowing the thing away.

"I'll take that as a no, you're not okay, then?" He squats down beside me, careful to keep his sword over his lap and easily drawn if needed. "I see you found your girl?"

All of my blood fizzes, rising to the surface of my skin, ready to implode from sheer panic at the thought of having to explain what happened. Having to relive it.

Then I notice the trajectory of his gaze has settled on Sable. I've misunderstood him. He's not asking about the female noctis.

Not yet anyway.

Sable is safe enough territory though that I feel comfortable answering. "Couldn't leave her behind."

"Of course not," he says. "The moment that bolt flew by, I knew exactly where you'd be headed. You've had that crossbow as long as I've known you."

"That's not true. I only had it after…"

It's a painful reminder for both of us. Somehow everything always leads us back to that day.

"Right… I can't believe I forgot it belonged to your mother." The way he leans, one arm propped over a bent knee, it's too casual. Especially for him. Something is wrong, but like me, he isn't ready to broach the subject. "I've seen you with it so many times—every time I've seen you, really—I think I convinced myself it had been yours, even when we were younger."

Impossibly, he manages to make me laugh. "Can you imagine? My father allowing seven-year-old me to wield this thing around Hulbeck?"

"In the cathedral, nonetheless." He smirks to himself, lost in a life so distant and yet so familiar. "How are you doing? With...all of it."

He doesn't specify and he doesn't have to. The past week has been a nightmarish ride, and he leaves it open for me to elaborate on all of it. Unfortunately, I don't even know where to begin. Being ambushed by the prince and his noctis friends while I was trying to save the mother of Rowland's unborn child? Being caged and starved? Abandoning my cellmates in a panic of survival, only to discover that I left one of them—the mother of his unborn child—to die?

Do I tell him about what it was like to bash a noctis' skull in, or to stab one in the belly and watch as the life faded from her eyes the same way it would any human being's?

I can't bring myself to say any of it. Instead, I just shake my head, my hands beginning to tremble again. "You?"

His chest rises as he inhales, but I can almost see the heavy boulder pressing down on him.

"We killed the big one. But he got to Julian first. He—" The muscles in Rowland's jaw contract as he buries his face in one hand. "He ripped his throat out and spat it at me. He didn't even—He didn't even feed on him, he just—He did it to kill him. To make a point."

My own encounter with the female noctis starts clouding my mind, Rowland's words beginning to disappear behind a fog. I have to fight to stay with him. I can tell by the tremble in his voice that he needs me.

"But," I interject. "You killed him?"

He lifts his head, stares at the closed doors. "I killed him."

Slowly, I nod.

He turns to me. "And you killed the—"

I nod again, as vigorously as I can to make him stop before finishing that sentence.

If he notices my strange behavior, he doesn't say anything about it.

"Good. At least we don't have to worry about those two hunting us down while we rest a bit."

For the first time since they all came in, I'm finally able to pull myself away from my own personal bubble of misery and take stock of the others with us.

In the corner diagonal from us, Dunce stands in front of one of the shattered windows. He glances nervously from one direction to the next, his bowl-cut hair whipping his head each time he moves it so suddenly. If he's trying to keep a lookout, he's doing a poor job of it. Not only is he standing right in the open, where anyone would be able to spot him, but he's hardly looking in any direction long enough to be able to see whether there's a threat.

My attention roams to the other corner of the room where there is more commotion.

Lewis leans back on the floor, legs stretched out. As he winces and clutches his thigh, I remember that Ursulette had shot him. Mira is crouched over his bloody thigh now, seemingly unharmed, and busy at work to patch him up.

"I never thought you'd come back here," Rowland says after a long moment has passed. At first, I'm not sure what he's talking about. The former Shadowthorn? To our group? "I returned once; you know? Not immediately. But when I turned sixteen, I had to come back. I'd been forgetting faces, names. I wanted to be reminded of home. I didn't want to lose that. So I came back to see it for myself."

Suddenly my heart is a ball of ice. Each word that leaves his mouth is a hammer that keeps clang-clang-clanging away at its fragile surface.

I run back through my mind, return my thoughts to when

I'd sprung free from the forest and the town came into view. I'd only had sights for the bell tower and the cathedral then, but as I think back on it, everything becomes clearer. I recognize the fence bordering the village. I recognize the way the crisp air almost takes my breath away.

"I almost invited you to come with me, but I didn't think—"

I'm on my feet and barreling toward the door before he can finish.

"Charlotte! Wait!"

Nothing can stop me now though, not even myself.

I race outside of someone else's volition, someone who I thought had died years ago, in this very town. A younger version of me who never thought she'd see her home again.

Stumbling out into the open with Sable clutched firmly in my hand, I pivot around to gaze upon the fallen village of Hulbeck.

It's just as I remember it, only smaller. Like the buildings shrank and shriveled since the decade I've been gone. Aside from Lewis' hissing, and Rowland scrambling to chase after me, there's an eerie silence that's settled over the place I once called home, gutting out all the joy I remember hearing here, leaving it hollowed and miserable.

Then it takes an even darker turn. Although the streets are bare, covered only with the overgrowth of a forgotten town, I see them painted red. I see the dead bodies I had to run past, my eyes stinging and streaming. I hear their miserable cries as dozens upon dozens of the people I called family and friends are slaughtered.

I can still smell the blood and metal and fire.

My legs almost give out, but Rowland is there to catch me, to shield me under his arm the way he hadn't been able to that day. I have never been able to forgive him for that. Maybe I never will. I know I should though. Who knows what would've happened if we had stayed together. Maybe we'd both be dead.

Today is not the day I find it within me to face my demons though.

I shrug out of his grasp and dazedly stagger back into the cathedral where my memories can stay just that.

"Is everything alright?" Mira asks as I storm by.

"Never better," I bite out, hating myself even more for how caustic I've become.

"It's just been...a lot," Rowland tells her, trying to soothe things over. "This place was where we grew up. I don't think she noticed we were here until..."

He doesn't finish his thought because I glare at him in a way that suggests I'll kill him if he ever dares to speak for me again.

I return to where I'd been earlier, collapse to the floor, and fold my arms over myself and Sable. I'm like that little girl again, curled up like a babe trying to soothe herself while blood rains down around her.

The comparison makes me stubbornly toss my arms to my sides. I refuse to be that weak little girl ever again.

"I'm...so sorry," Mira says from across the room.

"Can you focus on this?" Lewis grumbles. "You know, before I bleed out like a fucking pig?"

He picked the wrong day to treat her so poorly in front of me.

I'm back on my feet before I know it, Sable aimed at his other leg.

"Charlotte!" Mira yelps.

I ignore her. There's no bolt nocked anyway. I'm not *that* crazy. This isn't about hurting him, as much as I'd like to. All I want to do is scare him into showing her some respect.

"Speak to her like that again, I dare you."

It's not in his nature to back down, especially from a woman, I imagine. And I can see the effort it takes for him to keep himself silent.

I almost wish he wouldn't.

To my dismay, Lewis holds his palms high.

When I don't lower Sable of my own volition, Rowland does it for me. I hadn't even known he was beside me, and I wonder why he let me get this far. It's not like him to turn a blind eye to my chaos.

Then I notice his smirk and realize he knew all along.

Mira glances between the two of us, the tension in the air making her shoulders bunch and her lips worry. "I...should probably try to find some herbs for his wound. The bleeding is slowing, but there could be infection if not treated properly."

Rowland beats me to denying her. "It's unsafe out there alone, and we don't have enough time to scavenge for medicinal plants. We stay here only as long as we have to. We rest. We form a plan. We leave."

"What about me?" Lewis says, anger boiling up and turning his neck fiery red. Nervously, he glances at me, trying to make sure not to incur my wrath again. "What about my leg?"

"You'll have to make do," Rowland tells him. "When we're somewhere safe, we'll find you the help you need."

"Somewhere safe?" All signs of restraint leave Lewis now. "And where's that? I haven't been safe my entire life. I'll lose my fucking leg if it gets infected. And then what? You just gonna hack it off?"

"That's not—"

"Drag me around like a maimed donkey that should've been put out of everyone's misery? You can get fucked if you think I'm letting that happen."

Everyone's quiet, and frankly, I have no argument.

Even if we attempt to go back to Rowland's community, it'll take us days to walk there. I'm no healer by practice, but I imagine Lewis' leg can't afford that kind of journey, and we can't afford to be dragging him around like dead weight anyway.

Our only options are to leave him or to treat him.

When I start to convince myself that leaving him might be best for everyone, my chest tightens. Only monsters would abandon the living to their deaths. And a monster is what I've been for most of the past decade.

I can no longer afford to lose touch with my humanity. Not like them.

But I also don't like the thought of Mira wandering out there alone on a fool's errand for an herb that might not even grow here. The Blight tampered with the forest. It changed the flora that grew here ever since its inception. The trees, the vines, the flowers, even some of the wild animals that dwell in the Shadowthorn can only thrive in these woods. Unless she's specialized in Shadowthorn medicinal plants like the Crusaders had been, I doubt she'll be able to find what she needs to heal him.

Suddenly, a new idea comes to mind.

Shoving Sable into Rowland's chest, my fingers float up to graze the side of my neck where the bite marks are gone.

"Maybe you don't need herbs to heal him. Maybe...maybe I can do it with my blood."

Rowland blinks. "What?"

"The fuck you will!" Lewis growls, grimacing as he tries to put some distance between us, but he only manages to drag the back of the wound through rogue shards of stained glass. There's almost no escaping it.

"What are you saying?" There's no accusation in Mira's tone. No judgment. Her only aim in this is to aid a man who doesn't even deserve her generosity. "This is about that noctis, isn't it? The one who bit you. There was no bite mark after. It was like...like it never happened."

Suddenly reminded of the gaping wound that should be etched into the side of my neck, Rowland takes my head into his hand and tilts it back, examining the place where the wound should be. Blood has dried on the collar of my blouse, but there is no wound. Not even a scar of one, if my fingers are to be any sort of judge on the matter.

"That's impossible," he says, releasing me, maybe a little too firmly. "I saw him bite you. I saw him drinking your blood—"

Lewis' concern increases, his temper skipping along with it. "You were bitten? By one of them?" He blinks, staring at all of us before exclaiming, "Then let me repeat myself: the fuck you will. You keep your vile blood away from me. I don't want to— Oh shit!" His eyes bulge with understanding. And something else. Something that makes me feel as if I will soon be running from a mob with pitchforks. "You'll be one of them soon. You'll be a ghoul. You guys! We have to kill her. Before it's too late!"

"No one's killing anyone," Rowland warns, voice low and guttural.

"*She* will if we don't do something about her first! She'll kill us all and then we'll all turn into ghouls!"

Rowland jumps between us, acting like an impenetrable wall. "I said, you're not touching her. Don't make me remind you again."

"Stop it," I say, shoving him aside. "Both of you. I don't think we have anything to worry about. I feel fine. I don't exactly understand what happened or why, but I think I might be...immune."

The room goes silent.

Lewis eyes me warily. "Bullshit. You're lying."

Rowland agrees. "He's right. I would've learned about it by now."

This strikes me as odd, but then I remember the resources Rowland has at his disposal. For all I know, this has been part of his research of the noctis, testing their toxins against human blood, searching for a cure or something close to it.

"Look," I say harshly. "We don't have time to discuss it. Lewis, you want to keep your leg? Well, this is all we've got right now. You're a dead man walking without a healer's touch and, I'm sure you are already aware, but none of the medicinal plants we're familiar with grow in this forest. Without my help, at best you'll lose your leg. At worst? Maybe your life."

Lewis works his face into a gnarled frown.

Mira attempts a soft smile. "What harm could it do to try?"

His laugh is a humorless thing. "That's easy for you to say."

The fight in him is waning though, and so I don't move until he tells me to.

In his own time, he finally jerks his head, beckoning me forward. I squat beside him, unsure of what I'm doing, or even if it'll work.

There's only one way to know for sure though.

Reaching behind me, I grab a shard of glass from the ground. I drag its sharpest edge along my finger. Blood beads along the cut and I bring it over to the gash in his leg. He jerks as the droplets fall, seeping into his flesh.

And then we wait.

A handful of seconds is all it takes for the flesh to begin knitting itself back together before our eyes.

"Fuck-fuck-fuck!" Lewis jumps back like he's trying to get away from the leg attached to his own body.

A soft gasp escapes Mira's lips, but she holds her ground, the curiosity of a healer holding her in place. Rowland doesn't move either, but his is a stiff stance, one that makes me uneasy, makes me worry that he's judging me and my strange newfound ability.

Until he opens his mouth to say what's plaguing his mind. "Your blood has healing properties," he says, watching Lewis' leg but gazing somewhere far beyond it. "And the noctis we killed had your blood inside him—"

"Who fucking cares!" Lewis exclaims. He has his leg cradled up to his chest now, examining the new flesh like a small boy who's just discovered the wonders of fire. "So what if he healed after you gutted him like a pig. He's not our problem anymore! He's gone. And we will be soon now!"

But as Lewis springs to his feet to test his freshly healed leg, he makes me realize the gravity of his words.

Rowland realizes it at the same time. "Where did you say you killed the female noctis?"

My wide eyes are the only response I can give him before I snatch Sable out of his grasp and bolt up the stairs, Rowland hot on my heels.

I search everywhere. Every corner of the attic. Every shadow that could conceal a full-grown woman—and even the ones that couldn't. Her body is gone. All that I find where I left her corpse sprawled on the dusty floorboards is a pool of blood.

Rowland and I exchange a worried glance.

"Where is she?" he asks, each word a slow wheeze of wind through dingy shutters.

I shake my head. "She was here. She...she must be gone."

Downstairs, the double doors burst open. The scent of death putrefies the air and curdles my blood, and I can feel my pulse rattle my bones.

The noctis have risen. And I can only assume they're back for revenge.

2 8

MOUNTAIN

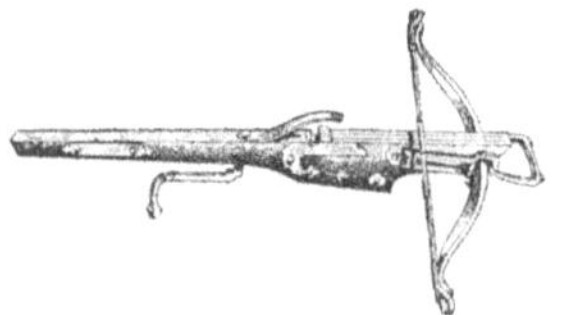

Rowland and I take the stairs two or three rungs at a time. It's still too slow.

The time it takes for each stride to land is filled with an eon of screams and hollering, of glass crunching beneath boots that shuffle from one side of the lower cathedral level to the other.

I just keep thinking about Mira, hoping she's okay. I never had a sister. I don't pretend to know what having one is like. But I feel a kinship toward her, one that I can't describe or explain.

As we reach the landing in the middle of the staircase before it loops around to the lower half of stairs, I'm finally able to see her. To see all of them.

The main entrance doors are wide open, and in the middle of the room cower Mira and Dunce.

They're crouched together, arms looped through one another's the way small children might clutch onto each other before venturing into a dark room. There's something in Dunce's arms, a makeshift shield of some sort that he's using to defend himself and Mira, though with their backs turned to us, I can't make out what it is.

Lewis stands just in front of them, fists raised and ready for a brawl.

The looming figure in the doorway, the one everyone is slowly backing away from, is as hulking as a bull. Every inch of Harland's body is taut, every part of him ready to charge. The corded muscles that bulge from his shoulders and around his back remind me of the angry hills of the Unresting Mountains, a terrain so brutal that it's been known to swallow up even the most skillful of climbers.

I fear the same could be said of those who dare face Harland in battle.

Rowland's already survived one fight. He even managed to kill him…for a time. Until my blood repaired the damage that had been done.

I wonder what that means for my own immortality.

I wonder what it means for Harland's.

The fire in the noctis' eyes is set low as he prowls into the room, searching for something—or someone. My first thought is Rowland. He is, after all, responsible for landing the killing blow earlier, as well as killing one of Harland's brothers.

But Harland doesn't know that. He still blames only one person for the deaths of Gregor and Boris.

"Where is she!?" His voice has an inhuman quality, a gravelly edge that doesn't belong to any living thing.

Rowland grabs my arm and tugs me backward.

No one has noticed us yet. Now that the sun has fallen, the only light down below is what the moon can offer through the broken windows, and it doesn't quite reach this high on the staircase.

I glare at Rowland, regardless of whether he can see it. I don't understand what he's doing. If he's even suggesting for one second that we leave the three of them to die, then he has everything wrong.

Sable lifts in my hands and it takes me a moment to realize it's of his doing. It takes me even longer to understand his meaning. But Rowland and I are from the same cloth, even if I haven't known it as long as he has.

When the people we care about are in danger, we fight to protect them.

"I won't ask again!" Harland bellows, something like bones and dirt in his throat. "Give her to me and the rest of you can leave with your hearts in your chests."

For the briefest second, Lewis' stance falters. His weapon lowers just an inch, almost imperceptibly.

But then Lewis surprises me. His posture returns to that of a defender, and he squares off with the fuming noctis towering over him.

"That's not how this works. You see, this is war. And you're on the wrong side. Human"—Lewis points to himself with condescending flair, and then to Harland—"Noctis filth. Didn't we teach you this lesson already when we stuck you like a pig?"

It's in that moment that I realize what Rowland has been trying to explain to me since the day our paths crossed after the fall of Hulbeck.

Sometimes, it's worth fighting for others. Because they'll fight back for you.

My knee thuds against the floorboards as I take aim, but the sound is lost behind Lewis' taunting. For whatever reason he seems to think he's big and mighty now, even though he has no business feeling as such in the presence of the male noctis before him.

His arrogance will be his undoing.

Without warning, Harland throws his arms back to unleash a bellow that I can only imagine contended with the lungs of one of the ancient, gargantuan Primordials.

Everyone flinches, including Rowland and I, but it's Lewis who loses his balance in the mighty roar.

Harland lunges before anyone can recover, fist the size of an anvil cocked back. When it cracks into the top of Lewis' head, I can hear the crunch, even from this distance. His knees buckle, his body falling like wet dough into a plume of dust.

Mira screams. She tries crawling over to him, likely to check if he's still breathing, but Dunce pulls her back before she can reach him.

My blood had been inside him though. A few droplets at least. Will it be enough to save him?

That's when Harland finds his next mark. Dunce, a scrawny man who has likely always struggled to stand on his own two legs. They wobble now, even where he sits, knees clacking to the staccato beat of his thumping heart.

Somehow, he finds enough bravery within his shaking body to release Mira from their locked arms. He pushes himself to his feet and takes a step away from her, a valiant gesture that I have no doubt he hopes will remove her from the direct line of sight of the ravenous noctis and give her enough space and time to escape. Because now that Harland's focus has shifted to Dunce who's slowly backing away toward the windows, it's leaving Mira a wide, safe path through the front entrance.

He's giving her an opportunity to run.

And she isn't taking it.

Harland's boots rattle the shattered shards of glass on the floor as he stomps over toward the young man. A sound like a gasp wrenches from Mira's lips where she remains frozen in place, her hands clutching her chest as Harland pulls back his fist and prepares to break Dunce's face next.

I want to take my shot. But there's a beam between us that's blocking all of the usual weak spots. Besides, shooting Harland will only enrage him, and as long Mira is still down there, I can't afford to anger him further.

I need Mira out of there.

With only two bolts left, I need a clean shot.

It goes against my previous decade of better judgment, but I call to my friend. "Mira, run! Just go!"

Harland's attention snaps in my direction like a shark aiming for his dinner.

He's been looking for me? Well, now he's found me. He can let the others go.

Looking over her shoulder, Mira's expression turns watery, the regret in her eyes unwarranted but understood. Being the sole survivor of a noctis attack is a heavy burden to bear. I would know since it's a dark cloud I've had tethered to me since I was eight.

But the truth is, she's the only one who is assured survival here today. She is the only one who can make it to the door before Harland will have a chance to stop her.

I shake my head at her in answer, until I realize she can't see me up here in the shadows.

"It's alright," I tell her. "We'll find you after. For now, save yourself. Make sure one of us survives."

Survival is all that matters.

Her lips press together in a firm line. Barely able to contain her sobbing, she finally obeys my pleas, dashing across the rainbow glass that shimmers in the moonlight and racing out the front door.

A flag of midnight hair whipping at her nape is the last I see of her. My cellmate. My…friend.

I'd stare at the door for an eternity, confounded by the realization that *I* actually considered her something so close as a friend, but the monster has been pushed over the edge now.

In his eyes, I killed his brothers.

I killed Rhain.

He's hunted me across the Shadowthorn and died at the hands of my friend.

Tormented, taunted, and thwarted. Harland has come for vengeance, and the grin he flashes is a demented thing that makes me quake where I stand.

He dives for the stairs.

With no time to aim a perfect shot and only one way to go, I spin on my heels and stampede back up the steps with Rowland at my side. We run into the room and slam the door behind us as if it will grant us any amount of safety. The slant of the attic walls is smothering, the dimness disorienting.

We run as far as our feet will take us, across the room to the single window. Throwing Sable over my shoulder, I shove the shutters open.

Rowland catches the crook of my arm. "What are you doing?"

"Knitting fucking scarves. What does it look like I'm doing? I'm getting out of here."

The rolling of his eyes is almost hidden by the way he glances over his shoulder. Behind us, Harland bounds up the steps. By the sounds of it, he's as lumbering as a rhinoceros.

Rowland peers out the window. "The fall's too far. We won't make it."

"Yeah, well? We won't make it in here either."

Nostrils flaring, I shrug out of his grasp. As I stare out the window, at the freedom that's so close but so far away, I look for Mira. I hope she's alright. I hope that any of the noctis nearby will come for us and that she'll somehow manage to find a way out of this place. She's survived this long, after all.

Instead of her dark head of hair and sienna skin, I find the opposite. A pale woman in a dark cloak limps toward the tree line, a curtain of white hair billowing behind her and shimmering in the bright moonlight.

You know, I thought it was a gift to have blood that could heal, but now I'm beginning to wonder if it's not the dumbest thing in the entire realm. The last thing humans needed was for their blood to revive noctis from the fucking dead.

With Harland's boots thundering on the steps just outside our door and my heart hammering in my chest, I tear my mind away from my botched evolution, and back to our escape.

Maybe Rowland is right though. Maybe jumping from the window is a bit hasty. After all, *the Devonshire bitch* was limping, likely an injury she sustained from the fall, and one that neither Rowland nor I could afford if we have a rampaging monster on our heels.

But escape isn't our only option.

Grabbing Sable from my shoulder, I twist back around to face the stairs and ready fire.

The moment I do, Harland stops stomping.

I stare into the blackness, the gaping dark that threatens to pull us in and swallow us whole. Only my breathes reach my ears—and a creak or two from downstairs where Dunce is presumably making a cautious beeline for the exit.

The door creaks open, but in the darkness, I see nothing. And somehow every floorboard that creaks sounds as if it's coming from every direction.

But Harland is as thick as the ancient oaks of this forest. If I unleashed my bolt now, chances are I'd strike him somewhere. Slow him down.

But I don't want to just *slow him down*. With only two bolts left, I can't risk anything but a kill shot.

A voice like smoke sifts into the air. "What did you do to me?"

My eyes bulge, trying to see deeper into the darkness, to find any hint of his location. But I find none. Not even his talking helps me pinpoint exactly where he is. But maybe if I can keep him talking...

"It looks like I saved your life," I counter. "Is that why you've come here? To thank me?"

The growl of a hibernating bear who's just been prematurely disturbed from his slumber rises from the ether.

"Do you have a shot?" Rowland whispers from the side of his mouth.

I want to tell him that I don't, but I also have the distinct feeling that Harland can hear our every word, and he doesn't need any other advantages.

Another floorboard creaks, feet shuffling. In the darkness, I focus on the place where I think I heard him last, and then I see it. Barely. There, a crimson patch scarcely visible in the black abyss.

My aim is steady, my finger confident in its pull.

It's too dark to see the quarrel fly, but there is no mistaking the deadly whistle of it as it slices across the room and—

Thunk.

A moment later, Harland roars and charges from the darkness like a black avalanche.

My bolt is jutting out of his eye—the patched one. A perfect shot. Except that it doesn't seems to bother or slow him.

He barrels after me, arms outstretched, sausage fingers grasping, and I drop Sable to the ground. She'll do me no good now, not in such close quarters.

That was my last chance to save us, and I've failed. I couldn't even fight his brother who was half his size. What chance do I have at fighting him?

Rowland leaps in front of me before Harland can reach me. Throwing his shoulder into the meaty noctis, he tries knocking the two of them back, but Harland is too big. It's like the guy is part of the cathedral itself, as erect and unmoving as the beams that have stood here and faced not only a demon scourge but also a noctis invasion.

Rowland collides into him with a wince, but he recovers quickly, prepared to fight my battles for me, yet again.

I won't just stand here and do nothing. Let the men fight while I cower like a little girl?

Not a chance.

As long as he's distracted, I can—

Before I can bend to retrieve Sable from the dusty floor, Harland dodges one of Rowland's right hooks, and delivers a devastating uppercut to his stomach—gods, it seems to reach his spine.

The sound that escapes Rowland as he's thrust into the air is wet and hollow. Using the momentum, Harland hurls Rowland behind him, and he disappears down the dark stairwell, tumbling helplessly.

I don't have time to worry about whether his neck is broken. Or how badly he might be bleeding.

My fingers fumble for Sable. They slide over the last remaining bolt. Crouched on my knees, I press the weapon into my lap and draw the bowstring back, a feeling of panicked triumph consuming me.

But fingers close around my neck. The air is squeezed right out of my throat as I'm lifted off the floor.

I drop Sable again and start hammering against Harland's arms. Each one seems as formidable as a hundred noctis a piece. His grip doesn't relent. In fact, his fingers tighten, cutting off the last hairs-width of space left in my windpipe.

I gag on nothing, choking on what feels like a rock lodged into my throat.

I strain for anything, for even the slightest breath.

I barter and beg and plead to no one for just one more taste of air.

My head begins to pound. I can't tell if my vision is fading or if it's just so dark in here that I can no longer see a thing.

"Char—" I hear Rowland wheezing from somewhere in the room. I wish I could hold his hand. I wish I had never left Valor's Rest that day. I wish for so many things.

My ability to lift my own arms weakens, fingers dragging limply across Harland's forearms instead of the pounding I was giving them just moments before.

My eyelids grow heavy, and soon I fear I won't be able to open my eyes at all.

After all these years of running, there was no evading death at the hands of a noctis.

I'm only slightly aware of a thud, followed by a sound caught somewhere between a groan and a gasp.

To my surprise, and great relief, Harland's fingers loosen from around my neck, much like the way Gregor's had in Gravenburg. I fall to the ground at his feet, gasping and coughing, only mildly aware of his staggering footsteps as he hobbles away from me.

When the massive weight of him crashes to the ground, shaking the entire attic, I'm finally able to lift my gaze.

I prepare to give thanks to Rowland for saving me, yet again. But he isn't the one standing before me.

A woman with bright, shaggy red hair squats down to my level.

Resting her arms atop her knees, she clasps her mangled fingers together and leans in and smiles. "There. That ought to make us even for me getting you captured."

HUNGER, NO MORE

"Something's coming."

Caz stops abruptly. Thrusting an arm behind him, the flat of his palm thumps Renee in the shoulder and we stop with him. The three of us crouch behind together in the underbrush, watching, waiting, listening.

All I hear is the quiet that's followed us all throughout these forsaken woods. A dreary sense of foreboding has only worsened since nightfall consumed the sky.

It's like the earth here is alive. Like every tree is watching us, waiting to grab us with its spider leg branches and drag us down into the ground.

A shudder skitters down my spine at the thought.

I can only hope that for as long as I live, I will never find myself inside these woods again.

Renee, Caz, and I strain to listen, and after a few moments, I finally hear the rhythmic pounding that caught Caz's attention.

Footsteps. And they're coming right at us.

"Not something," I say.

Caz has already surmised as much and nods his agreement. "Some*one*. They sound injured."

I don't pretend to be able to pick up on the same details that he can, but I trust his judgment.

"Are they human?" Renee asks, wetting her lips. "I could go for another bite."

Somehow, I manage to refrain from snapping at her.

There were only three young women who were released in this area, only one of them seeming capable enough of surviving long into the Hunt. I won't allow Renee to sink her fangs into *her*. No matter how hungry all of us are.

Caz flashes us a wicked, toothy grin. "I guess we'll find out soon. They're coming this way."

I'm about to launch into a counterargument about how we should remain focused on finding Ursulette and keep trekking forward, when someone bursts through the trees.

Night has fallen, making in near impossible to see anything in the darkness cast down by the forest canopy. But the river of white that flows behind her is a dead giveaway, and the truest mark of any Devonshire.

The only question is, what is she running from?

Before she can limp too far out of earshot, I whisper-shout at her. "Ursy?"

I hear Ursulette's lopsided gait stagger to a stop, and then as she turns to search for us. "Malachi? Was that you?"

The three of us rise and, using the ethereal glow of her pal hair, we meet her where she's leaning on a tree.

"You're alright!" Renee cries, throwing her arms around her.

Ursulette winces. "Mostly, I suppose."

Through her panting, I hear the injury Caz alluded to, a heavy quality that drags every one of her words down. Some of it, I have no doubt, has to do with losing Rhain. But there's something else now too, something physical.

Releasing Renee from where they embrace, Ursulette stands on her own, clearly favoring one side of her body. "They...they killed him."

"We know. We found his—we found him."

I reach for her shoulder and give it a comforting squeeze, but she jerks out of my hold, clutching her ribcage as she staggers into the shadows. It reminds me of the way a dying animal retreats into isolation for its final moments alive, and that makes something sharp twist in my gut.

"What's wrong?" I ask her, coming to her aid even if she doesn't want it. "What happened to you?"

To my relief, when I grab her elbows to steady her, she doesn't fight me. But her pulse is like a geyser beneath her skin, powerful and burning. I have to force myself not to jerk away from her.

Stifling something that sounds like a cough but could also be the tail end of a sob into her shoulder, she manages to regain her balance, then her composure.

"I had to jump out a window. I didn't land as gracefully as I would've liked."

Renee pulls Ursulette's cloak away and lifts the blouse underneath it to inspect the wound. It's no use though. The Shadowthorn forest is too dark to see much of anything.

"We should get her back to the castle," Renee suggests.

I'm inclined to agree with her.

Except then I remember I can't go back there. I might not ever be able to return again.

Not that my friends know that yet. I haven't had time to tell them. We've been too focused on finding Ursulette, making sure she was safe from herself.

Maybe the time has come.

Before I can muster the courage to say anything, I notice Caz beside us. He hasn't said a word since she arrived, and although I can't see him through the pitch blackness, I can feel his unsettled mind beside me like something still isn't adding up.

"What's on your mind, Caz?"

He's quiet for a moment, considering. "Who were you running from?"

"What are you going on about?" Renee asks with her usual impatient grumble. She lets Ursulette's clothes fall back into place, shielding her skin from the crisp night air. "She wasn't running from anyone—she was the one doing the chasing. Remember?"

"She *was*," he admits. "But no one else ran through this way. Just you" The direction of his voice shifts, aimed at Ursulette now instead. "What happened to the people you were chasing? And who or what are you running from."

The thought is almost too absurd to think about. Never since meeting any of them have I known Ursulette to run from a fight. I'm not even sure what sort of creature it would take to make her flee. I once saw her stand up to Harland and both of his brothers when they were teasing Rhain for being so boyishly-figured. She fought all three of them until she was a bloodied pulp and refused to let anyone else come to her aid until all three of the brothers forfeited the match. Which they did.

But her silence says it's not so farfetched of an idea as I think it is.

"What were you running from?" I ask her again, a cool breeze wafting over my skin and making it prick with anticipation. Perhaps fear.

Ursulette turns away. For a long moment, she doesn't answer, the words too difficult to surmise.

"It was that girl," she says at last, like she has to wrestle every word from her mouth. "The one we caught in Gravenburg."

Charlotte…

My heart leaps in my chest. Suddenly I feel like I've just tumbled over the ledge of a rocky cliff overhanging the ocean.

"What about the girl?" I ask, trying to maintain my composure and grateful that no one can see my face. "What happened?"

I always pegged her for a fighter, but I can't imagine what she could've done to frighten away Ursulette.

My cousin hugs herself, rubbing her arms for comfort. "She...she let me bite her."

No worse report could've been given…

Bitten.

Condemned.

As good as dead.

My chest becomes as cold and tumultuous as the ocean, my heart bruised and broken.

I knew this would happen. I knew that it was the only possible outcome for her once she entered these woods. And yet...I'd hoped there could be another ending for her, one that didn't end with her dead or worse, wandering the forest as a ghoul.

"What do you mean she *let* you?" Caz clarifies.

It's not until then that I, too, notice the odd choice of words.

No human would just *let* a noctis bite them. It would mean their imminent death.

Even the ones in my employ don't allow my fangs near them—and I wouldn't want them to. I have no interest in creating ghouls and further depleting our dwindling source of food by unleashing a ravenous, unstoppable creature upon the realm.

Ursulette's mouth hangs agape. "I…I mean just that. I think she let me bite her. She could've stopped me or fought it, but she just stood there. And she didn't… She tasted wrong."

Hope sparks in my heart like cinders to dry logs. It hasn't always been that humans turned to ghouls when they were bitten. Some of them had a different fate. Some of them became noctis.

"You think she has druid blood?" I ask, maybe too eagerly

considering the side-eye I feel emitting from Renee. "She's becoming one a noctis?"

I don't care who judges me though, especially not Renee. If Charlotte is a noctis, then there's no longer anything weird about the connection I feel toward her anyway.

But Ursulette snuffs out all vestiges of hope I had left.

"No." My tortured heart erupts so violently that I almost can't hear her. "No, not druid blood."

Caz cocks his head. "Then what?"

"I haven't the slightest clue," she admits. "And…there's more."

Impatience exudes from Renee. I can feel her tapping her foot through the tremor in the earth. "Like what?"

Once more, Ursulette is slow to find the strength to tell us. I have to remind myself that she's been through a lot in the past few hours: she lost her mate, she might have a broken rib or two, and she's shaken up about something else, something that happened with Charlotte.

We let her speak in her own time.

"After I bit her—" Ursulette swallows. "She—I died."

Caz snorts. "Well obviously not. You're very much alive right now."

"No. You don't understand," she insists. She pulls back her cloak again, grabs my hand and places it on something sticky on her abdomen. "I died. She stabbed me in the stomach, and I bled-out in the attic of some abandoned cathedral. I remember."

I feel her flinch beside me, the memory so painful that she has to take a few ragged breaths to steady herself before she can continue.

"I remember fading away. I remember the dark. The cold. The absolute nothingness. And he—" the sobs thrash within her now, those pale eyes searching ours in despair— "He wasn't there. Rhain wasn't there. He wasn't—"

I catch her just before she falls, pressing her firmly against my chest where she unleashes every heart-wrenching howl.

I thought the screams I'd heard earlier had been awful, but at least those had been fueled with rage and agony.

These are the wails of someone who has nothing left to spend. Of someone with no hope left.

Renee leans in, drawing Caz and I near as if she's afraid the forest might be listening.

"If she died, then why is she very clearly alive now?"

"I don't know," Caz admits. "But she seems to think it has something to do with your girl's blood."

My face pales, but I'm sure Renee's finds all the color I've lost.

"Stop joking," I snap at him. "Now is hardly the time—"

He throws his arms up in defense. "I'm not joking! Ursulette said she didn't taste like human blood. She didn't taste like druid blood either. And next thing she knows, after biting into the Gravenburg girl, she dies and wakes up again, miraculously alive."

My mouth opens to protest or defend, but nothing comes out. I'm not even sure what I'd say because none of this makes any sense.

Finally, I settle on, "I've never heard of anyone's blood having that effect."

"You think?" Renee chirps. "Do you know how many humans we've sampled? As a species. Someone is bound to have discovered this before. Right?"

Caz shrugs. "Unless people like her have been in hiding. Like the Shadow Crusade seem to have been."

"I don't think she's part of the Shadow Crusade," I argue.

"I'm not saying she is. Just that a lot happened when the noctis took over the realm and no one knows why. The Shadow Crusade disappeared. The Magistrate went missing. Magic vanished. All these things had to have gone somewhere."

"You make it sound like something big is happening," Renee adds.

"Maybe it is," I say softly, the pieces of the puzzle finally aligning in my thoughts. "What if that's why the Shadow Crusade is choosing to fight now? Maybe something is changing and that's why Charlotte's blood brought Ursulette back to life? What if the druids have found a way to return magic to the land, or change humans, or something—I'm not sure what."

We're all silent for a while, even Ursulette who has pulled herself out of my arms and has started dabbing her damp face dry.

Finally, Caz lets out a low whistle. "Then we're in for a hell of a ride."

I shudder at the thought of it all. The last time our people went to war, mankind and noctis alike faced near extinction on both sides. Only the ghouls thrived. Could we endure another magic-infused war? Does it have to come to that?

Then I realize, this might be the answer I've been waiting for, the discovery that could help me talk my way out of the exile that awaits me.

"There's something else you should know."

Ursulette's voice, meek and frail, breaks me away from my excitement.

She hangs her head in shame, as if what she's about to say next could somehow possibly be worse than any of the previous news she's given us. I don't see how that's possible, and it makes me all the more worried about what's about to come out of her mouth next.

"Ever since I rose from the dead," she continues. "I haven't been…hungry."

Their wide eyes reflect the pale moonlight all around the circle, the only thing just barely visible in the darkness.

Caz and Renee brim with questions, concern, and fear.

All I can think about, however, is that our plight might finally be coming to an end.

A cure? Long ago I stopped dreaming of such a thing. But now? Now maybe there's a way to rid ourselves of the blood-lust that has plagued our kind and the realm.

Maybe I don't need to earn back my father's trust. Maybe this new path I'm on has put me in a position to reunite human and noctis once more.

And Charlotte's blood is key.

"We have to find her," I say to the others, cutting off from their heated debate. No one dares interrupt me, not when I'm using my royal voice. Turning to Ursulette, I have one more command. "Show us where you last saw Charlotte."

FORGOTTEN IN THE DEPTHS

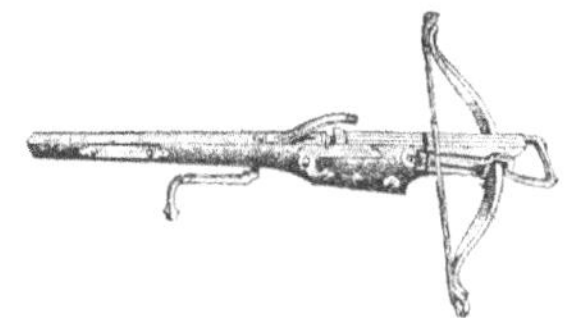

"Even?" Flames lick the back of my throat as I rage at the red-haired woman. "You baited me into a noctis trap! You're the entire reason I'm in this mess! And you have the audacity to stand there and tell me that we're even remotely *even*?"

My throat it's still trying to recover from where Harland's fingers had it clamped so my voice is harsher than I'm used to. But I don't need it to sound pretty. I just need Fox to know that she's fucking batshit crazy if she thinks that saving my life from a threat that she put in my path to begin with makes us anything close to allies.

I don't care how many fingers they cut from her hands. Or the kind of leverage they had over her.

She betrayed her own people the moment she let the noctis use her.

How many girls did she help them ensnare? How many parents did she strip away from children?

On shaking legs, I shove myself to my feet and glare down into her big, blue eyes.

And she has the nerve to look at me like *I'm* the crazy one. Like she has any right to judge me.

"Don't blame your poor choices on me," she says, eyes locked on mine. "You've lived in this world long enough to know better than to aid a stranger in the street. I know you weren't born yesterday."

I balk, unable to form words from the fire on my tongue.

"In some ways," she continues, rising with me. "You might even say you were lucky. If it hadn't been Prince Malachi who baited you, who knows the kind of sickos who might've snatched you up otherwise."

Almost none of my strength has returned, but my anger makes me believe otherwise.

I lunge for her, fists balled and thrashing.

Before I can reach her, firm hands yank me back.

"Wait," Rowland hisses in my ear. I'm so shocked to hear his voice that I actually listen. He's alive. He's conscious. He's here. "You...have your differences," he says. "But she *did* just save our lives."

"Oh, for fuck's sake..." I roll out of his grasp, suddenly less pleased to see him alive. "You know she's the reason you're here too, right? If I hadn't been taken, you wouldn't have had to bring your men to the castle to try to break us out."

He's quiet for a long, uncomfortable moment.

"It doesn't matter," he says at last, his voice stiff and ragged. It's only then that I remember he had more than one reason to infiltrate the castle, and she's no longer among us. "All of that already happened. The noctis used her to bait you. You were captured. Now you're here. And now we need to think about what comes next."

"Your knight here is right," she says.

Before I can lash out at her again, footsteps sound up the stairs and Fox retreats to greet the people walking up them.

Two small figures appear first—children, by the looks of it—and then another figure.

They lunge forward, arms wrapping around my neck.

"Oh Charlotte! You're alive!"

"Mira?" I gasp, squeezing her tight, only dimly aware that it is only one of a handful of embraces I've shared in the past decade. "What are you doing here? I told you to run."

"I did run," she admits. "But then I ran into her, and when I told her about Harland, she insisted we come back here."

"That piece of—" Fox stops herself, likely realizing her children are listening— "that *brute* needed to die."

At least that's one thing we can agree on.

In the darkness, I hear someone striking tinder, and then a flame sparks. A dull light seeps into the room and I release Mira to watch Fox close the lantern on the small fire she's just created inside.

Part of me wants to hate her for what she did to me, what she did to countless others. But seeing her, now, here with her two sons, it sparks a forlorn longing in me that I have never been able to shake whenever I see mothers with their children.

They're lucky. Truly.

Not everyone is so fortunate to be reunited.

I look upon the two children, the smaller nestled into the folds of her prisoner garb, but his features recognizable every time he sneaks a peek out. Even in the dimness, he could easily be mistaken as her double, if not for being two decades or more younger. The other one, a young boy on the cusp of the awkward stage between boyhood and manhood, has sharper features, the shadows under his eyes darker. He reminds me of myself for some reason, and I have to look away.

"Thank you for saving us," I say.

"We should get going," Rowland says, and then nods at Harland's body in the center of the room. "Before he awakens."

As I twist around, heading for the stairs, I notice Dunce

has staggered up the stairs too. I flash him a grateful smile and wonder how Lewis is fairing too. The blow to his head seemed bad, but with my blood inside him, maybe it was survivable…

Mira catches my wrist gently before I can go further.

"What is it?" I ask, but it's Fox who answers.

"He won't be awakening. Not anymore." She flips a wooden stake in her hand, the precision impressive and unimpeded by her missing fingers. "Stake through the heart should do it."

Tossing Sable over my shoulder, I take the offered piece of wood. I feel the grain on my fingers, run my thumb over the sharp tip.

"This thing is supposed to kill him? Like…for good?"

"If they're invigorated with *your* blood? Yes. Decapitation works too. Or setting them on fire. But I don't think any of us feel like sawing through his spine or burning down this place. So, stake it is."

"Hang on," I say, realizing she isn't at all thrown off by us suggesting that the bloodied, unbreathing noctis isn't dead. "You know about…"

I trail off, unsure of what to say.

"Of course I do," she says. But then her brow furrows. "But it seems like this is new information to you. What do you know then?"

Suddenly, I'm aware of everyone's gaze upon me, Rowland's heaviest of all. He's known me my entire life, and to learn this thing about me, it must feel like a betrayal of trust.

For that reason, I look to him when I answer her.

"I don't know much at all. The noctis you just killed bit me a couple of hours ago, but the bite healed itself. Within seconds. Then another noctis bit me and it was the same thing. No mark was left behind and I…I didn't turn."

"And when we killed the noctis," Rowland adds. "Once they had Charlotte's blood in them, they came back to life."

Rowland takes my hand then and my heart beats like the wings of a hummingbird.

Mira pipes up next. "She also healed a man downstairs, just with a few drops of blood."

"So, I don't know much," I conclude. "Nothing concrete anyway. But I'm guessing I have some special healing blood or something?"

I turn my gaze to Fox, hope bright in my eyes but doubt shrouding my heart.

"Something like that." Her smirk twitches up a notch. "Tell me, have you heard of the tales of sirens?"

It's about as far from what I expected her to say as she could get.

"S-sirens?" I say, dumbly blinking. "Like...the evil fish people?"

Rowland inches closer. "I remember people talking about them. When we lived in Hulbeck, right before...right before the town fell. There had been talk about someone who had committed murder and what the town should do with him. I remember my mother saying that before the Capital fell, the Magistrate had a deal with the sirens and that he would send all the prisoners who had committed atrocious crimes to the underwater colonies. She said our people were debating on doing the same, but they weren't sure how. Even living on the coastline, no one had seen or heard from the sirens since the War of Blood and Night."

Fox's eyes bulge. "I'm impressed someone so young, and who has lived through such a chaotic time, knows so much of the United Realm's history."

"We had teachers before everything fell apart," he tells her, and gives my hand another squeeze.

Our proximity, this intimacy, it makes me want to run. This time I fight it though. This time, I try to be different. To be better. To be someone worthy of his time and attention.

I squeeze his fingers in return, and address Fox. "What does this have to do with anything?"

Over her eldest son's head, she glances out the open window to the moonlit night. It's nothing but darkness out there, and a moaning wind that is starting to pick up.

Returning her attention inside, she nods to Harland's dead body.

"I will answer your questions," she says at last. "I promise, I'll tell you everything I know, and everything that's happening. But not while we're here, waiting around like sitting ducks for the noctis to come for us."

Rowland nods. "I agree."

"Where do you suggest we go then?" I ask, frustration rippling off me like a heat wave. "We can try to make our way back through the Shadowthorn, but we'll have to fight our way through a noctis army. And according to King Tor, the rest of the Shadowthorn doesn't seem to be much safer."

"That's why we're leaving the Shadowthorn," Fox says, giving her youngest son a gentle squeeze. "To the same place we were headed before your friend found us. Somewhere where the noctis won't be able to follow."

"And where's that?" I ask, my patience growing thin.

"The Shadow Crusade."

The room collectively gasps.

"The Shadow Crusade?" Rowland says. "I thought they all died."

"Not all of them," Fox tells us. "There's a faction residing nearby. They were only expecting the three of us, but I'm sure they would take the rest of you in, especially given your bloodline." She nods at me pointedly.

"My *bloodline*? What's that supposed to mean?"

"Later," Rowland reminds me.

As stern as his voice is, there's a gentleness in his eyes that makes me decide not to bristle. He's right anyway. We need to find a safe place to rest, and if she knows where one is, then there's no point wasting time here.

"Okay, fine," I say at last. Rotating the stake in my hand, I step over Harland's unmoving body. Before that menacing eye can open again, before another single breath of air can fill his lungs and pump the vile blood in his veins, I drive the stake down through his heart. When I stand, wiping the blood on the thigh of my already filthy trousers, I fix my attention on Fox. "We follow you to the Shadow Crusade. Then, once we're safe and rested, you tell us everything."

A relieved smile curls one side of her mouth as she says, "Okay. Let's go introduce you to the Crusaders and the sirens."

Continue reading in: *Death & Wicked Monsters*
PREORDER NOW:
https://geni.us/DeathAndWickedMonsters

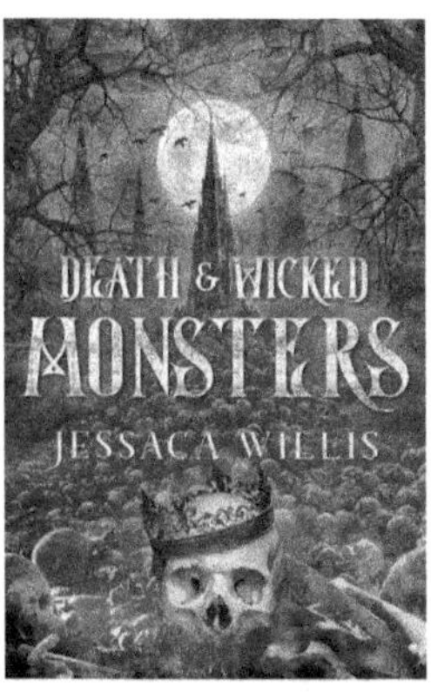

Thank you for reading *Blood & Magic Eternal*!

<u>Leave a Review</u>
Help other readers find this dark saga by leaving a review on Amazon, Goodreads, Bookbub, or any other reading website. Even a simple "I loved it!" can really help!

ARC Team

If you're someone who loves leaving reviews and you're excited by the idea of having early access to all of my books, check out my website for more information on how to join my ARC Team: www.jessacawillis.com/ARC

Social Media

And last but not least, if you'd like to stay connected, you can find my social media links here: https://linktr.ee/jessaca_with_an_a

PRIMORDIALS OF SHADOWTHORN
Epic Dark Fantasy Romance

Ruled by tyrants. Hunted by demons.
This vengeful huntress is ready to fight back.

When Halira's parents are slaughtered by the horrifying demons that plague her lands, she joins the Shadow Crusade, a legion of warriors determined to slay the last living Primordial, end its reign of darkness, and destroy demon-kind once and for all.

But as her training begins, Halira soon discovers a secret about the forgotten magic that once thrived throughout the lands, one that could threaten her very survival.

Will Halira be the savior her country needs, or will her own dark secret force her to hide in the shadows?

Check out the Primordials of Shadowthorn series—the prelude to Blood & Magic Eternal—on Amazon

ACKNOWLEDGMENTS

This might be the first book that I debated skipping the acknowledgments section. Not because I don't believe in acknowledging the many people who played a part in ensuring this book came to fruition—because, believe me, there are *numerous*—but because I always fear that the acknowledgments rarely come across as genuine and heartfelt as I intend.

The truth is, these books would never leave my imagination if it weren't for the tremendous amount of love and support I have around me, and I never quite know how to encapture that in the few words on this page.

But here I am, giving it a go again.

To Kieran, who inspires me daily to make my dreams come true so that I might be a good example for him as he embarks on attaining his own.

To my readers, who have lifted me up when I've struggled with imposter syndrome. Thank you for falling in love with my characters and my worlds.

To my editor, Kate, for always cheering me on, for being gentle but firm with her feedback, and for being the most accommodating and flexible person in the business.

For my Platypi Writing Group friends—Reina, Dani, Dee, Tiff, Chani, Colby, & Cass—you are always there for me when I can't be there for myself. You give me strength, and show me love, and from you, I find the courage to keep telling my stories.

To my cover designer, Silviya with Dark Imaginarium Covers, working with you is always a joy, but the covers for this series are my favorites yet. I am so grateful you brought to life the concepts we had in mind for this gothic vampire series.

To my brother, who has heard me say this a million times but I'll say it a million more: you've got creative spark, dude! Thanks for letting me siphon it during our mind meld sessions. No one leaves me as creatively invigorated than you.

To my mother, who still puts up with me, after all these years.

To all the other artists and creators who bring their visions to life through story, music, visuals, and entertainment—you make the world brighter, and you inspire me to do the same.

To everyone else in my life, know that I am grateful for every way you show up for me, and that it all leads back to books like this. You fuel me.

Jessaca is a fantasy writer with an inclination toward the dark, epic, and adventure sub-genres. She draws inspiration from books like the Nevernight Chronicles & ACOTAR, videogames like Dark Souls III, and television shows like Game of Thrones and The Chilling Adventures of Sabrina. She is a self-proclaimed nerd who loves cosplay, video games, and comics, and if you live in the PNW, you just might see her at one of the local comic conventions in one of her favorite RWBY cosplays!